THE SEETHING

"*Midsummer* meets *The Mist* in The *Seething*, a slow-burn tale of creeping terror and a pressure cooker of a novel from horror's rising star Ben Monroe. Not your usual summer vacation by the lake, *The Seething* is irresistibly ominous."
—Lee Murray, four-time Bram Stoker Award®-winner and author of *Grotesque: Monster Stories*

Monroe has managed to seamlessly intertwine a number of beloved horror tropes into a complex, page-turning…story that takes place in an eerie mountain town surrounded by a mysterious lake. Definitely worth a read if you like sitting around a campfire and sharing spooky stories.
—Francesca Maria, author of *They Hide: Short Stories to Tell in the Dark*

THE SEETHING

by Ben Monroe

This one's for Aidan and Charlie

Content warnings are given at the end of the book

CHAPTER ONE

Golden Oaks was a resort town, and busiest during the summer when people came from all around Northern California to enjoy the mountain lake nearby. But as summer waned, a calm descended over the town. The bustle and noise of summer visitors was slowly replaced with the everyday quiet comings and goings of the people who lived there year-round. A sense of relief blanketed the town as the residents began to feel like they could return to their normal lives.

On the first day of autumn, Mike Barnes woke up to the quick jerk and shudder of an earthquake. He wasn't sleeping well anyway, or he'd probably have slept right through it. And he'd been a Californian long enough that it didn't faze him. He lay still in his bed for a minute or so after the shaking stopped. He probably would have gone back to bed if he hadn't heard a crash of glass from downstairs.

Mike grudgingly got out of bed, and when he went downstairs to investigate, he found a framed picture of him and June had fallen off the wall, the glass shattered across the hardwood floor. He carefully picked up the frame, carried it over to the trash and turned it over the bin, letting loose glass shards and slivers tumble into the can. The photo had been on the wall for years; so long that it had become part of the background. For the first time in a long time, he looked at it, looked at the frozen moment in time when his wife had still been healthy and full of joy.

"Miss you," he whispered, and placed the frame on the kitchen counter.

After he swept up the glass and tidied up a few other things that had been shaken off-kilter by the quake, he was restless, cooped up in his home on the edge of Oro Lake. For the last couple of weeks, he'd been thinking about renting a rowboat and taking it out for the day. He decided today was as good a time as any and was soon looking forward to a quiet day of fishing and drinking on the water.

The last year had been difficult for him. A couple of winters back, his wife of forty years had died, and he'd never really recovered from that. Their marriage hadn't always been easy, but he'd loved her and was still hollowed out from her death. Their son, Gabe, his wife, Laurie, and their daughter, Kimmie lived a few hours away and came to visit from time to time, and that was good.

Mike often wondered if maybe he and June shouldn't have moved away from Golden Oaks when they got married. June had wanted bigger things, more excitement, more life. Just more. More than she ever got in Golden Oaks, anyway. They'd talked when they were first married about moving to San Francisco or Los Angeles. Somewhere with excitement and bustle. But this was where he'd found a job, and they had made a home, and in time she had come to love it too. They'd raised Gabe here in Golden Oaks, and even though he'd moved away to go to college and start his own life, he still came back to visit.

It was slow and quaint, but that was fine with Mike. They'd been mostly happy here. And even without June, he still loved the funny little town. But he missed her an awful lot. On the rare occasion that anyone asked him how he was doing, he'd force a smile, maybe crack a joke. And cry himself to sleep when he got home.

After June died, Mike took an early retirement from his job at the bank in nearby Keyford and took part-time work at the hardware store in town. The commute to Keyford had been killing him, and he found he liked helping customers with their house projects a lot more than pushing pencils all day anyway. He could even ride his bike to work if he felt like it. He still visited June's grave almost every day, but the visits had dulled from melancholy monologues to quiet contemplation. Mike called once in a while to talk to his son, but even those calls were becoming fewer and farther between.

Now he lived alone in the house he'd raised a family in, the house where Mike's marriage had started and ended, and he kept to himself. It was quiet, and nobody bothered him, and that was okay. Sometimes he missed his kid, and his granddaughter. He occasionally thought about selling the place in Golden Oaks, giving most of the money to Gabe to put a down payment on a house in Alcosta. Mike thought maybe he could find an apartment nearer to his son. But he knew the boy had his own troubles, and Mike didn't want to be a burden. Maybe he'd invite Gabe, Laurie, and Kimmie to stay with him over the Christmas holidays. Golden Oaks was too low in the mountains for a proper White Christmas, but it was still nice to be around family for the holidays.

But for that first day of fall, Mike had an itch to be alone on the lake. He wanted to crack a few beers, maybe catch a few trout.

There was a path behind the property, overgrown with weeds and poison oak, which ran across a little rill of a creek and right down to the lake's edge.

During recent years, the creek was always low, and with the dry summer they'd had, it was pretty much dry clay, and he could cross it on foot. There was even a little pier on the edge of the lake that the previous owner had installed. It was a little rickety though, and Mike had been meaning to replace it ever since Gabe had been a kid.

He'd done the short hike plenty of times in the past, but today he didn't feel like it. He didn't want to spend the extra time hiking through the bracken and bush, dodging poison oak.

He could see the lake from his back porch, the vague snaking shape of the path that ran toward the beach lost in weeds and scrub. The path used to be clear, used to be a short walk to the water. But it took time to clear it, and when June got sick, Mike sort of let it slide. Taking care of her had been all he really cared about, and the path became neglected. Maybe next spring he'd clear that path. Maybe if he cleared the path next summer, he'd buy a boat he could leave alongside the pier, so he could go out on the water whenever he wanted. Maybe.

With a six-pack of Bud and a few sandwiches he'd picked up at the Raley's downtown on the way home from work the night before in one small plastic cooler, and an extra empty cooler for anything he caught, he was ready for the day. He threw the coolers, his rod, reel, and tackle box into the storage area in the back of his little sun-faded Toyota Tacoma. He slammed down the rear hatch, just as he saw a bicycle wobbling toward him from up the road. The bike came closer, wobbling on the rough asphalt, weaving around a few potholes, and soon he recognized Peter Guilford, a local teenager who lived a few miles further north. Peter didn't cause anyone any real trouble, and Mike had gotten used to seeing him tooling up and down Ringgold Drive on his venerable old Schwinn. Peter was always the athletic type, and even though his family owned a spare car, Peter was always getting around on his mountain bike.

"Hey, Peter, how's things?" Mike said, as he circled around the side of the car to open the driver's side door.

"Good-good!" Peter called back. He looked left-right-left and right again for good measure before he veered across the street between them. "Goin' fishing?" he asked, as he brought his bike to a slow stop, and propped his dusty green Oakland A's cap from his forehead.

"Yeah," Mike replied, as he opened the latch to the car's door. "Warm days won't last forever. Felt like getting out on the lake before the cold and rain comes in."

Peter peered around Mike into the back of his car. "Yeah, nice day for it, I suppose." He stood up straighter and hitched up his faded jeans. "What kinda bait you using?"

Christ, Mike thought, *I'll never get out of here now.* "Yeah, don't know. Figured I'd stop by the store on the way to the lake and see what they had. Maybe some PowerBait or something."

"My dad says worms are best," Peter replied, hands in his pockets.

Mike braced himself for a lecture.

"Worms wiggle and thrash, see? The fish like going after something that squirms. They don't want any of that purple stuff that floats there. He says fish're mean sons of bitches." He looked up at Mike, realizing he'd sworn in front of a grownup, not his pals from school. "Least, that's what I heard, you know?"

Mike opened the Tacoma's door, and slid into the driver's seat. "Good to know, Peter," he said, closing the door. He rolled down the window with one hand as he slid the key into the ignition with the other. "I tell you what," he said as the window fully opened. "I'll get some live bait, and some of the goop, and see which works best."

"Now you're talking!" Peter laughed. "You'll see what the fish go for. Hell, maybe you can write an article for *Field & Stream* about it when you're done."

"Well, I don't know about that," Mike said, and turned the key in the ignition. The engine shuddered to life. Mike raised his voice above the engine's dull thrum. "But I'll get dinner out of it. Hey, aren't you off to school soon?"

Peter nodded and ran his hand through his hair to get it out of his eyes. "Yeah, leaving for Davis next week actually."

"That's great," Mike said. "Any idea what you'll be studying yet?"

"I'm kinda leaning toward Entomology or Botany right now," he said. "But haven't decided yet."

Mike nodded thoughtfully. "Well, you won't have to declare at first. Get your solid biology foundation classes in, and you'll figure it out. Davis, huh? Good school, I hear."

"I was accepted to Davis and Cal State Alcosta, but in the end, Davis won out."

"Well, that's great," Mike said, as he threw the engine into gear. "Davis'll be lucky to have you. Alright, well those fish won't wait all day. Say hi to your mom for me, okay?" he said.

"I will Mr. Barnes, sure thing!" Peter said.

Mike smiled and waved as he pulled out from his driveway. In the rear-view mirror, he could see Peter waving after him.

He turned on the radio where Bob Seger was growling about lost highways and shattered dreams, and Mike felt like he would have a pretty good day for a change. He cracked open a can of Bud, took a long swallow and thought, *Maybe things are looking up.*

***

Mike stopped in town and picked up a jar of purple "garlic flavored" bait that felt like Play-Doh, a tub of pile worms, and another of salmon eggs. He rented a little plastic rowboat as well and dragged it into the back of the Tacoma.

By the time he made it to Oro Lake, it was about nine thirty. Later than he'd have liked, but considering it was a spur of the moment decision, he didn't really care. Even if the fishing was better earlier in the morning, he was mostly happy to be on the water at all. He'd avoided it for most of the summer while the lake was filled with summer people.

The rowboat cut across Oro Lake, the first chill breezes of autumn whispering across the rippling water. Eddies of cool air snaked between the gusts of lingering summer heat, mirroring the undulating lake water below. Silence surrounded him, the susurrant hiss of the boat cutting through water, and the occasional intermittent splash of his paddles slicing the lake's surface. He was warming up already, and decided to remove his life jacket, since it made him hotter and restricted his movement as he rowed. Tossing it to the floor of the rowboat, he cracked another beer and drank it down in three long swallows. He was already getting a nice buzz and felt like it was going to be a pretty good day.

He pulled against the oars, and could soon see Deer Island, a small island at the center of the lake about a mile away. Deer Island was the only landmass within the otherwise clear lake. It was covered with clusters of oaks, and as he looked toward it, Mike saw one of the eponymous California mule deer dart between the trees. Mike often wondered how the deer got to the island. He never saw any swimming out, and it was too small for any to live there. He guessed anyway. Maybe he'd ask a ranger someday.

The boat was gliding freely through the water as he neared the island when he hit something with a dull *thud*. Something sharp that scraped along the outside of the boat's hull as the water dragged it past. The boat shuddered as a gnarled shaft, slimed and black with algae pierced the rowboat. A branch maybe, or something similar. "Fuckety-shitballs," Mike muttered as water began to flow into the boat through the puncture. He remembered reading in the paper that, thanks to the summer drought and the resulting lowered water levels of the lake, all kinds of things long-forgotten had come closer to the surface.

He tried covering the leak with his foot, but water instantly sluiced around his sneaker. Looking back toward shore, he guessed the island at the center of the lake was closer. Despite the "Keep Off!" signs posted on it, he rowed there to get out of the water and try to patch the hull. He thought briefly of putting on his life jacket, but decided it'd be better to quickly get to shore and patch up the boat. He could call for help when he got to the island. Mike had his cheap little cellphone in his pocket, and it was fully charged. He was glad now that Gabe had insisted he get one.

It was a struggle against the water pouring into the shell of the boat, but with effort, Mike managed to get the boat to the island beach. He jumped out of the boat, landing in cold water up to his waist, and began dragging the boat toward shore when it caught on something. Mike gave it two quick tugs, as the craft listed to one side, filled with water, and sank beneath the surface, sliding backward, away from the island and into the deep water.

Within moments, it had vanished along with his fishing gear. The coolers floated on the surface though, and he dashed back into the water. Wading out awkwardly until he was up to his waist, he reached out and grabbed one. The other floated out of reach, but the one in his hand was heavy. It was the one with the sandwiches and beer inside; at least he wouldn't go full on Robinson Crusoe—for a few hours anyway.

He had turned and began splashing back to shore, dragging the cooler behind him, when his foot caught on something under the water, a root maybe, and he went under. The water was green and cold, and he hated it already. Regaining his footing, he stumbled to shore. Mike fell to the island's sandy beach, his feet still in a few inches of the lapping water and took a deep breath, spitting out lake water as he did. He wiped his wet hair out of his eyes and peered into the silty water of the lake.

"Fucking-A," he muttered. Sunlight danced across the rippling surface of Oro Lake as he wondered how the hell he was going to get himself out of this mess. He drew his phone from his pocket. Water poured from the seam in the plastic, and the LCD screen was dead gray.

"Shit!" he yelled and arcing his hand overhead, tossed the phone across the sparkling water of the lake, where it disappeared with a quiet splash.

The sand was warm and slightly damp where he sat. He leaned back on his elbows, stretched out his legs, and sighed. A deep, weary sigh of frustration and resignation. He scanned across the rippling surface of the lake, hoping to see another boat nearby. Surely, he couldn't be the only person who'd decided to go fishing this morning?

His eyes drifted across the glittering lake water, but something seemed off to him. He stopped and peered into the water a dozen or more feet in front of him. Where the water began to get dark, and a submerged shelf gave way to the cool green depths of the lake, he glimpsed rippling lighter spots beneath the surface. They might have been light colored fish, but he couldn't tell for certain.

"Hope you choke on the bait," Mike muttered. He looked around, wondering where the rowboat had come to rest beneath the water, but couldn't see it at all.

He yelled for help. He banged sticks together and jumped around while waving his arms overhead, trying to alert anyone on the shore. Far in the distance, he could barely make out hikers, runners, happy couples walking their dogs and children on the distant trail which circled the lake. But none of them took any notice of him at all. He was as good as if lost at sea.

Maybe he could swim to shore, but he didn't think he'd make it. He was a decent swimmer form-wise but was out of shape. And it must be over a mile back to shore. He wished he'd kept up with his swimming.

So, he took a walk. He decided to see what was on the island after all, take a look around and see if he could find a better vantage point to signal for help. But after a few hours, he'd marched around the perimeter of the island a few times, eaten all the sandwiches he'd brought, and finished the last of the beers. He'd continued calling and waving, but no help had come.

He hiked over the top ridge of the small island, crossing from one side to the other. When he was about at the top, he found an area where the earth had been flattened down. It looked decidedly man-made, yet covered with a sprinkling of leaves and dirt. He trudged across it and noticed how hard the ground was. He kicked at the ground with the sole of his soggy sneaker and uncovered dingy concrete. "Weird," he muttered. He felt odd talking out loud where nobody could hear him. Mike looked around, left and right and behind him instinctively. He heard rustling in the trees and looking around, noticed a pair of ravens watching him. Perhaps waiting for him to drop a morsel of food. Or to keel over and die.

"Sorry birds," he said. "Got nothing for you."

He kicked again at the dirt, walking out toward the edges of the concrete. Mike tapped and poked with his foot until soon he was able to determine the edge of the slab and where it met the surrounding earth.

He circled around the perimeter, until he'd cleared away the edges completely. When he'd uncovered the edges, he could see that it was indeed a concrete slab, roughly ten or a dozen feet to a side. He was considering stepping onto it when he noticed a thin, jagged crack across the center of the concrete.

Mike was raising a foot to take a step onto the concrete when the ground shook. Jerked and bounced. The trees surrounding him shuddered and shook briefly, and he spread his feet to keep his footing. *Aftershock*, he thought.

A groaning *crack!* as the fracture in the concrete slab, began to spider-web out, then stopped. For a moment, everything was quiet and still. Suddenly the slab fell, a dull crumbling *thump* as the concrete collapsed inward in a cloud of pale gray, gritty dust.

Mike leapt back as the concrete caved in, rattling and echoing as it fell into a cavity below. He stood back from the lip of the hole, far enough where he thought he was safe, watching it, waiting for the edge to collapse further. But other than a cloud of dust kicked up by the falling concrete, all was still.

After a minute, the dust settled, and he approached the lip. The pit wasn't too deep, a conical shape maybe six or eight feet across, and twice that deep. It looked deliberate, like a chamber dug into the top of the island and then covered over with the slab. He saw the concrete rubble piled up in the bottom of the hole, and a few fissures in the surrounding walls leading into the depths of the earth: small passages so tiny only snakes and vermin could explore them.

Something about the pit unsettled him. The air wafting up from it carried a faint smell of trapped decay, and a strange hint of ozone. When he turned from it, he didn't like having it behind him. He had the distinct feeling of something predatory and malign at his back.

He rotated in a circle and saw that this vantage point probably once had a clear view of the entire lake. Or maybe it was still a valley when the concrete was laid down. The lake had been dammed up in the 1930s as part of a WPA project. A few trees blocked his view intermittently, but they were thin, surely fewer than fifty years old.

He retreated from the edge of the hole and circled it again, looking into the distance as he did. His foot hit something hard under a pile of brown rotting oak leaves. Mike kicked the decaying oak leaves away. They were wet slimy as he scraped deeper into the pile. When cleared away, he uncovered a chunk of old wood. It was squared off though, carved and shaped, not like a fallen log. Looked like maybe eight inches to each side, and it was a few feet long. He cleared the length before finding a splintered, rotten end.

Mike stood up, wondering how the beam got up here. And the slab. Maybe it was a surveyor's shack, or a fire station lookout tower back before the valley had been flooded to make the lake? The original survey team must have sealed off the cave or pit and used the concrete slab as the base for their survey tower.

He went back down the hill, sat on the shore, and glared out across the lake. More hours passed, and rain came. Cold and miserable, he moved back from the shore and sat under the oak boughs. The moon rose, night came, and a chill set in. By morning, he had a fever, and he was hungry and parched.

He opened his mouth to catch some rainwater, and sucked on his soaked shirt, but it wasn't enough. He got on his hands and knees at the edge of the lake and gulped a few mouthfuls of the cold water.

Slow, cold rain oozed down Mike's back as he sat on the shore, staring out across the lake. The sun rose, and golden ripples reflected off the lake's surface. The constant drizzle was irritating, and he felt wretched. Mike wished the rain would come harder, would pour out of the sky in bucketfuls and splash across the surface of the lake. At least he wouldn't have the false hope that the people he glimpsed on the far shore of the lake would notice him and send for help.

He lay in the rain-wet mud, shivering and coughing. A thick, wracking cough that ripped at the insides of his chest. Mike approached the water. Nobody was coming to help him. The day had barely broken, and most people hadn't even risen for their morning coffee yet. He would either die alone on the island in sight of the shore, or he could swim. He stepped closer to the water's edge and heard a rustling in the leaves nearby. Turning to look behind him, he saw a pair of ravens, midnight black, and staring at him from a branch in an old oak tree. "Least you can fly out of here," he said, before turning and walking toward the water. The ravens flapped down from the tree and onto the sand, hopping after him.

He stepped off the shore and his feet sank into soft, silty sand. The ravens flapped and cawed as he did. A cacophony of beating wings and furious noise.

In final desperation, he lurched out into the water. His head was pounding and thick as he strode into the lake. When the water was up to his thighs, he stepped off the shelf and began paddling toward shore. He reached and pulled at the water, kicked his legs to put the island as far behind him and as fast as possible. But his chest was thick and heavy, and breathing was agony. His muscles weakened fast, and he was reduced to treading water while trying to keep his head above the surface.

He bobbed under, taking in a mouthful of cold lake water, thrust up and spat it out, coughing. Mike rolled on to his back, arms and legs splayed out and stirring slightly to keep him afloat. He rested, his ears below the waterline, hearing the muffled ebb and flow of the low lapping waves.

Lying on his back, he leaned his head forward, and saw the island beyond his feet. He was about to turn over and begin a crawl-stroke when he saw something dark, sinuous, but indistinct through the haze of his fever vision, slithering through the tree line in the distance. Mike turned onto his stomach and began to pull at the water with weak strokes of his arms. His legs kicked behind him, and he sliced into the water, panic rising in his chest.

Something grabbed at his limbs, clutched with biting cold, slithered around his arm, dragging it back until the joints strained and popped from their sockets, pulling tight and digging into his skin. He took a final breath as his throat was encircled, and he was dragged under. His vision flooded with green lake water as a last breath of air exploded out of him, and his lungs filled with liquid as he was pulled down into the slime at the bottom of the lake.

A lancing, searing pain from his arms and legs, a cloud of crimson, and he saw nothing more.

***

Many miles away, in a small, two-bedroom apartment in Alcosta, California, Kimberly Barnes (Kimmie to her family and some friends) woke with a start. Her sheets and sleep shirt were damp with night sweat, her heart was racing, and she had the taste of lake water in her mouth. A vestigial memory from her dream. A dream of being dragged underwater, of cold, grasping darkness and indistinct forms slithering in the slime at the bottom of a lake.

And she knew that her grandfather was dead.

She wasn't sure how she knew, but she did. Kimmie often had strange insights, or hunches, that turned out to be true, but this was the strongest one she'd ever felt. It was as if she'd seen him dying in her dreams. No, not exactly seen him. It was almost like she *was* him. Like she was watching the events unfold through his eyes, through his body. Felt his fever, his wracking cough. His desperation and terror as he was dragged into the water of Oro Lake. The lake where she'd visited him with her parents so many times. She'd recognized the little island at the center of the lake, the one that, on a clear day, she could see from her grandfather's back yard. The one she'd asked him to take her to, but he'd said it was off-limits.

She looked out the window at the sunrise starting to creep over the hills to the east. It was still an hour before she had to leave for school. She usually liked to sleep in a little longer. But with her heart racing and blood pumping, there was no point in trying to get back to sleep now.

Kimmie stumbled out of bed and got into the shower. The hot water washed away the tension and nightmare sweat, and by the time she'd toweled off and gotten dressed for school, she was starting to feel almost normal.

She came out into the apartment's hallway and was greeted with the smell of freshly brewing coffee. She'd never liked the taste of it but loved the smell. Something about it felt homey and comforting to her. She came into the kitchen where her father, Gabe, was scrambling eggs over the stove.

"Morning, sunshine," he whispered as she came in. "Mom worked late last night, so shhhh!" he put his finger over his lips and smiled at her. "Got time for breakfast with your old man before you jet off to school?"

She nodded before pulling up a seat at the small wooden table in the breakfast nook in the corner of the kitchen. She scooted her chair up as Gabe placed a plate of eggs in front of her.

"Hey, kiddo," he said. "You've got your worried face on. Everything okay?"

She looked up at him, her dark hair falling forward and framing her face. "Dad," she said sheepishly. "I think you should check in on Grampa."

CHAPTER TWO

Three Years Later ...

The sun was barely above the horizon, and already the city was sweltering. It had been a hot summer, and according to the weather reports, the next few weeks were going to be dry and scorching.

Gabe was working on his third trip from the apartment to the car and back when his cell phone chirped in his pocket. He put the suitcase next to their blue Corolla and fished the phone out of his pocket. When he raised the screen, he saw it was a call from Steve Bridges. "For cripes sake," Gabe said, and thumbed the button to pick up the call and placed the phone next to his ear, and leaned his head to sandwich it in the crook between his ear and shoulder. "Hello?"

"Gabe? Hi, it's Steve," the voice on the other end said, loudly. Gabe could hear the roar of the freeway beyond the voice.

"Hang on, Steve." Gabe opened the trunk of the Corolla with one hand as he awkwardly lifted the suitcase up to place it inside. When it was settled in the trunk, Gabe took the phone in one hand and relaxed his neck. "Yeah, what's going on?"

"Gabe, hey you're still coming in tonight?"

"Yeah, that's the plan," Gabe said. "We're packing the last of it now but should be on our way soon."

"That's great," Steve said. "Listen, I've got tri-tips marinating for dinner tonight. You guys want to come over?"

Gabe paused. "Ah, yeah, sure. That'd be great."

"Good deal," Steve said. "Take your time, drive safe. Once you're settled in, give us a call and I'll start up the grill."

"It'll be a few hours, but we should be in Golden Oaks by later in the afternoon. But yeah, we'll give you a call once we've arrived and sort it out."

"Perfect," Steve said. "Kay's chomping at the bit to see Laurie and Kimmie. Figured we'd offer dinner your first night, so you don't have to deal with cooking."

Gabe looked down the street at the cars zipping by. He let out a slow sigh, barely audible. He was planning on picking up dinner at the Get Up and Go diner in downtown Golden Oaks, but he knew Laurie would love to see Kay and Steve, and it'd give Kimmie a chance to meet their kids and make some friends.

"Okay, sounds great. I was planning to run into town and do some quick shopping once we get settled. But if you need me to pick up anything for dinner on the way in, let me know and we'll stop at the grocery store in town," he said as he was walking up the steps toward the house.

He shuffled to the side of the stairway as he saw Laurie exiting with a large cardboard box in her hands. When he passed her, he smiled, leaned forward, and kissed her on her cheek. She smiled back and skipped down to the car.

Gabe entered the apartment and looked around. "Guess we'll see you in a couple of hours."

"Okay, perfect," Steve said.

Gabe scanned the small living room. He kept thinking there was something he was forgetting but couldn't put his finger on it. "Look. I gotta go, finish packing up and hit the road."

"Great," Steve said. "Oh, hey, I was going to stop by the BevMo and stock up. Any requests?"

Gabe thought about that and realized whatever he said, if it wasn't some sort of weird small batch organic IPA, Steve would tell him he didn't know anything about beer and get what he wanted anyway. "No, whatever you want is fine." And made a mental note to bring some Coors or something to piss him off.

"Hey, are you okay? You sound kind of distracted."

"No, everything's fine," Gabe said. "Doing one last check of the apartment."

"Well," Steve said, and Gabe could hear amusement in his voice. "It'll be good to see you guys."

"Sure," Gabe said. He was getting antsy. He wanted to get on the road and get out of the city. It was too hot for chit-chat. "Hey, Steve, we have to get going. I'm going to lock up. I'll see you in a couple of hours, okay?"

"Yeah, sounds good," Steve said. "See you soon." The line went silent.

Gabe took the phone from his ear, checked the screen to make sure the call was done, and put the phone in his pocket as Laurie came back in the house.

"Was that Steve?" she asked. "He sure can talk."

"Seriously," Gabe said, smiling. "And now we're going to spend two weeks living only a few miles from Mr. Mouth?"

"Oh, he's not that bad," she said and came over to Gabe, putting her arms around his shoulders. She kissed him playfully. "And if he gets on our nerves, we can simply kill him and dump him in the lake."

Gabe laughed. "Okay, deal," he said as she slid off, her hands lingering over his shoulders. "Reminds me, hey Kimmie, have you seen my hockey mask?"

Kimmie had entered the room, dragging a suitcase behind her. She pulled one earbud from its nesting place behind her long hair and said, "What?"

He looked at her deadpan. "My hockey mask. Do you know where it is in case I need to murder someone in the woods?"

She put the earbud back in and stared at him. "You are so weird, Dad."

And then she was out the door.

He heard the suitcase bonking down the steps as she dragged it toward the car. He turned to Laurie and shrugged. "Wonder if there's any money in being a psycho ax-murderer?"

She laughed, a bright, crystal trill that cut the edge off of Gabe's melancholy. "It's going to be fine," Laurie said, looking him in his eyes. "Really."

"Oh, I know," Gabe said. "If he really starts bugging me, I can always make an excuse to run into town for something."

"No, not that. You. Us. You'll find something else, it'll be fine," she said and smiled back at him. But Gabe could see the concern in her eyes. "Fresh start, right?"

"Right," he said. "It'll all work out." He kissed her forehead, and playfully smacked her backside. "Come on, let's get out of here before the traffic gets bad."

***

State Route 346 wound from the flatlands of the central valleys, up into the peaks of the Sierras. It was a familiar road to Gabe, as he'd ridden or driven along it for most of his life. When he was a kid he would have been nose into a book or comic, only occasionally looking up when his mom pointed out something of interest along the side of the road. It was an older road, the kind that moved with the flow of the land instead of plowing through it.

The Corolla meandered around a curve in the low hills, when Gabe saw a herd of black and brown cattle in the fields on the other side of a long, barbed wire fence along the side of the road. A few sat under the shade of a cluster of live oak, lazily swatting flies with their long tails.

Gabe smiled as he thought about seeing similar cows along the same route as a kid, and his mom never failing to announce, "Look Gabe! Cows! Mooooo!" And Gabe would sometimes look up from whatever held his interest and see the cows. When Kimmie was little, he could even get her to 'moo' at them. He was about to carry on the tradition, but when he looked toward her in the rear seat, he saw she was plugged into her headphones and dozing, so he went back to driving.

He was thinking about the last few months, the last few years really, and all the chaos. Three years ago, Gabe's dad had vanished without a trace, and the Golden Oaks PD suspected he'd died in a boating accident on Oro Lake. They'd never found the body, but they found the boat he'd rented submerged near the island at the center of the lake, and some of his gear washed up on the shore. That was enough evidence for them and the insurance company, in any case. Mike's house stood empty for a year, while Gabe halfheartedly hoped his dad would show up. Like maybe he'd gone on safari in Africa and forgot to tell anyone.

Eventually, Gabe and Laurie started fixing the house up and using it as a vacation home. Weekend getaways to the mountains at first, and then as a short-term rental property. There were always people looking to spend a weekend at Oro Lake, and they made a decent amount of extra cash renting it out for weekend and week-long stays. Enough to seed Kimmie's college fund, in any case.

But a few months later, Gabe lost his job at the advertising firm and he started thinking seriously about leaving Alcosta. He'd started talking to an out of state advertising company (and a competitor of his previous job, which was sort of cathartic for him), about managing some of their accounts, and all the work would be virtual. Only problem was it would be a trial run, and he'd only get paid for the hours he billed, so not stable work at first. And of course, Laurie loved her job in Alcosta, where she managed the office of an event planning firm, and all the project management and personnel issues that came along with it.

For Gabe, there was no need to be tied to an office anymore, he had options. And while Laurie liked her job, she had talked about maybe starting her own business. A little store or something. Moving into the old house in Golden Oaks where Gabe had grown up made sense to Gabe. He could work from there, and maybe Laurie could start her own business in Golden Oaks. But on the other hand, they could fix it up and get it ready for sale. That'd give them a nice little nest egg. They could stay in

Alcosta but with a little buffer. Gabe could be pickier about the jobs he chose, and Laurie could maybe open up her own shop, and none of it would impact Kimmie.

Either way, the place needed work, but Gabe was sure he could do most of the minor repairs himself or find local contractors to help out with anything bigger than he could handle.

A car horn blaring to his left brought him out of his thoughts. He turned his head to see a large red pickup truck barreling around him in the passing lane. The passenger stuck out his hand and gave Gabe a one-finger salute as the truck flew by.

Gabe, startled, swerved out of the way of the truck, then looked down at the dashboard, and saw that he was driving at 55.

"You okay, babe?" Laurie asked.

White-knuckled grip on the wheel, he steadied the car out, and pressed the accelerator, bringing the speed back up. He nodded. "Yeah, sorry," he said. "That guy startled me."

It wasn't yet noon, but the car was getting hot and stuffy. Laurie cracked the passenger side window, rolling it down a few inches to get a breeze going. But the air outside was hot and dry and uncomfortable, so she rolled it back up.

"Want me to turn on the AC?" Gabe asked and reached for the button.

"Sure, why not?" Laurie replied. She was watching the golden grass roll by outside her window. She'd leaned her chair back and was stretched out, relaxed. "I'm glad we're doing this," she said.

"Yeah, I am too," Gabe said, briefly taking his eyes off the road to smile at her. But it felt forced, almost false. He looked back toward the blacktop highway. A few cars (including the truck with the rude passenger) sped along a few hundred yards ahead of them, but the road was mostly clear. Golden Oaks and Oro Lake weren't as big for tourists as Reno or Yosemite, but still had a lot of visitors in the summer. "I hope you and Kimmie love it there," he said. "I've got some projects I want to tackle while we're there. I hope you two can find some things to keep you busy." He wanted to talk to her about the idea of moving to Golden Oaks permanently but couldn't figure out how to broach the subject. *When the time is right,* he thought.

Laurie smiled at him and put her hand on his shoulder. "We'll be fine," she said. She looked back out the window. "Can't wait to get my toes in the lake."

Gabe nodded, and wiped beads of sweat off his forehead. He adjusted his butt in the driver's seat, feeling his lower back pop as he did. "I hear you," he said. "We'll start settling in tomorrow, and maybe plan to take a hike to the lake in the afternoon." He looked at the temperature gauge and noticed it was 104° outside. He flipped on the A/C to cool the car down. "Oh, Kimmie, I didn't tell you earlier, but Steve and Kay invited us over for dinner tonight."

Kimmie didn't respond, her eyes focused on the screen in her palm.

"When are we supposed to be there?" Laurie asked.

"I told Steve we'd give him a call when we were settled in. He's not going to start the grill before we're on our way."

"It'll be nice not to have to cook our first night there," Laurie said.

"Agreed," Gabe replied, leaning forward, stretching out his sore back. He looked up at the rearview mirror so he could see Kimmie behind him. "Hey, kiddo, want to stop for lunch or anything?"

She looked up and shook her head. "No, I'm okay."

"You?" he said, turning to Laurie. "There's a decent burger joint up ahead."

"No, I'm fine," she said. "Let's get to the house and get settled in."

"Suits me," he said.

✳✳✳

The next two hours passed in ascent as they drove toward the mountains. Soon the gradual rise of the sloping low hills of the valley vaulted up abruptly as they approached the foothills of the Sierra Nevada mountains. Dry, golden grassland gave way to cool green on the side of the road; coastal live oaks replaced by the pine and aspen of higher altitude. And every so often they'd emerge from beneath the canopy of green to see scarred, apocalyptic blackened remains of the wildfires of the previous few summers. Intermittent scorched, dead tree trunks thrust skyward like spears; the ground bathed in drifts of ash and scattered green shoots where life was slowly returning. The patches of blackened earth seemed capricious and random, and disappeared behind the trees almost as soon as they'd appeared.

The tall trees stood clustered to either side of the road like ancient giants, stern and brooding, casting long shadows in the afternoon sun. Directly over the winding blacktop, the slimmest river of blue sky could be seen through the canopy of green.

Laurie sipped the last few drops of her milkshake, and pointed ahead where a green highway sign read simply *Golden Oaks—20* and below *Oro Lake—15*. "Hey, we're almost there," she said as the car sped past the sign. She tilted her head, looking at Gabe whose eyes were fixed on the road. She knew the look, had seen it many times before, called it his thousand-yard stare. He was lost in his thoughts again.

"Hey, Mister," she said, putting her hand on his shoulder, squeezing it lightly. "You okay?"

Gabe blinked and smiled at her. "Yeah, I'm good," he said, never taking his eyes from the road. Ahead of them, the road widened slightly, adding an extra lane in either direction. They came around a bend in the road and he saw the familiar sign *Golden Oaks—Population 3,487—Last Gas 75 miles*. Below that, another simple white sign proclaimed *35 MPH,* and below that, a board had been nailed up, painted white behind the road grime with *Slow Down!* stenciled on it in peeling black paint.

Laurie's eyes wandered to the sign as they neared the town. "You think there's really thirty-five-hundred people?" she asked. "I guess they're pretty spread out, but still."

"Oh, probably," Gabe said, and slowed to the requested top speed. "Technically, the town includes all the houses around the lake. And not everyone lives right downtown, of course."

Kimmie was watching out the window. "It really is a small town, huh?"

Gabe nodded, "It isn't much more than a speck on the map. If they didn't live there, the only reason anyone ever paid attention to it was for the camping and fishing at Oro. Maybe a little historical interest because of the WPA, but the Gold Rush was way before the town was founded. There are a few little shops downtown, but all in all, the town's pretty quiet."

A few people were out meandering along the narrow sidewalks, and only a handful of cars were parked downtown. What comprised the downtown area of Golden Oaks spread out briefly around them. A few small shops, a Raley's supermarket, two gas stations on opposite sides of the road, and the familiar green and gold sign letting travelers know they'd finally found *"Clarendon's Irish Pub."* A vibrant green shamrock design for emphasis. The five-block stretch of downtown was comfortingly familiar to him.

The last block before leaving town was dominated by the Raley's supermarket—it had been an independent grocery store until the mid-90s—next to that a tired-looking laundromat. "How late's the Raley's open?" Laurie asked as they drove past.

"Oh, not sure," Gabe said. "Man, I still remember when that was GG's," he said. He craned his neck to see the sign which showed the store hours. "Looks like maybe ten or eleven."

"We should probably stop." Laurie said. "Pick up stuff for breakfast and lunch at least. I can go back tomorrow and stock up."

"That makes sense," Gabe said as he slowed the car, flicking the turn-signal on. "Maybe pick up a bottle of wine or something to bring over to Steve and Kay's tonight." He looked into the rearview mirror and saw nobody behind him, so he pushed the accelerator and turned left across the lane. That's when he heard the horn blaring. He looked back to the road and saw a large pickup truck barreling right at them, getting larger in his vision like a charging predatory beast.

"Gabe!" Laurie yelled out, grabbing onto the arm rest next to her and bracing herself.

Kimmie grabbed the hook over the door in the back of the car and held on as the car swerved across the road.

Acting completely on instinct, Gabe floored the gas pedal, speeding across the lane as the truck raced by. Gabe slammed the brakes, skidding the car to a halt in the middle of the small parking lot in front of Raley's.

His hands were tight, white-knuckled on the steering wheel. When he realized he was holding his breath, he let it out in one large gasp.

"Jesus," he said. Distantly, Gabe heard a shriek of tires squealing on asphalt. A split second's cacophony, and then silence.

Laurie relaxed her grasp on the car door's hand grip. "I didn't even see it coming, did you?"

"No, it came around the curve so fast." Gabe relaxed his hands on the wheel and looked behind. The truck had skidded to a halt in the middle of the road, and now was backing up. "Son of a bitch," Gabe said. Looking carefully ahead, he saw nothing in front of him but the store, and pulled into a spot.

The truck reversed into the lot, and stopped abruptly. The door flew open, and a man stepped out. He was wearing faded, worn blue jeans and a dirty gray t-shirt with the American Flag on it. Below the flag was the motto, "These Colors Don't Run, Never Have, Never Will." A frayed black ball cap perched on his head, and he looked extremely pissed off. His scuffed leather boots pounded gravel as he stomped toward Gabe. A second later, another man jumped from the passenger side. He was wearing jeans, work boots, and a grimy black t-shirt.

Gabe turned to Laurie and Kimmie, "Stay in the car." He opened the door and got out, walking toward the man. "Hey, man, you okay? I didn't see you coming around the curve."

"Damn fool, coulda got yourself killed!" the guy wearing the cap said. He was ten feet away and closing. His companion was hustling up behind him, grabbing for his arm.

"Yeah, well, everyone's okay, right?" Gabe said, stopping where he was. Now the guy was right in front of Gabe, nostrils flared and face red. Gabe took a step back, raised his hands. "Hey, buddy, it was an honest mistake."

The guy plowed into him, shoved him hard with two open palms. Gabe took a step back, stumbled, and fell. His head bounced off the hood of his car with a dull metallic *thud!* as he fell to the gravel. He put a hand to his head, and it came away wet with blood. "Dude!" Gabe called out. His vision was swimming, pain throbbed in the side of his head. He heard a door slam and footsteps as Laurie came running around the side of the car.

"Back off, asshole!" she said. "Someone call a cop!" Gabe looked up to see her standing next to him, glaring at the guy.

"Screw you, bitch!" the guy said, and spat in the gravel at her feet. He looked down at Gabe and a cold smirk spread across his humorless face. "You need your woman to do your fightin', punk?"

"Arlen, forget it," his companion said, grabbing his shoulder and tugging at his shirt. He circled around in front of the guy in the grimy cap, Arlen, and tried to hold him back. "We don't got time for this bullshit."

Gabe leaned up on one elbow, started to rise, but the parking lot swam in his vision and he stumbled. "Hell, man. What the hell's your problem?"

"My problem," the guy said, "is that you almost got me killed, dumbass!"

An explosion of pain shot up Gabe's side as he felt the impact of shit-kicking boots into his ribs.

"Someone help!" Laurie yelled.

"Daddy!" Gabe heard Kimmie shout from inside the car.

"Stay in the car," Laurie shouted, and Gabe heard the door slam shut.

A double *woop-woop!* of a police siren, and Gabe saw a white-and-black sedan with a Golden Oaks Police Department decal on the side door pull into the lot. A stern, artificially amplified woman's voice boomed out from the sedan. "Back down, Arlen. It's too damn hot for any more of your trouble today."

"Goddamn it," the guy—Arlen, Gabe assumed—said, and ran for his truck. His companion ambled along behind him, a resigned slump to his shoulders.

Gabe watched a woman in a dark police uniform charge out of the vehicle, cross the gravel quickly, and grab Arlen by his shirt collar. Arlen's feet went out from under him, and he landed flat on his ass. With lightning speed, she had a pair of gleaming steel handcuffs around his wrists.

"Dammit, Arlen," the cop said, hauling him up. "Holy shit. You smell like you fell into a vat of beer. I sure hope you weren't the one driving that truck of yours." She spun him around and propped him up against the side of her sedan. "Don't go anywhere handsome," she said. The officer pointed to Arlen's companion. "Don't you go anywhere either, Darryl."

He held up his hands, shrugged, and went over to lean against the side of the truck.

Laurie sat down next to Gabe. "Let's look at your head, babe. How's it feel?"

"Pretty much like it bounced off the hood of a car," he said, and tried to sit up again. This time the dizziness passed in a brief wave, and Gabe was able to sit up fully. He could feel her fingers at his scalp. A crowd had begun to gather in front of the grocery store. A dozen or so locals milling about, cell phones at the ready and snapping pictures of the mayhem.

The trooper came toward Gabe and squatted down when she got near. She took off her dark sunglasses and took a good long look at his scalp. "One thing about police work in the modern world," she said looking from the wound to Laurie and back. "We can always count on witnesses. Never any help, but always plenty of witnesses. Sir, I'm Officer Shawna Lasher. Are you all right?"

Gabe slowly shook his head side to side, groaning at the throbbing ache. "I think I'll live."

"How's your head?" Lasher asked.

"Hurts," Gabe replied. He pressed his hand to his scalp, and when he removed it, a wet crimson stripe crossed his palm.

"Let's take a look at that," Lasher said, rising. She stood beside him and examined his scalp. "It doesn't look bad, sir. Just a scratch. I've got a first aid kit in my vehicle. Let's get you cleaned up a bit. You good here?"

"Hey! Hey Lasher, you got no right to keep me like this!" Arlen called out. Gabe turned to look toward him in time to see him slide off the hood of the police sedan and fall to the ground. "God-dammit! I got rights, you know!"

"I'll be okay," Gabe said.

Laurie stood up. "Officer, that man assaulted my husband, and you can be damned sure we'll be pressing charges."

Lasher nodded. "Yes, ma'am. I don't doubt it for one minute. But let's get your husband here cleaned up and get that wound dressed. You can tell me everything that happened while I'm doing that. Backup should be here any minute now too. Good thing I was already in town when this all went down."

She leaned over and peered into the back of the car. "You okay in there, honey?" she said to Kimmie.

Kimmie nodded silently, eyes wide with fear. "Is my dad okay?" she asked, sliding toward the window closer to Lasher.

"A few scrapes, honey. He'll be fine."

Laurie sat down next to Gabe again.

He leaned the unwounded side of his head on her shoulder. "Babe?" he said.

Laurie was watching Lasher rummaging in the trunk of her sedan, pulling out a large firetruck red plastic box with "First Aid" stenciled on the side in blocky white letters. "Yeah," she answered. "What's up?"

"Tell me again what a great idea coming up here was," Gabe said. And started laughing.

"Well," Laurie replied, and started to giggle. "I mean, I suppose it can't get much worse than this."

Gabe forced a smile. "Oh, don't say that." He started to laugh, as pain shot up his side and he hissed as he sucked in his breath. "Oh, don't make me laugh."

Lasher approached them both with a puzzled look on her face. "Well, you must not be at death's door with all that giggling going on." She dropped to one knee, placed the first aid kit next to Gabe and opened it. She took out a packet of antiseptic wipes and began to clean the area around Gabe's wound.

"It all happened so fast," Gabe said, wincing at the sting of alcohol near the gash.

"Sorry," Lasher said. "What happened?"

"We were coming through from Keyford, right?" Gabe said. "So, I was on the other side of the road. We came through town and we figured we'd stop and grab some groceries."

"We're from Alcosta. We're staying for a couple of weeks near the lake," Laurie interjected.

"Right, so we figured we'd pick up a few things," Gabe said. "I turned to cross the road, and I swear it was clear, and this guy comes plowing along, around the curve. I was already in the lane, so I floored it."

"Uh-huh," Lasher said, as she was applying a bandage. "What next?"

"Well, I pulled into the lot," Gabe said. "He blew past so fast, scared the crap out of me. I stopped the car, and that's when I saw him pulling off the road toward us."

"He drove right up," Laurie said. "Backed up right at us, and got out, screaming like a crazy person."

Gabe looked around Lasher, where Arlen was now sitting in the dirt, propped up against her car, Darryl was sitting next to him. Arlen's head was lowered to his chest, and Darryl looked like he was whispering a ration of grief at him.

"Right, he was raving about how I almost killed him, or could have gotten myself killed, or something," he said. "So, I got out of the car to apologize, figured nobody was hurt, just shook up. That's when the fucker shoved me down on my ass."

"Shoved you?" Lasher asked. "How'd you hurt your head?"

Laurie pointed to their car. "He hit the hood of our car as he was falling."

"Which one of them was driving?"

Laurie looked over at the two brothers, her eyes shooting daggers. "I honestly don't remember, it all happened so fast. Gabe, did you see?"

"I think it was the guy sitting in the dirt," Gabe said, indicating Arlen.

"I see," said Lasher. "Well, the good news is that this cut's minor. Scalp wounds always bleed a lot. You're going to want to get it checked out of course. I'm no doctor. How's it feel?"

"Hurts, but I'll live," Gabe said. "Thanks."

"Bad news is I'm going to need you both to come in to the police station, file a report," Lasher said, standing up, and snapping the first aid kit closed as she did. "Ma'am, if you're okay to drive, you can follow me to the station. It's not far at all."

Laurie stood up, offering her hands to Gabe, helping him to his feet. He stood unsteadily at first, took a few steps toward the car, dragging his fingertips across the hood for balance. He was moving slowly round the car when Gabe saw Lasher pulling his assailant to his feet.

"Which one of you was driving?" she asked the brothers.

Without missing a beat, Darryl spoke up. "I was officer." He glared at Arlen. "My brother'd had a couple of beers while we was fishing, so I drove."

"Uh huh," she replied, not believing him. She looked from one to the other. "Come on Arlen," she said, as she directed him to the back seat of her car. "We're going for a little ride."

"What about my truck?" Arlen whined. "I got fish in the cooler!"

"Well, seeing as I'm pretty sure it was you driving, I think the truck's going into impound for a couple of days." She turned to

Darryl. "Darryl, you're free to go. Call yourself a ride, and get those fish home before they start to stink up the town."

Darryl nodded, turned to go, and punched Arlen in the shoulder as he passed his brother. "Dumbass," he grunted. He dragged the cooler toward a payphone at the entrance of the Raley's, fishing for change in his pocket with his free hand.

Gabe and Laurie got back into the Corolla. Gabe saw the last few looky-loos leaving the area, scattering off to wherever they were on their way to before all the excitement started, and he wondered how many times in the next hour the phrase, "You won't believe what I saw down at the Raley's," would be whispered, texted, and posted.

"Are you okay, Daddy?" he heard from the back seat, and turned to see Kimmie behind him, her eyebrows stitched together in a look of worry.

"I'll be fine, kiddo," he said. "Just going to get checked out, make a statement, and we'll be back on the road."

Lasher signaled toward them out her window. "Stay behind me," she called out. "It's only a mile or so to the station."

Laurie gave a thumbs-up and drove out after the police sedan. She pulled toward the road and she made sure to double check the traffic coming from each direction. And a triple check to be sure. "Any idea how long this might take?" she asked Gabe.

"Not a clue," Gabe said. "Hopefully not long."

Gravel spat out behind the car as it rolled onto the blacktop. "Call Steve or Kay, will you? Let them know we might be late."

Gabe let out a sigh. "Yeah, sure thing." He reached into his back pocket to get out his phone. "Yowch!" He pulled his hand from his pocket. Thin beads of red welled up on the pads of his thumb and forefinger. "Oh, great."

"What?" Laurie asked, and spared a brief glance in his direction. "Oh, jeez," she said when she saw the blood.

Gabe braced his back against the car seat, arching his torso and raising his bottom up. He carefully reached into his back pocket to slide his iPhone out, gripping it by the edges. spiderweb of cracks was spread across the screen. "One damn thing after another."

Laurie just drove.

31

Chapter Three

After the incident in the supermarket parking lot, there had been a full hour of making statements, getting checked out by one of the on-call EMTs, and headaches both literal and figurative. Gabe and Laurie got out of the small Golden Oaks police station as the sun was inching toward the horizon, casting golden rays through the surrounding woods as it sank to the peaks of the distant hills.

From there, it was shopping at Raley's while trying to avoid stares and questions and finally, a drive straight through town and a few miles past it to the northwest shore of Oro Lake. Even once they got to the lake, they had to drive another five miles of winding road around it, over a perfectly safe, but suspiciously rickety, bridge that Gabe was still amazed hadn't fallen down. The sun hung low in the sky, slipping beyond the mountains in front of the horizon, and with a last brilliant blaze, it dropped fully behind the distant ridge and a shower of sparkles glimmered across the wide lake in its passing.

Finally, they turned onto Ringgold Lane, and in another five minutes of slow driving over the rough asphalt road, they pulled to a stop in front of the old house. It was a two-story building with a garage tucked to the right on the ground floor. The master bedroom Gabe and Laurie would occupy was over the garage. Topping the house was a slanted gable roof, not as steep as those up in the alpine areas of the Sierras further east.

Golden Oaks wasn't high enough up in the mountains that they got much snow, so nobody around there ever worried about it collapsing the houses. A light dusting, maybe an inch or two if it was a really cold winter.

It wasn't long before they were all settled in, the food was put away, and Kimmie was exploring the house while Gabe and Laurie got unpacked upstairs. Gabe was exhausted and wanted to take a shower and go to bed. But by the time they were unpacked, they were all hungry again and on their way across town to Steve and Kay's.

Soon they were sitting around the table surrounded by the rich scent of roasting beef, while Kimmie hung out on the back porch with Jill and Andrea, Steve and Kay's girls. Their youngest child, and only son, Jake, had come down to say a perfunctory hello before disappearing back to wherever his video games lurked. But when Kay called out that dinner was ready, the kids practically stampeded to scramble into chairs around the table.

"So, what's going to happen to the guy?" Kay asked as she placed a large wooden bowl filled with a green salad on the table.

"Beats the hell out of me," Gabe said, dishing salad on to his plate. "I didn't want to press charges. Let the local law enforcement do whatever they want. He's in jail for the weekend, at least."

"You should get yourself a good lawyer," Steve said, punctuating his thought with a bloody pink piece of rare steak impaled on a stainless-steel fork. "You want me to ask around for you?"

Gabe swallowed a mouthful of salad. "I don't know, guys," he said, putting his fork down on the table and reaching for a glass of beer to wash down the greens. "I mean, I don't want to deal with all that legal crap. Let the cops do their thing, keep him in the drunk tank or whatever. The cut on my head's not even deep. No stitches, nothing. Only a scrape."

"Sue his ass," Steve said around a mouth full of half-chewed steak. "Take everything he's got."

Kay glared at Steve and his choice of words. She turned to Gabe. "He sounds unhinged. Normal folks don't go around starting fights like that."

Laurie rose, taking her dishes to the sink. "Honestly, Steve, it didn't look like he had much."

"Right," Gabe said. "The cop, Officer Lasher, she said the guy's the local town asshole."

"Gabe!" Laurie said, and tilted her head, eyes comically wide indicating the kids. "Language."

Gabe's mouth dropped open a sliver and he looked at Kimmie. She was smirking. "Oh, yeah, sorry. No swears." He smiled at the girls. "Sometimes I have a big mouth, kiddo. Don't repeat it or you'll get me in trouble."

"Roger-dodger," Kimmie said, and took a drink of Coke from her glass. "No swears," she said, after swallowing, and gave him a big thumbs-up.

The other two girls whispered some secret between them, and Jake looked like he was trying to hold back raucous laughter.

Gabe suddenly didn't quite know what to make of Kimmie. Sometimes he still thought of her as a little kid, but in the past year she'd sprouted into a lanky fifteen-year-old. Not the little girl who'd fall for his 'pull my finger jokes' anymore, that's for sure. *Kim?* Gabe wondered. Should he be calling her Kim now that she was getting older? And what about still calling her 'kiddo'? He was wandering into uncharted territory. The mind of a teenager. *Terra incognita* indeed.

"You're too soft on people, that's your problem," Steve said. He put his fork down and pushed his chair back away from the table. "Gabe," he said, as if he were talking to a toddler. "That guy could've really hurt you. And it sounds like he was probably drunk. What if there'd been people crossing that road, or wherever the jackass is drunk-driving next? Sue him back to the stone age."

Gabe shot a glance at Laurie. "I'd rather forget it. Honestly, I'm beat and want to get a decent night's sleep." He stood and picked up his plate. Gesturing to Kay, he asked, "You done? Can I take your plate?"

"Sure, thanks," she said. "But let us do the dishes." She waved to Kimmie. "Give a hand, kiddo?"

Kimmie drank the last of her Coke in a few swallows. "Sure, no problem," she answered, and headed to the kitchen.

Gabe came back and sat down across from Steve. Looking out the window, Gabe saw he could barely make out the sky beyond the trees outside the house. He was taken aback by how profoundly dark it got at night in the country, with hardly any of the light pollution he'd gotten used to living in the city.

"I really want to put it in the past," Gabe said. "Don't feel like having this shadow hanging over me all week." He turned to Steve. "Anyway, I'll deal with it in the morning. I need to see if I can find somewhere in town to get the screen fixed on my phone, I can always swing by the station and press charges if I feel like it." He finished the last few swallows of beer from his glass and set it down in front of him. He was feeling a nice warm buzz now, relaxing after a long day.

"Hey, man," Steve said. "Look, do what you want. I'm telling you what I'd do." He popped the cap off another bottle of the Surly Bear IPAs he'd brought and poured it into the glass before him. "You sure I can't get you one of these?"

Gabe gazed out the window, looking into the darkening night. Thin moonlight glowed to the north, but he couldn't see the source behind the trees. he thought that maybe the new moon was coming sometime later in the week. "No, I'm good," he said, not wanting to continue the discussion. "I hear you. I'll figure it out eventually."

Steve picked up his beer and stood up. "Think I'll take this out onto the porch. Too nice a night to stay cooped up inside."

"Sounds like a plan," Gabe said, and stood again. "I'm going to check on the girls." He entered the kitchen as Steve opened the porch doors and wandered outside. Laurie was putting clean dishes away, and Gabe tapped her on the shoulder and gave her a kiss on the cheek when she turned to him. "I'm beat, babe," he said.

He turned to Kay. "Hope this doesn't come off as rude, but I think I want to crash."

Kay gave him a cordial hug. "Don't be silly. Nobody could have predicted the kind of day you had."

"That's for sure," Gabe said. "Okay, well I guess we should get rolling."

"I'll go find Kimmie," Laurie said.

***

After they got back to the house on Ringgold Lane, Kimmie said her goodnights and trudged up to bed. It had been such a long day and she wanted to go to bed. The drive had been dull, though she'd passed a little time texting with some friends from home. Kimmie had actually enjoyed the ride up with her folks, though she'd never admit it to them. But when they got to the Raley's the scuffle in the parking lot had taken the wind out of her sails completely.

She'd had fun hanging out with Jill, Steve and Kay's daughter, who'd promised to show her around town this week. They'd made plans to get together to go to the lake with Jill's little sister and brother in a couple of days. Kimmie hadn't been looking forward to the trip much, but at least now she had a sort of friend locally to hang out with. Even if for a little while. And she thought that was a pretty good thing, because she was kind of sure that her dad was going to propose moving the family up there permanently. He hadn't come right out and said it to her or her mom, of course. But sometimes Kimmie had an intuition like that, a little tickle at the back of her head that grew into a thought.

When she was little, Ms. Emmy—one of the teachers at her preschool—used to call her "the Bloodhound," because Kimmie was so good at finding lost things. Whenever a kid would lose a crayon or a toy or something, Ms. Emmy would smile and say, "Go find it, Bloodhound!" and more often than not, Kimmie would know right where the thing was.

As she got older though, she realized that talking about finding lost things or knowing secret things about other people sort of creeped people out. And since she had the dream about Grandpa Mike, the intuition or hunches, or whatever they were had become dim, like the last beats of a waning echo. Nothing much had come to her in a long time unless it was something really strong, something someone was dreadfully worried about. She'd gotten strong feelings of worry from her dad since he'd lost his job. But the feeling had started becoming strong again after her dad lost his job and he'd mentioned coming to stay at Golden Oaks.

Maybe living up here would be okay. She'd miss her friends back home, but she never really liked Alcosta. The city was too busy, too much noise and bustle. Even when it was quiet, it was too noisy.

The lake house was pretty old, and had kind of a weird smell, but her room was nice enough. And she hadn't known that her folks had installed Wi-Fi, so that was something. She'd had to promise her mom she wouldn't spend the whole trip Snapchatting with her friends or watching YouTube. And she'd try and stick to that, but when they drove through Golden Oaks, she remembered that this place really was the boonies. God help her if her dad, decided to try to teach her to fish.

The room was small, or cozy as she tried to think of it. A twin bed in one corner, chest of drawers along the adjacent wall, and an old oak writing desk next to it. Over the bed, on the wall across from the doorway a pair of casement windows looked out into the dark woods. She cranked them open enough to get a breeze in the room, thankful for the screen that would keep the inevitable barrage of night critters out. She smelled oak and pine on the night breeze, and the cool air off the nearby lake. She couldn't wait to go swimming at their own private beach. Kimmie pulled her phone from her pocket and connected to a charging cable, and plugged the cable into the wall beneath the desk. The battery had run down earlier in the evening, unnoticed. Now the screen was blank except for the icon which showed it was recharging. She left the phone on the desktop while she got ready for bed.

She was glad to get out of the clothes she'd spent all day in and change into the knee-length T-shirt she wore to bed. She'd be mortified if any of her friends saw it with its great big, silk-screened image of Taylor Swift's smiling face, but she'd had it for years, and it was worn down so soft that she couldn't imagine sleeping in a strange place without it.

For a few minutes she sat on the edge of the small bed, taking in the room, staring out the window. Five days wasn't so bad. More than that, she'd have to take it as it came.

And maybe there was something to do in town, or maybe she could convince her mom to go on a day trip somewhere further into or over the mountains that was more entertaining than what she'd seen of Golden Oaks as they drove through.

She left the room and went down the hall to the bathroom. She'd started brushing her teeth when she heard a series of faint pings and beeps from her bedroom. She rinsed and spat and almost ran back to her room. Her phone's screen was now glowing softly from where she'd left it on the small desk. She lifted it to check the screen, and as predicted, she had a couple of text messages waiting for her from friends back home.

Hailey missed her already, and Sydney was mad at Danara, and OMG did she know that Emily had a huge crush on Trey? Many three-letter acronyms and short messages were exchanged and slung through the ethereal pathways of the internet. But it was late, and Kimmie's eyes grew heavy. She wrapped the messages up, the conversations ending with some variation of *STFU LOL!!! OTB* and a sleepy-faced emoji for punctuation.

She turned off the overhead light, called "Goodnight!" softly out the door and got into bed. Faint moonlight glowed beyond the trees outside, casting thin blue fingers through the windows next to her bed. She fell asleep listening to the sound of creaking trees, the chirruping of distant night creatures, the occasional hoot of an owl, and the trickle of water from the nearby creek.

***

Gabe sat on a bench swing on the back porch of the lake house, the warm night surrounding him as he sipped at a glass of ice water and rocked gently. Laurie had gone to bed, and now it was only him holding down the porch swing. He'd intended to go right to bed once they got back but was feeling restless and couldn't sleep.

High overhead, the fingernail sliver of the waning moon glared down at him through the trees like a sleepy eye. And while the night was warm, he pulled his gray zip-up hoodie close around to fight off the thin fingers of chill air winding through the warmth. He felt a stinging at the back of his neck through his haze. When he dully slapped at it, he felt something slick and warm pop under his palm. Taking his hand away he saw a large mosquito flattened against his palm, its long limbs twitching in an awkward spasm. A smear of crimson emanated outward from the dead insect. He wiped his hand against the leg of his jeans, smearing the bug off. "Fuckin'-a," he muttered, and drained the last of the ice water.

The vacation was already off to a crappy start. Gabe had forgotten how tedious he found Steve. He could deal with Kay because she was a friend of his wife's. But Steve rubbed him the wrong way. The idea of spending five days trying to avoid him didn't thrill Gabe one bit. And the drama had already started before they'd even spent one day in the lake house. Gabe could tell Steve was sure that the fight Gabe had described earlier was probably Gabe's fault.

Gabe was also finding the quiet put him on edge. He'd lived in the city so long, he was now used to the comforting mechanical murmur of buses, cars, late night wanderers. Out here, it was dark and quiet, and the few noises that did permeate the woods felt weird to him. Creaking trees, insect songs, and the splashing of the lake in the distance. Still on edge from his encounter earlier in town, he knew it was going to take him some time to settle into the quiet.

Beyond the trees which surrounded the yard, Gabe could barely see moonlight glittering off the lake water, only a few dozen yards distant. He wondered if his dad had ever had the path cleared off. They'd talked about it but Gabe wasn't sure if Mike had ever hired anyone to do it. He remembered coming to visit years ago, and his dad getting pissed off lugging all his fishing gear down to the water to the little dock on the beach. He knew it was only a mile or two by car, taking the loop road off Ringgold Lane.

He'd figure it out tomorrow. The whole point of the trip was to decide what needed to be done to fix the house up. After all, like it or not, this was his place, so he ought to know something about it.

Gabe was tired now and thinking he should get upstairs to bed before he got any more wobbly than he was already feeling. He stood to leave, and as he turned to go into the house, Gabe heard another sound. A shifting, rustling. Like something or a few somethings, long and heavy, slipping through the underbrush, slithering beneath the dark foliage. Receding into the night. A wet slapping, splashing followed briefly, and then silence.

Despite the warmth of the evening, Gabe felt a chill up his spine. The hairs on the back of his neck twitched as gooseflesh puckered his skin. He entered the house, checking twice that the porch door locked behind him. He stumbled through the darkness of the building and double checked all the locks. Once he was sure they were secure, he went upstairs, undressed, and quietly slipped into bed next to Laurie. He lay in bed, listening, sure he wouldn't fall asleep any time soon. He was out in fifteen minutes.

CHAPTER FOUR

Gabe woke early, sneaking out of bed and going downstairs quietly so as not to wake anyone. He started the automatic drip coffee machine, silently thanking Laurie for picking up coffee when they were shopping the night before. While the machine hissed and dripped, Gabe leaned back against the island in the middle of the kitchen, where bar stools lined one side. His head and side still ached from his skirmish in town the day before. Maybe Steve had been right? Maybe he should press charges against the guy and sue him? But as Gabe started stewing over dealing with the inevitable legal hassle, while also coordinating fixing up the house and everything else, he felt exhausted and overwhelmed.

When he noticed the carafe in the coffee machine was full, he went to pour himself a mug and pulled a stool out from the kitchen counter. After adding milk and a sprinkle of sugar, he sat, hunkered over the counter and sipped at the warm, smoky liquid. *Today was going to be a long one,* he thought. He was mulling over what he was going to have to do about the assault when he heard Laurie coming down the stairs.

Laurie smiled when she saw him. "Coffee smells great, babe. Thanks for getting it started."

"Not a problem. Sorry if I woke you. I tried to let you sleep."

"No, that's fine," she said and came over and kissed him. She gave him a hug before moving away. "How's your head feeling?"

"Oh, totally fine. A little sore, but the headache's gone."

"That's good," Laurie said. She opened the fridge, peering inside. "Any thoughts about breakfast?"

Gabe sipped at his mug of coffee. Thready vapors rising from the cup and stinging his eyes as he did. "No, not really," he said after swallowing. "Thought I might go into town in a bit. See if I can find someplace to get my phone fixed. Maybe I'll grab something on the way. There's a diner sort of downtown-ish." He placed the mug back down on the counter in front of him.

"Well, downtown's not that big," Laurie said. She was at the fridge, getting out a small container of heavy cream for her cup. "Want some company, Mister?"

Gabe smiled and shrugged. "I'll be there and back in no time. You hang out with Kimmie. Get some girl time. Maybe call up Kay and see if she and the kids want to go to the beach or something?"

"You sure?" she asked, pouring cream into her cup. "Might be fun to explore town for a bit."

"Come along if you'd like," he said. "I'm always happy with your company, but it's no problem for me if you'd rather stay here. I mean, you haven't seen Kay in forever, and you have to look at my dopey mug every day."

Stirring cream into her coffee, Laurie looked at him like she was going to say something but thought better. "Yeah, well that's my favorite dopey mug, so try not to get in any more trouble and get your nose busted or something."

Gabe laughed, but it was false, a thin, forced wheeze. "Oh, I'll be fine," he said, and took his empty cup to the sink. But he didn't feel fine. "Officer Lasher's got that good ol' boy locked up tight, and I'm sure that's the last we'll hear of it."

Laurie turned toward him as he was rinsing his coffee cup under the running tap. "I'm sure it is, but keep your eyes out anyway, okay?"

"Promise," Gabe said. He wrapped the mug in a dishtowel, rubbing it dry. More than it needed. He didn't want to admit it, but he was full of nervous energy. Part of the reason he wanted to go into town was to make sure that Lasher had that Arlen guy locked up tight. Make sure he wasn't let out until their vacation was over. Something about him seemed like the kind of guy who'd hold a grudge and maybe come looking for them. His hand slipped on the mug, and it tumbled free of the washcloth. "Shit!" he hissed as it fell, tumbling through the air, and smashed to pieces at his feet.

"Son of a bitch," he muttered. He stared at the mug and took a deep breath.

"I'll get a broom," Laurie said, walking toward the utility closet in the kitchen.

"This is not my week," Gabe said.

Laurie stopped, turned toward him. She reached out her hand to him.

He took it in his, fingers clasping lightly. "One step at a time, Mister," she said, and squeezed his fingers. "I'll take care of this. You go explore the mysteries of downtown Golden Oaks, California," she said, smiling.

"Hey, you laugh, but Golden Oaks has a storied past. Gold miners, moonshiners. Guys used to brew booze up here and run it to the speakeasies in San Francisco, Sacramento, Alcosta, wherever. Hell, there wasn't even a lake here a hundred years ago, you know? It was a WPA project to dam up the rivers, I guess they hoped to make some sort of resort area out of the place, or at least encourage some businesses to settle here. Don't know why that never happened. There were rumors about mob guys from Reno and Tahoe setting up hideouts around here back in the 50s. No idea if that was true though. But the town grew up around the lake over time."

"Thank you for the history lesson, Professor Smarty-Pants," Laurie said, a sarcastic grin dimpling her cheek. "But you scoot and let me clean up your mess."

"You sure?" he said, as his fingers slipped from hers.

"Totally," she said, and got a broom and dustpan out of the closet. "Get out of here before I put you to work."

"Hey, all right," Gabe said. "Don't have to tell me twice." He gave her a kiss on the cheek, and she gave him a swat on the butt, and he was out the door.

***

Gabe stepped out onto the porch and took a deep breath as he closed the door behind him. His head still felt muddled, and his side ached, but the air was crisp and clean. Sun filtered through the surrounding forest, casting dappled shadows along the ground, making the rough asphalt of Ringgold Road seem less haphazard, and more rustic. And it was so quiet. In the distance, he could hear trickling water from the creek that ran by the property and shortly fed directly into Oro Lake and the scratchy *caw-keet!* of a scrub jay.

He stepped down the short stairs from the porch to the dirt path which led around to the garage, and as his foot crunched on the dirt, he saw a dull flutter of movement out of the corner of his eye. Looking that way, he saw a blackberry bush at the edge of the property line. And at the base of the bush the branches were shaking back and forth. He took a few steps toward them. The branches stopped moving.

He stepped forward again until he was standing in front of the bush and poked at it with the toe of his shoe. When he did, a large black bird erupted from the rear of the bush, flew straight into the woods, and rocketed off into the trees. Gabe wasn't sure if it was a raven or a crow, but it was big, and startled him. He stepped back quickly, tripping over his own feet and crashed onto the lawn.

"Shit," he grunted, as he clambered back up. His face was right in front of the bush, and he smelled a foulness. A rank, vinegary smell, rich and meaty. Smelled like something dead, maybe something in the bushes, or down by the creek. But underlying that, the faintest hint of the vaguely chlorinated smell of ozone. He stood up and poked at the blackberry bush looking for the source of the smell. If there was a dead animal or something in the bushes, better to get rid of it and not draw predators.

When he gingerly moved some of the branches of the bush aside, careful of the thorns, he saw the source of the smell. A few tufts of fur, and what looked like a good-sized rat or squirrel's paw rested on the dirt. Gabe got down on one knee to take a closer look and saw small clots of black slime tangled in the blades of grass, oozing around the paw and dripping from the leaves of the bush. Some kind of algae, Gabe decided, maybe some animal got caught in it and dragged it up from the lake. It sort of reminded him of the clots of lake weeds he often caught on his fishing line, the crud dredged up when his hook accidentally dragged along the bottom of the lake. And it smelled rank, whatever it was.

The smell was stronger as he leaned closer and reminded him of mildew, but with a strange, acrid, ozone-like tang underlying it. It was revolting.

He stood up and crossed the lawn to where a length of green garden hose was coiled up next to the house. Gabe turned on the spigot, uncoiled the hose, and dragged it across the lawn. When he got to the other side, he squeezed the trigger on the spray head and sprayed the bushes down thoroughly until they were dripping with crystal drops of clear water.

The smell abated in the spray, replaced by the clean scent of tap water.

He heard a voice behind him.

"Hey, thought you were going to town?"

He turned to see Laurie walking up to him, a steaming mug of coffee in her hands.

Gabe lowered the hose and released the trigger, the water stopped. "Hey, yeah, still going. Found something gross in the bushes, just cleaning it up."

"Something gross?" she said, leaning around him to take a look. "What was it?"

"Oh, not sure. Looked like something died in the blackberries, and a crow or raven or something was having its own breakfast."

"Well, I guess that's country living for you," she said. "Do you think we should we call animal control or something?"

He shook his head. "Nah. Circle of life and all."

She patted him on the back and turned to go back into the house. "Okay, well, I'll keep my eyes out for varmints and critters."

He sprayed the bushes down with water one more time for good measure. Almost as an afterthought, he adjusted the spray valve to its narrowest setting and hosed the ground under the blackberry bush. Really blasted at the area where he'd seen the slick dark matter earlier, and the lone, pale paw. When he looked again, there was nothing on the ground below the bush but mud.

He returned the hose to where it had hung before, wiped his wet hands off on his jeans, and left the yard, continuing along the side of the house to the front. He was fumbling in his pocket for his car keys when out of the corner of his eye, he saw a raven land on the eaves of the roof.

Gabe looked up at the bird which hopped along the mossy roof tiles toward him. He wondered if it was the same bird he'd startled (and had startled him) earlier. "Sorry I interrupted your breakfast," Gabe said.

The bird opened its beak and *cawed* at him a few times, flapping its wings.

"Yeah, well, same to you, buddy," he said, and got into the car.

Gabe backed the car out of the driveway, and with a quick three-point turn, he had the Corolla turned around and facing the way they'd come in last night. The sun was lost behind the trees of the woods around him, filtering through the canopy and casting ghostly patterns on the hood and windshield of his car. But as he drove toward town, he saw the large copse of pine trees and aspen begin to spread out further from the side of the road, clear cut to make way for the humans who'd taken over the valley. The forest thinned as he put the house behind him and drove toward Golden Oaks.

***

Gabe drove toward Golden Oaks, his mind wandering. He found himself thinking about how towns and cities are like living things. Despite the rock and steel construction, there's something organic about them. A flow, where the residents create whorls and patterns which almost replicate a living organism. He thought about how even though Alcosta and Golden Oaks were very different in many ways, they shared the commonalities of roads and streets, residences and commerce, areas of health and blight, which all combine into something recognizable and give each town its unique character.

He got closer to downtown and thought about how that's like the heart of any city. It's where the population—the town's lifeblood—enters, takes care of business, and passes through to carry on the life of the town. Downtown is where the action happens, where people from all around the town meet in passing or on purpose. It's where decisions are made and plans enacted. It's the place that the old folks in town complain has changed too much over the years, and that the young people find boring because it's always the same and nothing ever happens there.

That morning, the small town, a strangely living thing in the Sierra foothills, was drawing sluggishly awake. Gabe noticed how empty the town was.

Only a few people were walking the street, and not much was open when he got into town. He realized he hadn't taken into account that it was still early on a Sunday morning, and most of the few businesses downtown wouldn't be opening for a few hours.

Gabe parked in the middle of town and decided to wander a bit. Hunger was creeping up on him, and when he found the Get Up and Go Diner, he figured it would have to do, and it did. He'd eaten there many times in the past. It was as close to a "hangout" as he and his friends had had when they were teenagers, and nostalgia made his decision for him.

When he stepped inside, he was amused to see it hadn't changed a bit since the last time he'd been there a few years previous. Pale turquoise wallpaper surrounded him, along with the haphazard assorted knick-knacks found at most roadside diners. Strange expressions of the owners' style and sense of humor were expressed through the medium of dusty tchotchkes. The wide white eyes of a Felix the Cat wall clock peered from side to side as its tail wagged in unison. A poster with a cat clutching a branch and "Hang In There, Baby!" next to the cash register, with a single dusty strand of spiderweb running across a curling tear in the bottom edge. Aside from him, it was almost empty, with only an older couple sitting at a corner table, eating eggs and toast and speaking to each other quietly. They looked imminently comfortable in the booth, and Gabe found himself wondering how many hundreds of breakfasts they'd had right there over the years.

He got a decent breakfast, along with a recommendation for a place to get his phone fixed. The waitress, a jaded middle-aged woman named Emily told him about the old Ace Hardware over by the police station. The owner's son was good with computers and did repairs for most folks in town when they'd gotten a virus on their computer, or busted their phone screen like Gabe had. He'd set up a spot in the back of the shop and called it "Hardware Support."

"Hardware Support? Get it?" Emily asked, while freshening up his coffee.

"Yeah, sure," Gabe said. "That's a good one. Weird having a tech support shop in the hardware store though. How'd they come up with that idea?"

She finished pouring the coffee. "The owner's son, Eddie, lost his job during the shelter-in-place from the Corona in 2020. He was working up in Reno at a computer fix-it place that closed down. So, he came back to Golden Oaks and set up shop in the Ace with his dad."

"Oh, well, glad he landed on his feet," Gabe said.

She pointed at his forehead. "What happened to your bean, fella?"

Confused at first, Gabe suddenly realized she was talking about his head. His hand went to his forehead where he felt the thin strip of plastic bandage stuck to it. "Oh, yeah. I, um, oh nothing, really. Slipped and banged it yesterday."

"Lot of that going around, I guess," she said. "Heard about a fella yesterday got into a fistfight in the parking lot at the Raley's, split his head open on a car or something."

Gabe's chest tightened. Word sure travels fast in a small town. "Yeah, that was me. Not as bad as you heard, obviously." He tapped the bandage with one finger. "A scratch, really."

Emily squinted to get a better look at his bandaid. "Well, heck. Way people were talking, you'd think you'd have your brains leaking out your ears."

"Not that I'm using them for much, but my brains are fortunately still in my head," Gabe said.

"Well, looks like you'll be fine," she said. "So you're the one who pissed off Arlen so bad?"

Gabe was mid-swallow when she said that and gagged on his coffee. After a cough, he nodded, reaching for a napkin. "Yeah, I guess I am."

"Don't worry about it too much," Emily replied. "Chances are you weren't even the first person to piss him off yesterday. Arlen's pissed off at the whole world. That boy doesn't have a chip on his shoulder. He's got a whole damn tree."

Gabe chuckled at that. "It was a misunderstanding that got blown out of proportion."

Emily put her hand on one hip, and looked at Gabe like he was a particularly stubborn five-year-old refusing to eat his vegetables. "Well, you listen to me, and stay clear of Arlen McEwen."

"That bad, huh?" Gabe said, leaning back into his chair. His head was starting to hurt again, not from the scrape, but from the thought of the ongoing drama in what was supposed to be a relaxing week.

"Him and his brother. They both hold onto grudges like angry dogs," she said. "So take my advice, and keep away from them."

"Well, I'll do my best," Gabe said, and drained the rest of his coffee. "Chances are I won't be coming into town much."

"Probably for the best," Emily said. "Not that I'm trying to run you off or anything. But one run-in with the McEwen brothers is enough for anybody."

Gabe was getting antsy. Starting to feel like maybe coming into town this morning was a bad idea. Or at least that it was time to see about getting his phone fixed and get back to Laurie and the lake house. Put as much distance between him and either of the McEwens as he could. "Thanks for the warning. We're staying up near the lake for a few days, so I don't really think I'll be getting into town often."

"McEwen's live out past the lake," she said. "Where abouts you staying?"

"On Ringgold Road," Gabe said. "It's off the main road around the lake." He reached for his coffee cup.

She paused and gave him a look up and down. "Well, hell. You're Mike's boy, aren't you?"

Gabe's hand stopped halfway to his mouth. He put his coffee back on the table. "Yeah, that's right. You knew my dad?"

She nodded, smiling, but with a sad turn to her eyes. "Oh, yeah. Mike was a great guy. Used to talk about you all the time. And your daughter, what's her name?"

"Kimmie," he replied.

"That's right, Kimmie. He thought the world of you."

Gabe smiled, swallowing a lump in his throat. "That's really kind of you to say."

"We were all so sorry when he went missing like that," she said. "He's been missed around town."

"Thanks," Gabe replied, quietly.

"You ever thought about selling the house?"

Gabe leaned back in the booth seat, feeling the vinyl cushion soften behind his back. "Maybe. I really don't know; it'd need a little work if we decided to sell it. I need to take stock of the place and get some idea what can be done with it. Might hit up one of the local realtors while I'm in town for a few days and see if they've any thoughts."

"That makes good sense," she said. "Well, anyway, listen. Don't you worry about the McEwens. I mean, not that Darryl or Arlen would even know where you were, but that's on the whole other side of the lake from them, and they're back off a ways into the woods, I hear. Almost back to the other side of the lake, I think, but not quite."

Gabe felt a little relief at that. "In that case, I'm not going to worry about it. Out of sight, out of mind."

"Sounds good," Emily said. "Can I get you another cup of coffee?" She raised the coffee pot to pour, but Gabe shook his head.

"No, thanks," he replied. "I've really got to get going. See about getting my phone fixed if I can."

Emily nodded and took her check pad out from her apron pocket.

"I'll leave this here," she said sliding the green and white meal receipt across the table to him. "Hope you have a good time while you're up here. Stop by for dinner sometime, we make a mean meatloaf on Wednesdays."

"Oh, I remember the meatloaf," Gabe said. "Charlie still making it?"

"You know Charlie Gaines, the owner?"

Gabe nodded. "Oh, sure," he said. "Man, I'm glad to know he's still around. Too much in the world's changed. Nice to have some continuity."

Emily smiled. "I suppose that's true."

"Where is he, anyway?" Gabe asked, looking around the diner.

"He took the day off today and went fishing. Might have some fresh-caught catfish on the special tonight."

Gabe reached for the check, as he was getting out his wallet with his other hand. "I'll spread the word. I'll have to come back and say hi to Charlie. And never let it be said I turned down a mean meatloaf."

Emily laughed at that and strolled back to the kitchen.

Gabe placed a few bills on the check, leaving an ample tip for Emily, and placed his empty coffee cup on top of them. He caught Emily's eye as he left and waved goodbye.

When he stepped outside the diner, a wave of heat pounded into him. It had been warm already when he left the cabin, and it had warmed up significantly even in the time he'd been eating breakfast. He could tell it was going to be a hot day and was glad he was getting his errands taken care of early.

***

Gabe found Hardware Support without a hitch. It was right where he'd recalled the hardware store being. Down the block from the police station where he'd been yesterday, right where Emily had told him, and he was able to walk there from the Get Up and Go Coffee Shop. Most places in downtown Golden Oaks proper were within walking distance of each other, and Gabe felt a growing fondness for the town begin to take hold. It had been a long time since he'd meandered the streets of the town, and he took some comfort in seeing how most of the place remained unchanged since his youth, though the occasional new business had cropped up here and there.

Sliding glass doors opened and an electronic bell pinged as Gabe entered Hardware Support. Stepping inside and out of the growing heat off the street, he was glad of the air conditioner. The shop was narrow but long. Only a few aisles wide and stretching back a dozen yards or more were shelves instead filled with every imaginable item one could use for home repair. Gabe recalled buying model kits from this store when he was younger, but it looked like the hobby section had disappeared long ago. Gabe was standing in the entrance to the store, staring at the aisle signage overhead and wondering how many trips he'd make to the hardware store over the next few days, when an older man came toward him.

"You look lost. What can I help you with?" the man said. He was tall and lean, with the sort of rough hands that looked like they had experience with any sort of project the store could supply equipment for, and many more. He was wearing the ubiquitous red Ace Hardware apron. The ID tag pinned to the apron read "Mitch." He looked vaguely familiar to Gabe, another anchor to the town's past, and Gabe wondered how many times he'd come into this store as a teenager to buy model glue and paints from probably this very guy.

Gabe's gaze was down the aisle in front of him as he turned toward Mitch. "Yeah, I was told you had a phone screen repair service?"

"Yup, sure do," Mitch replied and started walking down the center aisle. "Only place to get a smartphone fixed for fifty miles in either direction," he called over his shoulder.

Gabe followed Mitch down the aisle, past racks of plumbing supplies which gave way to camping gear, and finally to a key duplicating machine and a desk with a pair of iMacs glowing softly on it. Behind the monitors sat a skinny kid, probably in his early twenties, who was clicking disinterestedly on the mouse clutched in his hand.

"Hey, Eddie," Mitch said as he approached the desk. "Fella here needs his phone fixed."

Eddie looked up from the computer screen, taking a moment to refocus on Mitch and Gabe. "What's wrong with it?" he asked.

Without a word, Mitch left, walking back up the aisle to the front of the store. Gabe passed him as he did so, pulling his phone from his back pocket. "Just a cracked screen," he said. He pressed the home button and the screen glowed to life, showing a kaleidoscope of multicolored app icons refracted through the spiderweb cracks in the glass.

"That's all?" Eddie asked. He took the phone from Gabe, peered at it, turned it over and scanned the case with the practiced eye of someone who'd done this particular operation many times before. "It's a 12, right?"

Gabe had to think. "Uh, yeah, 11 or 12, I think. Probably a 12."

"It's a 12," Eddie said, and turned back to the computer. He clicked the mouse a few times, and Gabe saw an inventory database spring to life on the screen. Eddie scrolled madly, tapped out a series of numbers on the keyboard, staring at the screen. "Yeah, I've got a screen in stock. Give me an hour and I'll have it ready for you."

"Oh, yeah, that'd be great," Gabe said, getting out his wallet. "How much?"

"Sixty bucks for the screen and labor. More if I find anything else wrong, but that doesn't seem likely."

"Great. Do I pay you now, or later?"

"Pay when you pick the item up," Eddie said. An electronic hum and a whir, and he pulled two sheets of paper out from under the desk. He gave one to Gabe, and set the other aside, placing the phone on top of it. "That's your work order. Bring it back in an hour."

"Sounds great," Gabe said. "Okay, well, I'll be back in a bit."

"Great," Eddie said, and turned back to the screen of his iMac.

Gabe stood by, not really sure if the conversation was done, but feeling like it most likely was. "Hey, this place used to have a great hobby section," he said. "You still carry anything like that?"

Eddie looked up at him without moving his head, rolled his eyes as if he couldn't be bothered. "Nobody builds models or any of that stuff anymore. We got rid of it all years ago."

"Oh," Gabe said. "That's a shame." He turned away toward the front of the store. He was nearing the exit doors when he saw Mitch helping a scruffy-looking man with some plumbing. The man was wearing a sweat-stained T-shirt and grease-splotched jeans and was mulling over the differences between two different shutoff valves in the plumbing aisle. He looked vaguely familiar.

And then Gabe recognized him: Darryl McEwen. The brother of the guy who'd punched Gabe yesterday. He felt his stomach flop and a cold sweat break out along his spine. He hoped the guy didn't recognize him. "Eddie get you all sorted out?" Mitch said as Gabe approached.

"Yeah, he's working on it. Said it'll be an hour."

"The kid's good with his hands when it comes to that little detail stuff," Mitch said. "I coulda helped you with a busted phone if it was an old rotary job. But these new cell phones, that's beyond me."

Gabe nodded, and noticed that the guy Mitch was talking to was eyeing the bandage on his forehead.

"Hey, ain't you the fella from yesterday?" the guy asked.

"Yes, I am," Gabe replied, and tried to worm his way around the guy.

"Hey, I'm sorry about that," Darryl said. "My brother's kind of got a temper, you know?"

Gabe slid past him. "Yeah, no worries," he said, trying to avoid another conflict.

"You from around here? Don't think I've ever seen you in town before."

Gabe stopped. "Yes, I am. But I moved away a while ago. Twenty years or so."

"Uh-huh," Darryl said. "When'd you say you come back to town?"

"I didn't," Gabe said, feeling defensive. "What's it to you?"

"What's it to me? Nothin', I suppose." The guy looked Gabe up and down, like he was sizing him up. "Only askin' questions. Wonderin' about things."

"Yeah, well, maybe wonder about your own business," Gabe replied.

"Now, Darryl," Mitch said, steering the conversation. "Fella doesn't have to justify himself to anyone." He turned to Gabe, a dry, mirthless smile across his face. "Glad Eddie could take care of your phone for you."

Gabe strode past the pair. "Sure. Thanks for the help. I'll be back in an hour or so."

Mitch nodded, smiled, and turned back to helping Darryl McEwen. Gabe moved toward the store's exit, and the glass doors slid open again with a *ping!* He turned, and saw that Darryl was still glaring at him.

This town's getting weird, he thought as he stepped back outside. With an hour to kill, he wandered. Strolled along the street, taking his time, with nowhere particular in mind.

CHAPTER FIVE

Laurie sat on the back porch, feet curled up under her, the swing bench rocking gently in the morning breeze. She had a warm mug of coffee—her second of the morning so far cradled between her hands, wisps of steam rising from the dark surface as she sipped at it. The mug was light gray with a dark, speckled pattern on it. An abstract image of mountain peaks and woodland trees decorated the side of it, along with the slogan "Camping Hair, Don't Care" stenciled over the image. Laurie smiled at it. It was the kind of thing her mother-in-law would've had squirreled away in the cupboard.

A copy of last month's *Sunset* magazine had held her interest for a few minutes after Gabe went into town, but now lay discarded on the porch floor below her. Laurie was enjoying the whispering murmur of the woods, the growing warmth of the day, the sense of calm which surrounded her. A metallic squeak caused her to look up, and she saw Kimmie stepping onto the porch, closing the screen door behind her. "Morning," Kimmie said.

"Morning, kiddo," Laurie replied, and sat up a little straighter, making room on the bench. "Come to keep me company?"

Kimmie took the offered space, sitting next to Laurie and drawing her feet up cross-legged.

"It sure is quiet here. Where's Dad?"

Laurie sipped her coffee. "He went into town for a bit. He wanted to find someplace to see about getting his phone fixed and look around town, I guess."

She looked over at Kimmie and could tell the teenager was worried about something from her furrowed brow, and the way she was chewing at her lower lip. "You okay?" she asked.

Kimmie shook her head. "I guess I'm kind of worried about Dad. That was scary yesterday."

"It was," Laurie said, nodding. She reached out and put her hand over Kimmie's and squeezed it gently. "Your dad's okay, kiddo. I think he probably hurt his pride more than anything."

"Has Dad ever been in a fight before?" Kimmie asked, looking up sheepishly at her mom from under her bangs.

Laurie mulled that over, while sipping at her coffee. She shook her head as she swallowed. "I don't think so. I don't think people really get in fights as often as you'd think from watching TV."

"I guess," Kimmie said. "Anyway, it was fun seeing Jill and everyone last night. I'm going to see if they want to go to the lake sometime next week."

"That sounds great," Laurie said. "We'll make a day of it. You two figure it out and let me know. I'll give you a ride to the public beach whenever you want. There's a great place to swim there, and you might meet some other kids from town. Oh, nuts. Well, except for today, I guess. Your dad took the car into town."

"No problem," Kimmie said. "I guess I can hang around here for today. Maybe tomorrow or something."

"Sounds good," Laurie said. "But hey, after breakfast, why don't we take a walk down to the lake from here? There's a back trail that goes right from the yard to a little bit of beach. There's a pier your grandpa had put in years ago."

"Oh, that'd be fun," Kimmie said. "I think I kind of remember that."

"Let's get some grub started. I slept in way too long," Laurie said, and turned back into the kitchen, calling out behind her. "Come on, let's see what's for breakfast."

Kimmie followed her as Laurie was getting a carton of eggs from the recesses of the refrigerator. "Can you start up the stove?" Laurie asked.

Kimmie placed a large Teflon-coated skillet on the stove, and, with a click and a whiff of gas, got a flame going under it.

"How do you want your eggs?" Laurie said, finishing off the last few swallows of her coffee. "I picked up some cinnamon-raisin bread too. It's in the pantry if you want toast."

Kimmie nodded and went to the pantry to retrieve the loaf. "Scrambled is fine. Where's the toaster?" she said, as she began unwrapping the plastic bag containing the bread.

"Crap," Laurie muttered. "I forgot. I know it's around here somewhere."

Kimmie began rummaging through the shelves and cupboards in the kitchen.

Laurie had cracked four eggs into the pan, and was stirring them, watching the clear liquid mass turn white, clot, and form solids as she scraped at the pan. She looked up and toward the wooden cupboard doors next to the refrigerator. "Maybe up there somewhere?"

With a triumphant, "Aha!" Kimmie pulled a dusty chrome toaster out from behind a bag of paper napkins. She put the toaster on the linoleum island at the center of the kitchen, plopped a slice of bread in both slots, and pressed the lifter knob down until it clicked. Almost instantly, the smell of warm cinnamon began to fill the kitchen. While the toast warmed, Kimmie took down three plates, found utensils, and began to set the table.

Outside the sun was rising over the trees; the lawn was bathed in golden morning sun. In the far distance, past the trees, Laurie saw the faint glitter of sunlight on the lake. "Going to be a beautiful day," she said. She scraped the eggs into a green and white porcelain bowl and brought it over to the table. She sat and started dishing eggs onto the two plates.

Kimmie cleared her throat. "You ever think about what it would be like to live up here?"

Laurie knew the look in Kimmie's eyes. A combination of pity and worry. The toaster pinged, and two slices of warm cinnamon raisin toast rose from it. Laurie took the toast and dropped two more slices of bread into the toaster.

"Well," Laurie said, taking a seat across from her. "Yes, I have. I bet it would be nice. Slower paced than back home, anyway. Why do you ask?"

"Oh, just thinking."

"Any reason?" Laurie asked.

Because I know Dad wants to move here, and thinks we'd like it, but he hasn't gotten up the nerve to talk about it with us yet, Kimmie thought. But what she said was, "I thought it might be nice. You know, in case you and Dad are thinking about it or anything. I guess that if you were, I suppose I'd be okay with it."

Laurie nodded as she ate. "Well, it's not something we've talked about, but I'm glad you like it up here." Laurie realized that she was getting so used to thinking of Kimmie as almost an adult, but she was still figuring out how the world worked.

"Yeah, I guess," Kimmie said.

She got up to go to the refrigerator and pulled out a carton of milk. She started pouring milk into the cup and looked out the kitchen window across the lawn, and toward the woods beyond. "I can kind of see the lake from here. Through the trees that way," she said, pointing across the lawn with her chin. "We can really walk straight to it?"

Laurie was caught mid-bite. She swallowed the eggs and replied, "Absolutely. It's like having our own private beach. Cut through the woods, and there we are. We'll pack a lunch and take it with us. Make an afternoon of it."

"Awesome!" Kimmie said, raising her voice in an excited almost-shout. "When can we go?"

Laurie finished the last of her eggs and took a bite of toast as the toaster pinged again. "Whenever you want. Let's clean up breakfast and we can pack lunch."

Kimmie wolfed down the last of her eggs and followed it with the last few bits of the cinnamon toast. "Okay!" she said, as she got up from the table and practically sprinted upstairs to her room.

Laurie watched her go, smiling. She started to gather up the breakfast dishes and was thinking about what sort of picnic they could pack, when she was startled by the galumphing sound of teenaged feet running back toward the kitchen. Kimmie burst back into the kitchen. She was wearing a one-piece dark blue swimsuit, and had a towel tossed over her left shoulder. Swim goggles were propped up over her forehead, and bright green flip-flops adorned her feet. Laurie once again marveled at how grown up Kimmie looked lately. She was growing tall and lean, yet still with the awkwardness inherent to all fifteen-year-olds.

"What are you waiting for?" Kimmie said. "Let's get to the lake!" She drew out "lake" like a wrestling announcer exhorting a crowd to get ready to rumble.

Laurie laughed and gave Kimmie a hug. "You go play outside. I still have to change into my swimsuit and get lunch together."

Kimmie squirmed out of her mom's embrace, gave her a quick kiss on the cheek, and said, "Okay! Don't take too long." She was out the back door before Laurie had a chance to answer.

***

Kimmie sat on the bottom step of the stairs leading from the porch down to the back lawn. She'd kicked off her green flip-flops and was worming her toes in the grass. She was humming the Lumineers's song "Ho-hey!" and keeping time by tapping her fingers on her knees. Looking across the lawn, she saw the blackberry bushes, still glittering with water where Gabe had sprayed them earlier. Kimmie stood up and wandered over to the bushes, where she saw that the branches were heavy with berries. She carefully plucked a few from the bush, scraping the knuckles of her left hand slightly on the tiny thorns.

"Yowch," she muttered, pulling her hand away, a pair of juicy blackberries clutched between her forefinger and thumb.

The berries were fat, dark, and glistening. They looked perfect to her, but she didn't think she'd ever seen real berries in the wild before. Lots at Safeway or Trader Joe's, but she'd never picked them right off the plant before. She reached out with her other hand to snitch a few more as she popped them into her mouth. But when she bit down on them, a wave of revulsion hit her, and she spat them out.

They weren't the tart, yet sweet flavor Kimmie was used to or expecting. They were bitter, slightly salty, yet with a musty aftertaste.

She was reminded of getting an old book down from a high shelf at the school library. A book nobody had checked out in a long time, and accidentally breathing in the dust on top of it when she tried to blow it clean. The berry wasn't juicy at all, but rather had a chalky, putty-like texture. It was as if the fruit was long dead, not rotten but desiccated, and yet looked perfectly fine.

Kimmie spat again, trying to get the taste out of her mouth. She plucked another berry from the plant, and bringing it closer to her face, squeezed it until it split open, releasing a faint foul smell. It smeared between her thumb and finger, slick like liquid soap, not sticky or juicy.

"Gross," Kimmie said, flicking it away and wiping her hand on the grass. She strode along the edge of the grass, looking suspiciously at the berry bushes as she did. Wondering if the rest of the fruit was as foul as the ones she'd already tried, or maybe that was a diseased plant. A few more steps and she saw a bare patch between two bushes. Wide enough for her to walk through without scraping her legs, for sure. Beyond that, a thin patchy trail led down into a gully where a stream trickled and gurgled along. "Cool!" she whispered excitedly.

A hollow *bang!* behind her and she turned to see Laurie waving to her from the porch.

"Looks like you found the trail, hey kiddo?" Laurie called, as she stepped down to the grass. "It winds through the woods back there. It's a bit of a hike, but it shouldn't be too bad."

She looked down at Kimmie's bare feet. "Did you bring shoes?"

"Are flip-flops okay?" Kimmie asked, looking back to where she'd left the spongy green shoes and felt like a dope. Those were beach shoes, pool shoes. Not hiking shoes. She noticed that her mom was wearing sandals and felt a little better.

"Oh, those'll be fine," Laurie said, picking them up and bringing them over to Kimmie. "Alright kiddo, you found the trail; you lead the way!"

Kimmie smiled and slid her feet into the flip-flops. "Roger that!" she said with a mock salute and turned back to the wide spot between the bushes. Her eyes stopped on the berries. "Hey, Mom?"

"Yeah, what's up?"

"Those are blackberry bushes, right?" Kimmie asked.

Laurie looked where Kimmie was pointing. "I think so. Why do you ask?"

Kimmie turned back to the trail, and began to walk down the slope. "Oh, I tried one earlier, and it was nasty. Maybe they're not ripe yet?"

"Probably past ripe," Laurie said. "They look pretty good, don't they?"

"That's what I thought too, but they're nasty," Kimmie said while carefully walking down to the stream. Her feet skidded on rough gravel, and she slid the last two feet to the sandy bank edging the stream.

"Woah!" she said, looking back up toward Laurie. "Watch your feet here." She pointed at the ground where she'd slid.

"You okay?" Laurie asked, hiking down the narrow path behind her. She hopped the last foot and landed on the sand.

"Oh, I'm fine," Kimmie said. She looked up and down the stream. It wasn't much, but a trickle of water ran past them. A rich, earthy smell rose from the gully, and while the earth nearest the water was still soft and moist, she saw it drying and cracking a few feet away.

When she got to the bottom, Laurie said, "It wasn't a very wet winter, and it's been a dry summer." She pointed up to a line where grasses and scrub grew across the stream. "That's how high the stream got in winter. In a few weeks this whole gully will be dry as bone."

"How do we get to the lake from here?" Kimmie asked, searching the far side for a trail through the woods.

"There's a trail that cuts through the woods. Right there, see?" Laurie pointed across the stream bed. There was a wide patch in the dirt, next to a gnarled oak, boughs heavy and drooping. They wound through the woods and Kimmie asked if they had to worry about poison oak, but Laurie was able to assure her they were too high up for that. So they tramped around knots of oak and aspen, sunlight dappling the trail through the intertwined leaves and canopy of branches overhead.

The trail wasn't hard to follow, even if it was somewhat overgrown from disuse. They came around a bend in the track, and suddenly Kimmie stopped, completely still.

Up ahead a few yards, a deer and her fawn were stepping lightly across the trail. Thin beams of sunlight rippled across the deer's golden-brown fur, highlighting the snowflake-like spots on the fawn's hide. The deer carefully made their way across the path and into the bushes beyond. Laurie slowed and stopped next to Kimmie and watched as the doe and fawn turned first to look at them, before walking into the woods.

And then they vaulted, bounding up the hill and disappearing into the trees.

Kimmie turned, wide-eyed, to Laurie. "Mom! Did you see?"

Laurie put her hand on Kimmie's shoulder and hugged her. "I did!" she said. "How special, right?"

"Oh, I wish I had my phone with me," Kimmie said. "I wish I'd been able to get a picture to send to my friends back home." *Home*, she thought. *Not for much longer.* She began walking again, and her mom followed along.

"I'm sure we'll see them again," Laurie said. "Besides, there isn't any cell reception out here anyway."

"Oh, really?" Kimmie asked. "Nowhere around here?"

"Well, it's spotty," Laurie said. "There are towers on the other side of the lake, I think, but I've never been able to get a signal on this side. I leave my phone at home, or I'll end up wearing out the battery for nothing."

Kimmie looked ahead and picked up her pace. "I think we're almost there!" She jogged ahead.

"The lake should be right ahead of us. Kimmie, don't go in the water until I'm there, too! Okay?" she called out.

In response, Kimmie raised a big thumbs-up in the air for her to see. Laurie strolled along behind her, but after a minute, Kimmie was lost from sight. She followed on in silence. The creak of trees waving in the slight breeze and the muffled thudding of her feet on the trail below them the only sound.

Laurie crested a rise in the trail and saw that it dipped down ahead and weaved through a copse of trees.

In the distance, the golden shimmer of sunlight glittered off the green lake water. Moments later, she emerged from the trailhead onto the smooth sandy beach which crept into the waters of Oro Lake.

The beach stretched away from her in both directions. To her left, it curved around in the distance. The other side of the lake was far enough away that it was not much more than a blur of green and spindly tree trunks reaching skyward. She knew the lake in its entirety was sort of a horseshoe shape. One point of the lake was right here, where it curved around on itself. Closer to town was the public beach run by the city where there was a lawn, a swimming area, and a few piers with boats tethered to them. To her right, the beach meandered away and disappeared around a curve. Somewhere back there it curved around and formed the other part of the horseshoe shaped lake.

Laurie was catching her breath, while Kimmie had already dropped her towel and sandals and dove off the pier into the cool green water as soon as she saw her mom approaching. She was watching Kimmie splashing in the water, and then her eyes were drawn to the small island in the center of the lake. A few boats were out; people paddling around and a few fishing. Across the lake, there were a handful of people fishing off the small docks.

All in all, she thought it was an altogether lovely day.

***

Kimmie swam. Arms and legs slicing against the water and powering her forward. Pulling and kicking against the cool green water while the warm summer sun beat down on her back. And when her arms grew tired, she'd roll over and float, staring up into the bright blue sky. Laurie was sitting in the sand on the edge of the water, the woods behind her from where they'd emerged not long before. Treading water, her legs and arms forming slow circles, Kimmie looked around to get her bearing. She saw Laurie dozens of yards away and waved to her.

Laurie waved back enthusiastically. She'd warned Kimmie not to swim out too far, and Kimmie figured she was getting to the edge of that vague radius. To Kimmie, it was like they had the whole lake to themselves. There were people picnicking and swimming on the other side of the lake, a few paddle boats, and even a larger motorboat within sight. Kimmie saw a man fishing from the rear of the boat and could vaguely hear the muttering of the gas engine. The man saw her and waved slowly, while taking a drag from the beer can he held in his other hand. Kimmie waved back, but with less enthusiasm than she'd put into her wave to Laurie and Kay. She noticed the name painted on the side of the boat, *Shadowfax*.

"Cool," she said to nobody. "Like in *Lord of the Rings*."

But there was nobody on *their* side of the lake. Kimmie liked that and decided that it *was* their side. Nobody else on the beach anywhere near her or Laurie. Their own little secret spot, and they could swim, or fish, or build sandcastles, or sit and listen to the waves if they wanted to.

And that funny little island in the center of the lake. She wondered if anyone had ever been out there before, and took a few paddling strokes toward it. Laurie had told her not to go that far, and that the island was off-limits, but no reason she couldn't get a closer look.

She dipped underwater, letting the green surround her entirely and shot toward the island with the strong pull of a breaststroke. A few more strokes underwater and she came to the surface, caught her breath, and quickly dropped back underwater. She pulled against the water, feeling her body shoot forward effortlessly.

She kicked backward with her legs when something scraped against her foot. She shot up to the surface, and spat water, yelping in surprise. She looked behind her but didn't see anything. Had she kicked a branch, or log maybe? Treading water, she slowly floated herself away from the area where she thought she'd kicked whatever it was. The water did look a little darker there, like something lurking a few feet below the surface. She looked up and saw the man on the boat looking in her direction. He waved toward her again, and looked like he was calling out to her, but she couldn't make out what he was saying.

Something slithery and cold circled around her ankle and pulled her below the surface. Hard and fast, before she had a chance to cry out. Her arms shot straight up as cool water surrounded her, large bubbles of breath volcanoed out of her lungs in a muffled shout as she plummeted down. She was topsy-turvy, losing her orientation as bubbles filled her vision. The water was getting darker, and when she looked up, she saw the glittering lake's surface dwindling. Pain lanced her leg and she felt strong, slimy coils winding around her calf, grabbing her other foot. She kicked, violently shoving against whatever it was that gripped her, pulled her toward the lakebed.

And then she was on the muddy, sandy floor of the lake. Green light surrounded her, beams filtering through the lake water, the reeds and detritus reaching up from the fine silty mud below her. Her chest was getting tight, black spots swimming before her eyes as she held her breath. Kimmie reached down to try and free her legs, and through the haze of lake water saw black, root-like vines or tendrils of something wrapping around her ankle and winding up her leg. Her other foot was caught in a black, ridged mass. She pulled against it, reaching down with one hand to free her foot.

Her thumb slipped under the web-like mass and pried against it. Her fingers gripped it, piercing the dark tendrils' surface, slick with rot, twitching against her foot. She screamed, soundlessly, taking in a lungful of water. Panic filled her as soon as the water did. She kicked against the hand, ripped the ropy pseudopod from her leg. Stamped and kicked and heaved against the water surrounding and invading her. Suddenly she was loose, floating upward, away from the twitching and grasping below her.

Distantly, a shadow slid across her overhead, and a chill shrouded her as the water's temperature dropped by degrees. And a great crash and churn of bubbles. Kimmie's body was suddenly encircled, engulfed. Something grabbed her around her torso, and she had no energy to fight.

Darkness swallowed her.

CHAPTER SIX

Gabe parked the car on the side of the house and came through the back, letting the screen door slam against the frame as he did. The house was quiet, and he called out, "Laurie! Kimmie! Anyone here?" When he came into the house, he saw a scrap of paper in the middle of the otherwise empty breakfast table and went over to take a look.

"Gone to the lake, back later!—L&K!" written on it in skipping blue ink. Gabe smiled at that. He was glad the girls were having a chance to have their fun. He poured himself a glass of iced lemonade from the fridge and found a pad of paper and a pen in the junk drawer in the kitchen, and went to sit on the back porch.

Gabe sat, rocking on the swing and staring out into the woods. He heard little more than birdsong and creaking trees on the soft breeze. He'd almost forgotten how still it was up here. How quiet life was in Golden Oaks compared to the noise and bustle of Alcosta, Oakland, or any of the other cities he'd spent his adult life in.

He stared at the yellow pad of paper, the thin green lines wanted to be filled with ideas and tasks for getting the house back in order, sorting out what needed to be done to get it ready to sell. He half-heartedly began a list, but his heart and mind weren't in it. Within a few minutes he had absent-mindedly flipped to a blank page and was sketching the trees in the distance. After a few minutes of that, Gabe went back to the list. He picked up the pad and took a walk around the small house, checking it out. It could use some work, a little TLC, but it had potential. The rough planks of the dark wood exterior certainly had some charm. Gabe's dad had done most of the basic maintenance himself, so those tasks had fallen by the wayside years ago. Patches of moss on the roof sprouted from beneath and between plank tiles. Twigs and leaves poked up over the edges of the rain gutter. A mass of them caught in the top of the downspout, reaching over the edge like so many spindly spider legs.

Around the front, he toed at a few loose flagstones leading from the street to the front steps. Yeah, it could use some work, a little curb appeal. But it was a solid house. He was pretty sure they could sell the place if they decided to. Or move into it. He decided he'd talk to Laurie about that idea soon. He'd even seen a little vacant shop in his meanderings downtown, which he thought might interest her.

Gabe had underlined "roof" when he heard a car coming down the road. He turned and saw a large, pickup truck, gray with dust and trundling toward him.

It slowed to a halt, and through the bug-specked windshield he saw Kimmie and Laurie in the front seat next to an older man who looked vaguely familiar.

Kimmie's hair was in disarray, plastered to her face, her head resting on Laurie's shoulder. Laurie waved at Gabe as they pulled to a stop.

The guy driving nodded in Gabe's direction, opened the door, and stepped out. "Heya, you this little girl's daddy?"

Gabe rushed forward, confused. "Yeah, I am. What's going on?" Suddenly, he recognized the man from his childhood. "Oh, Charlie, right? From the diner?"

"Guilty as charged," Charlie said. "Give me a hand." He opened the passenger door to his truck. Gabe followed, and as he got to the open door, Kimmie scooted toward him.

"Help her upstairs, will you Gabe?" Laurie said as she followed Kimmie out.

Kimmie slid from the truck and fell into Gabe's arms. "What's going on?" Gabe asked, looking first to Laurie, then Charlie. "What happened?"

"She's okay. Let's get her inside, I'll explain everything," Laurie said.

Gabe picked Kimmie up in his arms and headed toward the door to the house.

Laurie turned back to the driver. "Thanks again for everything," she said, shaking his hand and hugging him. "You saved her life."

"Glad I was so close when she went under. Lucky they haven't closed the lake to boats yet, either. Go on in and take care of your girl. Here's my number in case you need anything else." He scrawled his name and number in slightly shaky black ink on a scrap of paper and handed it to her.

"Thank you again," Laurie said, and turned to hustle into the house, closing the door behind her.

Charlie got back in his truck, shaking his head. "People should stick to the beach with the lifeguards," he muttered as he turned around and drove off down Ringgold Lane. His tires kicked up a cloud of fine dust as he disappeared around the bend.

***

"Put her down there on the couch," Laurie said, and Gabe did, gently. He brushed Kimmie's hair from her face with his hand as he lay her back on the couch, placing a pillow behind her head. "What happened, babe?"

Laurie quickly crossed the room and sat next to Kimmie on the edge of the couch. "Are you okay, honey?" she said, taking Kimmie's hand in hers. She looked around, saw a soft green cable-knit blanket tossed over the back of a chair. "Gabe, hand me that blanket?"

Gabe pulled it from the chair, brought it over, and draped it over Kimmie, who smiled at him, and coughed, a deep wracking cough that shook her whole body. She shivered in front of him, and Gabe noticed the deep purple bruise which encircled her ankle. Swollen and scratched, thin lines of dried crusted blood circled it in lateral stripes.

"So, what happened?" he said, his stomach knotting, and fear raising the pitch of his voice.

Laurie took a deep breath. "Kimmie had a scare in the lake." She turned to him. "Babe, can you put on a pot of tea, or coffee or something? Anything warm."

Gabe felt a wave of relief wash over him. "Sure. Kimmie, should I get some ice for your ankle?"

Kimmie nodded.

He went to fill a ziplock bag with ice from the freezer.

"Kimmie got her foot caught on something in the lake," Laurie said. "She couldn't get free and started drowning. Thank God that guy was there."

Gabe was standing near the stove, getting a mug down from the cupboard. "He runs the diner in town. Charlie Gaines. I stopped there for breakfast and the waitress said he was out on the lake fishing for tonight's special."

"Well, thank God for small miracles," Laurie said. She had her hand on Kimmie's forehead, a look of concern on her face. "You don't feel hot, sweetie. How do you feel?"

"Crappy," Kimmie said, and coughed again.

Laurie smiled. "Well, that's understandable, I guess." She turned as Gabe approached, sitting on the edge of the sofa by Kimmie's feet.

He handed the bag of ice, wrapped in a dishtowel, to Kimmie. "Here, put this under your ankle. It should help a little."

Laurie lifted Kimmie's leg onto a small pillow, putting the bag of ice between her foot and the cushion. "Thanks babe," she said. "So, he was fishing nearby. Closer than I was anyway. When he saw Kimmie thrashing under the water, he zoomed over in his boat and jumped into the lake after her. Swam down and pulled her free."

"Wow," Gabe said. "Lucky break he was there. Where were you?"

Laurie's eyes suddenly filled with tears. "I was right on the shore, Gabe. It all happened so fast I didn't even have a chance to jump in the water before Gaines was jumping from his boat."

"Hey, it could've happened to anyone," Gabe interrupted. "Count our blessings she's okay. Kimmie, how's your foot? Any better?"

She nodded. "Hurts, but I think it'll be okay."

A whistle grew louder on the stove, and Gabe looked up to see the teakettle steaming. He went over to it, turned the oven knob to off; the flame disappeared under the kettle, and the whistle dwindled to a thin sputtering hiss.

Gabe opened a cupboard next to the fridge. Inside were boxes of instant oatmeal, cans of beans, olives, and a glass jar full of tea bags. A random assortment of items left behind by his dad and previous weekenders. He suddenly felt very small, and very tired. The realization that his parents were both gone, and that he could have lost his daughter hit him as he watched Kimmie, small and fragile herself on the couch.

Gabe carried a cup with a Lipton tea bag steeping in it over to Kimmie. He placed it on the coffee table in front of the couch. "Here. Hope this warms you up a little."

"Thanks, Dad," Kimmie said, pulling the blanket up tighter around her.

"You think you need an ibuprofen? I think I've got some in my travel bag," Laurie said.

"Sure, that'd be great," Kimmie said.

Laurie turned to leave the room, then stopped. "Do you think we oughta take her to a hospital or something?"

"I don't know," Gabe said. "I think there's an urgent care in town."

"Okay, let me get the ibuprofen, and we'll see how it goes." She turned to leave the room.

"Did you want anything in your tea, Kimmie? Sugar, milk?"

She reached for the cup. "No, it's fine plain. Thanks." Kimmie took the cup, blew across the lip, and took a sip.

"How is it? Too hot?" Gabe asked.

She shook her head slightly. "No, it's fine."

"And your foot? How's the ankle doing?"

She peeked toward her ankle and saw the bruising. "It's sore, but the ice helps."

"What do you think you caught it on? A root or branch or something?"

"I don't know. Maybe," Kimmie said, and sipped the tea. "How would a root or branch get all the way down there, anyway?"

Gabe leaned back in his chair. "Oro Lake was part of the forest before it was flooded back in the 30s. It was a WPA project. It's really more of a reservoir than an actual lake. It's dammed off at one end."

"Oh, yeah?" she said. "I didn't know that."

She scooted her foot back under the blanket. "Dad," she said, hesitantly. "If I tell you something, do you promise not to get weird about it?"

Gabe shifted uncomfortably in his seat. "I mean, I guess I can't really say until you tell me. Is anything wrong?"

"It's ..." she dropped her eyes, embarrassed. "I know this sounds weird, but I swear something under the water grabbed me. Not like I caught it on a root or a branch, but like something really grabbed my foot."

"Well," he said, looking at Kimmie. She suddenly looked like a scared child, not a strangely confident teenager. "I guess that is pretty weird. But it'd be hard to be sure about something like that, don't you think? With the water murky and all, and I'm sure you were pretty scared."

She nodded but didn't say anything.

"I mean, do you think it was like a crawfish or snapping turtle or something?" he asked.

Kimmie shook her head. "No, nothing like that."

She looked up at him, scared eyes peering out from behind the long hair spilling over her face. "Like a hand. It's nothing. Probably letting my imagination get away with me."

Gabe smiled and ruffled her hair. "Too many scary movies with your friends. I'm sure it was nothing to worry about. But let's keep an eye on your ankle, make sure it doesn't get infected or anything, deal?"

"Deal," she said, and finished the last of her tea.

***

"Jesus, Gabe, it was terrifying," Laurie said as she pulled her jeans up over her swimsuit bottom. Gabe was sitting on the edge of the bed as Laurie spoke. "She was swimming along, having a great time, and suddenly she was gone. Vanished under the water. I thought she'd dived down below the surface until I saw the water frothing, and her hand shoot out. Then she was right back under."

Gabe leaned back on his elbows, lying across the bed. "Wow. And Gaines happened to be there?"

"Lucky for us, yes." She opened her black leather travel bag and began rummaging around in it before withdrawing a small bottle of generic ibuprofen pills. "Bingo.

Gabe sat back up. "I'm sorry I wasn't there with you."

"No, it's fine," Laurie replied. "You wouldn't have been able to act any faster than I did. And you were in town anyway, so don't beat yourself up about it."

"I know it's awful, but I keep thinking what if nobody'd been able to get her unstuck? I keep running it through my head."

Laurie wiped tears from her eyes. "Me too. I can't unsee it. But it's a good reminder for us all not to go into that lake on our own, I suppose."

Gabe leaned back on his elbows on the bed. "Kimmie seems fine now, and I guess that's all that's important.

"She's shook up, but I think she'll be okay," Laurie said, and sat down on the bed next to Gabe. She put an arm around his waist, and lowering her head to his shoulder, took a deep breath, and let it out slowly.

"I'll get the info for the urgent care in case we need it," Gabe said.

Laurie raised her head and Gabe felt her hand slip from his waist. "Perfect ... Oh, hey, did you find anyone to fix your phone?"

"Huh? ... Oh, yeah, crap I did." He leaned back and slid his hand into his pocket, pulling his phone out. "Good as new. Need to charge it up, though. I couldn't find the cable in the car."

"Oh, my bad," Laurie said. "I brought it inside and plugged it into a charger next to the bed last night. Hang on." She leaned over the side of the bed and pulled up a plastic cable. She reached out with her other hand and Gabe gave her his phone. She snapped it onto the cable, and the little familiar Apple logo appeared as it powered up. "Hopefully you didn't miss any important calls."

Gabe stretched and stood up. "Who's going to call me but you? And you're right here, so who cares about anyone else?"

"Smooth talker," she said. "Keep it up, and you might get lucky tonight."

"Hey now," Gabe said, smiling, and moving in close to kiss her. "That sounds like a challenge."

Laurie put her arms over his shoulders, tugging him toward her. Suddenly, her mouth was on his, and he felt her breath, hot and warm, mingle with his own.

Laurie gave him a hug, and a kiss on the cheek and then said, "I'm going to check on the girl."

"Sure, I'll be right down," he replied.

She left the room, closing the door behind her. Gabe stood next to the bed. He glanced briefly at his phone, then placed it back on the nightstand and let it keep charging. He pulled back the thin gauzy curtains, before opening the windows. A soft breeze washed through the insect screens and the smell of pine, oak, and summer dust trickled into the room. Outside the windows, the forest stretched on. In the distance, he could barely make out the lake, sunlight glittering off its surface like a shower of diamonds. He heard the distant creak of trees waving in the light wind, the rustle of oak leaves and pine needles rubbing together. He could smell the warm scent of sap on the breeze, the dry underlying smell of the dirt floor of the forest. He took a long breath, held it, and let it out slowly. Felt his heartbeat slow and his frustration slide away.

They had some decent savings and could maybe make it work up here. He'd been glad to get away in his twenties, but Golden Oaks, Oro Lake, they weren't so bad, really. Gabe sighed again and left the room, knowing that he needed to either give up the idea, or have a serious talk with Laurie. Probably best to talk it over with her in any case. They'd figure it out somehow.

Chapter Seven

In addition to picking up plumbing supplies for the backed-up sink, Darryl McEwen had been in town to try and post bail for his brother. Arlen spending a night in the drunk tank wasn't an uncommon occurrence, and Darryl knew the drill. He'd expected the usual: talking Officer Lasher into letting him go, being told to keep a better eye on his brother next time. Same old song and dance, and a drunk and disorderly to deal with.

But this time, Lasher had told Darryl off in some particularly unpolice-like terms. She was keeping his brother for at least the weekend, so Arlen was going to have to stew in jail for a while. Darryl asked him if he wanted anything from home and promised he'd bring him his toothbrush and some dirty magazines later in the day. He was pretty sure he could sneak them in, despite the contraband nature of the request.

Well, at least Arlen's getting three squares and AC. Darryl figured Arlen was getting a pretty good deal when it came down to it. Darryl was going to be on his own for a while. He figured he'd come to town, may as well make the best of it. He picked up the essentials at Raley's while he was in town (beer, a couple loaves of day-old bread, and a few pounds of hamburger marked down because it was nearing its "sell by" date).

Afer that, he meandered over to the hardware store to find a replacement shutoff valve for the crapper in their bathroom. The old one had finally rusted through a week ago, and the toilet couldn't flush without it. He and Arlen had been shitting in the woods, but since he was in town anyway, Darryl figured he'd get the part to fix it.

Good thing, too, because running into the guy who'd got Arlen put in jail was an unexpected bonus. He followed Gabe through Golden Oaks for a bit until he realized the guy wasn't doing a damn thing but killing time. When Gabe had picked his phone up from the nerd at the hardware store and headed out of town, Darryl followed him in his dusty forest green 1987 Ford Thunderbird. The car was almost more rust than steel, but it still ran. Could keep up with Gabe's Corolla, anyway.

Darryl followed far enough behind that he thought Gabe wouldn't notice him. Rolled along behind him for a few miles out of town until the blue Corolla took a left onto Ringgold Lane. Darryl didn't bother following after that. Ringgold only went a couple miles around the lake, and there weren't many roads coming off it. He knew what Gabe's car looked like now, and could come back and look for it later after he'd had time to decide what he wanted to do.

If Arlen knew he'd found the guy, he'd sure as hell want Darryl to do something about it. When he got home, he found a scrap of paper and scrawled a quick note: "Blue Corolla—Ringgold Lane." He moved some old copies of *Hustler*, *Guns & Ammo*, and a few empty beer bottles out of the way and left it on the coffee table in the ramshackle living room.

Damn it's hot, Darryl thought. He went to the fridge and got himself a beer, drained it in a couple of gulps, and went back for another.

The clicking of nails on linoleum alerted him to the arrival of Arlen's dog, Barney. Darryl looked toward the dog as he entered the living room. Barney sat on his haunches and *whuffed* at Darryl, eyebrows arching and turning his head to the side. The dog was mostly brown with a few dark spots along its flanks, and a dusting of gray around its muzzle. A Heinz-57 breed if there ever was one.

"What do you want, dog? Hungry?"

Woof! Barney replied and wagged his tail, tongue lolling from his snout.

"Alright, you stupid dog," Darryl said. "Let's find something for you to eat before you start chewing up the furniture."

*****

An hour later, Barney was fed, and Darryl had a couple beers in him and was lying on his back on the floor next to the toilet. The bowl stank, a musk of stale urine from when he'd forgotten the damn valve was shut off. Darryl cranked the wrench clutched in his hand. Nothing moved.

"Damnit!" he shouted into the silence.

Sweat dripped along his scalp, running through his thin dark hair and down toward the nape of his neck. It was "sonofabitchin' hot" as their dad used to say. One of these days maybe he'd get around to setting up an AC unit. The money he made doing odd jobs and playing the lotto didn't afford him the luxury of cooling, but on still, hot, miserable summer days like this one, he thought it was worth it. Shit, maybe he'd sell some of Arlen's stuff while he was in stir.

He leaned into the pipe again, and with no warning, the valve came loose with a snap. The damn pipe cracked, sluicing thin threads of foul-smelling water along the length of the pipe.

"Fuck a nut!" Darryl yelled again. The pipe was cracked on the outside of the tank at least, saving the house from getting flooded. Darryl leaned up onto one elbow, squeezing around the grimy toilet bowl.

He kicked the wrench and replacement parts to the side, then stood staring at the toilet. "Dammit," he grunted. "Was looking forward to shittin' in my own damn crapper."

He heard a rhythmic clicking from beyond the bathroom door out in the hallway, and the large slobbering dog came trundling through. Darryl turned to the dog, reached out and gave it a rub behind its ears.

The dog squatted back on its haunches, laid out its front paws, put its head on them and stared up at him.

"Well, Barney," Darryl said, sitting on the edge of the bathtub and petting the dog's head again. "Guess we better hope the Queen of France don't stop by anytime soon. She would not approve of the state of this shitter."

The dog yawned wide, closing its mouth with a slight *whuff,* and a drizzle of slobber on the linoleum floor.

"You probably need to go too, huh?" Darryl said.

Barney's eyebrows arched a bit.

"Ready for a walk, buddy?"

Barney clambered to his feet, long nails rattling on the linoleum. He turned to walk from the room. Darryl had a sudden memory of when Barney was a pup and would race around the house at the sound of the word "walk." But that was years ago, before the white around Barney's muzzle had begun to match the grey at Darryl's temples.

"Alright boy," Darryl said, wiping his hands on his jeans. "Give me a second and let's go for a walk."

Flies lazily buzzed and bumped through the kitchen as Darryl got Barney's leash off a nail pounded into the wall next to the back door which led out from the kitchen in the back of the house. There was a sour smell to the room. Stale beer and unwashed dishes. Darryl figured he should probably take care of them at some point.

"Come here, boy," he said to Barney, and latched the leash to his collar. "Alright, buddy. Let's stretch our legs, okay?"

He grabbed a cold beer out of the fridge and pressed the can against his forehead. *Good lord it's hot,* he thought. He drained the beer, crunched the can, and tossed it onto the kitchen table to deal with later. He took out another for the walk, feeling the coldness of the can pressing it like a balm on the back of his neck.

He closed the fridge door and looked at his watch. "Dinnertime in a few hours," he said. He opened the freezer side door and stared into the cold depths for a minute, letting the frigid air wash over him. There were a couple of frozen steaks in a ziplock baggie shoved up at the top of the freezer and he pulled them out.

"Let's fire up the grill and have us some steaks tonight, boy," he said to the dog. Barney looked up at him and licked his chops. Darryl leaned over and rubbed the dog's head. "Yeah, why should Arlen get to enjoy these, anyway? Been saving 'em for a special occasion and having dumbass Arlen out of the house for the night is about as special as it's gonna get."

He put them on the counter next to the sink in a puddle of sunlight. Before closing the refrigerator, he slipped his fingers through the plastic loop rings on a six-pack of Coors to take with him.

The torn screen door slammed shut with a bang and a clack as they trundled down the three creaky stairs to the bare dirt patch beyond. Car parts, stacks of warping plywood and loose boards, and other junk littered what the McEwen's called their "yard." A low post and rail fence marked the edge of their property, weatherworn wooden beams attached to rough posts. Darryl had replaced the loose rails many times over the years. But there were great gaps between the beams, and it wouldn't keep anyone or anything in or out of the yard, but it did mark their property line. And the rusty metal signs nailed to the sides of their house with slogans like "Trespassers Will be Shot; Survivors Will be Shot Again" and "Due To Increasing Costs of Ammunition, We No Longer Offer Warning Shots" made their intention pretty clear.

Even so, they always made sure Barney was tethered when he was in the yard. Once when he was a pup, the dog saw, a squirrel or something, and took off through the fence, barking up a storm. It had taken the better part of an afternoon of Darryl and Arlen wandering around the woods to find him.

Barney was shuffling back and forth in front of the gate. "Hang on, you dumb dog," Darryl muttered. He unlatched the rusty gate latch, and swung the it open. It *skreeked* loudly on rusted hinges, the noise alarming in the calm quiet of the summer afternoon.

"Come on, boy." He pulled a can from the six-pack, laced two fingers through the empty ring, and gripped the dog's leash in the same hand. He popped the freed can open and took a swig. Barney strolled through the gate after him and it slammed shut with a bang.

A dirt path led from the gate back around to the front of the house and petered out a dozen yards into the woods, turning into patched grass and clear spaces between bush and scrub.

If it wasn't for them using the path to sometimes go down to the lake to go fishing, it probably would have grown over completely. Darryl found himself thinking that in a couple of months he'd probably have to come out here with the loppers and cut back some of the branches that were getting close to blocking the trail.

Barney started to whimper and scratch at the dirt, looking back at Darryl.

"Okay, this is as good as anywhere, I guess," Darryl said, and led Barney off the trail to do his business. When he was done, Darryl kicked some dirt and leaves over the stinking mess, drained the rest of the beer and tossed the can into the woods. He wiped sweat from his forehead with his free hand.

"Wanna go to the lake, boy?" Darryl asked.

Barney's tail wagged faster at that, and he let out a snuffling *whuff!* of enthusiasm.

"Alright," he said. "Let's go."

***

The trail didn't take long to get them there, though Darryl did have to stop along the way to piss in the woods.

"You don't buy beer, buddy," he said to Barney. "You rent it." To reiterate the point, after he zipped up, he pulled another can from the six-pack he carried, popped the top and chugged it.

Following a long belch, he crushed the can in his fist and tossed it into the trees.

"Come on," he said to Barney, and kept hiking toward the lake. Soon they were out of the woods, and climbing down a rocky slope to a small beach on the edge of Oro Lake. At the edge of the sandy shore, the land turned to clay, dry and cracked. He hiked down the deeper slope another dozen feet.

"Ain't seen the water this low in as long time, boy." He kicked off his Red Wing hiking boots and stepped into the cool water. "Go play, you dope," he said, but the dog wandered the edge of the water sniffing.

Darryl took a few more steps into the lake, the water lapping at his ankles and up toward his shins as he went in further. Soon it was wetting the cuff of his jeans. He pulled another beer from its plastic ring, and placed the remaining four beers in the water to keep cool. To make sure they wouldn't float away, he broke a thin branch off a nearby tree and speared it through one empty ring and into the muddy ground.

When he released them, the beers bobbed and floated in the lake water. This part of the lake was often teeming with crawdads, and he wandered out a few feet to take a peek, kicking himself for not bringing his fishing gear with him. A group of the little lobster-like creatures swarmed around in the shallows, which always meant there were more in the deeps.

"Coulda caught an appetizer for dinner, right Barney?" he said. He emptied the can, crushed it, and tossed it aside. Darryl and Barney were at a narrow point of Oro Lake, a couple of miles around the curve from where most people spent their days playing in the areas with lifeguards on duty. Fishing boats and paddle canoes only, very rarely came around this part of the lake, and that was fine with Darryl and his brother. It was narrower here, too. If he'd wanted to, and could be bothered to, Darryl could have swum across the spit to the other side. Or at least, that's what he told Arlen once on a dare. He'd gotten about halfway across before turning back, saying he didn't feel like going there anyway.

Darryl followed along the beach after Barney. Sure, he could swim across the lake if he wanted to. "You bet I could," he said. He looked out across the rippling water, to where the land sloped up on the far shore. Somewhere over there was the old miner's cabin he used to go get stoned at with friends back in high school. He wondered if kids today still did that. After weed was legalized in California a few years ago, he guessed the allure of the forbidden had worn off of it. But he thought teenagers still needed places to go to get in trouble out of the prying eyes of grownups.

And there it was, to the left of where he'd been looking. Back a bit from the lake's edge, up a sandy slope, and almost hidden behind some oaks and aspens. If he hadn't been looking for it, he didn't think he'd have noticed it at all. There wasn't much left of it, and it pretty much blended into the shadows of the forest. He was looking toward the splintered remains of the cabin when a brown and gray female mallard duck dropped from the sky, sending up a spray of water as it skidded to the surface of Oro Lake.

A bark broke his concentration.

"It's a duck, dumbass," he said, turning toward the noise. Barney was haunches down, snarling. The dog barked again, and turned to run behind Darryl.

"What the hell, dog?" Darryl said. He looked in the direction Barney had been glaring and barking at. The duck was gone, ripples on the surface where it had been a moment before. He turned around to pet the nervous dog's head. "It went fishing, dummy."

He waded along the shore, looking toward the spreading rings as they dissipated. Something bobbed to the surface. It was dark against the emerald green of the water, and when it rolled over, Darryl recognized the vague shape of a duck's body, crushed and broken. "Damn." Darryl backed out of the lake. "Must be one big-ass crawdad."

Darryl heard a whooshing sound and ducked as a large raven sped overhead. It flew over him to alight on a tree branch nearby, then turned to look at Darryl with a hearty *kaw!* "Fuck off, bird," Darryl hissed. The bird croaked again, and something about the noise caused the skin at the back of Darryl's neck to crawl. He picked up a stone from the beach and tossed it at the bird. The stone missed by inches, but the bird flew away. "Dumb bird."

Suddenly, Barney was barking madly again. He was back on his haunches, hackles raised, and growling at the lake. Darryl stepped quickly back toward the shore, arms out for balance. When he reached the shore, he turned back to the water as something else broke the surface. Long, thin shapes like roots or long, grasping fingers, dripping with slime and algae slipped from the water's surface. They encircled the dead bird, clutching around it until it was firmly within the bony knotted cage. He heard a crunching sound over the whisper of the lapping water as the clotted mass disappeared beneath the surface of Oro Lake, and nothing was left but rings of water spreading outward from the spot where the bird had disappeared.

Darryl stood at the water's edge, watching the rings ripple outward. A dark low, lumpish shape broke the surface, followed by two more. Soon there were three dome shapes risen barely above the surface, shiny and wet. Darryl stepped forward to get a better look at them, and stopped ankle-deep in the water, hands on his hips.

"What'dya think of that, dumbass?" he said to Barney. "Ain't seen turtles in the lake in a while. Huh."

He reached down and grabbed three round stones about the size of his palm in his hand. He tossed two into the other hand, then tossed the third a few inches straight up and caught it again.

"Think I can hit those little fuckers from here?"

Barney growled, low in his throat. Then he looked up at Darryl and whined.

"Don't be such a chicken-shit, dog. Just a bunch of fuckin' turtles." The low bulges slowly turned and began to move toward shore. Darryl adjusted the rock in his right hand, leaned back and hucked it at the nearest shape. It vanished in the water with a *plop!*

The shapes came closer. They were rising above the waterline by fractions of inches, and Darryl thought they were pretty weird-shaped turtles.

He tossed another rock from his left hand into his right. He reached back, took aim, and threw the rock straight at one of the shapes. A *crack!* and a hole appeared in the low dome. Thick gray slime oozed from the hole. Poured out in thick runnels, and clots of dark matter plopped into the water.

"What the fuck?" Darryl muttered and took a step back.

The three shapes floated toward him. The one closest to him rose from the water, twenty feet from shore. Sunken eye-sockets glared malevolently from a spongy gray brow. The eye-sockets split slightly open, revealing dead white eyes beyond the lids. White light flickered from the eyes, like cold moonlight in the dead of winter. The corpse-gray face rose further from the water, followed by two more algae-slicked, skull-like, water-logged faces. They came closer until their shoulders rose above the water, exposing sodden, rotting, workman-like shirts caked with scum and vegetation. Cold light glared from three pairs of dead eyes sunken into swollen dead faces. A finger-thick, glistening black worm squirmed from an empty eye socket in one's skull, crawled awkwardly across the dead thing's face, before tumbling into the water with a faint *plip*.

"Fuck this," Darryl said, turned around and started to run, but something grabbed his ankles and he fell face-first into the gravelly sand of the lake's shoreline.

He landed with a *whuff!* as the breath was knocked from his lungs, and pain shot through his mouth. Darryl realized immediately that he'd bitten his tongue. He flipped over onto his back, tried to kick away at whatever had him by the ankles, but they were held tight. He pushed away from the lake with his hands, but they slipped on the gravel. Inch by inch, he was dragged toward the water's edge.

Barney was going berserk. Barking, yapping, running in circles, then stopping at the shoreline and barking at the things in the lake.

When he looked toward the dead faces, he saw they hadn't moved any closer toward him. They were still out of reach, still only heads and shoulders poised above the water, empty, dead sockets glaring in his direction. He forced himself up with his hands until he was sitting up straight. He looked down at his ankles and saw they were tangled in black tendrils of slime, ropy tentacles of utter darkness emerging from the deeps of the lake, circling his ankles and crawling worm-like up his legs. Frantically, he shoved against the dry, dusty clay, pushing against the ropy lengths which clutched at his legs. He pushed, and kicked, and yelled, "Help! Someone help me!"

In a faction of a second, he was yanked into the water. Webs of darkness surrounded him, grabbed his arms, wrapped around his torso, twisted around his neck, and forced their way into his mouth. He choked on a mouthful of rot and lake water as he was dragged below the surface.

Barney yapped and barked from shore as the three dead faces glared at him. The hellish cold light reflected off the rippling lake surface, like the ghosts of skittering water bugs.

Dark, grasping pseudopods broke the surface and slithered across the shore toward him. Barney backed up, barking at the slimy lengths oozing from the water. One lashed out, with a stinging barbed point at the end. It slashed along Barney's flank, before he darted away, pulling free. He turned tail and ran into the woods, back toward home, barking and howling the whole way.

CHAPTER EIGHT

"We've got perfectly good toothbrushes here, Arlen," Officer Thomas Millsap said wearily through the bars of the jail cell. There were three cells in the Golden Oaks police department, and only one of them had a guest this weekend. "Happy to give you one, at taxpayer expense. Hell, you quiet down, maybe I'll even throw in a bar of soap and some mouthwash."

"Ain't the point, *Officer*," Arlen McEwen said with a sting of contempt. "I need to make sure Darryl feeds my dog, too."

Officer Millsap rubbed his temples, knowing it was going to be a long evening unless Arlen got what he wanted. "Darryl's a big boy, Arlen. I'm sure he'll feed your dog."

"Darryl's a dumbass, and you know it," Arlen said, sitting on the edge of the cell's slab bed. "Call him again."

Runs in the family, Officer Millsap thought. "I've already left a message for him, but I'll be happy to try again later tonight," he said.

"Yeah, but by then visiting hours'll be over, and he won't be able to bring it to me," Arlen said, standing up and approaching the door to his cell. "Come on, do me a favor, will ya?"

"Sorry, Arlen," Millsap said, turning his back to him and walking toward the door in the far wall which led back to the rest of the office.

"You're gonna have to stew a while. I'll bring you a toothbrush with your dinner."

"Thanks for nothin', pig," Arlen muttered.

Officer Millsap pretended not to hear that and closed the door behind him as he stepped out into the hall. He adjusted his belt which was being tugged down by his baton and service revolver. *Gotta lose a few pounds,* he thought as he locked the door to the holding cells. *Too much time in the cruiser, not enough walking.* He entered the main office and found Officer Lasher staring at her computer screen. Just the two of them in the office as the afternoon wound down. Josie Phelps, the office manager, had left early for the day, and Officer Bill West wouldn't be in until later in the evening.

Lasher looked up as he poured himself a cup of coffee from the machine in the pantry in the corner of the room. The smell of fresh coffee wafted across the small room, and she breathed it in; the fragrance stirred an automatic response in her, and she suddenly really wanted a cup. "How's our VIP in the Penthouse Suite?" she asked.

"Our VIP's a PITA as usual," Millsap said. "You want a cup?" He pointed at the coffee maker.

She nodded. "Absolutely. What's bugging him now?"

Millsap poured the hot coffee into the disposable styrofoam cup. They'd worked together long enough he didn't even need to ask what she took in it, because she took it black. Coffee was a staple, even on a hot day like today, with the AC blasting. The coffee kept them going during the long dull hours of paperwork that comprised most of their day. "Wants his toothbrush, and his brother hasn't brought it yet. And he's convinced Darryl's going to forget to feed their dog."

He picked up both cups and brought them over to her desk, and pulled up the chair at his own desk which faced hers. He sat heavily in the black cushioned office chair. The hydraulic support wheezed as it adjusted to his weight. Lasher blew the wisps of steam rising from her cup, and took a sip.

"Well, I wouldn't put it past him," she said after swallowing. "Did you call him?"

"Yeah," Millsap replied. "Rang, no answer."

He drank a swallow of coffee, thick with cream and sugar. "You'd think with all the junk they haul, they'd have come across a working answering machine at some point."

"Call him again," Lasher said. "It's slow, and maybe it'll get Arlen to shut up."

Millsap lifted the receiver on his desk phone, punched "9" to get an outside line, and realized he couldn't find their number. "You got his folder?" he asked Lasher. "I think I tossed the Post-it I had his number on."

Lasher picked Arlen's file off her desk and folded it open. "Intake's on top," she said, and handed Millsap the folder. She sat back in front of her computer as he punched the McEwens' number into his phone.

Millsap waited, listening to the phone ring on the other end. He noticed Lasher staring intently at her computer's screen again. "Something interesting?" he asked her as the phone continued ringing.

She looked up from the screen. "Maybe. Maybe not." She leaned back in her desk chair, putting her hands behind her head. "That guy that Arlen punched yesterday?"

Millsap tapped his fingers on the green blotter atop his desk. "Barnes, right? Gabriel?"

"Bingo. You'll make detective yet."

"Har," Millsap said flatly, and hung up the phone. "No answer. What about him?"

Lasher sat forward, hands back on the keyboard of her computer. "The name sounded familiar after he gave me the address where they were staying. Barnes, Ringgold Lane. Ring any bells?"

"None at all. Should they?"

"They should," Lasher said. "Turns out our friend Barnes isn't a tourist. He owns the place."

"Oh, yeah?" Millsap said, getting curious. "Is there something we should know about him? Nothing special about a guy who owns a rental on the lake. Is there?"

"It's his dad that got my interest. Missing persons from a few summers back? Mike Barnes, his dad, owned that place. Guess he left it to Gabriel in his will. Last anyone saw of Mike, he'd rented a rowboat to go fishing on Oro, then," she raised her right hand and spread her fingers out like an explosion, "Poof! Vanished right off the face of the Earth."

Millsap took a slow sip of his coffee. "Oh, yeah," he said, clearly interested in where this story was going. "Sure. They dragged part of the lake, stirred up a whole bunch of muck, pulled up a bunch of dead trees and the boat he'd rented, but never found a sign of the guy. He was declared dead without finding the body."

She shook her head. "That's right. Not even a hair on his chinny-chin-chin. Found his car by the lake, some of his fishing gear washed up on Deer Island, and that was the only sign anyone ever saw of Mr. Mike Barnes ever again."

"So, where's all this going?" Millsap asked.

Lasher closed the file and pushed back from her desk. "Oh, nowhere, probably. An interesting coincidence, I suppose." She stood up. "No answer at the McEwen place, huh?"

"Nope," Millsap said. "I can keep trying for a while if you want, though. I'm on 'til midnight, and things seem slow."

Lasher grabbed her jacket from a coat rack near the side doors to the station. "I'm going on a quick patrol. Maybe I'll swing out that way and see if Darryl's home."

"You think something's wrong?" Millsap asked. "Want me to come along?"

"No, it's probably nothing," she said. "But when Darryl came by this morning to visit with Arlen, he seemed like he was planning on coming back before lunch. Maybe he got drunk and forgot, but maybe not."

"Gotcha," Millsap said.

"I'll take a quick turn around Oro, and if things look funny at the McEwen's, I'll see what I can see," she said. "Okay, Millsap, you're in charge while I'm gone. Try not to burn the place down."

"No promises," Millsap said, punctuated with a casual salute.

Lasher stepped away from her desk, and started down the hall to the exit bay. The hydraulic door openers sighed as the door closed behind her. Millsap was alone in the tiny Golden Oaks police station, except for Arlen in his cell. He got up, poured himself another cup of coffee, took it back to his desk, and kicked back with a beat to hell paperback copy of Cormac McCarthy's *Blood Meridian*.

"Hope it's a slow night," he said. But only the cinderblock walls heard him.

***

Officer Lasher stepped from the little air-conditioned police station into the waning heat outside. The sun was making its slow descent toward the welcoming horizon, kissing the distant treetops to the northwest and preparing to fall entirely into their embrace. Soon, the town would be cast in the golden glow of early evening, thick with gloom and long shadows. She descended the steps to the asphalt lot on the side of the plain single-story building where two patrol cars were locked and secured by the tall chain-link fence surrounding the lot.

Lasher entered the closest vehicle, the one she used the most frequently on her patrols. Inside it was swelteringly hot. She left the door and rolled down the opposite window to try and get a cross-breeze going. The pine tree-shaped air freshener hanging from the rear-view mirror had long since lost its potency, and the car had a strong smell of old french fries and burger wrappers, made more potent by the heat.

In short order, the car had cooled off slightly. She closed it up, started the engine, and cranked the air-conditioning up to max. She drove toward the gate in the fence, and stopped a few feet in front of it.

The transponder connected, and the gate slowly rolled open. Lasher always smiled when the gate slid open on its state-of-the-art trolley and transponder system. It reminded her of when she first started in the Golden Oaks police department.

After 9/11, when the Department of Homeland Security was sending money for anti-terrorist equipment to every police department in the country, Golden Oaks had gotten its share. Lasher's predecessor, Chief Miles "General" Pershing, had made the wise decision that Islamic extremists probably weren't going to blow up Golden Oaks. He'd always said he was more worried about someone deciding to start cooking meth in the forest, or a faulty power line going down and burning the town down, than someone halfway around the world with a grudge. So instead of the Lenco BearCat that Mayor Chris Haines had been pushing for, Pershing had used the money mostly for capital improvements. He was a smart guy, but fundamentally lazy about what he called "little stuff." Always trying to find more efficient ways to get the job done. He'd hated having to unlock the gate, drive out, park, lock the gate behind him when going on patrol, and doing it all over in reverse when returning. So, some of that DHS money went to the automatic transponder system to open and close the gates. The rest of it went to some flak jackets that had never come out of storage, the two patrol cars which were new seventeen years ago, and now had tens of thousands of miles on them and probably needed replacing again sometime soon. And the coffee machine in the Station office. Pershing loved his coffee, and that machine was a workhorse.

As Lasher drove out of the lot, and the gate slid closed behind her, she wondered what her legacy in Golden Oaks was going to be. Pershing had retired and moved away to Florida a few years ago. Most residents of the town could tell a story or two about him, but his real impact was on the department, the station, the way they did things. Lasher drove through downtown, past the Ace Hardware, and the Get Up and Go. She waved at some teenagers riding their bikes through town while she tried to remember all their names. One of the things she liked about police work in a small town was how everyone knew her, and she knew everyone. At least the locals. Tourists and summer people were a different story, but she had a pretty good handle on the regular rental properties, of which there were only a handful around the lake anyway.

But when she moved on, either retired or needing a change of scenery, would anyone in town remember her for anything? Had she put her stamp on the department, on the town? And was that really important? Often, she thought it was enough in life simply to do her job well, break up the occasional fight, help Mrs. Granger with her grocery shopping, and generally keep Golden Oaks quiet and peaceful. Like Mellencamp said, a small town was good enough for her.

She drove past the Raley's, she made a mental note that she needed to do some shopping once her patrol was over. The larder was getting bare back at her house, and it wasn't like the magic grocery fairies were going to fill up her cupboards for her.

The sun dwindled behind the tall trees surrounding the town and lake as she drove SR 346 out of town and toward Oro Lake. There were backroads through town that would get her there, but her normal patrol route was to go out this way, and before circling back through town. If it was earlier in the day, she might even stop at the boat launch and swimming area of the lake where the little cafe had a decent grill, and the cook, Harlan Jespries, made a pretty mean cheeseburger.

She continued until she saw the sign for Oro Lake, dutifully clicked her left turn signal on, checked for oncoming traffic, and pulled across the highway. Her car bumped and juddered as it hit the ramp leading to Oro Lake Road, the prosaically-named road around the lake. One of these days, she'd have to bug Mayor Haines about getting that ramp smoothed out. She turned left again onto Oro Lake Road and was reminded of how the lake and town got their names. The sun was almost gone beyond the tree-covered hills on the other side of Oro Lake, and golden light sparkled and danced off the surface. It dappled through the oak leaves which were brown and summer dry, but when the sunlight hit them, they glowed like pirate gold. Golden light surrounded and suffused the lake, the trees, and blazed from the hills across from her as the sun made its final decent. Soon, the blaze dwindled to a soft glow, and the sun vanished behind the hills.

***

Lasher drove along the edge of the lake as the sunlight dwindled. It was still another hour or more until full dark, but something about the gloom chilled her spirits a bit. She crested around the lake near the swimming area, but only saw half a dozen cars in the small parking lot. A small SUV towing a boat pulled out of the lot, drove up the side road, and passed her as she approached. The driver smiled and waved, a friendly-looking man with a deep sunburned face. Next to him in the passenger seat, a pretty woman about the same age was looking at something on her phone. Officer Lasher waved back, and noticed that behind the driver, in the back seat, a child with an ice cream-smeared face had already fallen asleep. *Good day on the Lake,* she thought as she drove by.

She drove past the public entrance to the beach, where the asphalt turned into a rough dirt road and the trees lining Oro Lake Road became noticeably thicker, wilder. Not many people lived on this curve of the lake, and those that did were pretty spread apart. She drove her patrol car along the winding road, turning and roaming with the flow of the snaking rutted dirt, taking hairpin turns slowly, and skillfully navigating the switchbacks.

It wasn't long at all before she came to a yellow metal sign, edges dark with rust which read "Private Road." Below that, a gray, weather-worn plank of wood onto which was carved "Nothing Here's Worth Your Life." The letters of the carving had once been bright, shiny enamel red, but had long since weathered away. Next to that, a dingy metal mailbox with "McEwen" painted on the door. A series of rainbow-colored hippy teddy bears stenciled on it, dancing along the side.

The light was almost gone now, and she flicked her headlights on, casting twin cones of illumination yards ahead of her. After a minute the road turned slightly to the right, and the McEwen's house came into view. A car was parked in front of the house, and Lasher recognized it as Darryl's Thunderbird.

It was a small, one-story place. Dark wood paneled the outside, and moss clung to the walls in patches. The shingle roof was in need of repair, and even from the car she could see that the rain gutters surrounding it were clogged with dead oak leaves and pine needles. She picked up the radio handset hanging from a hook on her dashboard and clicked it on. "Hey, Millsap! You there? Over." Waited, listening.

The channel opened on the other end with a click and a hollow, echoey hiss. "I'm here, Lasher. What's up? Over."

"You ever get ahold of Darryl McEwen? Over."

"Negative. Tried a few times, but no answer. Why? Over."

Lasher sighed, craning her neck around to get a better look at the house. The place was dark. No lights were on inside that she could see, nor a porch light. "I'm out at their place. His car's out front. I'll see if he's home. Over."

"Sounds good," Millsap said. "I'm logging you at the McEwen's at 8:25 p.m. Over."

"Okay, I'll let you know if I find anything. Out." She clicked off the radio with finality. Placed it back on its clip and got out of the patrol car. She stood and stretched, cracking her back and working the knots out of her lower back with the knuckles of her balled up fists. Lasher adjusted her scuffed, worn belt as she approached the house. It always got uncomfortable when she'd been driving a while. All the little pouches and equipment strapped to it poked into her back and sides.

She was approaching the front porch when she heard a muffled *whuff!* from her left. She took her Mag-Lite from where it was slung on her hip, flicked it on, and shone it in that direction. The light skimmed along the wooden slats of the fence around the makeshift backyard, she continued moving the circle of light along the fence toward the back corner. The pale white glow had dwindled to a semi-circle at the fence's edge, when she saw a dog's face peek out into the light. "Hey, Barney," she said, walking toward the dog. "What're you doing out of your pen?"

At the sound of her voice, Barney came around the side of the fence, limping toward her. She could see a cut along his rear flank. He was favoring his rear right leg, and his hip was matted with a dark patch. Officer Lasher approached the dog, and when she got closer she squatted down, holding out a hand to him. "Oh, hey, Barney, what's the matter, buddy?" Barney took one more step then lay down in front of her. He was panting, whining. She rubbed his head, behind his ears, and looked down at the wound on his hip.

"What'd you get into, buddy?" she said while she pulled a pair of sky-blue nitrile rubber gloves from a pouch on her belt. Putting them on, she probed around the wound in Barney's side. She'd almost expected him to bark or lash out at her. She knew Barney, knew he was a pretty good dog, even if the McEwen's didn't treat him well. But Barney whined pitifully as she used her fingers to move the hair on his side away from the wound; a small hole, no wider across than her finger, like he'd been jabbed with a stick. A trickle of blood oozed from the wound. She noticed the smell. A faint whiff of chlorine or ozone, more apparent when she lowered her head toward the dog for a closer look. Not a sick dog smell, for sure.

She took off the gloves, folded them up and tucked them into her pocket. "You went and got yourself pretty hurt, didn't you boy?"

She petted Barney's head, smoothing down the hair and rubbing his ears. He looked tired, eyes staring into the distance. He yawned, and Officer Lasher noticed his gums were pale. "Okay, buddy, you stay here. Let's see if we can find your person." She scratched him behind the ears again and stood up.

Officer Lasher stepped up the short staircase, only two wobbly wooden steps, and up onto the porch. Rough wooden slats for a floor, and a rickety-looking bench sat below the wide window next to the door.

She was about to press the front doorbell when she saw a hand-written note on it: "Ringer's Broke Knock." The wooden door rattled in its frame as she rapped on it.

"Darryl!" she called out. "Darryl, this is Officer Shawna Lasher from Golden Oaks, PD. You in there?" She waited, then knocked again, calling out, "Darryl McEwen, you in there?"

Nothing.

She stepped to the side, shone her flashlight through the window. Dingy curtains blocked most of the window, but there was a crack between them where they hadn't been pulled completely together. She shone the light through the crack and peered through the dirty window. The slim beam of light lanced through the slit between the curtains and illuminated the sparsely furnished room. A TV on a table against one wall, a dark sofa with a blanket tossed over the back. A few other chairs and general clutter.

She stalked the perimeter of the McEwen house, shining her flashlight along the walls, into the fenced-off yard. Her boots crunched on fallen leaves and dry grass as she passed, the only sound except for creaking trees and a distant chorus of frog croaks. She went around the perimeter of the house, shining her light into the windows of the kitchen and one of the bedrooms, looking for any sign of inhabitance.

"Shit," she said as she approached the front of the house again.

Barney was breathing hard now. He lifted his head as he saw her approach where he was sprawled out in front of her cruiser.

She removed a pad of paper and pen from her belt and started a note:

Darryl,

Came by because we couldn't reach you on the phone. Your brother needs to talk to you, come by during visiting hours tomorrow.

Barney's hurt, and not doing well. I'm taking him in to the station, and I'll see if I can get a vet to look him over.

She signed it off at the bottom, folded her business card into the note, and tucked the paper in the thin space between the door and the jamb. She turned toward her car.

"Okay, Barney," she said to the dog lying pitifully at her feet. "Let's see if we can help you out back at the station." She lifted the dog, who went limp in her arms. He curled his head into the crook of her arm and whined as she did. He didn't put up a struggle, though, and it didn't take her long to get him into her cruiser, lowering him onto the back seat slowly so as not to jostle his wound.

She backed her car away from the house, still expecting Darryl to come walking out of the woods, appearing out of the darkness. Officer Lasher drove through the night, made darker by the forest around her, blocking out the stars overhead. She drove the long road back toward the Golden Oaks police station, and couldn't help the feeling that something was off. She decided that if she hadn't heard from Darryl by morning, they might have to spend some time searching the woods.

CHAPTER NINE

The house on Ringgold Lane was quiet, dark. Gabe and Laurie rocked slowly on the back porch swing, listening to the sparse night sounds of distant frogs, trees creaking and rubbing against each other in the light wind.

It was a little after nine o'clock, but the whole house was still. After a long, stressful day, the evening had been quiet and sedate. A nearly silent dinner, followed by a tense evening of reading, listening to quiet music, and a general feeling of quiet unease. Kimmie had insisted she didn't need to see a doctor and had spent the evening quietly reading. After she said her goodnights and took her book to bed, Gabe and Laurie found themselves with glasses of iced lemonade in hand, rocking slowly on the swing on the back porch.

Gabe stared into the night, eyes half-closed, but despite the stillness of the night, he couldn't relax.

"Hey, Mister," Laurie said, putting her hand on his knee and giving it a gentle squeeze. "What'cha thinking about?"

Gabe sighed, long and deep. "I don't know. So many things."

"Like what? Talk to me?" she said, turning toward him.

First the run-in with that asshole yesterday, then Kimmie getting tangled up and almost drowned this morning, Gabe thought.

"I guess I feel like this is turning into a total shitstorm of a vacation, you know?" he said.

Laurie nodded. "Yeah, you know I can't say as I disagree," she said.

"I've been thinking about maybe you two should head home, you know? Call it a wash, and I'll stick around and work on the house for a few days. Get things settled and figured out."

Laurie put her hand on his shoulder and rubbed his back. "Oh, no, let's not do that. Things'll turn around. You'll see."

"Yeah. I guess." He turned to her. "So something else I've been thinking of. I know this is totally out of left field, but I've been thinking about this place. This old house."

"Yeah, what about it?" she asked.

"I was thinking maybe instead of looking for another company, it's time to strike out on my own. Maybe start my own agency, you know?"

"Really?" she said. "After the day we've had, you decide now's the time to drop that bomb?"

"Look, it's only an idea. But it might be a good move."

"For *you*," Laurie replied. "You've got connections, you know the right people to do the work, and probably could take a few of your old clients with you. Enough to get you started, at least. But what about for Kimmie and I? Gabe, I actually like my job. And Kimmie's got all her friends in Alcosta. It's the only place she's ever known."

"Right," Gabe said, feeling worse about his idea already. "Forget it. I'm being selfish."

She let out a long sigh. "No, you're not. I mean, it's not a terrible idea, but it's something we're going to have to think about for more than an evening or two. It's a *big* change."

"Yeah, I get it," Gabe said. "It's not something we can decide on tonight, anyway. I mean, it's something I've been mulling over. And I know you're not exactly a small-town girl. It would be a big adjustment."

"Right," she said. "I mean, I love it when we come up here, I always have." She stared out into the woods, taking in the quiet, the distant starlight.

"You don't get any of this peacefulness in Alcosta, that's for sure."

"True," Gabe said. "And I know you're settled in your job there, and that's a big thing to think about."

"Yeah, I am. Did you mention this to Kimmie?"

He took a sip of his lemonade. "No, why?"

"She mentioned earlier that if we decided to move up here, she'd be okay with it. You sure you didn't say anything to her?"

He shook his head. "Nothing I can think of, that's for sure."

One of her hunches, Laurie thought. "I wonder if she'd really be okay. She'd hate to lose all her friends back home, but I'm sure they'd still keep in touch."

"Well, think on it," Gabe said. "But it's nothing we have to decide on right now. The other option could be to sell the place outright. Use the cash as seed money to start something back home."

"Maybe there's something halfway, too, you know?" she said. "Sell the place, and move somewhere a little quieter for you, but with more opportunities for me."

"Sure," he said. "We'll figure it out."

"We always do."

She leaned over and kissed him on the cheek. "It'll be okay, you know?"

"Yeah, I know."

Laurie got up from the swing. "Okay, Mister," she said. "I've had enough excitement for one day. Oh, I was also thinking tomorrow maybe we go say thanks to Mr. Gaines, the guy who got Kimmie out of the water? Bring him a cake or something?"

Gabe paused. "Yeah, that'd be nice. Do you know where he lives?"

She tweaked his nose and gave him a kiss on the forehead. "I'm sure we can find him online. Or swing by his restaurant. If we do decide to stick around here, can't hurt to meet some of the neighbors."

"That's not a bad idea at all, really."

"Course not," Laurie said, smiling. "I thought of it."

"There you go," Gabe said, amused.

Laurie ruffled his hair, then stepped away from the swing. "Off to bed with me. You coming?"

He smiled at her, and took a moment to take her in. He was reminded of how beautiful she was, how much he loved her. How he always felt like he'd be lost without her. "Yeah, I'll be up in a little. Going to finish this"—he rattled the ice cubes in his glass for emphasis—"I'll be up after."

"Okay," she said, slipping away. "But don't be too long. Told you, you might get lucky tonight."

He laughed. "Well, then I'll definitely have to be right up."

She stepped through the screen door and into the house. It banged closed behind her, and Gabe heard her feet padding away into the house, and he was suddenly very much alone on the porch.

He was mulling over the idea of selling the house again when he heard a rustle in the trees, and then raven-calls. *Caw! Caw-caw-caw!* hastily repeated, and unnervingly loud. He got up and stepped to the edge of the porch, looking out into the woods. Past the lawn, gnarled oak trees rose into the night, their small leaves glowing softly, washed in dim moonlight. He heard the raven's cry again, *Caw! Caw!* He looked up into one of the trees, branches spreading from the thick trunk, making it look like a knobby giant's hand bursting from the dead earth. Along one of the branches, a raven sat, something clutched in its claw, pressed against the tree bark. It swiveled its head to glare directly at Gabe and called out again, *Caw! Caw! Caaaaaww!*

Gabe stepped down the steps to the lawn to get a closer look. when it dawned on him that he'd never seen a raven at night before. He'd always assumed they were daytime predators. That made him pause. If ravens normally hunt during the day, what's this one doing up in a tree in the middle of the night? Gabe stopped in mid-stride, wondering if it was sick. He looked up at it, trying to get a better view. He thought about something he'd read years ago about how sick animals act counter to their nature. Rabid bats flying around haphazardly during the daytime. Or mad dogs turning on their owners. Ravens hunting at night could be something similar. He reached for his phone to look it up on Google, before realizing he'd left it upstairs.

A flurry of wings, and another six ravens lit on the branch next to the first. All turned to Gabe and started screeching that maddening chorus of *Caw! Caw! Caw!*

He took a few steps backward, until his foot touched the porch steps. "Okay," he said to the night. "Think I've had enough nature for one night."

Gabe went back into the house, where Laurie waited upstairs for him, and he hoped she was still awake.

He was glad to find that she was.

***

They made love later that night. Slow and hesitant at first, building to a passionate climax. An hour later, Laurie was sleeping soundly on her side of the mattress. Her red hair fanned across the pillow glowed like copper in the thin moonlight which shone softly through the sheer curtains of their bedroom window. Gabe couldn't sleep. He alternated between staring at the ceiling and lying on his side to watch her. He envied her peaceful slumber.

His mind rattled with anxious thoughts. Worries of dwindling savings accounts, bills to pay. Gabe sat up in bed, swiveled to the side, and dropped his feet to the cold hardwood floor. He quietly crossed the room, took his flannel bathrobe from where it lay over the edge of a clothes hamper and wrapped it around himself, tying the belt loosely. He left the room, closing the door quietly behind him.

Walking downstairs into the kitchen, he opened the fridge and let his eyes adjust to the light. Peering into the white shelves sparsely filled with the meager assortment of groceries they'd picked up earlier didn't fill him with any sense of satisfaction. He wasn't even hungry really, only restless. Taking two cans of beer from the fridge, he stepped out onto the back porch and sat on the swing. He cracked one open, took a long drink and let it flow down his throat. Another couple of quick gulps and the can was empty. He put the empty can on the bench next to him and stared out into the night. When he was little, his dad used to call empty beer bottles and cans "dead soldiers." Gabe thought that was funny as a child, but the memory made him more melancholy now.

The warm breeze, quiet night, good sex, and cold beer should have relaxed him, but instead, his mind was playing out every possible disaster to come. Ruminating over the events of the day. He went over the scuffle in the parking lot time and again, fantasizing about punching the bastard in his stupid smug face. He played out endless scenarios where he'd come out the victor and impressed his wife and daughter.

This vacation will be good, he thought as he cracked open the second beer. *A chance to clear my head.* They'd spend a few days on the lake, hang out with Steve and Kay. Laurie and Kay always had a great time when they were able to get together. Steve was kind of an insufferable know-it-all, and never listened to a word anyone else had to say, and Gabe never could figure out what Kay saw in him. But he knew how much Kay meant to Laurie, so he kept his opinions to himself. And at least their kids were around Kimmie's age, so if Kimmie got bored she'd have someone to talk to.

Maybe he'd do some fishing, which he hadn't done since he was a teenager. If he sold it right, he could probably teach Kimmie to fish. She might like that, and if nothing else the vacation would be a good chance for them to bond a little.

Lost in his thoughts, he didn't notice he'd finished the second beer until he brought it to his lips, tipped back the can and only a few sad drops dripped out onto his tongue. He was feeling a little buzz now, mellowing out quite nicely. He put the dead soldier next to its fallen comrade and sat back in the chair.

It's nice to be out of the city for a few days, he thought. *Away from the stink and noise for a bit. Sure. It'll be good for us. Take a few days to collect my head, explore Golden Oaks a little, and relax.*

***

The blue glow of moonlight and a cool breeze washed through Kimmie's room, bringing the scent of the forest and a hint of dry heat with it. Kimmie lay on her side in bed, eyes open a crack, tired but not sleeping. She stared out the open windows, the forest and stars beyond. Past the forest she imagined the lake, the low rippling waves, cool waters, green depths, and what lay beneath.

Her ankle pulsed and throbbed. She'd taken a long bath before bed, lying in the water until it had gone from steaming hot to tepid, then cold. Finally, Laurie had made her get out and helped her limp to bed. An ibuprofen tablet had taken the edge off for a while but didn't really help. They'd wrapped her ankle in an elastic bandage to immobilize it, but it still ached.

Her phone had a few alerts from her friends back home on it, but she wasn't interested in replying, so she turned it off. Maybe tomorrow she'd get back to them. Maybe not. What would she tell them, anyway? *OMG, almost drowned when something grabbed my foot in the stupid lake TTYL.* They'd think she was nuts.

Chimes rang out from her phone and broke her out of her thoughts. She lifted the phone and saw an incoming FaceTime request from Jill. She framed the phone so it only showed her face, masking her embarrassing Taylor Swift shirt, and thumbed the little green icon to take the call.

"Hi," she said.

"Hey, Kimmie!" Jill squealed in the tiny screen. She paused. "You okay? You don't look so hot."

"I'm fine," she said. "I hurt my ankle today."

"Oh, ugh," Jill replied. "You still up for the lake tomorrow? We can do it some other time if you want?"

Kimmie thought about the green water and the squirming darkness under it. She forced herself to nod and replied, "Yeah, sure. I might not go swimming, but I'd love to hang out. I can work on my tan," she said.

"Neat!" Jill said. "My parents are working though, so I've got to bring Andrea and Jake with me. Is that okay?"

Kimmie shrugged. "I guess, sure."

"If it's a problem, I can probably let them wander around in town or something. They don't have to come." But from the tone of Jill's voice, Kimmie could tell they pretty much did.

Kimmie forced a wan smile. "No, it's fine. I'm feeling kind of crappy tonight. Sorry to be a bummer."

"No worries," Jill replied. "I'll let you go, and we'll talk tomorrow, 'kay?"

"'Kay," Kimmie replied. "Talk to you soon."

Jill cheerily waved goodbye and ended the call.

Kimmie turned onto her back, staring at the ceiling with half-closed eyes. A fat, black spider crawled across the wooden planks to the corner of the room where it took up a sentinel seat in a circle of webs. Funny she hadn't noticed it when she unpacked her stuff yesterday. Maybe tomorrow she'd tell Dad. Or get a broom and knock it down herself. Serve the stupid spider right; it should be outside catching mosquitos or something. What could it feed on in here?

Her foot itched. A weird stinging irritation under the wraps that sort of reminded her of the time she rubbed her arm against stinging nettle once.

She reached down under the blanket, curving her spine and bringing her ankle toward her so she could get to it, when her fingers felt wet cloth. "Ugh. What now?"

Pulling back the covers, she leaned up on one elbow, lifted the comforter, and looked under it toward the end of the bed. Kimmie saw that both the bandages wrapping her foot and the sheets below it were soaking wet. Otherwise, she was dry, her Taylor Swift shirt twisted a bit from her tossing and turning. But when she patted herself down, she felt nothing damp. She sat up fully, back against the bed's headboard, and threw aside the covers. She bent her leg, bringing her sore ankle over her other leg to get a better look.

The bandage was sodden, like she'd stepped into a bucket of water with it. Pale, bath-wrinkly toes poked out of the edge of the wrappings. Probing with her fingers, she untucked the terminal end of the bandage and began to gently unwrap it. Layer by layer, the bandages came off, spiraling to a wet heap beside her bed. And then her foot was free. The strange long bruises had formed one full purple and black mass, but the swelling had gone down a bit from earlier in the evening. Where before there had been thin long scratches, quickly scabbed over, now there was a web of dark threads dimly visible under her skin. "Oh, shit," she whispered.

She pressed her finger against the bulge and clear fluid seeped from her skin like sweat. It had an acrid, bleachy smell. A small depression remained in the puffy bruise when she removed her finger, but soon swelled full again. Her foot continued to seep.

The itch was becoming maddening. She lightly scratched her nails against the thin, scabbed-over scratches that were the area of most of the discomfort. With the scratching came the relief that often does, even though she knew she was probably making it worse. The nail of her index finger caught on something. An electric twinge shot through her ankle and her hand snapped away reflexively. She looked closer and saw a tiny splinter, dark and thin as a hair poking from her skin. She bent over her foot to get a closer look at the scratches and noticed another half dozen or so slivers just like it. She flicked one with her nail and it stung, a low buzzing throb, like a biting insect.

Taking a deep breath, she gripped the splinter between the nails of her forefinger and thumb and pulled on it. It stung. It *hurt*. Kimmie gritted her teeth and tugged on it, slowly and firmly. She felt something loosen under her skin. The splinter slipped a few millimeters, coming loose with a drop of scarlet behind it. The blood disappeared as fluid oozed up around it, washing it away in a pink runnel that drizzled down her ankle.

She took another breath, gripped the splinter again closer to her ankle and pulled with one smooth, fluid tugging motion, like pulling a violin bow back across the strings. Except in place of a violin's screech, she hissed through her teeth as she drew the splinter out. And as it came loose, she saw one of the dark lines spreading out under her skin disappear with it. She pulled it out in a slow, long stroke. When it finally came free, it was almost as long as her finger.

She felt sick to her stomach, and sweat had beaded up on her brow. She took a deep breath, turned on the lamp next to her bed and brought the splinter over to the light. It was long and thin. Slick and glossy like a length of black wire or fishing line, narrow and needle-like at one end, ragged at the other like loose threads.

Her ankle was now red and puffier than before. She went to pull the next splinter out and had to press her nails into the swelling to find where it exited her skin. One by one she pulled three other lengths of splinter from her ankle. There were still dark lines under her skin, but she couldn't find where they came out. Her foot was a swollen angry red mass, and she was exhausted. And scared.

She put both feet on the floor and began to stand up. She wanted her mom. No, her *mommy*. Kimmie was scared like she hadn't been since she was little and the world was large and full of dark places and strange people.

But suddenly, inexplicably, exhaustion found her. She tried to stand, hand on the nightstand beside her bed to steady her. Darkness swam before her eyes, her knees wobbled, and she lurched back to bed. She lay on top of the rumpled covers, sprawling out in a pool of blue moonlight. Her eyes drooped and she was on the edge of sleep while she watched the fat black spider in its wheel-like web in the corner of her room. The creature crawled along the strands of its opus, circling along the webbing, spiraling closer and closer toward something caught up and twitching in the center.

She slept, and she dreamed of winding roads, of absent friends. She turned and tossed, and dreamed of snakes and roots undulating through the detritus of the forest floor, winding out, searching. She saw a great wheel in the sky. It rolled across the heavens, and as it rumbled toward her, she realized it was rolling across the surface of the world, grinding everything in its path to dust. Its spokes were endless cables of spider silk, and there were blackened, dead worlds caught in the webs. It ground overhead, and she saw holes, rotted pits in the surface of the wheel. It rolled over her, and she was in one of the pits of the wheel's surface. Suddenly, all around her was darkness, silence. In her night's eyes, she saw a black lake in the middle of a dark wood, steely gray moonlight glinting dully off the low, rippling waves. And at the center of the lake, an island, full of menace and malignancy. A hunger radiated from the island, tugging at her mind. A hungry void, corrupt and bleak.

Chapter Ten

Charlie Gaines's boots tramped and crunched drying grass and fallen oak leaves in the still, quiet morning as he wandered a game trail which wound through the forest. A riot of greens and yellows, rich with the fecund promise of reborn life. The morning air was clear and crisp, and as he hiked farther and his heart rate increased, his lungs ached from breathing in the chill.

In a few weeks, with summer at its peak, the grass would be dry and yellow, and the trees would be casting deep shadows; the type of warm summer shadows where you might want to sit with a book and spend an afternoon lost in thought. But now, in early summer, the woods were still cool, perfect for morning walks.

Charlie and his wife had run the Get Up and Go diner in town for the last thirty years, but since she'd died, he'd lost a lot of his motivation. He'd been thinking about selling the place off recently but wasn't really sure how to go about doing something like that. Maybe Florence Hansen over at the ReMax knew something about commercial real estate. *He'd have to call her later,* he thought. Charlie had been having trouble sleeping lately too, and a few months ago had stopped coming in for the morning shift.

He was usually in the diner by lunchtime though and worked into the evening. That was his plan this morning, take a hike in the woods, before going in for the lunch crowd. Usually not much of a crowd on a Monday, but it was as good a time to start his workday as any. Yesterday he'd hoped for a nice quiet day on the lake, tooling around in *Shadowfax* with a few beers, and maybe catch some catfish for the dinner special. His wife had named the boat after some guy or a guy's horse or something in those fantasy books she'd liked so much. He couldn't remember which guy it was. Charlie'd tried to watch the movies they'd made from them, but he never could figure out which guy was which. There were the short scruffy, dirty guys, and the tall dirty, scruffy guys, and damned if he could keep any of them straight.

He was glad he'd been out on the lake though when he saw that little girl starting to drown. Wasn't even a second thought for him to turn the boat her way and jump in the water after her. Poor girl was near to drowned when he got her unstuck, but coughed up a lungful of water as soon as he heaved her up onto *Shadowfax's* deck. Lucky the lake was still open to boats, too. There was talk that they were probably going to have to close it off soon, since the waterline was getting so low. He decided he should check in on her and her folks later today, make sure they were doing okay. Maybe swing by on his way into the diner after his walk.

When he'd started out on his early morning hike, a wispy caul of mist had obscured his sight, closing his range of vision down to only a dozen or more yards in front of him. But after he'd continued on for a while, the gray mist had lifted, leaving a pale morning-blue sky overhead. He'd hiked this trail hundreds of times in his life. More when he was younger, but plenty over the last year or so. He'd started a few months after the Big C took his wife. "Cancer, not the 'rona," he often had to clarify to people when the subject came up.

He'd gone far at first. Only from the front stoop of his house down to the end of the lane to get the mail and back. Then down to the corner.

Every day a little more. Every day another few steps recorded on his FitBit. And now, almost a year to the day she died, he was up to three miles every day. He thought he owed it to Gail to stay fit and healthy.

He sometimes found himself thinking he should get a treadmill for when the winter got too bad, but it wasn't a priority.

The weather never got too bad up there in Golden Oaks. Hot and dry in the summer, cold and sometimes rainy in winter. Besides, when the rains came, they never lasted more than a couple of days at a time, and he'd call those cheat days. Sometimes he'd walk laps around the living room.

But when the sky was clear, he preferred to take long walks outside. He'd found this old game trail when he was a kid with some of his friends. Now he lived far enough away that he had to drive to the head of it, but he still thought it was worth the trouble. When he was a kid, he and his pals would tramp this forest all summer long, pretending to be pirates, cowboys, and spacemen.

Charlie came around a bend in the path, when he thought of a story his friends used to tell when he was filled with the fire of youth. Up ahead, and a bit off the path into the forest, they used to whisper of the bootlegger's shack. A ramshackle squalid hut lost among the groping boughs of the coastal oak trees deep in the woods. Charlie's friend Bobby said he'd been to the shack once. Said he'd peeked through a tear in the waxy paper windows and peered into the darkness beyond. Bobby had claimed that the place was occupied, but he couldn't see the inhabitant. He said he'd seen a rowboat next to it. Inside were a Coleman stove, some empty tin cans, and what he described as "a raggedy-ass sleeping bag." And that was it.

Charlie's friends were obsessed with the shack after that. But Bobby wouldn't take them to see it, so they mythologized it in the way boys with the barest traces of peach-fuzz on their lips tend to do. They were convinced it was the home of a bootlegger from the prohibition era. Or maybe a mafia stooge from Vegas, hiding out from hit men. And obviously it had a treasure stash buried under it. Charlie had thought the whole story was stupid Greg, Reggie, and a couple other hangers-on begged Bobby to take them, but he wouldn't. "The place is weird," Bobby had said.

"What do you mean, 'weird'?" Greg had asked. "Like, is it haunted or something?"

Bobby had punched him jokingly in the shoulder, told him not to be such a chump, and there were no such things as ghosts. But Charlie had seen a tickle of fear in Bobby's eyes when he told them. The faintest dash of movement, as if Bobby was briefly looking back the way he'd came. The tiniest trace of worry crossing his face. Charlie noticed it then, and thought about it now. The others hadn't said anything about it at the time, of course.

But later that day, Bobby had quietly confessed to Charlie that the shack had freaked him out more than he'd wanted to let on earlier.

Charlie had tried to get more details out of him, but Bobby laughed and told him not to worry about it. But also, not to go looking for the place. "Not worth the effort," he'd said. "A bunch of old hobo junk probably. I only said that other stuff to creep out the guys."

A few weeks later, late in that faded golden summer, Bobby creeped the guys out good when the laces of his Chuck Taylors wrapped around the gears of his dirt bike (the last birthday present he'd ever get), sending him ass over teakettle across the handlebars and into the grill of an oncoming Coca-Cola delivery truck.

Charlie often wondered what sort of life Bobby might have had if it weren't for that single instance of bad luck. He sometimes told himself it would have been something filled with glory. That Bobby had been the kind of kid that others flocked around, and that he would have been that kind of grownup, too. But he knew that, more likely, Bobby would have had the same type of life everyone else did. As Garrison Keillor often said on that show he and his wife used to listen to, it more than likely would have been "pretty good, mostly."

Being out in the woods thinking about Bobby got Charlie ruminating about that old cabin again. While they'd mythologized like it was the home of pirates as kids, as an adult he thought if it existed, it was probably one of the workers' huts from when the

WPA came in and dammed off the Oro River to make Oro Lake. He was lost in thought when he realized the side trail was right up ahead. The old post that used to signal the direction of that path was gone. The trail was weedy and becoming lost to the crawl of time, but it was still there. He marched a few dozen steps forward, feeling the uneven dirt and dust under his feet. Heard his worn hiking boots crunching gravel underneath. And then he was standing at the trailhead, looking down the path which had been such a strangely important place to his youth.

He looked down the trail, realizing that the direction post wasn't simply missing. It had either decayed away or been removed at some point in the past. Sticking out of a patch of grass and a few spindly branches of red-leaved poison oak was a square-shaped stump of broken wood, dry-rotted gray splinters pointing skyward. He bent over, reached down, and plucked a thick splinter of old wood from the stump. Charlie looked at the splinter, felt its dry roughness against his fingertips. The dryness of time's passage, of memories slowly turning to dust. He rolled it between his fingers, squeezed slightly, and the splinter crumbled to fine powder, and the powder was lost on the breeze.

Standing up straight again, he felt joints pop and creak in his back and knees. He was getting sore from his walk but wanted to go further. His eyes travelled up the scrubby game trail, wondering what was beyond. Was this the way to the shack?

He took a few hesitant steps forward. The trail meandered ahead, slowly rising up before disappearing around a slope in the hill. He looked down the overgrown path and wondered if kids still came out this way. Did teenagers slink off to the cabin to fool around out of the prying eyes of judgmental adults? Charlie continued along, feet crunching on the gravel and dry leaves which littered the hard dirt path. The day was growing warm, and clouds of gnats buzzed in rays of sunlight streaming intermittently between the boughs of the coastal oaks which made up the majority of the woods. The gnats made Charlie think he was going in the right direction. Bobby had once told him the cabin was set back a bit from the shore of Oro Lake. The trail widened out slightly and soon he could barely make out the tracks of bicycle tires in the path dried into the dirt, which got Charlie thinking about his childhood friends again. Maybe he should try and track some of the old gang down again. Look them up on Facebook, or Google or something. He wondered if he'd left one of those tread marks. But that was impossible.

A whole lifetime of rain and wind had washed away any trace of his childhood. Sure, someone had ridden this way back in spring when the rains turned the dirt to mud, and the mud it dried out over the summer. The ossified remains of a lone traveler on this forgotten trail.

So, he kept walking. His legs began to feel the delicious ache of use, going up and down the hilly slopes, pushing himself farther than he had in months. The warmth, the solitude, being this far outside of town for the first time in a while, lifted his spirits.

When he came around a bend in the trail and saw the first actual sign of the old cabin, he felt a mix of excitement and disappointment. He'd half believed the cabin was a figment of Bobby's imagination, but there it was. What was left of it, anyway. The tiny shack was way off the trail, maybe a hundred or more yards distant. He could see it through a cluster of trees, but the ground was cleared around it.

Charlie stepped off the trail, skittered down a slight slope of summer-dry grass. He felt that he was about to lose his balance, but hopped down to the uneven floor of the forest below. From there, the cabin was harder to see than it had been back on the trail, but he could still make out the general shape of it in the distance.

He tramped toward it, weaving between the trunks of oaks, stepping through clusters of wide-bladed bracken fern, and the strange shivering pods of rattlesnake grass. All his summer camp training as a kid of staying on the trail, not disturbing the natural world around him came back to him. He chuckled to himself, wondering what the counsellors at his old day camp would do if they saw him now.

Charlie rounded another oak, ducking under the low, thick, twisting boughs, and came out in the clearing around the cabin. He approached it slowly, taking it all in. It was ramshackle, for sure. A low porch stretched sideways before the open doorway, the slats crooked and pointing. The roof was mostly collapsed into the old shack, and one corner had fallen in. The low structure was a collection of wooden slats and upright beams. A heap of stones at one end showed where he assumed a chimney and fireplace had once stood.

As he came closer, a pair of large ravens fluttered from overhead and landed on the ramshackle roof. One dipped its beak down and snatched at something between two boards of the moss-covered roof. Whatever it was, the raven liked it. Charlie watched as the bird raised its head and swallowed. When he got closer to the building, the ravens hopped forward and cawed at him. When he didn't stop walking, they took wing, circling overhead, disappearing behind a large oak. He heard once last croaking *caw!* and they were gone.

He knew he was getting close when he heard the distant lapping of the water of Oro Lake. When his nose caught the clean smell of fresh water over the dry, woody smell of the forest in summer, he felt a rush of memories, a twinge of nostalgia for those old summer days and those old summertime friends. Charlie went closer to the cabin, and as he did, he saw Oro Lake past it where the ground sloped down slightly twenty feet beyond it. Trees along the shore still obscured a clear view, but he could make out golden sparkles of sunlight rippling on the lake's green surface.

Charlie stood with his hands in the pockets of his jeans, taking it all in. This was really it. The crazy old cabin that Bobby had claimed to have visited, and yet been so reluctant to talk about. A funny old thing not even that far off the trail, barely still standing after who knew how many years. The lake was beyond it, where people fished and swam, ran their boats all summer long. There was an orange and black "Keep Out!" sign nailed up next to the door, and he suddenly found himself wondering why the city hadn't torn the place down. It looked like it was ready to collapse at any time. He approached the porch and stepped up, careful not to lose his balance or twist an ankle on the loose boards. The doorway was clear, and he could see the old door fallen inside.

Cautiously, he stepped inside, taking only a few careful steps into the building before stopping. Barely even a building now that he was seeing it from within. A single room, a tangle of boards, leaves, and branches. Vines grew up the far wall, light filtering through where he assumed a window must once have been.

The room had a strange smell to it, an animal musk underlay the earthy smell of decaying wood. And under that, the faint smell of stagnant water. Charlie took a step forward, and there was a loud cracking sound as the boards gave way underfoot. He reached out to catch his balance, and tumbling into darkness. A searing pain as he hit his forehead on something hard and cold. A black swoon of unconsciousness overcame him.

***

Charlie woke in a dark chamber, lying on his back in a shallow pool of muddy, brackish water. A small circle of light shone down from the hole above him, casting a bright glow across his torso. He rose slowly from unconsciousness, only fully regaining his senses when he felt prickling spreading over his bruised hands. He itched the back of one with the other and was revolted to feel the squelching pop of chitinous bodies, and something slick and vile slimed his fingers. His eyes opened immediately and saw that his hands and arms were swarming with fat white spiders, wobbling along on tiny swollen legs. They crawled in crazy drunken patterns over his exposed skin, while their bodies extruded sticky strands of webbing. With a sharp, almost barking yelp, he sprang to his feet, cracking his head on a beam in the ceiling of the low vault;

the under-flooring of the shack above. Looking up, he saw blue sky overhead through the ruined floorboards through which he'd fallen.

Charlie slapped his hands together, wiping the strange arachnids from his hands, swatting them off his legs. The creatures fell to the muddy pool and rotten splintered planks around him and tried to make their escape. He stamped and splashed madly, his foot landing on a dry patch of ground where they crunched underfoot, and he felt their bodies split and squirt viscous fluid as he crushed them.

The last of the strange, pale spiders crawled away into the muck and he took a few breaths and felt himself relax. The wind groaned above, rattling against the thin walls. Thin eddies of air seeped down past the boards like searching fingers and caused a handful of dry oak leaves to flutter down into the pit with him. His eyes adjusted slowly to the darkness surrounding him.

The pit was at least ten feet deep, a hollowed-out basin below the cabin. He raised his hands toward the lip of the hole above him but couldn't quite reach the splintered wood. The walls were wet and smooth, almost clay-like, and the pool of water filled one end of the small chamber where the walls went straight down into it. Across from that, closer to below the hole, the ground sloped up gradually for a few feet, ending in a solid wall of dirt.

While he was taking in his grim, slimy surroundings, he heard a furtive splashing noise from across the small chamber. Instantly alert, his breath caught in his chest. He waited, and he listened. The sound came again, a bubbling splash from the far end of the pool. His heartbeat pounded in his chest, his breath still caught in his throat. His blood flushed with adrenaline, and every instinct urged him to flee. There was a brief moment of stillness, and he released his pent-up breath.

And a frothing, berserk seething as the water churned around and over him. His eyes burst wide with terror as he felt something like icy claws grasping at his legs, firm and sharp, and something unseen burbled in the murk and muck. A growling, chattering, furious cacophony of nonsense howling and gibbering from under the murky water.

Charlie pulled against the force gripping his legs, his fingers clawed desperately at the clay walls as he was dragged into the murk. Tears of fear rolled down his cheeks in thick, fat streams.

"Help!" he screamed to the hole above him, watching it pull away inch by excruciating inch. "God, somebody help me!"

Slimy and threadlike tendrils slid with excruciating deliberateness around his face and throat, like roots or fingers, encircling him, pulling tight, forcing their freezing cold lengths between his teeth as his mouth filled with a foul, bitter taste. Fiery pain exploded in his mouth as the sharp, rigid things pierced his tongue, lanced through his cheeks. The barbed lengths ripped at his limbs and body, squeezing, tearing.

And with one final tug, whatever unseen force was below the water dragged him under. Murky green haze washed across his vision as his eyes filled with stinging water, and he was pulled into the darkness.

Chapter Eleven

She wasn't scheduled to be back in the office until 9:00 a.m. Monday morning, but Shawna Lasher was in early anyway. They didn't have 24/7 coverage in the station in Golden Oaks, but the city was so small they rarely needed it. Millsap had left at midnight as planned, relieving West for the graveyard shift. When Lasher arrived in the morning, West had already finished off his first pot of coffee and was starting on the next. Outside, the sky was brightening, and cones of light cast by the streetlights winked off one by one. "You must be planning one hell of a trip with all that luggage," Lasher said, pointing to the dark circles under West's eyes.

West drained his cup of coffee and mock-saluted her with the empty cup. "Oh, yeah. You know I've been thinking about a long trip to the Bahamas. Kick back on a warm beach with a cold drink and watch the waves go by."

"Sounds great to me, West. What's stopping you?"

"Well, you know, I think the taxpayers might have something to say about me using their hard-earned money for something so frivolous."

Lasher nodded, smirking. This was a game they'd played many times before, with differing details and cadence. "Well, I guess that's true."

"So instead, I think I'll grab a six-pack and stick my feet in the inflatable pool in the back yard. Reminds me of something my brother used to say to me when I was a kid."

"What's that?" Lasher said.

West rose from his chair, and walked across to the coffee machine. "'Billy,' he used to say, 'You think you're hot shit on a silver platter, but you're really a cold turd in a Dixie cup.'"

Lasher snorted. "Okay, you got me. Good one, West."

Again, he saluted her with the empty cup, before refilling it. "In any case. Your patient has been dozing quietly."

Lasher went around the desk to find Barney sprawled out on a pile of folded up blankets. With another thin yellow fleece blanket spread over him keeping him warm. He was panting slowly but raised his head to look at her when she came forward. "Hey, Barney, how you doin', buddy?"

A weak *whuff* … was the dog's only response. Barney put his head back down over his paws on the blankets.

She drew back the thin yellow blanket covering him and took a look at the wound on his leg. The blood around the gash hadn't spread, but the fur around it had darkened, slick and glossy with moisture. The blankets folded up below him were likewise dark with damp. She ruffled his ears and stroked his skull. The dog raised his eyebrows, stared at her, then closed his eyes. She caught a faint whiff of a smell emanating from the dog. Like ozone, or chlorine. "Well, my friend, I've lined you up an appointment with Dr. Hoeger. He's gonna take a look at that scratch and see what's going on."

West turned to her, sipping his coffee. "That really our responsibility?"

She stood up and turned to him. "Funny thing about small-town policing. You end up doing a lot of things that aren't really your responsibility. You know that part in the job description where it says 'Other duties as needed'? Well, Barney here's become an 'other duty'."

West put down his coffee. "Okay, I get it. You want me to take him to the vet for you? My shift's almost over anyway."

"No, I want to see this one through. I've got some questions about Barney for Hoeger. In the meantime, let our illustrious guest know what's going on with his dog. And try to ring up his brother again, will you?"

"You got it," West said. "Millsap's not due in till the afternoon, but Josie and I'll cover the desk until you get back. She should be in with Monday Morning Donuts any minute now anyway."

"Perfect," she said.

"Hoeger's office doesn't open for another hour or so, though," West noted, as Lasher was bending to pick up Barney.

She shook her head. "No, he's coming in early today. Payback for an old favor."

"Oh yeah," West said, taking a sip of coffee. "What's that?"

"Fixed his parking tickets," Lasher said, and lifted the pitiful dog up, blanket cushion and all. "Okay, buddy. Let's get you fixed up."

***

"So, any ideas, doc?" Lasher said, sitting on a wheeled stool in the corner of the exam room. Barney was still and sedated, laid out on a metal table under harsh white overhead lights. The green tiles of the wall and floor cast a strange pallor over the room's occupants. Clarence Hoeger, the town vet, hunched over the table, examining the prostrate dog. He'd shaved the area around the wound bare, down to a downy fluff of stubble. The skin around the puncture hole was damp, seeping clear fluid, and a thick trickle of pink oozed from the wound.

Hoeger's brow furrowed as he probed the wound in Barney's flank with one gloved finger. "Any idea what happened? This wound is pretty deep."

Lasher stood up and stepped toward the operating table. "None at all. Found him last night, and he was limping. Figured I'd bring him into the station until I could get him in here."

Hoeger nodded. "Good idea. This wound could've gotten infected if he stayed outside all night." He picked up a thin metal probe from an instrument tray nearby. He poked and scraped at one of half a dozen thin black splinters which emerged from the skin near the wound. "Feels weird."

He slid a pair of scissor-like forceps over his thumb and forefinger. "Let's see what we've got here."

He opened the forceps slightly and used the gripping tines to grasp the black sliver poking from the skin. Slowly and gently, but with constant force, Hoeger pulled and a thin length of a dark, stiff substance slid forth. Once it was free of the dog's flank, a small bead of crimson blossomed from where it had exited, and constricted closed to a small, puckered hole. A few red droplets of blood slid down its length. The sliver was six inches long, and only a few millimeters in diameter. With his free hand, he pressed a cloth bandage against the opening and applied pressure.

He held the forceps up into the light of the multiple white light bulbs of the surgical lamp overhead. The twine-thin sliver came to a needle-like point but was also fringed with hair-like roots or shoots. He brought it close, trying to get a better look at the strands protruding from the trunk.

One of the strands twitched. They all spasmed once, twice, then were still. Slowly, all of the strands began to flutter downward, curling through the air like thin cloth in a light breeze until they hung limp and still.

Lasher leaned in to take a look. "What do you think of that, doc? Some kind of lake plant? A reed maybe?"

Hoeger gestured to a cabinet over the sink along one wall. "In there. Grab me a specimen jar."

Lasher opened the cupboard, rifled through the contents until she found a clear plastic jar with a blue lid. She unscrewed the lid, ripping a strip of sticky paper which crossed the seam between jar and lid for sterility. She held the jar out to Hoeger, who dropped the sliver into it. A dull rattle as it hit the bottom of the jar.

"Put it there," Hoeger said, pointing to the instrument tray with the bloody-tipped forceps.

"So, what do you think it is?" Lasher said, holding the jar to her face for a closer look.

"I honestly haven't a clue," Hoeger said, turning back to the wound on Barney's leg. He spread it open again with the forceps and swiveled an overhead light over it to get a better look. Lasher turned the jar in her hands, holding it up to the light. The sliver rolled along the lip of the jar, leaving trickles of red along the inside as it moved. The thread-like extrusions hung limp, twisted and tangled as it turned in the jar. "What are those threads? Maybe some kind of parasite?"

Hoeger stood up straight. "Look, Officer Lasher, I appreciate your concern about the dog, but for now, why don't you let me do my job? Let me close up this wound, and we can take a look at that later?"

Lasher put the plastic jar on the instrument tray. "Okay, deal. But if it's all the same to you, I'll wait outside."

"That's fine," Hoeger said, turning back to his canine patient. "I don't think I'll be long. You know where the door is."

"That I do," Lasher said, and showed herself out.

Hoeger smoothed out the fur over Barney's head, patting him gently. The dog looked so vulnerable on the operating table, oxygen tubes in his nostrils, and IV in his foreleg. "Alright, Barney," Hoeger said. "What did you get yourself into this time?"

He pressed a pedal below the table with his foot and the metal slab moved up a few inches, letting him get a better look at his patient. Peering closer at the wound, he saw the edges were clean, not ragged. Whatever had punctured the dog's skin had done so cleanly, and come out the same, without any additional tearing. The wound was pink and slightly inflamed around the circumference, but it seemed to Hoeger that the puncture was clean. But there were more of those strands poking out from around it. Black and stubbly. One by one he removed them, until the specimen jar held six of the things.

"But what's going on inside you, buddy?" he asked quietly. "Let's not take any chances."

***

Officer Lasher was starting on her second cup of complimentary waiting room coffee, and it wasn't any better than the first.

Her face must have given away her feelings about it, because as she was putting it down on the side table next to her seat, the receptionist said, "Try the mocha creamer. It makes it almost drinkable."

Lasher looked up and smiled at the girl, a teenager named Abby. Good kid. Lasher knew her from around town and had never had any trouble with her. 'Never gave me any trouble' was pretty much Lasher's only requirement for being a 'good kid.'

"Thanks, I'll try that," she said, stood up, and reached for a little plastic tub of mocha creamer in the black plastic rack of creamers and tea packets over the coffee machine. She popped the tub open, poured it into her coffee, and gave it a stir with a wooden coffee stirrer. Taking the stirrer out of her cup, she licked it clean before tossing it into the trash bin. She took a sip of the newly-sweetened coffee and thought, *Yeah, that made it worse; tastes like chocolatey gym socks.*

Abby asked, "What do you think? Any better?"

Lasher raised the cup and smiled. "Absolutely. Thanks." She returned the cup to the side table, where it rested among the waiting room magazines and week-old newspapers.

"In awfully early, aren't you?" Abby said, smiling at Officer Lasher.

Don't you have any paperwork to file? Lasher thought. "The Doc opened up early for me."

"What happened to Barney, anyway?"

"Beats me," Lasher said. "Got into something last night, looks like. Maybe got tangled in a bush chasing a skunk or running away from a mountain lion."

"Hope he'll be okay," Abby said. "He's a good boy."

"I'm sure the Doc'll fix him right up. He been in here before?"

Abby nodded, her long blond hair bobbing against her shoulders. "Yeah, a couple of times. But I've seen him around town, too. Like him a lot better than his owners. The McEwen's are a couple of creeps, if you ask me."

"No comment," Officer Lasher said, took another sip of coffee and instantly regretted both speaking and drinking.

She picked up last week's *Mountain Herald*, the local weekly paper, and skimmed the local news, all of which she was aware of. She was close to pulling out her smartphone and checking her work email when the door to the operating room opened, and Dr. Hoeger emerged.

Hoeger was drying his hands with a paper towel. "Well, looks like Barney's going to pull through."

"Good to hear," Lasher said as she dropped the paper coffee cup into the trash. She could see Abby smiling.

"So, the puncture was deep, but went in laterally under the skin. It doesn't look like it penetrated the muscle tissue at all. I flushed it with saline and checked for pocketing, but it looks clean." Hoeger wadded up the paper towel and tossed it into the trash bin near the coffee maker.

"What's pocketing?" Lasher asked.

"A cavity in the tissue that can be formed by a tear," Hoeger said. "But he looks fine. I'd like to keep him overnight, if that's okay with you. We can keep an eye on the wound, but I'm sure he's fine."

Lasher nodded in agreement. "If you think that's necessary."

"I want to watch for any sign of infection. No offense to the cleaning crew at the station, but it's probably more sterile here. And I don't want to send him home to the McEwen's right now."

"Not an option anyway, really," Lasher said. "No sign of Darryl, and Arlen's under my supervision for a few days."

"I see," said Hoeger. "So that's settled for now. He'll stay here tonight at least. We'll let you know if there are any changes."

"Thanks again, doc," Lasher said, holding out her hand. He took it in his and they shook briefly.

"Any time, Officer," he said, turning his back to her and walking toward the operating room. "Happy to help." The door swung shut behind him.

Lasher hesitated, then turned to Abby. "Thanks again," she said and handed the teenager her card. "Any trouble, any changes, here's how to get ahold of me."

"Okay," Abby said. "Or, 'Roger that'!"

Lasher forced a smile. "Roger that," she said and went through the door back onto the street. The day was already hot, and beads of sweat broke out on her forehead.

Chapter Twelve

Gabe was halfway up the pull-down attic ladder when Laurie stepped onto the second-floor landing with a pile of folded towels in her hands. "Watcha doin' up there, Mister?" she said as she approached.

He looked down at her and almost lost his balance on the rickety ladder. "Jesus," he said, reaching out with his left hand to the wall to steady himself. Laurie dropped the towels and grabbed the ladder. "You're like a freakin' cat when you're sneaking around like that," he said. The ladder stopped quivering as he regained his balance. He stepped down, taking three careful steps before he was on the landing.

"You okay?" Laurie asked, bending to pick up the towels. "Sorry to startle you."

"Yeah, no, I'm fine. Didn't hear you coming up the stairs."

She placed the last towel on top of the stack and picked them up. "So, what're you doing up in the attic?"

He caught the faint warm smell of vanilla drifting from the kitchen. Laurie had been baking. "Just going to go through some old stuff," he said. "I was telling Kimmie about how Oro Lake was an old WPA project originally and thought there might be some old newspaper clippings or something about that up there. Dad used to find and save stuff like that. Never threw anything away. Mom tossed a ton of stuff before she died, but I know Dad kept some old boxes in storage. Besides, I haven't been up there to really root around in years. Never know what I might find. Also, I want to make sure nothing's crawled in and taken up residence since the last time we visited."

Laurie gave him a kiss on the cheek as she slipped by. "Okay, well don't be up there too long. The fog's burning off, and it's going to get hot soon. No AC in the attic."

"No worries," Gabe said and began scaling the ladder again.

Halfway up he stopped again and asked, "How's Kimmie doing?"

She stopped right before she was disappeared around a corner. She looked at the wall, at the fading retro floral print wallpaper.

"Oh, I think she's okay. Sleeping. I checked in on her earlier and she said she wasn't hungry for breakfast yet. Oh, that reminds me." She stepped back into the hall. "There was a funky smell in her room this morning. Moldy, like a gross animal smell. Check over her room will you?"

Gabe nodded. "Sure, I'll take a look. Think something might've died up there?"

"Could you look? I opened the window and aired most of the smell out, but take a look anyway."

"Will do," Gabe replied and once again started up the ladder.

Laurie turned to walk around the corner and then stopped. "Oh, I almost forgot. I took some cookies out of the oven. Kimmie and I are going to run them over to Mr. Gaines when they've cooled. Sort of a thank you for pulling her out of the water yesterday."

"Nice," Gabe said. "Your snickerdoodles?"

"How'd you guess?" Laurie said, smiling.

"Hell, I can smell them from here," Gabe replied. "Save a few for me, will you? Manna from heaven ain't got nuttin' on your snickerdoodles."

Laurie laughed and nodded. "Okay, deal. I made way too many anyway."

"You better be careful, though," Gabe said as he continued up the ladder.

"Why's that?"

"Charlie gets one bite of those cookies, he'll probably try and talk you into baking them for his diner. Big money in snickerdoodle, you know?"

She laughed and turned to walk down the hall. Then she stopped and turned back to him. "Oh, and Gabe?" she called out.

He stopped. "Yeah?" he called back down as he stared up at the opening to the attic. He took another step up toward the dark opening. The dry musty smell of the forgotten past whirled through the warm vanilla smell coming from the kitchen.

"If we do move up here," she said, looking at the walls again. "We're going to do some serious redecorating."

Gabe laughed. "Okay, yeah, deal," he said and climbed the last few steps up the ladder. Heaped before him were the stored objects collected over the course of his parents' life together. He wondered if he'd have the fortitude to go through all this old stuff.

He put his hands onto the pine slats which lined the attic floor and pushed himself up into the dark, dingy chamber. Gabe propped himself on his knees and swiveled around so that he was sitting at the edge of the opening, his feet on the topmost step of the ladder below.

The light from below illuminated less than a dozen feet around the opening. He could vaguely see the underside of the roof overhead, but the wall of the other side of the house was a cloud of darkness. He knew there were boxes and cases toward that end but could only make out the vaguest shapes. He was closer to the front of the house and could see the interior walls in that direction; slats of rough, dark wood. His dad had once said the frame of the house was made with redwood, from back when it was more common to build with that.

Overhead was the same dark wood, and nails shoved through from where they held the shingles on the outside of the slanted roof. When he was a kid, Gabe had always wanted to get up into the attic. He was sure it held a secret stash of toys, old comic books, all the sorts of things that are like pirate's treasure to a young boy. But his mom would never let him in. She was worried he'd hurt himself on the nails, crack his skull on the low joists, fall through the access hole, or make a mess of things.

Gabe stooped under the gabled roof, his head inches away from the interior panels. Somewhere nearby, he knew there was a pull-string to turn the attic light on. He reached out and slowly waved his hand back and forth until he felt the thin cord that dangled from overhead. A quick pull and a pale white line shone out from bulb in a bare porcelain fixture overhead.

The attic wasn't any more inviting when it was lit up. Bare plywood floors, cardboard cartons piled haphazardly along the far wall. There were old toys, but it was stuff of Gabe's childhood. A cobweb-strewn tricycle, a cracking plastic laundry tub full of toy cars, trucks, and wooden blocks. He wondered why his folks had saved any of that, or hadn't given them to him for Kimmie when she was little.

A length of copper pipe was attached from one ceiling joist to another five or six feet away, and a dozen or more dresses in dry-cleaning bags hung from it like a clothes rack. Gabe had spoken to his dad about donating them after his mom's funeral, but he'd clearly never gotten around to it. More boxes were stacked along the floor where it met the roof. Some reused and adorned with the logos of long-forgotten brands. Others with simple notes scrawled in black magic marker: "Cookbooks" or "Christmas lights" and "Train set."

Maybe this would be the summer he finally got around to clearing all this out. Call one of those junk places and let them deal with it all. His dad had said essentially the same thing every summer since his mother died.

Gabe hunched down as he inched toward the stack of boxes, bending lower under the slope of the roof. He thought about how thin the plywood flooring laid over the floor's frame was. He could feel it flexing underfoot as he crossed it, adding an uncomfortable spring to his step as he stooped to avoid impaling himself on the roof nails or cracking his head as he ducked below the joists.

He came closer the dusty cardboard cartons and noticed a sour smell. He looked around, trying to place the layout of the house's second story to where he was standing. Kimmie's room was on the other side of the attic. If there was a smell drifting into her room, it wasn't coming from around where he stood. He got down onto one knee, bent his face to a crack between two plywood sheets and took a sniff. A slight musty, dusty smell, but faint. No mold or rot, for sure. He got back to his feet and continued to the back wall, approaching a grimy pyramid of boxes almost as tall as he was.

Gabe opened a box at random and found a collection of old linens. Flipping through a few inches of them he saw they were the tablecloths and napkins his folks would bring out for special occasions. "Company napkins," he wistfully recalled his mother calling them. They were something his grandmother had brought out from back east when she came to California.

The next boxes were equally uninteresting. Old trophies from forgotten sporting events, a box of his dad's old woodburning supplies from the summer he'd tried a hobby, endless report cards, schoolwork. Gabe found some poems he'd written in 8th grade English and was amazed how good the grades were for such terrible work.

He'd shuffled half the boxes to the side when he lifted one that was heavier than the others. He picked it up and set it on top of the ones he'd moved already, keeping it at about waist height to get a better view of the insides. He picked the carton lid open, when he heard Laurie's voice behind him.

"Gabe?" she called out softly.

He turned around to see her head poking up through the hatch leading back downstairs.

She smiled at him as he armed grimy sweat from his forehead. "Find anything good?"

Gabe turned away from the carton. "Nothing yet. Bunch of old schoolwork, Mom's fancy linens." He wiped his fingers across the boxes next to him. "It's a mess, though."

"Well, keep digging. Maybe you'll find Jimmy Hoffa."

Gabe gave her a thumbs-up. "Yeah, I'm going to go through the rest of these, and then I think it's lunchtime for me."

"You're a mess," she said. "Make sure you shower first, if you're going anywhere."

He gave her a double thumbs-up. "Okay, so noted."

She lifted a plate with a small pile of cookies up over the entryway and slid it toward him. "I'm going to take Kimmie to the lake to go swimming with the Bridges kids. We'll take those cookies over to Mr. Gaines on the way. Here's a few for you." She put her finger to her lips in a shushing motion. "Don't tell the ghosts."

He laughed. "Okay, deal."

"Alright Mister. Have fun messing around in your dirty old attic."

"It's a thrill a minute, let me tell you."

Laurie smiled at him, and disappeared below the access hatch. "Don't be too much longer!" she called as she vanished. Gabe heard her steps lightly on the ladder rungs, the hinges creaking as they flexed when she hopped off the ladder.

He turned back to the box he'd placed on top of the heap. Opening it, he looked inside and found a photo album. When he reached in to remove it, he saw it sitting on top of a few binders and old composition books, their mottled blue card stock covers brittle and faded when he picked one out to examine it.

Opening the photo album, he saw the first page had a newspaper clipping pasted in it. A front page from the *Mountain Herald,* dated May 14th, 1958. "Oro Lake Reservoir Open for Business!" the headline read in faded, yet bold, black ink. Flipping through the album, he found more newspaper clippings, most from the *Herald,* some from other papers as far away as the *Sacramento Bee.*

"Bingo," he said, placing it all back in the box and closing the lid. He lifted the carton and carried it toward the hatch where he set it down. "Okay. Let's see what else you've got."

***

Gabe carried the dusty cardboard box into the kitchen, where he placed it on the floor next to the kitchen table. He ran his hands under the faucet, letting the cool water rinse most of the attic dirt off before pumping a couple of squirts of soap into his palms and working them into a lather. He cupped his hands and caught water in them, splashing it on his face, washing the sweat and dirt off. Gabe washed his face again, and then wiped it dry with a hand towel.

When he felt properly cleaned, Gabe pulled a chair up to the table and sat down, opened the box back up, and started flipping through it. He pulled out a stack of dusty old notebooks, loose papers, and carefully folded newspaper clippings. He pulled folded newspapers out of the box; old issues of the *Mountain Herald*. He put the one proclaiming "Oro Lake Open For Business!" to the side and thumbed through a few more.

Gabe carefully unfolded a sheet of one newspaper and wiped the dust from his fingers onto his jeans. The headline said, "WPA Breaks Ground On New Dam." He glanced at the photo at the top of the clipping that showed a lonely hill in the center of the valley, a wide creek or narrow river coursed around its base, cutting through the valley floor. Trees had been cleared from around the top of the hill where a small lookout station was, being erected stood on spindly legs.

He tapped the photo. It was the same island that he remembered being in the middle of the lake, but he didn't recall there being a watchtower anywhere on it. He wondered if it had fallen down over time or been pulled down after the construction project ended.

He skimmed the page and scanned the article, stopping about halfway down the page to read. 'Local Indians have avoided the valley for years, and gave no trouble to the workers on the project. They call it the Empty Valley, and say there's nothing to hunt here.'

He thought that was strange. He hadn't been all that interested in the material about the local native tribes when he was in school, but was pretty sure they were the Sierra Miwoks. Maybe some Yokut, Paiute, or Mono too? He suddenly wished he'd paid more attention to those lessons. Gabe was looking at all the papers spread out in front of him when he remembered there was a local history museum downtown, adjacent to the library. Maybe after Laurie and Kimmie got back, he'd take a trip into town and do some digging around.

With nothing else to do until his girls came back, he made himself lunch and dug into the old newspapers. There were plenty of old articles about the building of the dam, the formation of the reservoir, and how the little town of Golden Oaks grew into a slightly larger town over the years. For the most part, the project went smoothly from start to finish, though it ran a few months over the deadline and a bit over budget.

He found an article about the ribbon-cutting ceremony once the reservoir was deemed "Open for Business!" with a great big photo of the town council and the mayor cutting a ribbon with a pair of shears.

He went through the papers and articles, finding photos of the island at the center of the lake. The watchtower was more or less clear and standing tall in the early ones but seemed to have disappeared by the 60s or so. Eventually, he found a brief article mentioning that it had fallen down during an unseasonable storm in the winter of 1963. By then it had fallen to disrepair anyway, and the city had the remains torn down and mostly removed.

He wondered how long it would take to get out there by boat. When he was a kid, one of his friends had claimed to have camped out on the island, but Gabe was pretty sure he'd been making that up. Everything he'd ever read told him that the island had been closed off to everyone for as long as long as Golden Oaks had been there. Would be interesting to find out what was on the island, though. He'd have to ask when he got to the history room later.

Chapter Thirteen

"It's got to be around here somewhere, you think?" Laurie muttered as she guided the car through the woods. The windows were down, and her hair fluttered in the breeze. She'd rather have the AC on, but after they left the house, she'd noticed a funny smell in the car. Like they'd run over something the day before, and it had been ripening in the undercarriage for a day or two.

She craned her head side to side, but all she saw was a sprawl of oaks reaching up overhead, nearly blocking the sky from view. She looked in the rearview mirror, checking to see if anyone was following them.

Laurie hated looking for an address when someone was behind her. She worried that she was driving too slow, holding up traffic. Or that she might see the address too late, slam on the brakes, and end up getting rear-ended.

Kimmie was transfixed by her phone in the seat next to her. She had been quiet all morning. She looked pale, her dark hair really drawing attention to her washed out skin.

Laurie turned her eyes back to the road. The trees were thinning out on the sides of the road ahead of them. Light dappled the road through the tops of the oaks to the side. "We must be getting close," she said. She slowed the car as she saw an approaching intersection. "Burney Road," she read, and glanced at the printed map in her lap. "I think we want the next turn after that, Aspen Lane." The car drove past Burney, and Kimmie gazed up the road as they passed. It went straight for a few yards, before veering sharply right and disappeared behind the trees. "You mind if I close the window?"

Laurie shook her head. "No, that's fine. Maybe we've gotten rid of the worst of the smell."

Kimmie flicked the window switch and held it while the window on her side slid closed.

Laurie glanced over at her daughter. "Kimmie, how you doing? You sure you want to go swimming?" Kimmie didn't respond. Laurie patted her on the knee, and Kimmie sluggishly raised her head. When she did, Laurie realized she had her earbuds in, and was deaf to the world. Laurie mimed plucking earbuds out of her own ears, and Kimmie got the point.

"Yeah?" Kimmie asked, her voice both tired and dismissive.

"I think we'll be there soon," Laurie asked. "We won't stay long, though, and then we'll get you right to the lake to see your friend. How are you feeling?"

Kimmie shrugged. "Fine."

"Ugh, whatever that smell is, it came back." She flicked the switch to lower her window again. "Maybe they have a car wash in town."

Kimmie shrugged, never looking up from her phone.

Laurie saw the sign for Aspen Lane coming up. A bank of rural mailboxes lined the edge of the road at the corner of the intersection. "I'm thinking we'll stop at the Raley's and pick up sandwiches from the deli after we drop off the cookies and say thanks to Mr. Gaines. Or would you rather find something else in town?"

Kimmie shrugged again. "Yeah, I guess. What do they have to eat in this shithole, anyway?"

"Hey, not okay," Laurie said, but she was trying not to laugh. "There's a café at the lake that makes decent burgers and fries and stuff."

"Sure, whatever," Kimmie replied, and moved to put her earbuds back into her ears with one hand and then lean forward and scratch at her hurt ankle with the other.

Laurie slowed down and veered onto the side road. When they turned on to it, she saw that the road split, going straight uphill in one direction, and winding to the left in the other. She saw a post almost completely hidden behind the mop of untidy scrub bushes growing around it. It had a series of addresses noted on it: *101-104* with an arrow pointing left *105* pointed right, in the direction of uphill. "The address I got from Google said he's number 101 Aspen Lane. So, looks like we go left."

She pulled the car to the left, felt it juddering over the rough, haphazardly-patched asphalt road. They drove for less than a minute more, the road sloping slightly down and the trees getting thicker again. A driveway shot off from the road ahead. A green post with a number 101 on it rose from a tightly trimmed lawn which edged both the road and the driveway. "Bingo," Laurie said as she pulled up the gravel driveway.

The car rattled and clacked as her tires rolled over the gravel. "His truck's not here," Laurie said. "Crap, we probably missed him."

"Looks like Grampa's place," Kimmie observed as they parked in front of the garage. It was a single-story house, but did look a lot like the house on Ringgold Lane.

"It does, huh," Laurie said, and opened the driver's side door and got out. "Kimmie, you up to coming along and saying hi?"

Kimmie plucked her earbuds out and nodded. "Sure." She lifted a plastic plate from where it rested between her feet off the floor below her, and slid out of the car. The plate was almost overflowing with snickerdoodles and covered in plastic wrap.

Kimmie was crossing the gravel driveway, while Laurie was already on the porch. Laurie knocked twice on the door and waited. Kimmie was catching up with her, and as she came toward the porch, Laurie noticed a slight limp as Kimmie walked. Almost as if she was trying to hide how much her foot hurt her.

Laurie asked her, "You sure you're okay? Sit while we wait." And pointed to a metal-framed bench with faded cloth cushions, surrounded by potted plants. They looked like once they had been bright, blooming flowers, black-eyed Susans, freesias. But now, long forgotten and neglected, they were drooping, dried up, straw-like husks. Kimmie shrugged and sat on the bench in a clearly decidedly grumpy manner, putting the plate of cookies on the seat next to her. She went back to her phone, hunkering over it, poking and prodding at the glass screen, her face hidden behind her hanging hair.

Laurie stepped to the side, peering through one of the pair of windows which framed the door. "Don't see anyone," she said, and knocked again on the door and pressed the ringer button for good measure. "Maybe he's out. Or taking a nap, or something."

"Maybe he's dead," Kimmie added.

"Not funny, Kim," Laurie said, and peered into the other window. "You think it's okay to leave the cookies here?"

Kimmie didn't answer.

"I don't want to leave them," Laurie said. "Might attract critters. And I don't want them sitting out all day."

Laurie picked up the cookies and tapped Kimmie on the shoulder to get her attention. "Why don't we go into town and meet your friends? We can stop by the diner, or maybe swing by here again on the way back." She brushed Kimmie's hair from her face. "Sound good, kiddo?"

Kimmie nodded, stood up and went back down to the car.

Laurie stepped after her then stopped. "I'm going to check around back, maybe there's someplace there I could leave them," she said, pointing to the plate in Kimmie's hand. "Or at least make sure he hasn't fallen and hurt himself or something."

Kimmie limped back and handed the plate to Laurie. "Sure, that's fine," she said. "I don't want to get back in that car yet anyway. What *is* that smell, anyway?"

Laurie shrugged as she handed the car keys to Kimmie. "I smelled it in the house, too. Maybe we've got a rodent problem. I bet something crawled into the trunk and died."

"*Eugh!*" Kimmie grimaced. "Well, you go check the back, I'll pop the trunk and take a look."

"Okay," Laurie said. "Back in a sec."

***

Kimmie sat in the car with the passenger side door wide open. It was too hot to be in the car with it closed. In the short time from when they arrived at Mr. Gaines' house to when she'd gotten back into it, it had already heated up to an uncomfortable degree.

Her face was bent over her lap where she held her phone, and her hair fluttered in a soft warm breeze. But Kimmie wasn't looking at her phone. The screen was dim, unanswered text messages barely visible. She was keeping a close eye on Laurie, who was walking around the side of the house, looking around. Part of Kimmie didn't really care. But another part of her, a deep, strange, unfamiliar animal cunning part of her really wanted to know. What was her mom really up to? Was she planning something about her?

Her ankle throbbed, warm and itching with infection. She reached down slowly, almost as if through water to rub her ankle. She felt wet where the bandage surrounded it. A sick, greasy moistness, uncomfortably damp. She pulled up the cuff of her jeans which were also damp. Her leg was red, inflamed. And over the top of the bandage, she saw black threads under her skin. Creeping upward again, like the night before. A puff of outside air brought a smell upward toward her face, she caught a whiff of rot, of decay, and of stagnant water. A flutter of motion to her right startled her. She turned to see a raven taking flight from a nearby oak bough, finally coming to rest on the grass across the driveway to stare at her. It hopped forward, opened its mouth, and let out a reedy croak as if challenging her, staring her down.

Kimmie stared back at the black bird, feeling strangely angry at it. Antagonistic. And in a flurry of wings, the bird careened forward, tumbling into the grass and beating the blades flat with its wings. When it came up, Kimmie saw that it had a mouse trapped in its beak. The pitiful little gray thing twitched and shivered, and then was still.

The raven looked again at Kimmie. It hopped forward once, twice, until it was almost next to the open door. She waved her hand at it and hissed, "Scram, bird!"

The raven tilted its head to the side, then lowered it to the ground. It grabbed the mouse by the hindquarters with one shiny black talon and pecked and tore at it until the head came free. It looked up again, the mouse's body in its beak, and flapped off into the sky.

Suddenly her skin went chill. She shivered as cold sweat trickled down from the nape of her neck, slithering down between her shoulders before soaking into her shirt. She saw the tiny mouse head outside the car door, and fought back her gorge. *Why did the bird leave the mouse's head behind? Only cats do things like that,* she thought.

"I hate this place," she muttered, and went to sit in the shade of the porch.

***

Laurie came around the other side of the house, having found no further sign of Mr. Gaines or a place to leave the cookies. She was almost to the car in the driveway when a large black bird flew past her, then soared off into the sky. Ascending higher and higher until it was nothing more than a black mote in a sea of blue. Laurie thumbed the trunk lock button on the Corolla's electronic key fob and it sprang open, slowly rising. She bent forward and took a good long whiff of the open trunk. It smelled of nothing in particular. Maybe a hint of oily chip smell from some Fritos spilled in the corner and a little of the old rubber smell found in all cars. But it was mostly clean. It had been filled with luggage and food for the trip on the way up but was empty now. She reached in and peeled the black rubber cargo liner aside, revealing the spare tire, jack, and tire iron in the small compartment below.

"No rats," she muttered. "I guess that's something."

She heard footsteps crunching gravel and looking up, saw Kimmie coming toward her.

"Anything?" Kimmie said.

Laurie shook her head. "No, no sign of him."

Kimmie peeked into the trunk. "Whatcha looking for?"

Laurie let the cargo liner flap back down. "Oh, wondering if maybe there was something in the trunk causing that smell." She dropped the trunk lid, which closed with a satisfying *thunk*. "Aside from some chip crumbs and the spare tire and stuff, nothing. No rats or anything anyway."

Laurie swatted as a fly buzzed around her face. Beads of sweat glinted sunlight on her forehead. "Okay, well, we'll figure it out. Let's get lunch? I have to get out of this heat."

"Sure," Kimmie said, and slid back into the car. "Maybe we should leave a note or something? Let him know we'd stopped by?"

Laurie opened the door and slid the plate of cookies onto the backseat. "I guess. You have anything to write with?"

Kimmie dug through the glove box. "A pen. You have any paper?"

Laurie shook her head, "No. I don't think so. Okay, we can stop by here on the way back from town." She took a look at Kimmie, noting the sweat glistening on her face.

"Kimmie, you okay? I've got a bottle of water if you want it."

Kimmie shook her head, her hair swaying as she did. "No, I'm okay. But it"s too hot. Are we going to get lunch now?"

"Yeah, sure thing, kiddo," Laurie said. "What time are we supposed to meet your friends?"

"Not until two," Kimmie replied.

Laurie looked at her watch, saw it was barely noon. "Oh, well, we should get moving. We'll pick up a picnic lunch at the grocery deli."

Laurie stood up, closed the door, and took a deep breath. The air was hot and dry. A bead of sweat trickled down the back of her neck and she fanned herself with one hand. She opened the car door, slid into the driver's seat, and cranked the car window open. Laurie put the car in reverse and slowly backed out of the driveway, the crunching of tires on gravel breaking the silence. Laurie turned left off Aspen and accelerated. The car sped along the road back to town. Laurie had her hand out the window and was catching the air currents like an airplane, staring out the window, watching the distant hills dotted with oak and aspen. Mottled greens swaying in the light summer breeze. "It is gorgeous up here," she said.

Kimmie looked up from her phone, saw the trees speeding by. The sunlight streaming through the green canopy overhead and around them. "Yeah, it's nice, I guess."

"Nice, I guess?" Laurie said, teasingly.

Kimmie force a fake smile. "I mean, yeah, it's really nice. Super nice, I mean."

"That's what I think, too. Listen, you mentioned it before, but your father and I talked last night about moving up here for a while. Maybe for good. How would you feel about that?"

Kimmie turned to look at Laurie. "Are you serious?" she asked, wide-eyed.

"It's something Dad and I were talking about," Laurie replied. "We own the house here and could move right in. Might be nice to have a change of scenery? But like I said, it's only something we're talking about, and I wanted to see how you felt, too."

Kimmie shrugged. "I don't know. It wouldn't be so bad, I guess."

"You'd be okay leaving Alcosta for the wild woolly wilderness of Golden Oaks?" Laurie asked. "Wouldn't you miss your friends?"

"I guess," Kimmie said. "But we can see each other online all the time anyway. But what about your job?"

"Well, like I said, we're not really even seriously talking about it yet. But think about it. The three of us should have a talk later."

"That's fine," Kimmie said. "How much longer 'til lunch?"

Laurie smile and patted her on her knee. "Shouldn't be long. I'm starving, too.

CHAPTER FOURTEEN

Glowing green numbers on the office microwave counted second by second down to zero. Lasher's finger was hovering over the oven's door latch, and as soon as the alarm beep rang out, she popped the door open. She hated that electronic chime. Lasher reached into the microwave and slid out a frozen dinner. Lasagna with green beans and a brownie. She set it on the counter next to the oven and let it sit and watched as steam from the heated meal fogged up the film of plastic over the container. It reminded her of the fog on the lake in the morning, that strange caul of mist that came before dawn no matter the season.

"Lunchtime?" Officer Millsap asked.

She peeled the cover off the tray, the cloying smells combining into one salty, sweet, and altogether unappetizing smell. Under the fluorescents of the commissary, the food looked like it had been leached of color. "Yeah, need to take Arlen his taxpayer-funded meal." She looked again at the plastic-wrapped tray and made a mental note that the next time she went shopping she needed to pick up some fresh food.

"I could've done that," he said. "Or Josie. Sort of below your pay grade, don't you think?"

She smiled at that, thought about lecturing him on small-town policing again. "Needed to stretch my legs anyway. I've got some questions for him, too." She placed the meal on a plastic tray, put a plastic-wrapped spork and napkin next to it, and finally a juice box.

"Fair enough," he said. "I'll be up front if you need anything."

The Oro Lake police station wasn't that big, and it didn't take her long to cross through the office and down the hall to the cells, balancing the tray the whole way. By the time she got to the cell where Arlen was sprawled out, she was starting to feel a little more like a waitress than a police officer. She chuckled, thinking about the long hours she'd spent bussing tables to pay her way through college. *Some skills stay with you,* she thought.

"Alrighty, sleeping beauty, lunchtime!" she called out.

Arlen was lying on the bottom cot of a bunk bed against the far wall. He hadn't combed his hair in the two days he'd been in the cell, and she wasn't sure if that was out of some sort of strange form of protest, or his general slovenliness.

His eyes opened a slit. Lasher noticed that Arlen was one of those sorts of people who could glare at you with their eyes barely open at all. She thought he had the kind of face that would be fun to punch. There was an opening at the bottom of the cell door, and she slid the tray in. "Lasagna today, Arlen. Just like you asked for."

He rolled onto his side and propped himself up to sitting. "Oh, hey, groovy."

Lasher stepped back from the cell door, Arlen took the tray and brought it back to sit on the edge of the bed. "You hear anything from Darryl?" he asked around a mouthful of brownie.

"You're eating dessert first?"

"It's the best part," he said, stuffing another sporkful into his mouth.

"Suit yourself," Lasher replied. "No, nothing from Darryl. You sure he didn't say anything about going on a trip? Maybe visit some friends? Or over to Reno or something?"

"Hell if I know," he said. He shoveled some limp green beans into his mouth.

Arlen started to laugh. "I ain't my brother's keeper!"

There was a metal and plastic chair against the wall across from the cell door. Lasher dragged it forward and sat on it, leaning forward on her elbows. "Good one, Arlen."

"I just thought of it," he said around the green mush. He swallowed. "So, when can I get out of here?"

"Keep up your good behavior, and we'll let you out this afternoon, probably. The guy you assaulted decided not to press charges."

"Good," he said and started in on the lasagna. "It was his fault anyway."

Lasher wondered what kind of food the McEwen's normally ate that made Arlen so happy to be eating frozen microwave dinners. She decided she didn't really want to know. "You know, Arlen, the way I see it, you really dodged a bullet this time. If they'd decided to press charges, you'd be in here for a lot longer than a weekend. You could wind up in Folsom or somewhere."

"Three squares and a bed, you know?" he said, shrugging as he poked at the lasagna.

But Lasher thought she saw a tinge of nervousness come over him when she mentioned the Folsom prison. Like storm clouds appearing to darken a blue sky.

She stood up to leave. "I'll let you know if we hear anything from Darryl. Oh, and your dog's with Doc Hoeger."

Arlen looked up at that. "Why, what's wrong with him?"

She shrugged. "Looks like he got into a fight or something. Found him when I went out looking for Darryl last night. Took him in to see the vet."

Arlen cocked his head and glared at her, then chewed and swallowed the mouthful of lasagna he'd been working on. "Okay, well, I appreciate that. I think I owe you one now."

"Keep your nose clean from now on."

He hissed a thin laugh. "Yeah, well, no promises."

"No promises," she returned, and left him to the rest of his dinner.

***

After she'd fed and questioned Arlen, Lasher began to feel the pangs of hunger herself. She'd initially planned to do a working lunch as usual; catch up on some paperwork at her desk and return a few calls. But the tuna sandwich she'd brought with her for lunch didn't thrill her. She picked at it a little before giving up and tossing it in the trash. She decided to take a walk through town and find lunch while she was out and about. She pulled her short blond ponytail tight and put it through the hole at the back of her dark blue police cap as she put it on.

"Josie, I'm taking lunch out today," Lasher said as she crossed the office. She was almost out the door when she stopped, turned, and called out to officer Millsap. "Hey Tom! Grabbing lunch, you coming?"

Millsap prairie-dogged over the top of his cube wall. She saw he had his phone handset cradled between ear and shoulder. He covered the mouthpiece with his free hand. "Give me a minute, will you? Almost done here."

Lasher nodded and gave him a thumbs-up. She returned to where Josie was leaning back in her chair, slowly swiveling back and forth and staring at her computer.

Lasher leaned one elbow on the counter in front of Josie. "Hey, Millsap and I are going to grab lunch. You want us to bring you back anything?"

Josie looked up. "No thanks." Then seemed to think better of her response. "Actually, where are you going?"

"Not sure," Lasher said. "Probably Get Up and Go, or maybe Clarendon's."

"Well, if you go to Get Up and Go, you think you could bring me back a chocolate shake?" Josie asked.

"Sure, that all?"

Josie nodded. "Yeah, I brought lunch today. But a chocolate shake would be nice."

"You got it," Lasher said and stood up. She heard the telltale rattle and click of Millsap hanging up the desk phone.

He stood up and left his cube. "Alright," he said as he stepped into the main floor of the office. "Where we going?"

"Let's take a walk," Lasher said. "We'll decide as we go."

Millsap stepped out into the hot, dry summer air and held the door as Lasher stepped through. "Walk? In this heat? You're gonna make me work for my lunch, aren't you?"

"Do you some good," she said. "When was the last time you hit the gym?"

"I refuse to answer that on the grounds that it might incriminate me." He looked up and down the street. Only a handful of people were walking through town at midday. *People who all should have known better,* he thought.

Lasher started up the street, and he hustled to catch up. When they came to a stop at the corner of a T-intersection, she waved at a group of four teens going the other way. Two girls, and a boy who seemed a little younger and unhappy to be there. He had the look of a little brother who didn't want to be stuck tagging along with his big sister and her friend. They were all wearing bathing suits and flip-flop with towels thrown over their shoulders. One of the girls, a tall, thin blonde waved at the pair of police, then turned to one of her friends—equally thin, equally blonde, but slightly less tall—and whispered something behind her hand. The girls burst out laughing. The boy rolled his eyes and looked embarrassed. They crossed the street and scampered away toward the lake.

"What was that about?" Millsap said, arming sweat from his forehead.

"Well," Lasher continued across the street. "Knowing teenage girls the way I do, I'm guessing one of two things. Either they think we're dating, or they think you're cute. Probably both."

Millsap missed a step. "Wait, what?"

"Don't let it go to your head," Lasher said.

They had gone a few blocks toward what passed for Golden Oaks' downtown when the smell of burgers and fries tickled Lasher's nose. The Get Up and Go diner was around the corner, and she knew the smell was coming from there. The smell of a year's worth of char-broiled burger residue over the dusty dry summer air reminded Lasher of summer cookouts, twilight tag, and first kisses at summer camp. She hoped those girls would have a great summer. But not so great it got them into any trouble that she'd have to clean up. "Get Up and Go?" she said to Millsap.

"As long as the AC's working, sure."

"I promised Josie I'd bring her back a shake anyway," she said. They came around the corner and entered the diner. The lunchtime crowd was thin, and Lasher remembered it was a Monday. But the air conditioning was in fact working fine and cut the desperate heat as soon as they entered.

Emily, the head waitress and co-owner of the diner, waved as they entered. "Your usual booth, Officers?" She smiled.

"Thanks, Em," Lasher said, and stopped, realizing she was already on her way to a booth next to a large window which looked out onto the street. Emily hustled ahead, wiping down the table with a damp cloth as Lasher and Millsap took their seats.

"You know what you want, or do you need menus?" Emily asked, casually looking out the window as she spoke to them.

"Burger and fries for me," Lasher said.

"Same," Millsap said. "And a Coke."

"You want anything to drink, hon?" Emily asked Lasher.

She shook her head. "Just water, thanks."

Emily scribbled the order down and took another look out the window, pausing slightly before turning to go. She shook her head, looked up at the clock and began to walk back toward the kitchen.

"Is everything okay, Em?" Lasher asked.

Emily stopped and turned back toward the police. "I don't know," she said. "Charlie's usually in by now, and he's almost an hour late. I called his cell, but it went straight to voicemail."

Lasher checked her watch. "Well, maybe he's caught up somewhere."

Emily's hands went to her hips. "Maybe," she said. "But he always calls if something comes up. Must've slipped his mind."

Lasher nodded in agreement. "I'm sure that's it. Oh, Em, do me a favor and let me get a chocolate milkshake to go when we leave?"

Emily scratched another note onto her pad. "You got it. I'll have it ready for you whenever you're set." She turned and went back to the kitchen. "I'm going to try Charlie's cell again," she said as she left. "I'll let you know if I get through."

Lasher leaned back in the booth bench. It was red vinyl imprinted with speckles of glitter, torn in spots, and Lasher wondered how long ago exactly its better days had been. "How well do you know Darryl McEwen?" she asked.

Millsap had been staring out the window, watching a car inch by. "Well enough to know he's not the sort of guy I'd want to grab a beer with."

"What do you mean by that?" Lasher asked.

Millsap turned from the window. "You know, like how you always hear in elections about a guy who's maybe not the best candidate, or the sharpest tool in the shed, so people try to think of anything positive to say to show he's a decent guy, and the best they come up with is 'The kind of guy you could have a beer with'."

"So, you're saying he's not," she said.

"I think Arlen's a bigger pain in the ass, but I wouldn't trust either one of them with the keys to my car," he replied.

"He's definitely been a thorn in the side of the Golden Oaks PD for long enough," she said. "Both of them, sure."

"What's on your mind?" he asked.

"Something's not adding up. Arlen's in jail for a couple of days, and Darryl disappears. And they may be a couple of dipshits, but those two took care of their dog. Maybe like property to them, but if Darryl was going to spontaneously decide to take a vacation—permanent or otherwise—I figure he'd either have taken Barney along or kenneled him somewhere."

"Okay," said Millsap. "And you said there was no sign of him last night?"

"Only his car out in front of their shack," she said. "And that's another thing. He's not exactly the type to take an Uber somewhere."

"I can always check it out again later," Millsap offered. "Swing by and see if he's sleeping off a bender or something."

"Here you go, darlins," Emily said, returning to the table with a tray laden with burgers, fries, and drinks. "I remembered your extra pickle, Officer," she said, winking at Millsap.

Lasher caught Millsap's eye and tried not to laugh.

Emily slid the plates in front of the two police officers. "Anything else I can get you?"

"Not for me, I'm good," Lasher said.

Millsap already had a mouthful of burger, so shook his head and gave Emily a big thumbs-up.

Lasher took a bite of her burger, followed it with a couple of fries. She'd been trying to eat better over the last few months, and this grease bomb was like manna from heaven. She chewed slowly while looking out the window. A few people strolling along the sidewalk in either direction and a single car drove past. Another quiet summer day in Golden Oaks, where most local folks were smart enough to stay inside where it was cool. "Getting to be the fightin' hot part of the summer, you know?"

Millsap looked at her quizzically. "What do you mean?"

"Oh, just the hot. Maybe the thin air up here, too. Who knows? This is the time of year people seem to be short tempered. Pershing used to call it the 'fightin' hot' time of summer, and I guess it stuck."

"Yeah?" he said. "You thinking about the McEwens?"

She nodded, shrugged. "Maybe. Thinking about a few years ago, before your time. A few months before Pershing took his retirement. Same time of year, though a little after Independence Day, I guess. That's my least favorite day around here. Too many folks from out of town, drinking and blowing stuff up around the lake. You've been around for a few of those, so you know what I'm talking about."

Millsap blew out a slow stream of air, and followed with a "Yeah, sure do."

"But this was a week or so past that, I guess," Lasher continued. "Got called out on a domestic on the north shore of the lake. A neighbor had heard all hell breaking loose from a house nearby, and called it in. When we got there—Pershing and I, did I mention he was there?"

"No," Millsap replied.

"Okay, well, yeah it was the both of us. So, we get there and this guy, Timmy Francis, local loser, is going full on Mike Tyson on his own mother. He's screaming nonsense at the top of his lungs. I tried to restrain him, but he had a knife and came at me." She paused. A memory of the acrid stink of gunpowder and blood. "Pershing was a hell of a shot, you know?"

She dabbed a fry in ketchup, raised it to her mouth, but when she saw the redness of the sauce, she tossed the fry back onto her plate. "Anyway, neither one of them made it. The mother had ruptured organs. The husband had a ruptured head." After a moment she said, "Found his dad upstairs in his bed. Sledgehammer stuck in his head."

Millsap kept eating. "Shit. That's messed up."

"Yeah," she replied. "We get domestic stuff up here from time to time, but this was the worst I've ever seen." She looked out the window, eyes on something a hundred miles, or a couple of years, distant. "You know, Pershing told me after that, that in the entire time he'd been sheriff here, he'd never once had to draw his weapon except when he was at the range. Put in for retirement a couple of weeks later." Lasher raised her hand and waved briefly at Emily. She pushed the plate away.

"So, what was he screaming about, anyway? The killer?"

"Bunch of nonsense, like I said," Lasher replied. "The guy was nuts. Stuff about the … what was it? The ravens were following him, I think. Whatever that means."

She paused to think. There was something else, something gnawing at the edges of her mind like a rat trapped in the walls, scratching to get out. Indistinct, but irritating. She waved toward Emily. "Let's get that shake back to Josie."

Emily came over with a large chocolate shake in a styrofoam to-go cup. "Here you go," she said, placing it on the table in front of them. "Can I get you anything else?"

Lasher opened her wallet and fished out her Visa card. "No, nothing. Did you get ahold of Charlie?"

Emily took the card. "Still no luck. Maybe he overslept. I know he's been having trouble sleeping since his wife passed."

She went to the register, rang up their check, and came back with the receipt. "I'll let you know if he calls, though. Don't want you to worry."

Lasher signed the receipt and handed a copy back to Emily. "That'd be great, thanks."

She and Millsap stood up and headed toward the exit. "Thanks again for the grub, Em. Always good."

***

After dropping off the slightly melted, but nonetheless very much appreciated chocolate milkshake with Josie, Lasher made a beeline to the records storage room. All the way at the back of the building behind a sturdy locked door. Lasher moved a few boxes, handing them to Millsap as she travelled back in time year after year. By the time she got to the 2014 box, she had worked up a sweat from the heat in the close quarters of the room.

"You think there's something in that old file relevant to the McEwens?" Millsap asked, as he put the last of the 2015 boxes on top of the others.

Lasher slid the first 2014 box to the side on the shelf where it rested. She pulled the one behind it forward: "2014: Jun-Dec" was written in black marker on the front of the box. Lasher recognized her own handwriting. "Talking about Tim Francis got me thinking. In some ways, they remind me of him, but this guy made the McEwens look like a couple of geniuses."

"Why do we have hardcopies of all this stuff anyway?" he asked. "Isn't it in the computer?"

"Just the last few years. Anything past that, we weren't really up to speed with the computers yet. Pershing didn't trust them, so we still worked mostly with hard copy." She dragged the box forward and popped the lid. Inside it, the box was about half filled with manila folders, each with a date, case number, and name written in blue pen on the tab.

She flipped through the folders until she was in the handful of cases from June and July. "Mostly misdemeanors, drunk and disorderlies, that sort of stuff," she said. "Dumb to keep most of this anyway." Then she pulled a file out. "Bingo." She flipped it open and started skimming the report, tracing her index finger down the lines of laser printed text. Not much to say, but then she tapped her finger on a few lines almost toward the end. "Right here, Francis was talking about the ravens. And something about how he could 'feel it in my head'."

"Feel what in his head?" Millsap asked. "Any idea?"

She shook her head. "None, but how weird is that?" She looked at the date on the report: July 20th, 2014. "Yeah, that was the summer the lake was so low. Not as low as it is right now, but still low."

"What's that got to do with the McEwens?"

"Thinking about their dog, Barney," she said. "When I took him into see Doc Hoeger, there was something under his skin. Looked like he'd picked up a parasite, maybe. But there were these sort of threads hanging off it. What do you call them? Cilia?"

"Cilia?" he said. "What's that?"

She closed the box and slid it back onto the shelf. "Didn't you take biology in high school?"

"Been a while," he said.

"Cilia are parts of some microscopic organisms. These sort of threads or strands that twitch or vibrate and help the organism to move."

"Move in what?"

"Whatever they're in. That's how the microscopic critters get around in lake water when they're not floating along in the currents," she said and turned to walk out of the room.

"What critters?" Millsap said, following after her.

"Whatever critters are down there." She smacked the light switch, and the room went dark. "Come on," she said as she left the room. "Lock up, but leave the boxes for now. We'll put them away when we're done with this file."

Chapter Fifteen

Kimmie stood in front of the deli counter staring at the lunchmeat, sliced cheeses, all the ingredients arrayed palatably before her, but nothing looked good. Half-heartedly, she picked up a premade tuna sandwich and dropped it into the hand basket with a bag of barbecue chips and a bottle of Coke. She turned from the counter and she saw Laurie coming from around the corner of one nearby aisle.

Laurie waved at her as she approached. "Find anything good?"

Kimmie shrugged. "Just a sandwich and some chips. Not super hungry, I guess."

Laurie looked into the basket. "That all you want to get? Why don't you pick up a bigger bag of chips so you can share with your friend?"

"Okay," Kimmie said flatly, and went off toward the aisle of chips and snacks, Laurie followed along behind her.

"I'm thinking of maybe spaghetti for dinner tonight," Laurie said. "Go on ahead, I'll catch up," she waved to Kimmie as she disappeared down the aisle holding pastas and sauces. "Get a big bag of whatever you already chose," she suggested.

Kimmie wandered down the snacks aisle, then put the small bag back on the shelf, and replaced it in her basket with a large bag of barbecue chips.

Laurie caught up to her. "All set?"

Kimmie nodded. "I grabbed a couple of tuna sandwiches. Unless you want something else."

"Tuna's fine," Laurie said.

Kimmie came down the aisle, and Laurie noticed her slight limp. "You sure you want to go to the lake? How's your leg doing?"

"It's okay, Mom," Kimmie replied. "Still sore, but no biggie." She started walking back to the front of the store. "Come on, I don't want to keep them waiting anymore."

"I'm sure they'd understand if you weren't feeling up to it. You could tell Jill you hurt your foot and want to rest."

Kimmie rolled her eyes and emptied her basket on the checkout conveyor belt. "It's fine, Mom. It's a sprain or whatever. I'm not even planning on going in the water; just going to hang out."

Laurie gave her a tired smile. "Okay, if that's what you want. I think we've got everything we need. Let's get to the lake."

***

"Kimmie!" Jill shrieked as she saw her friend getting out of the car. She barreled over, grabbing Kimmie up in a bear hug. Kimmie laughed and squeaked as Jill lifted her a few inches off the ground.

"Oh, my god, put me down, you big dork!" Kimmie said, laughing.

Jill lowered her to the asphalt of the parking lot. "I was starting to worry you might not show."

"Sorry," Kimmie said. "We had a couple stops on the way." She brushed her hair back from her face and inclined her head toward Laurie to indicate it was her mom's fault.

"Gotcha," Jill said, smiling.

They got out of the car, and Laurie raised her hand to give Jill a high-five. "Hey, Jill! How are you?" she said, enthusiastically.

Jill stared at her upraised hand.

Laurie lowered her hand, feeling distinctly old and uncool.

"Fine, Mrs. Barnes," Jill said, finally. "Real good, I guess."

"Well, that's good to hear," Laurie said. "Glad we were able to make this work out; Kimmie's been looking forward to seeing you again."

"Yeah, me too," Jill said. "My sister and brother are here too, but they already went in."

"Oh, I'm so sorry we were late," Laurie said. "We had someone to visit, and then we stopped by the Raley's to get lunch." She turned back to the car, "Actually, Kimmie, give me a hand, will you?"

"Sure, Mom," Kimmie said.

Laurie dragged two grocery bags out of the back seat of the Corolla, handing one to Kimmie. "Here's yours, and we didn't know what kind of chips you like," she said to Jill. "But figured everyone likes barbecue, right?"

"Jake loves them," Jill replied. "Thanks."

"Okay, enough chitchat," Laurie said. She started walking toward the front gate. "Let's go see if they have any cute lifeguards here."

"Mom!" Kimmie said, mortified.

Jill laughed. They paid their entrance fees and strolled along the path to the beach area. The sandy beach was a wide crescent, the entrance kiosk roughly at about the center. A strip of asphalt, then grass bordered the sandy beach. The asphalt snaked all the way from one side of the public area to the other, making it easy for people with rolling coolers or other bric-a-brac to get their gear close to wherever they were going to sprawl out for the day.

It was still hot, almost uncomfortably so, but a cool breeze drifted across the lake bringing some relief. "Jill, where are your brother and sister?" Laurie asked.

Jill pointed to the left, down the beach. "They're hanging out on the pier over there."

Laurie looked in the direction she was pointing. In the distance, she saw a small floating pier, a lifeguard station nearby. Scanning across the lake, Laurie saw it was mirrored with another pier, another lifeguard station across at the other arm of the crescent.

"Okay, I'm going to camp out here," she said. "Kimmie, you can go play with your friends, and if you need me, I'll be here with my book."

Kimmie nodded. "Sure, okay. Thanks, Mom." She and Jill rushed off in the direction of the pier.

As the girls got closer to the small dock, a girl who'd been lying on the pier stood up and waved to them. Laurie smiled, happy that Kimmie would have some kids her own age to talk to for a while. Being stuck with her folks all week was probably getting old already.

Laurie spread out her towel and picnic and got a copy of *Crazy Rich Asians* out of her beach bag. She looked around thinking that the beach was pretty empty for a summer day. There were maybe fifty other people on the beach, and lots of space to run on the sand. Little kids played by the shore, making sandcastles under the watchful gaze of their parents. Older couples sat on beach chairs under large umbrellas. A middle-aged man wearing jean shorts, a tie-dye tank top, and a Sacramento Kings ball cap meandered along the beach waving a metal detector in front of him like a modern-day dowsing rod. He passed by her, intent on anticipatory treasures lurking under the sand and never sparing a glance away from the readout panel of his device. Laurie watched him, thinking that there are infinite clones of that same guy on every beach in the world. Only the team on his hat changed. She wondered if anyone ever found anything with one of those metal detectors. If there really were any secrets buried out of sight in a town like Golden Oaks.

She shrugged and lay down on her towel. "Least he's having fun."

***

Jill licked a trickle of melted chocolate ice cream running down her forearm. She and Kimmie were sitting at the end of the pier, Jill's feet dangled over the edge, splashing the lake water. "It's melting faster than I can eat it!" she squealed, and scarfed the last globs of ice cream off the wooden stick she held. Kimmie laughed and dropped her own ice cream stick into the grocery bag next to her. Jill flicked her fingers, tossing hers from the pier. It landed in the water with a thin *plip!* and floated away. Jill's younger brother Jake, and her sister Andrea were splashing in the lake a few yards out from the dock.

Kimmie leaned back on her elbows and stretched her legs out in front of her. "I'm glad I was able to get my mom to drive me here," she said. "It's only been two days, but I'm already going stir-crazy in the cabin with them."

"I'm glad you could, too," Jill said. "If you hadn't called, I'd probably be stuck babysitting Jake and Andrea since my parents are both working today." She looked out at them splashing in the water. "That would have been so lame," she said. Jill's dad, Steve, managed a local auto parts store, and her mom, Kay, was the day shift manager at the single hotel in town, the Golden Grove. Jill was hoping her dad was planning on fixing up a car for her sixteenth birthday coming up in the fall.

Jake had been pretty vocal about not wanting to spend time with any of them the night before when his parents had told him he couldn't stay home by himself. He'd have been happy staying at home playing *Star Wars* on the Nintendo Switch, but his mom had promised she'd give them all money so they could buy lunch and ice cream and sodas at the snack shack, and he finally had to admit to himself that that was better than spending the whole day by himself at home.

Under Jill's supervision, the Bridges kids had come through town to get to the lake. They lived on the far side of town, but still within walking distance of the public beach at Oro Lake. By the time they'd gotten to the lake, they were all sweating from the terrifically hot summer weather.

Now from the small pier, Jill watched Andrea and Jake splashing in the water. Jake had been acting like a brat earlier, but as soon as they got to the water, he started his favorite game of swimming straight down, trying to touch the floor of the lake. He'd come up gasping after a few seconds, tread water, and try again. "We saw the cutest cop on our way over," Jill whispered to Kimmie with a tone of conspiracy.

"Oh, yeah?" Kimmie said, but with a distinct lack of interest.

"Totally," Jill said. "I wonder how big his nightstick is?"

Kimmie laughed at that. "You're terrible!"

Jill saw Jake's head break the surface. He took in a great gulp of air and waved at her.

"I think I almost touched the bottom that time Jill!" he shouted.

"Well, keep trying," she yelled back. She noticed the lifeguard on his beach tower was watching them. At least she thought he was, then his head turned and she realized he was doing his scan back and forth across the small beach. He was one of three lifeguards on duty. The other guard stands were set in the center and far side of the crescent-shaped beach and had a lifeguard stationed in each, all scanning their section of the beach. On busy weekends, there were two other guards who'd patrol from the beach on foot.

"Do you know the lifeguard?" Kimmie asked.

Jill's blonde hair—still dry, and probably going to stay that way—fluttered in the soft breeze as she nodded slightly. "Yeah," she whispered. "That's Peter Guilford. He's going to Davis."

"College boy, huh?" Kimmie smiled.

"Yeah. I don't know what he's majoring in, though," Jill said. "But he's come back to town the last few summers to work."

Andrea grabbed on to the edge of the pier and slithered up out of the water. She skipped quickly across to her towel and flounced down, splattering water on Jill as she did. Jill screeched as the cold water dripped on her sun-warmed skin. "Eek!" She sat up straight. "Andrea! You got me all wet, you brat!"

Andrea shook her head back and forth, water droplets spraying from her short hair. Jill and Kimmie shrieked again and this time the lifeguard was definitely looking their way.

"It's a lake, Jilly," Andrea said. "You're supposed to get wet, not lie around on the pier hoping boys'll look at you. Jeez Kimmie, aren't you hot in your jeans?"

"No, I'm fine."

"How come you're not swimming, anyway?" Andrea asked as she squeezed water from her hair.

Kimmie looked at the water and felt her skin crawl. She shuddered as she thought of the clutching, icy roots, of grasping tendrils unseen below the surface, of water flooding into her lungs. "Don't feel like it, is all."

"Shut up, Andrea," Jill said. "She doesn't have to swim if she doesn't want to." She rolled over onto her stomach facing the water, her body propped up on her elbows. Kimmie did the same.

Jake popped to the surface like a cork again, spitting out a mouthful of water in a glistening stream.

"Gross," Jill said. He smiled and waved again and swam toward the pier. When he reached the edge, he held on with one hand.

"I think I felt a fish!" he said, excitedly. "I was swimming back up, and something swished by my leg. I bet it was a catfish. Kimmie, did you know they have catfish in this lake? I'm going to try and catch one, and we can have it for dinner."

"You don't even have a pole, squirt," Jill said. "What're you going to catch it with?"

"I'll grab it!" he said, as he launched his free hand into the air like a rocket, then brought it crashing down into the lake water. "Like Aquaman!"

"Aquaman is hella hot," Jill said, and the girls started giggling again.

"Watch me!" Jake said. "Who wants to bet I can catch a fish with my hands?"

Andrea rolled her eyes and lay on her towel. Kimmie laughed and said, "If you catch a catfish with your hands, next ice cream's on me."

Jill added, "And I'll buy you a Coke."

"Deal!" Jake said, and sluiced back into the cool green water, disappearing with a glittering spray as he kicked down.

Jill dropped down onto her towel, crossing her hands under her head.

Kimmie was peeking at the nearby lifeguard again. "I'm going to go talk to him."

Jill popped back up onto her elbows. "Oh, my god, you are not."

"Watch me," Kimmie said. She stood up awkwardly, the floating pier wobbling as she rose, and wandered toward the lifeguard stand. "Hi!" she called up, and looked back to see if Jill and Andrea were watching her. They were.

"Hi, what's up?" Peter the lifeguard said, leaning slightly toward her, but not looking directly at her. He was still scanning the lake. Kimmie didn't know what for as there were maybe only a dozen people actually in the water, and half of them were little kids near the shore.

"Hi, yeah," she said. "I was wondering if it was busy here today? Like, is this a lot of people for the beach?"

"No, pretty quiet today. Not as many as on a weekend, but still pretty crowded for a Monday afternoon."

Kimmie nodded. "Was it a busy weekend?"

The lifeguard looked down at her, but then turned his attention back to the rippling water and the people swimming in it. "Saturday sure was. The lake was at capacity, lots of folks out on their boats. Sunday was less than that, but still pretty busy."

"That's cool." She turned back to Jill and Andrea, who were watching her exchange with the lifeguard and trying to hold in squeals of laughter.

Kimmie was about to turn back to ask another question when two huge ravens, black and gleaming, swooped from the sky and landed on the pier. They hopped to the water's edge and started croaking at the shimmering green lake water.

Jill shrieked and scooted away from the birds. Kimmie rushed toward her friends, and the lifeguard hopped down from his perch. He jogged toward the girls who were flapping their towels at the ravens.

"Scram, birds!" Jill shouted, followed by a burst of laughter. One of the ravens hopped to the side, shot a dark-eyed look at her and a *caw!* Then Jill stopped and stepped to the edge of the pier. "Hey, Andrea, have you seen Jake?"

Andrea stopped shaking her towel and looked toward the water. "He was right there a minute ago. Right before these dumb birds showed up."

Jill rushed to the edge, dropped to her hands and knees and peered into the water. "Jake!" she yelled. "Jake where are you?"

Suddenly the lifeguard was next to her. "What's going on?" he said, shooing the birds away. They both cawed at him and took off into the air, gliding around the pier in a low, lazy circle.

"My brother," Jill said. "He was diving in the water and now I can't see him."

Kimmie and Andrea had both dropped to the edge of the pier and were calling out, "Jake! Jakey!"

The lifeguard jumped from the edge of the pier, disappearing almost instantly into the green water. A breathless few seconds passed as the girls watched after him. The water was cloudy enough that anything vanished a few feet under the surface.

"Do you see him?" Jill asked, panic rising in her voice, choking off the last word. "I don't see him!"

"What's going on?" Jake said behind her, and she spun around.

"Oh, my God, Jake!" She rushed to him, grabbed him in a bear hug and squeezed. Kimmie and Andrea hustled over alongside him. Jill broke the hug, pushing him back and holding him at arm's length. "Jake, where the hell were you?" she said, as tears of relief began to stream down her cheeks. "You scared the shit out of me!"

He shrugged out of her grip. "I had to go to the bathroom. I told you, but you were looking at the lifeguard. Don't blame me for being too horny to hear me."

Kimmie shrieked with laughter.

"Oh God, Jake, you had us worried. Next time pee in the lake, you little turd." Jake looked at Kimmie and Andrea, then leaned in so only Jill would hear. "I had to poo, Jill," he said.

She ruffled his hair, and hugged him close again. "Okay, but next time, you have to make sure one of us hears you before you go running off, okay?"

"Yeah, okay."

Andrea turned toward them, then back toward the water and said, "You guys, the lifeguard still hasn't come up."

"What?" Jill said, walking to the edge of the pier. The three girls stood at the edge, staring down into the water. It lapped rhythmically at the edge of the pier, a wet slapping, as the pier bobbed on the low waves.

Peter's body slid out from the dock under them. They were looking right into his face, an inch or so below the water's surface. Sunlight glinted in his bulging eyes, the cobalt blue irises rolled back in their sockets. His mouth was wide open, and a dark ring surrounded his neck, like a bruise that wrapped around his throat entirely. The ring slithered tighter, like a coiled black rope or a noose of algae being pulled tight.

Kimmie screamed. Jill turned and, grabbing Jake so he wouldn't see, dropped to her knees. Andrea stood, staring at the floating corpse, then she turned and ran from the pier, to find the other lifeguards, waving her arms overhead and screaming for help.

Across the beach, the other two lifeguards leapt from their posts and began running toward them, whistles blaring against the summer sounds of laughter and dim music from distant CD players. Laurie was torn from her book, and when she saw the lifeguards running in the direction of the kids, she scrambled to her feet, instantly following as fast as she could.

Kimmie watched as Peter's body floated a few feet further out from under the pier. His entire torso now exposed from beneath the pier as it bobbed below the surface. And she saw dark tendrils, sinuous and malign, slither around his body, curling around his arms, circling his neck. A dark shape rose from beneath the body, from the green of the lake's deeps, and Kimmie felt a wave of malignant energy wash over her. There was the vaguest hint of a face, horribly bloated, black, lank hair trailing from a piebald skull as it broke the surface.

Suddenly the shriek of the ravens circling overhead broke through the air. Kimmie looked up numbly to see the ravens slicing through the air toward her. Toward her? The dead lifeguard floating in the water? Or the ghastly face floating above the water next to the lifeguard's prone form?

The first raven lanced from the sky, Kimmie felt a whoosh of air as it passed inches away from her face and in a dark flash of feathers it was attacking the thing's skull, clawing and pecking before taking off into the sky again. A second raven repeated the action, stabbing its beak deep into the thing's empty eye socket before rocketing into the sky. The black birds arced up, circled, and began to descend again, cawing madly the whole way.

The ravens plummeted, but this time the thing in the lake reacted. One raven shot downward, and the thing lashed out with a blackened, slime-crusted arm. Fingers, long and claw-like, plucked the raven out of the sky, snatching it with an iron grip. A flurry of wings, a last *caw!* Kimmie heard a crunching of tiny hollow bones, and the bird was still.

She never took her eyes off the dead face in the lake. It turned to stare directly at her with empty eyes, and slowly, a rictus grin smiled menacingly at her. It opened its mouth wide, and with one fluid motion, it popped the entire raven into its maw. The bird disappeared behind a wall of long, white teeth. A crawfish clambered out of one dead, hollow eye socket, wriggled on the thing's dead cheek, then fell into the water with a faint *plip!* The corpse raised its black, clawed hands, slick with slime and putrescence, grabbed Peter's head, drew it close, and sank back beneath the water. And the water was once again still.

Kimmie felt the blood drain from her face, saw spots before her eyes, and felt a falling sensation as everything went dark.

Chapter Sixteen

Gabe had gotten restless waiting for the girls, so decided to ping an Uber driver to give him a ride into town. He figured he could either meet up with Laurie somewhere or get another Uber back later in the day. The ride was quiet, though Gabe tried a few times to strike up a conversation. The driver, an older man with a graying braided ponytail peeking out from the back of his faded brown felt fedora, didn't seem interested in engaging in conversation. In fact, when Gabe tried to get him talking about fishing at the lake, he turned up the radio louder, and let Jerry Garcia drown him out.

So, the ride was quiet, and awkward, at least for Gabe. When the driver let him off in front of the history museum, Gabe thanked him and said he'd leave a good rating, and the driver grunted a dull "thanks" and drove away. Sweat trickled down Gabe's back instantly, soaking into his shirt. The "Oro Lake History Room" was tucked neatly behind a strip mall, next to the equally small public library, on the edge of downtown Golden Oaks.

A wash of mercifully cool air conditioning flowed over Gabe as he stepped into the small museum. He took a deep breath of the cool air as the teenager behind the check-in counter looked up from her phone.

"How hot is it out there?" she asked.

"It's a scorcher," Gabe replied, stepping up to the counter and taking a brochure. "Be happy you're in here where it's cool."

She nodded. "Totally."

Gabe looked around the small space, noticed a little walking path around one edge with the "History of Oro Lake" etched on a placard at the opening. The other side of the room was wide open with a couple of dozen folding chairs set out in front of a small stage. Beyond the chairs, glass doors opened onto a patio.

"Thought it'd be bigger, honestly," Gabe said to the teenager.

She smiled. "Well, you know, the town's less than a hundred years old. Not a lot of history, really. But you're welcome to take a look at what we've got. Is there anything specific you were interested in?"

Gabe turned slowly around, taking in the room again. "I was wondering about the WPA project that created the dam. Oh, also, anything you might have about the natives who lived around the area before all that."

She pointed to the start of the path around the perimeter of the room. "Start there. It'll only take you a few minutes to see it all, but if you want to know anything more, we might have some papers or books in storage you can look through. If you want, I can see if the museum director is free to chat."

"Actually, that'd be great." He fished his wallet from his back pocket, pulled out a ten-dollar bill, and dropped it in the plexiglass "Donations" box on the counter. "Thanks again," he said, and went over toward the entrance to the walking tour.

Next to the placard noting the entrance to the main exhibit was a blown-up etching of three Native Americans hiking through the mountains. One had a long pole slung over his shoulder, a brace of rabbits hanging from the end. A pair of ravens flew high over their heads. There was an insert note which explained, "A trio of Miwok hunters, with the Oro Valley in the distance."

Gabe took a step back to take in the whole image and saw that there was indeed a valley in the background of the etching. And as he looked closer at that part of the etching, he noticed a steep hill in the middle of the valley. "Hey," he said, turning to the girl at the entrance counter. "Is that the little island at the center of Oro Lake?" She was rising to come over when a woman stepped out of an office door tucked behind a display of miner paraphernalia a little further in. The woman was in her mid-forties, wearing jeans and a crimson blouse, her hair pulled back in a braid. She smiled as she approached him.

"Yeah, you got it. Deer Island," she said, walking toward the etching. "Hi, I'm Jean Fowlis, the director here." She held out her hand, and Gabe shook it.

"So, this is what the valley looked like before it was flooded by the WPA?" he asked.

Her shoulders rose and fell in a slight shrug. "More or less. You know, artistic license and all."

"I found some old photos of that island in the *Mountain Times*. When the reservoir first opened, there was a watch tower of some sort on it. Know anything about that?"

Jean nodded, and motioned Gabe over to another small section of the room. This one had photos of the valley during the construction of the Oro Dam. "Yeah, it was a central point. Once the project was really underway, they put a surveyor's watchtower up there so they could observe the whole operation unfold, see?" She pointed to a photo which clearly showed the tower he'd seen in the newspaper photo earlier. A group of guys standing around in front of it, mugging for the camera. They were wearing hardhats and coveralls and giving a big thumbs-up with leather-gloved hands. "The tower fell into disuse back in the 60s, and it was torn down. Though the remains of the foundation slab is still there. Nobody's really allowed to go out on the island, though I'm sure someone has from time to time."

"Oh yeah?" Gabe said. "What makes you think that?"

"Oh, natural curiosity, I suppose," she said. "Gotta figure anything right there with a big "Keep Off" sign on it is going to draw some attention. Wouldn't surprise me to find out the local teenagers have come up with all sorts of ghost stories about it, and probably dare each other to row out there."

"Speaking of ghost stories, the article I read mentioned that the local Indians called this place the Empty Valley and avoided it. Any idea why?"

Jean smirked. "For some reason they didn't really hunt the valley much. Not a lot of animals in the valley worth hunting was what I heard. Maybe has something to do with how many ravens we get around here. Those birds can be pretty territorial and aggressive."

"Was it Miwoks or Ohlone?"

"The Sierra Miwoks lived to the south of the general area," Jean replied. "All through central California really. If you're interested, I could recommend you some books."

"No, just wondering."

"Fair enough," she said. "Well, if you have any questions, feel free to ask. Otherwise, I'll leave you to it." She turned to walk away.

"Hey," he said. "You know since you mentioned it, has the area always had so many ravens?"

"Oh, yeah," she said, turning back toward him. "A lot of them flew away when the WPA first flooded the valley. All the noise of the workers, the explosions, construction sounds, all that. Over time the population's come back, of course. But yeah, the area has always had a greater population of them than you'd expect."

"What do you mean by that?" Gabe said.

"Well, like I said, according to the stories, the Miwoks called it the Empty Valley because of the poor hunting, right? No big game at all really, and not a lot of small game, either. And carrion, hare, etc. that's the sort of stuff ravens thrive on. It's a weird ecosystem balance. Things are different since the valley was flooded, of course. The water in the reservoir has brought some deer, and the town seeds the lake a few times a year with fish."

"Weird," Gabe said.

"Here, check this out," Jean said and led him back to the display area about the WPA's building of the dam and the flooding of the valley. A plaque on the wall near some woven baskets was titled "Miwoks and Ravens."

Gabe leaned forward to read it: "The ancient Miwok people believed a flood destroyed the world years ago during the time of the First People. Some of the First People survived when they climbed to the top of a mountain to avoid the flood. But when the waters receded and they descended the mountain, they were unable to find food and died. Ravens flew down from the sky and landed on the places where the people died. Those ravens became new people, the Miwoks."

Below that, the plaque said: "Another story tells that the ravens who landed in the Oro Valley (which the Miwok called the Empty Valley) did not become people. They decided to stay ravens to guard the land."

"Guard it from what?" Gabe asked.

Jean shrugged. "Who knows?"

"Right," Gabe said. "Well, cool story anyway."

"So, if you have any more questions, let me know."

"Yeah, thanks, I will," Gabe replied. He wandered through the rest of the small exhibit, taking in the displays of photos, some old food tins, and building tools forming a display about the WPA workers. There wasn't much of historical note past the WPA. A few photos of the town through the late twentieth century, and a final plaque about the bright future of Oro Lake and Golden Oaks. All in all, Gabe thought the museum might make for a semi-interesting field trip for the local 6th graders.

He waved at the girl at the front desk as he exited the building. "Thanks again," he said before stepping out into the oppressive summer heat.

The door closed behind him, and he crossed the street to where it was shadier on the other side. He had barely stepped beneath the awning of a small bookstore entrance when the wail of sirens split the still air. He jumped, startled as a police car, sirens blazing, sped around the corner and shot off down the street. An ambulance came streaking down the main road, flying toward the lake. The ambulance rocketed past Gabe when he felt his phone buzz in his pocket. When he pulled it out, he saw he had a missed call from Laurie a minute before. The sirens had drowned out the chime. He thumbed the play button on his voicemail. "Hey, babe," her voice said. "Kimmie's had a bit of a scare. We're at the lake, and it looks like a lifeguard's drowned right by where she and her friends were swimming."

Gabe watched as a raven landed on the roof of the history museum across the street. It was followed by two more, and then a fourth, larger than the rest. The birds hopped along the roof, pecking at the moss growing between the dry wooden tiles.

"Someone's called emergency services already. But Kimmie's pretty shook up. We're leaving the beach, and going back to the house. Might take her to the urgent care in a bit if she's still not feeling well. Just a heads up. Talk to you soon. Love you," she said, and the line went dead.

Gabe thumbed the call-back icon on his phone and lifted it to his ear.

After two rings, Laurie answered, "Hey, we're still at the lake. Where are you?"

He started walking toward the main road. "I just got your call, is Kimmie okay?"

"She's shook up a little, but I think she'll be fine. We're heading back to the house after we talk to the lifeguards and the police."

Gabe approached the corner of the intersection. A few people were standing on the sidewalk, staring in the direction the ambulance had gone. "I'm actually downtown. On Main. Do you think you could pick me up on your way?"

"Oh, sure," she said. "I didn't realize you were coming into town today."

"Kind of a spur of the moment thing. Listen, I'll start walking toward the lake, and keep an eye out for you. Don't rush, and I'll either meet you at the parking lot, or you can pull over if you see me."

There was a pause on the other end, a muffled conversation, as if Laurie was holding the phone to her chest. "That's fine," she said. "We have to make a statement to the cops or something anyway."

"We're definitely getting to know the local law this week, aren't we?"

"As long as we're staying on their good side, I guess," she said.

"Here's hoping. Okay, well, be safe, and I'll see you in a bit."

"You too," she said. The phone was silent.

He slipped the phone into his hip pocket and began to stroll through town toward the lake. He was struck by the little changes, as well as how static Golden Oaks was. The Get Up and Go diner was a fixture he remembered since he was a kid. But he still had trouble thinking of the supermarket as anything other than the "Golden Oaks Grocery" anymore, having been replaced with the Raley's sometime in the last decade.

Some shops were nothing but empty storefronts now, and then there were places like the "Golden Oaks Antiques" which had been absorbed by a strip mall and was bordered by shiny new sporting goods stores and chain restaurants. Golden Oaks was a town that changed slowly, almost reluctantly. But it did change. He wondered what it would be like in twenty years. Would it continue to grow, or curl up on itself even more?

Within a few minutes, he was heading out of town. The road sign alerted him to the direction of the public beach, but he knew the way. In about half a mile the sidewalk ended, the main road became SR 346 again, and he marched along the shoulder of the road against traffic. The highway traffic was light, but it still unsettled him when the occasional car blazed by, kicking up grit and a burst of wind in its passing. Off the side of the road to his left, a long fence of brown, rusty barbed wire ran parallel to the highway. Beyond that, he watched a few head of cattle grazing in the hilly fields. A handful of cows clustered together under the shade of a gnarled old oak tree. He passed by just as two ravens burst into the air from behind a low bush, cawing as they shot up into the sky. He caught a slight whiff of decay, something corrupt and stale on the breeze.

He was working up a sweat as he hiked along the side of the highway and was beginning to regret his decision to walk toward the lake when he came around a bend and saw the "Oro Lake: Public Beach Parking" sign across the road. He looked both ways and hustled across the highway after confirming there was no traffic coming from either direction. When Gabe was a kid he used to bike from his house to the lake almost every day during summertime, even though it had always made him incredibly nervous to ride along that road. He still couldn't believe his parents had let him do that. He sure wouldn't let Kimmie ride her bike along this stretch of road. Different times.

Gabe was soon walking into the parking lot. It was mostly empty, which didn't surprise him since it was a Monday afternoon. Maybe people would come down to the beach later for picnic dinners or twilight hiking.

Up ahead, he saw his car parked near the entrance to the beach, but no sign of Laurie or Kimmie. He saw that the road access gate was open next to the entrance kiosk, and when he craned his neck around, he could see a police car and ambulance parked alongside the lake in the distance.

Approaching the entrance, he got out his wallet to pay the meager entrance fee. "Beach is closed," said a teenage girl distractedly from behind the glass window in the booth. The teen was staring at the commotion on the beach, not giving Gabe a second look. Gabe looked past her and saw a couple of dozen people standing around on the sandy beach.

Gabe nodded. "Hey, I'm not going swimming. I'm here to meet my wife, my daughter, and her friends. They were going to give me a ride, but I guess they had to talk to the police or something."

The teen turned toward him. "Oh, well, swimming's closed for the day." She looked upset, worried. Her eyes were hidden behind a pair of dark sunglasses, but her red nose told Gabe she'd been crying.

"I heard one of the lifeguards was hurt?" Gabe said.

She nodded, took a deep shuddering breath. "Yeah, Peter. Nobody's telling me anything. The cops and EMTs blasted through and who knows what's going on."

Gabe forced a smile. "Well, let's let them do their jobs. I tell you what, I'll go find my wife, and I'll ask around. I'll be quick and give you a heads up as soon as I find out what's going on. Deal?"

She nodded, and grabbed a tissue and wiped at her nose. "Yeah, okay. Thanks."

"Hang tight," Gabe said. "I'm sure the police are doing everything they can."

She wiped her nose, and blotted the tears from her cheeks. "Sure." She didn't sound convinced.

Gabe gave her a smile and hustled along the asphalt path leading past the changing rooms, the concession stands, and toward the sand, when he saw Laurie standing back from a dock around the left side of the beach. An ambulance and police cruiser were parked close to the dock, their light bars flashing a silent warning to the small crowd gathering nearby. A pair of lifeguards were doing a half-hearted job of crowd control.

"You can't come through, sir," one of them said, her expression tired and anxious.

"That's my wife over there," he said, pointing to Laurie. "I want to make sure she's okay."

The lifeguard turned as Laurie waved and then rushed over to Gabe. Past her, he could see Kimmie and a handful of other kids talking to two police officers. Laurie stook his hand. "Hey, sorry we couldn't come get you," she said, a tired smile creasing her face.

He leaned in and kissed her cheek. "Don't sweat it. Are Kimmie and her friends alright?"

She nodded. "Kimmie's shook up, so are her friends. But they'll be okay."

"Is there anything I can do?" he said, squeezing her hand.

"I think we'll be able to leave soon. Can you go pack up our stuff?" She pointed over to where she had laid out their beach towels and picnic earlier.

"You got it," he said, gave her hand one more squeeze and shook his head. "This really is turning out to be the worst vacation ever."

She shrugged. "Yeah, can't really argue at this point."

"I'll meet you back at the car?" he asked, and she nodded. Gabe turned toward the lifeguard. "Hey, the girl at the entrance, I didn't catch her name, but she's pretty upset. Any news I can give her about … Peter?"

"Nothing," she said, and Gabe caught a hitch in her voice. "He dove in, and one of the girls said they saw him with something caught around his neck before he went under. We went after him but haven't found him yet."

As if in punctuation of her statement, Gabe saw a lifeguard pop up above the waterline, shaking his head, and clamber up onto the dock. He sat on the edge, catching his breath as another dove in, resuming the search.

Gabe sighed. "I'm sorry to hear that. I told her I'd let her know if I heard anything on the way out."

The lifeguard was staring toward the dock, supervising as her colleagues searching the deep water as she was stuck on crowd control. Gabe could sense her impotent frustration, her yearning to be doing something useful. "Thanks for passing that on, I suppose," she said. "Let her know one of us will spread the word if there are any developments."

"Gotcha," he said, and awkwardly added, "Good luck." He pushed his way through the throng across the beach until he found where Laurie had been camped out. It only took him a minute to pack up their stuff, shake the sand from their towels, and fold them up. The late afternoon sun was high in the sky, and the day was still hot, but he was starting to feel a chill trickling off the lake and along the breeze. He turned back toward the lake, saw Kimmie finally break free of the police. Laurie put her arm around her daughter and started walking back to the beach. He couldn't hear what she was saying from where he stood, but the slump of her shoulders and the resignation in her step told the story.

Gabe collected all the gear and carried it back to the parking lot, trying to figure out how he was going to tell the girl at the entrance kiosk about her friend as he did.

CHAPTER SEVENTEEN

It was still early afternoon, but Abby Clayton was getting antsy to go home. She was already daydreaming about leaving work and hoping to skip out a little early since it was slow in the vet's office today. She was still thinking about the fight she'd had with her boyfriend Roger over the weekend. They'd been arguing about where they were going to spend their vacation at the end of the month. She wanted to go to Disneyland, but he wanted to save money and go camping. She'd called him a cheapskate, and he'd been extra hurt by that, and she was still fuming when she'd left for work that morning. And a full day of worry and stress had resulted in a pounding headache that no amount of Tylenol or caffeine seemed to help.

But the day was coming to a close, and she'd simmered down over the course of the day. Now she'd finally gotten to a place where she really didn't care where they went for vacation as long as it was together. After tucking her chair back under her desk and slinging her purse over her shoulder, she walked down the short hallway from the front desk to the exam area of the small veterinarian's office on the edge of Golden Oaks.

"Doctor Hoeger?" she called out as she knocked on his office door. She leaned in and saw him huddled over his desk. "Doctor Hoeger, is it okay with you if I skip out a little early today? My head's killing me, and it's pretty slow this afternoon."

Clarence Hoeger looked up from his desk where he'd been examining the strange slivers he'd pulled from Barney's flank earlier in the day. The dog was resting in the kennel area still, quiet and content. But the sliver had consumed Hoeger's thoughts for much of the day.

He smiled at Abby as he saw her standing in the doorway. "Do we have any more appointments today?"

She shook her head. "No, Victor's checkup was your last one." Victor was an ancient cat who'd come and gone for his annual checkup an hour ago.

"Sounds great, Abby. Go home and rest up. Good work today, by the way."

"Thanks, doc," she said and stood up straighter in the doorway. "Anything I can get you before I go?"

He shook his head. "No, just lock the front door as you leave. Have a good evening."

She flashed him a smile and a thumbs-up. "Will do. Don't stay here too late though, okay?" she said as she turned to leave.

"I won't."

He picked up the specimen jar which held the slivers. When he'd removed them from Barney's side, they had been rigid, and needle-like. But over the course of the day, they seemed to be slowly dissolving or decaying. They had lost most of their rigidity and were now limp coils on the bottom of the jar. But they still had a sheen of moisture to them; the sealed jar had kept them from drying out completely, though the clear plastic was now filmed with greasy dark droplets of condensation. He watched as a cluster of the tiny beads threaded together, formed one larger drop, and drizzled to the base of the jar.

"You sure you don't want me to order you a pizza or something?" she asked.

"I'm fine, really," he said, looking up from the clear container. "I'll be on my way in under half an hour."

"Sounds good," she said. "Guess I'll see you in the morning." Abby stepped out of the doorway.

"Hang on," Clarence said. He looked up from the specimen jar and waved her over. "Come take a look at this, will you?" he said, holding the jar toward her. Abby took it from him and held it up to her face, peering into the glass at the tiny sliver.

"Is this what you pulled out of Barney?"

He nodded, and leaned back, the hydraulics of his chair wheezing and creaking as he did. "You ever seen anything like it?"

She turned the jar side to side to look at the sliver from different angles. "Not really. Looks like threads, or algae or something, I guess. Is there something weird about it? Where'd he pick it up, anyway?"

"Out in the woods, maybe near the lake, I suppose. Officer Lasher said she found Barney near his owner's house, which I think is on the west side of the lake."

"No, can't say as I've seen anything like it."

"No problem. Figured I'd ask."

"Alrighty, well I'll see you tomorrow," she said. "Gonna go say goodbye to Barney on the way out."

"He's been quiet today, for sure. No sign of infection, though. He should be okay to go home tomorrow or the next day." Hoeger checked his watch. "Crap, I should have had you call Officer Lasher and let her know."

"I can do it now, if you'd like."

Hoeger put the jar back on his desk and got up to follow along after her. "No, I'll give her a call now." They stood in the office's entryway; streams of light glowed through the venetian blinds which covered the large glass window looking out toward the street. During the summer, they always brought the blinds down in the afternoon, to cut down the glare and heat. The building faced west, and the afternoon sun poured right in through the windows.

Abby slipped into the kennel where a row of industrial shelves along the far wall held a variety of enclosures for various sizes of recuperating animals. Today, only a couple of cats and Barney were housed within the room. One of the cats was recovering from a tussle with a car, nursing a broken hip. The other was being housed while its owner was on holiday, visiting family out of state. Hoeger's office didn't normally kennel animals, but sometimes he made exceptions for long-time clients. Barney's cage was on the floor level toward the back of the room.

Abby approached and could hear Doctor Hoeger in the front room leaving a message with Officer Lasher. She gave scratches to the cats as she passed them, and they seemed both appreciative of the attention and fickle in their disinterest in the way only cats can pull off endearingly.

"And how are you doing, Barney?" she said, squatting down to get a good look at him. Barney was curled up in the back of his kennel, his face turned away from her in its protective cone. "Barney?" she said again. The dog twitched slightly, his leg spasming slightly. "Dreaming about chasing rabbits, I bet."

Abby hung her purse on a hook fixed to the wall, and opened the cage. Leaning in, she reached out and put her hand on Barney's flank, running her fingers along his smooth golden fur, felt his body shudder and heard a low growl. She pulled her hand away.

"Hey, doc?" she called out, not taking her eyes off the dog. "I think something's wrong with Barney."

"Hang on," Hoeger called from down the hall.

Abby heard him hanging up the office phone and walking toward her, his loafers padding on the linoleum.

She looked up as he came toward her. "He's kind of twitchy, growled at me."

Hoeger checked his wristwatch again, and looked at Barney's chart hanging on a clipboard on the cage. "The Carprofen shouldn't have worn off yet. Let's take a look."

He got down in front of the cage and reached in to where Barney was curled up in the back. With both hands, he slid the listless dog toward the front of the cage as he turned the animal toward him.

Barney growled. A low, raspy, thick growl, as if around a throatful of phlegm or slime. He turned his head toward the doctor and snarled, dregs of black dipping from his jaws.

Hoeger let go and stepped back from the cage, reaching to the screen door to latch it shut.

"What's wrong with him?" Abby asked, leaning in to take a look.

"Don't," Hoeger said, throwing the gate closed, trying to lock the dog back in the cage, but the gate bounced back open. With his other hand, he grabbed Abby by the shoulder and pulled her back.

He reached out to close the door again, and Barney opened his mouth wide. They heard a popping crack as the dog's jaw joint stretched past the limit. An unearthly howl erupted from the dog, followed by streamers of black slime like thin vines, or webs. The dark thready substance erupted from the dog's mouth, blasting through the gaps in the kennel gate.

Abby got the full force of the burst, the slime catching her across the side of her face. Streams of it shot past her and attached to Hoeger as well, stark black streaks clotting on his clean white lab coat. When Barney howled again, further streamers of the nightmare slime erupted at them.

Abby shrieked in pain as it began to crawl, wormlike across her skin, working its way into her mouth and nostrils. Burning like freezing ice and spreading across her face until it had covered her eyes, blocked her nose and throat. She fell to her knees, clawing at the viscous darkness which bound, blinded, and suffocated her.

Hoeger grabbed her head as she toppled over, cradling it so it wouldn't hit the floor. Then a piercing pain at his neck. He slapped at it and felt the ooze underneath his hand squirm. When he took his hand away, the blackness stretched threadlike between his throat and fingers. It clutched at his neck, entangling his throat with a coldness that burned as it inched along, strangling him as it froze his skin. His hand blistered with frostbite, and he tried to smear the substance off on his lab coat.

Below him, Abby twitched and thrashed, her heels kicking against the floor, pounding out an arrhythmic tattoo on the linoleum before she fell still.

Gasping for air, clutching at the ropy threads around his throat, Hoeger got to his feet, rushing toward the phone in the office. And then he was yanked off his feet by the cords coiled about his neck. He fell backwards, his head bouncing off the parquet floor with a hollow thud. The slime spread, oozing over his face, down his shoulders to constrict his arms, choking, burning. He saw dark spots in his vision as the oxygen was cut off from his brain.

Ribbons of slime continued to squeeze and choke until bones cracked, and skin split. Abby and Hoeger lay shapeless, twisted beyond recognition as the strands of darkness slithered over their lifeless bodies.

CHAPTER EIGHTEEN

Office Lasher brought the squad car to a stop just before the gate to the McEwen's driveway. "Hop out and get that, will you?" she grunted to Millsap. Without a word, he got out of the car and opened the gate, drawing it wide to make room for the car to drive through. He closed it and latched it in place as she passed, then hopped back in as she waited.

"So, what do you expect to find in the daylight that wasn't there in the dark?" he asked as he buckled in.

"No idea. Keep your eyes peeled."

They drove silently along the poorly kept road, dodging the worst of the lumps and rocks in the crumbling asphalt. Eventually, the asphalt gave way entirely to dirt ruts with weeds between them. With their windows down, they could smell a faint smoky tang in the air, evidence of camping or cook fires in the vicinity. A sense of stillness, of quiet suffused the woods as they wound through, following the dirt ruts until they came around a bend and saw the McEwen's property at the far end of the driveway. Darryl's dingy green Thunderbird was still parked out front.

Lasher thought the house didn't look much more inviting in the daylight.

Millsap took a look at the variety of "Trespassers will be shot" signs plastered along the side of the house and the fenced in yard and whistled. "I'm always amazed people spend money on dumb shit like that."

"Someone's going to buy the stuff, there'll always be a market for it," Lasher said, as she pulled the car up in front of the house and brought it to a halt.

"That's their car?" Millsap said, pointing at the Thunderbird.

She nodded. "Yeah, Darryl's heap." She scanned the property right and left, looking for anything out of the ordinary. "Okay, let's see what we can see."

They got out of the car and approached the house. Lasher pointed toward the windows next to the front door on the porch. "I checked in the windows, checked the perimeter, but no sign of Darryl when I was out last night. I was about to go home when Barney found me."

"He's probably sleeping one off," Millsap said. He stepped up onto the porch and banged on the front door. "Hey, Darryl! It's the Police! You're not in any trouble. We want to ask you a few questions." He waited and when there was no answer, he turned back to Lasher and shrugged. Millsap peeked in the window and craned his head back and forth to try and look into the living room. The window was partially blocked by ragged gray curtains, but he could see enough to warrant a comment. "Who the hell lives like this?"

"Can it," Lasher said. She walked toward the side of the house, where the backyard fence met the edge of the dwelling, and followed along the length of the fence as it curved around the yard. Millsap hustled up behind her. When they got to the gate in the back fence, Lasher reached over the top, threw the latch, and opened it.

The two police officers stepped into the small yard, which had seen better days. The concrete slab in front of the porch leading into the house was crumbling, dandelions and patches of crabgrass creeping out of cracks between the broken slabs. Car parts, a broken refrigerator, other junk, and bric-a-brac were piled in a nonsensical heap in one area against the fence wall. If there was one thing the McEwen's took pride in, however, it was their barbecue. A gleaming, stainless-steel drum-style job attached to a propane tank was propped up to the side of the back door. A matching metal cooler next to that.

Lasher stepped onto the slab, crushing weeds underfoot as she approached the patio. "Notice anything odd?" she asked Millsap.

When he looked in the direction she was walking, Millsap saw that the back door was wide open and only the screen door was closed between the yard and kitchen. Even from where he stood, he could see the screen was crawling with flies. "Oh, jeez."

"Stand back," Lasher said, and opened the screen door, dislodging a few of the flies. She shook the frame to dislodge the rest of the insects, which slowly flew off into the warm afternoon sky like a stinking, stinging miasma.

When she stepped into the small kitchen, the stink was the first thing Lasher noticed. Not overpowering, but a rank, sour smell. *The smell of meat gone bad,* she thought. And then she saw a ziplock bag of steaks turning gray on the counter nearby. She pointed to the bag. "That, my friend," she said to Millsap. "Is what we sometimes call a 'Clue' in police work."

Millsap wandered over to look at the bag. The slabs of meat inside were graying, the bloody juice had leaked out and dripped into a drying puddle on the countertop. Flies lapped at the fluid and Millsap waved them away, the sour stink of rotting meat rising up with them to sting his nostrils. "These've definitely been out longer than a few hours."

Lasher was pacing the kitchen. "Check this out," she said, and pointed to an empty beer can, crushed and tossed absently onto the grimy table which served as an eating area in the kitchen. "None of this looks like he was heading out for an extended vacation." With one hand on her hip, she tapped her upper lip with the finger of her other hand, thinking. "Let's check the rest of the house." From the kitchen, they went down a short hallway, passed the bathroom door and headed toward the living room. Lasher stepped into the bathroom and instantly saw the mess around the toilet, smelled the musty stink of the dry tank. "What's this look like to you?"

Millsap peered around her at the toilet, saw the broken pipe, the array of plumbing tools spread around the floor. "Looks like they were working on fixing the toilet," he said, a hint of disgust in his voice. The bathroom was as grimy as the rest of the house. "Must've gotten bored or decided it wasn't worth it."

"Something like that, I suppose," she said, and left of the room. A few more steps and she was in the living room. Flies buzzed around in lazy circles in the close heat of the room. She marveled at how a room could feel sparse and cluttered at the same time. The few pieces of furniture covered with laundry, magazines, junk mail. She stepped toward the coffee table in the center of the room and took a look at the papers sprawled across it. Next to a stack of magazines and a few beer bottles, a hastily scrawled note on lined green notepad paper caught her eye. "Interesting," she said, tilting her head and leaning in to read it. "Blue Corolla—Ringgold Lane," she muttered, reading the text.

"Ringgold Lane's where that guy the McEwens assaulted is staying, isn't it?" Millsap said.

Lasher nodded thoughtfully. "Yes. And I'm pretty sure the guy was driving a blue Corolla. Looks like maybe Darryl was planning on paying them a visit sometime."

"Think we should go check in on the guy?" Millsap asked.

Lasher scanned around the living room one more time. "Couldn't hurt, I suppose."

A few minutes later, after giving the rest of the house a cursory check, they were walking outside. Leaving the back door open behind them, as it was when they arrived, Lasher made sure the screen door was shut tight. They stepped carefully across the squalid, cluttered yard and through the back gate.

When she closed the gate after Millsap, Lasher noticed a pathway meandering through the woods away from the house.

"That's the direction Barney was coming from when I found him last night"—she gestured toward the rough dirt path —"Where do you think that leads?" She took a few strides along it.

Millsap peered down the path until it disappeared in a bend around some aspen a few yards distant. He looked up at the sun overhead and turned around a few times to get his bearings. "I think it's going toward the lake," he said after coming to a stop.

"Come on." Lasher started off down the path.

Following the path was easy in the daylight. It wasn't marked or paved, but clear from use. "They must use this a lot," Lasher said, as they hiked along the weedy rut.

"I saw some fishing gear back in their house," Millsap said. "If this leads to the lake, that's basically free food for them, I guess."

"Sure," Lasher said. She was watching the woods, scanning back and forth as they hiked along the rough trail. She was treading heavily, kicking brush and weeds. Lasher was fully aware that while uncommon, there were mountain lions spotted in the area from time to time. Rattlesnakes, too, especially during the warmer months of summer. She didn't feel like taking any chances for her or Millsap's safety over the McEwens. The critters in the woods didn't want any trouble with people and she knew that, so she was making a little extra noise to warn anything off.

A few minutes later, they'd broken through the edge of the woods and clambered down a short rocky ledge to the sandy beach below. The clay of the lakebed was exposed by the low waterline, a series of fissures and cracks in the dry mud like a spiderweb leading down to the water. Millsap pointed down to where the water was slowly lapping at the muddy shore.

"Hey, check that out," he said, walking toward a branch sticking up a few feet out of the water. It was stuck through the plastic ring of a six-pack of Coors which was missing a couple of beers. The cans were floating at the surface of the water, bobbing and dipping as the water rose and fell with the slight wind. A crushed empty can rested in the sand nearby.

"And over here," Lasher said, walking toward the shoreline where the sand was churned and two deep furrows were gouged into it, trailing a few feet until they disappeared under the lake's surface. "Like something was dragged into the water."

She scanned the surface of the lake. Sunlight glittered off the low ripples of the surface, but the water was calm. A sinuous darkness slithered by about twenty feet off-shore. A ripple of shadow below the surface. She stepped forward to get a better look, but was startled by the sudden flutter of wings and croaking caw of a raven landing in a tree nearby. The bird thrust its head forward, cawing at the distance. When she looked back, the shadow was gone.

"Good fishing this time of year?" she asked Millsap. Staring at the area where the puddle of darkness had vanished just seconds before.

"Okay, I guess," he said as he retrieved the beer fixed in the lake water. "Depends on where around the lake you are, really." He turned the cans over and read the expiration date on the bottom. "These're pretty fresh. I don't think they've been out here long."

"Well, bring 'em along," Lasher said. "They're either litter, or evidence."

Millsap picked up the mangled beer can off the shore. He pulled a folded plastic bag from his back pocket and dropped it and the cans on rings inside. "You know what's stuck in my craw?" he asked as he spun the bag closed and tied a loose knot in it.

"What's that?"

"I keep thinking it's weird, you know?" he said. "That Darryl's disappeared, and then Em saying that Charlie Gaines didn't come in to work today. Didn't leave a message or anything, either."

Taking one last look at the lake, Lasher turned and marched back up across the beach. "Come on. I want to go talk to Gabe Barnes."

"The glamor of police work," he muttered as he clambered up the rocky slope to the path leading back to the McEwen's shack.

When he got to the top of the ledge, he heard a splash behind him and turned back to see ripples in the water, like something had plunged below the surface. The raven was still perched on a branch which dipped over the water. The carrion bird shuffled a few inches further up the branch, sunlight glinting dully off its blue-black plumage. It cawed once before taking flight, its strong wings beating against the warm summer air as it flew across the lake, disappearing around a sloping curve in the hilly distance. A sudden chill crawled up Millsap's back between his shoulders, and he shivered slightly. By the time they returned through the woods to their patrol car, both Lasher and Millsap had worked up a sweat.

"What should I do with this?" he asked, holding the cans of beer in the plastic sack out to Lasher.

She stopped to look as she was opening the door. "Probably trash, but could be evidence. Toss it in the back for now. Come on."

Minutes later, they were back on the road and barreling back toward town. They were nearing the intersection to SR 346 which would take them through town when Officer Lasher's phone pinged to alert her to a voicemail. She glanced briefly at the screen mounted on her dashboard and saw that Doctor Hoeger had called her earlier.

She tapped the phone's screen, and the voicemail droned from the car's Bluetooth-connected speakers. "Hi, Officer Lasher, this is Clarence Hoeger … the vet …" Hoeger's voice droned. "Wanted to let you know Barney's resting fine. Come on by and visit him any time if you'd like. I'll be in the office for the next few hours probably, or feel free to drop by during office hours tomorrow." A woman's voice called distantly, "Hey, doc? I think something's wrong with Barney." A pause before Hoeger replied, as if speaking to the other voice, "Hang on … Sounds like I better go check on him. Anyway, swing by any time." The voicemail shut off.

"You want to stop by the vet's on the way to check in on Barney?" Millsap asked, settling into his chair.

"I think Barney can survive one night in the kennel. Let him rest up, and we can check in on him in the morning." She turned onto SR 326, gliding into the trickle of crossing traffic. "I'm thinking if Arlen keeps his nose clean tonight, we'll let him out in the morning. I think he's paid his debt to society for the D&D by now. He can pick up his own damn dog."

"Sick of listening to his bitching anyway." He fell silent, watching the trees flow by as they drove toward town.

CHAPTER NINETEEN

Kimmie swung gently in the slight breeze. She was sitting on the swing bench on the back porch of her grandfather's house, a dog-eared copy of *Mockingjay* in her lap. She'd been reading it for a while after they came home from the lake but was feeling anxious and distracted and couldn't focus on the exploits of Katniss Everdeen today. A light *clink* took her out of her thoughts, as the ice cubes in the tumbler she'd placed on the porch below her melted and settled.

The sun was arcing overhead and starting to dip toward the distant tree line in the late afternoon sky. Someone was grilling burgers or meat in the general vicinity—she could smell the smoke and distinct tang of charbroiling beef on the air but had no idea where it was coming from. Her dad hadn't gotten the BBQ grill out of storage yet. She wondered how close the nearest neighbors were.

That got her thinking about Jill, and she picked up her phone and sent her a text: *You guys all okay? That was kinda scary today, huh?* She got up from the swing bench and left the porch, taking the steps slowly as she stepped out onto the small lawn beyond. She wasn't wearing any shoes and felt the soft grass tickling the soles of her feet. Her ankle still itched, and she absent-mindedly reached down to scratch it. She sat down on the lawn, rubbing her ankle, pulling the cuff of her jeans up to scratch at the inflammation. She felt something slick and wet on her ankle, and when she looked down to investigate, she noticed threads of shiny dark ooze slicking her fingertips, smeared across her ankle. When the breeze shifted, Kimmie caught a whiff of the acrid smell emanating from the rash. She wondered if she should show it to her mom or dad, maybe see about going to a doctor? But when she thought about that, her head got fuzzy. She suddenly felt as if something unseen and distant was gently but forcefully turning her mind away from the thought, reassuring her in strange silent whispers that she'd be fine, she didn't need a doctor. She looked back toward the lake, felt a longing for the coolness, the still calm of the water. Kimmie wiped her fingers on the grass beside her absently.

Her phone pinged and she glanced at the screen. *Totally,* the message said. *My parents were freaking out. They won't let me go back to the lake until the cops say it's safe.*

Sounds like they're overreacting a bit, Kimmie wrote back.

Of course they are, Jill replied. *That's what parents do.*

Kimmie shot back an emoji of a laughing face with tears streaming out of its eyes. *Yeah.*

Bet the town closes the lake, Jill wrote. *They've been talking about it for a while, anyway. The water's getting so low.*

Kimmie looked up from her phone, across the creek and the stretch of woods to where the lake glittered in the distance. The day was so hot, and she thought about how it would have been nice to have cooled off in the lake earlier, to drift in the cool green. The distant sparkles grew hazy, and her head became fuzzy with heat.

"Mom!" she called out, turning her head over her shoulder. "Mom!"

She heard the creak of the screen door behind her and turned to see Laurie step onto the porch. "Yes, honey, what's up?" Laurie said, walking down toward her.

Kimmie rolled onto her side and stood up. "Thinking about hiking to the lake and sticking my feet in the water."

Laurie looked over Kimmie's shoulder toward the lake. A concerned furrow crossed her brow. "That's okay, but only your feet, 'kay? I don't want you going swimming without your father or I there."

Kimmie nodded. "Just my feet, promise. I want to cool off a little."

Laurie gave her a hug and a kiss on the side of her forehead. "Okay, that's fine. But don't stay too long."

"I won't," Kimmie said, squirming from her mother's embrace. She was anxious to get moving toward the lake. She felt a distant compulsion almost. An annoying itch growing in the back of her mind, and the only relief for it was in the lake water.

Laurie looked down at her watch, noticing it was almost four thirty. "Don't stay more than an hour or so. I'll start something cool for dinner when you get back."

"Sure, Mom," Kimmie said as she turned away, only the barest hint of disdain in her voice. She tromped across the lawn, past the blackberry bushes, and toward the lake. She got closer and could hear the water lapping at the shore, smell the cool, clean breeze cutting between the trees and through the dusty haze of the woods.

Kimmie was halfway to the water when she heard her phone ping. *Still there?* a text from Jill said.

Yes, she tapped back. *Taking a walk to the lake.* Up ahead, the trees ended shortly before the beach, and just a few quick steps later she was standing on the sand. She raised the phone and took a photo of the lake, the tiny dock jutting out from the shore, and the small rowboat tethered to its far end. *You should come visit sometime,* she wrote. *We've got a little stretch of beach attached to our property. Less crowded than the other place.*

Kimmie went to the end of the dock and sat down on the edge. She kicked off her sneakers and pulled off her ankle socks. She placed the socks inside her sneakers and set them aside, dangled her feet off the edge of the dock. Her legs were long enough that her feet barely submerged under the water. The water was up to her ankles and felt amazingly cool after being trapped in her shoes for the whole day.

The water was calm, lapping languidly against the beams of the dock, and the faint slap of water rolling up the sandy shore was followed by the rustling hiss of its retreat. She could barely make out the sounds of the public beach to the south. Kimmie scanned the horizon, the far shore was a distant haze of dark greens and browns. Too far to swim, but still clear in the late afternoon sunshine. She watched the trees rustling on the strange island in the center of the lake. She picked up her phone, took a photo of the island and sent it off to Jill. She asked, *You know anyone who's ever gone out there?*

Now that she was at the lake, Kimmie was feeling calmer. Maybe it was the stress of the day, or her sore ankle, or how hot it was this afternoon. But she felt out of sorts, like the sort of muzzy, fuzzy feeling that might precede a cold. Sort of jittery and anxious, short-tempered, and headachey. Her phone pinged again. *Yeah,* the text from Jill said. *My friend Kevin said he and some friends messed around there once. But it's been off limits as long as I can remember.*

Kimmie stared at the island. *I want to go there,* she texted back. *Do you think Kevin could take us? Does he have a boat? I bet we could get out and back before anyone noticed. You want to come?*

Now? came the reply.

Kimmie pulled her feet up from the water, and crossed them in front of her, letting the sunlight warm them up. *Not now,* she typed. *I dunno. Soon?*

Maybe, Jill replied. *I'll let you know.*

Okay. Kimmie slid her phone into her pocket. She scooched forward on the dock and dropped her feet back into the water. She was splashing her sore feet softly back and forth, when she noticed a darkness, a shadowy patch moving in the water a few yards offshore. Like a school of dark fish moving together or as if something flew overhead, casting a shadow on the water's surface. Or maybe something tenebrous roiling below the surface. She watched as it floated toward her. But whether it was carried along by the rippling water or moving of its own accord, she could not tell.

She leaned forward over the edge of the dock to get a better look. She was strangely drawn to the shadow. Her foot began to throb, to ache as it drew nearer, and the shadow was reaching out coils of darkness beneath the surface of the lake. Snakelike tendrils slithered around her feet, but she felt no fear now. They caressed her injured ankle, cold threads probed her wounded foot like fine threads of algae or sea grass. She suddenly felt cold, an aching chill despite the heat of the afternoon. Her breathing slowed, she gasped, trying to take in deep lungfuls of air, but her chest was tightening, her heartbeat slowing. Her vision tunneled, constricted to mere pinpoints.

Tendrils of shadow rose from the lake, threading around her ankle and creeping up her leg. Where they touched her, she felt the cold void of absolute malice. Of a predator's keen desire for the kill. A craving for revenge. Light and warmth fell into these tendrils, the probing lengths of absolute blackness, as if the darkness was swallowing everything good, leaving nothing but a black rip in the fabric of reality. The shadow threads slid beneath her skin, inching into the cuts and scrapes around her legs from her struggle in the lake the day before.

Suddenly heat sluiced back into her. She took a deep gasping breath of warm air as light flooded her vision. Kimmie fell back against the dock, staring at the pale blue summer sky. Her head throbbed, her teeth ached, pulsing in time with her heart pounding in her chest, sending ripples through her body. Painful waves at first, but eventually a cold calmness settled her. Soon, she didn't notice the aches or twinges at all.

Kimmie rose onto her elbows, and sat up straight again. When she peered over the edge of the dock, the shadow around her feet was gone.

Everything seemed brighter than before. The sunlight glowed off the water's surface, off leaves of the surrounding trees, even the dock and the sandy beach like a strange phosphorescence. It made her think of how her eyes felt after swimming in an over-chlorinated pool, a strange, hazy luminescence born of distorted vision. She closed her eyes tight, shielding them from the prismatic sparkle.

Her eyes fell on the island at the center of the lake. It looked calm, cool. The light didn't dance around it like ribbons of flame scorching her eyes. She stood and stepped off the side of the dock, feeling the warm beach sand between her toes. She stepped into the water, and suddenly the light wasn't as bright, the glittering threads didn't glare so harshly. She kept walking along the side of the dock, and soon the water was creeping up past her knees. Her phone pinged. She fumbled it out of her pocket and saw a text from her mom. *Having fun, kiddo?*

Sure, she typed back quickly. *Just messing around, be back in a bit.*

She stepped into the water along the shore. The only sound was the soft splashing of her feet as she continued calf-deep through the water and the distant rustle of the trees. When she looked toward Deer Island, she felt the tugging call again, like a needling whisper in the deep fathoms of her mind.

"What the hell am I doing?" she whispered.

Suddenly she felt a wave of fear break through her clouded mind, as if she were rising from a half-sleep to find her hand over a stove burner. Kimmie jolted upright, turned her back to the island and began the walk back home.

***

After returning from town and all the chaos at the lake, Gabe decided he needed to clear his head a little. He was about to fall into crawling through old newspapers again when instead he decided to see about doing a little work on the house. He was perched on top of a Gorilla Ladder he'd dragged out of the garage and placed up against the side of the house when the police car pulled into his driveway. He scooped one more double handful of leaves and needles from the rain gutters and tossed it down into the mulch which ran around the house's perimeter, then descended the ladder. He hopped the last rung to the ground and saw the squad car's doors open. Officer Lasher—whom he recognized from the incident in the Raley's parking lot—stepped out first. He didn't recognize the other officer who followed after her. "Mr. Barnes, hello!" Lasher called out, waving to him.

He pulled one of the grimy, tan work gloves off and offered his hand to her. "Hi, Officer Lasher, right? Everything okay?"

She took his hand and shook it briefly. "Yes sir. At least, I hope so. I was in the area and had a few questions." She indicated the officer standing to her side who was looking around the yard while trying to look like he wasn't. "This is my partner, Officer Millsap." Millsap waved and returned to looking around.

"Sure, hi," Gabe said. "So, what can I do for you?" Gabe took off the other glove, and tucked the pair into his back pocket. Something about these cops coming out of the blue unnerved him. He didn't have anything to hide, but he still didn't like the idea of cops poking around unannounced.

Lasher took a look at the ladder. "Cleaning the gutters?"

Gabe nodded. "Yeah, I don't think they've been cleaned in a while. Lots of crud in there. I was up in the attic earlier and smelled something weird, like a rat smell or something. But couldn't find anything. Figured I'd check the gutters and downspouts, make sure there wasn't something stuck in there."

She nodded. "Good idea. Hey, you haven't seen or heard anything from Darryl McEwen in the last day or so, have you?"

"The brother of the guy who hit me?" Gabe asked.

"One and the same." She looked up as the front door opened and Laurie stepped out.

"Everything okay?" Laurie asked, taking in the scene.

Gabe turned to her. "Fine, babe. Hey, you haven't seen the brother of the guy who hit me lately, have you?"

Laurie crossed her arms in front of her as she stopped next to him. "No. Why, what's he done now?"

Gabe shrugged. "Beats me"—he turned to Officer Lasher—"No, I haven't seen him since the parking lot. No, wait. I did see him at the hardware store the next day. Why?"

"Seems like he's gone missing, is all," Lasher replied.

"And you think I might have something to do with it?" Gabe asked. "What could I have possibly done to him? And why?"

Lasher turned to look directly at him. "I was wondering if he'd been around. Look, he was supposed to bring some stuff in to the jail for his brother. Toothbrush, comic books, I don't know. He never showed, and when I went to check on him, he was gone, and their dog was limping around the property, pretty beat up."

"Oh, poor thing," Laurie said, sincerely. "Is the dog okay?"

"Far as I know," Lasher said. "I took him to the vet to get checked out. And now nobody's seen Darryl for a couple of days, which seems weirder."

Gabe rubbed sweat from his forehead. "Gotcha, well, I haven't seen him around, but I guess if I do, I'll call you, or tell him to call you."

"Thanks," Lasher said. "I'd appreciate that."

"Well, if there's nothing else we can help you with," Gabe said, "it's been kind of a long day and I'd like to finish this up before dark."

"No, that's all. I appreciate your time. Mrs. Barnes," she said, nodding at Laurie, and turned to go.

"Oh, Officer Lasher, that reminds me," Laurie said. "Have you heard anything about the lifeguard at the lake today?" she paused, as if unsure how to ask the next question tactfully. "Did they find the body?"

Lasher stopped. "Word travels fast. How'd you hear about that?"

"I was there when it happened," Laurie said. "Our daughter and her friends were there on the dock when he dove in."

"I wasn't aware of that," Lasher said. "But no, I haven't heard anything new about it yet. Millsap?"

He shook his head. "No, but I've been listening to the same radio, so ..."

Lasher scowled at him. "If I hear anything, I'll make sure someone gives you a call."

"You don't have to trouble anyone," Laurie said. "I thought you might have heard."

"How's your daughter doing? You said she was on the dock when it happened."

"She seems okay," Laurie replied. "She spent most of the rest of the afternoon reading in the backyard, before she took a walk down to the lake. Should be home soon, I hope. I was surprised actually, we've had our share of mishaps with the lake already this weekend."

"How's that?" Millsap asked.

Laurie turned to him. "Well, this afternoon, obviously. And the other day, Kimmie was swimming and got tangled up in something. Could have drowned if someone hadn't happened to be nearby on his boat. Mr. Gaines, he runs the diner downtown? He was fishing nearby when she went under."

"Lucky," Lasher replied. "Charlie's a good guy to have around in a pinch."

Laurie smiled. "Yeah, we were lucky. Tried to take him some cookies this morning as a thank you, but he wasn't at his house, or at the diner. Seemed like he threw the waitress for a loop too."

"Huh," Lasher said. "Doesn't sound like Charlie to miss work."

"That's what the waitress said," Laurie added. "Another mystery for you, I guess."

"Right," Lasher said. "Well, thanks again, and we'll let you get back to your evening. If we have any other questions, we'll call next time."

Gabe smiled and reached out to shake Lasher's and then Millsap's hand in succession. "Sure, no problem," he said, wishing they'd leave. "Anything we can do to help."

Lasher and Millsap got back in their cruiser, and sped away from the house.

Gabe felt a sense of relief as he watched the squad car's taillights curve around a bend in Ringgold Lane and disappear into the trees.

***

By the time she'd returned to the house, Kimmie's eyesight had returned to normal again. Her mom was sitting on the porch reading a book when Kimmie clambered up the embankment onto the back lawn. "Have fun, kiddo?" Laurie called.

The teenager shrugged. "Sure," she said and trudged up the stairs. "I'm going to take a nap. Wake me when dinner's ready?" She kissed Laurie on the cheek as she passed by. The screen door slammed shut behind her.

"Okay," Laurie muttered as Kimmie disappeared into the house. A moment later, Gabe came out. "Just saw Kimmie, she okay?" he asked.

"She seems tired," Laurie said. "She probably needs to rest."

Gabe took a seat next to her on the porch swing. He reached out and took her feet in his hands, stretched out her legs and put them in his lap. With his thumbs, he started to work at the knots in the arches of her feet. "Ooh, don't start that," she said and smiled. "You'll be there all night."

"Gotta earn my keep somehow," he said, and kept working at the soreness he knew from experience she had accumulated. "You want me to cook tonight? You've had a long day and I've been messing around."

"That'd be great."

"You think Kimmie's really just tired?" he asked. "She's been through an awful lot over the last couple of days."

"Stop worrying so much," Laurie said. "I'm sure she'll be fine. Nothing a pizza and ice cream won't fix right up, I'm sure."

"You're right," he said.

"How about we make some popcorn and let her pick a movie or something. A good old family movie night. We haven't done one of those in a while."

"Sure," Laurie said. She pulled her feet back and stood, stretching out her back. "Sounds like a great idea. A nice, quiet family evening at home."

"Deal," Gabe said. "Nice and quiet."

Chapter Twenty

"Call the Get up and Go, see if Gaines ever came in," Lasher said, as she pulled the squad car off of Ringgold Lane, over the rough bridge, and onto SR 346.

"Why, you already hungry for dinner?" Millsap replied, fishing out his cell phone. He had the diner's number in his phone's contacts, along with most of the other shops and restaurants in town.

"Don't be a smartass," she said. "Just call."

He shrugged and thumbed the call button, and after a brief pause he heard the phone begin ringing. Then an answering voice on the other end, "Get up and Go, this is Emily, how can I help you?"

"Hey, Em," he replied. "This is Officer Millsap. Did Charlie ever come in today?"

"No sir, he did not," Emily answered. He could detect a faint tone of concern in her voice. "You don't think there's something wrong, do you? I figured maybe something came up quick and it slipped his mind to call in."

"I don't know, Em," Millsap said. "Lasher asked me to call, but I'll let you know if I hear anything."

"Fair enough," Emily said.

Millsap said his goodbyes, and hung up.

"You think something's up?" he asked Lasher.

"I don't know," she said. "It seems weird. I mean, the day of his wife's funeral, Charlie Gaines closed up the shop in the morning, and was in slinging burgers an hour after the reception ended. The guy is dedicated to his work, and it's not like him to miss a day without telling anyone."

Millsap mulled over the information. "He got any family anywhere around here? Maybe out of town and he could have gone to visit? Or anyone we could call?"

"I'll check when we get back to the station," she said. They drove in silence for a few minutes. A burst of static exploded over the radio. "Possible double 10-54 or 187 at 15 Terrace View, any available unit please respond." It was Josie's voice, and Lasher could tell she was shaken.

Lasher grabbed the handset. "Car 012 responding, we're on it." She flipped on the lights and siren and accelerated into town.

"10-54?" Millsap said, incredulously. "That's a dead body."

"187's a homicide," Lasher said. "Which is it?"

The radio squawked again. "Roger that, car 012. Oh, Shawna, this is a bad one." She paused. "That poor girl, and Doc Hoeger."

Lasher squeezed the handset. "We'll be right there, Josie. You gotta keep the line clear. Over."

"Oh, sure," Josie said, trying to regain her composure. "Roger that. An ambulance is on the way, too. Um, out? I guess." The line clicked off.

Lasher couldn't remember the last time there'd been a murder in Golden Oaks, or anything that would constitute a major crime. Aside from Mike Barnes' disappearance, nothing came to mind as far back as when Pershing stopped Timmy Francis.

"What the hell is going on around here today?" she muttered. "Missing persons right and left, guy drowns in the lake, now two killings?"

Millsap sighed, "Is it a full moon tonight, or something?"

Lasher leaned forward and looked up into the sky as they sped along the empty road. "Just the opposite. New moon, I think."

"Must be something in the water," Millsap said, staring out the window as they barreled down the highway.

"Must be," she said.

***

The squad car took the turn onto Terrace View fast, tires screeching into the turn. There was a youngish man standing in front of the building, eyes wide and tears streaking down his face. He waved his hands frantically overhead as soon as he saw the car.

Lasher pulled the squad car to a screeching halt in front of 15 Terrace View, the same veterinarian's office she'd dropped Barney off at earlier. "Come on," she said, flipping the sirens off and leaping from the car, running toward the building when an ambulance came careening around the corner, sirens blaring.

A crowd was starting to form as people came out of the other shops which lined the streets. "Keep them back," Lasher snapped at Millsap. She approached the man in front of the veterinarian's office store front. "Who are you, and what's going on?" she said, hand on her gun.

"Inside," he said, choking back tears. "It's Abby and the doc, and, oh God," he turned, his knees buckling and fell to the ground, outstretched hand catching the side of the building for balance as he vomited the contents of his stomach onto the hot concrete sidewalk.

"Christ," Lasher said, and pushed the door open with her hip. An electronic bell overhead chimed incongruously as the door opened, and she stepped in. The smell hit her first, the meaty red smell of blood, and the underlying effluvium of human waste.

Next was the sound. Or lack of it. When she stepped into the small office it was quiet. No sounds of animals as would be expected in a vet's office. Quiet, and a faint buzzing. She recognized it as the somnolent thrum of flies hovering in lazy circles in the silence of the small, hot room. The air was still and thick.

The flies were buzzing beyond the countertop of the receptionist's desk in front of her. Down the hall to the exam rooms where she'd sat with Dr. Hoeger and Barney that morning. When she was standing before the front desk, she noticed the phone's handset was missing from its cradle next to the office computer.

She rounded the countertop, stepping around a filing cabinet, and turned to walk down the hallway when she saw the bodies. Nothing in her years of police work had prepared her for the state of the two corpses before her. Their faces were bloated and blue, veins bulging out on their foreheads, and eyes wide open with terror. Their limbs were folded and bent in directions no human body was meant to go. Black blistered marks like frost-burn encircled their throats, wrists, spread like a caul across Abby's entire face. Dr. Hoeger's hand was folded completely back, the tops of the fingers touching the skin of his forearm as if the wrist had been shattered out of joint.

She didn't bother checking their pulses. She took a few deep breaths. Tried to calm herself before investigating further. A slam behind her made her jump. Two EMTs banged the front door open and charged through with emergency bags in tow. She yelped.

She recognized them as Miles Grainger and Heidi Bogan, two of the half dozen or so paramedics in town. She hoped they had strong enough stomachs. "Save the first aid, guys," she said.

She spoke into her shoulder-mounted radio mic, "Millsap, you copy?"

Silence, then a crackle of static followed by, "Yeah, go for Millsap."

"Step somewhere quiet, will you?" she asked.

Another pause. "Okay, shoot."

"Get in touch with the station, see if someone can bring the crime scene camera down here. We've got some snapshots to take before we can move the bodies." She unlatched the safety strap over the butt of her service revolver and slid it from its holster as she stepped over Hoeger first, then Abby.

"Kee-rist," she heard one of the EMT's say behind her. She looked back over her shoulder and saw Heidi crouched down, examining the corpses. She quickly checked for pulses in the necks and wrists of each one.

"Confirm they're dead, and then go wait outside," Lasher said. "Don't touch anything else, got it?"

Heidi looked up at her and nodded. She rolled Abby's body up slightly off the ground, saw where the blood had already begun pooling into a blotchy purple and black bruise at the back of her neck and along her exposed shoulders where they'd lain against the ground. Checking Hoeger found similar marks of lividity. "Based on the lack of a pulse, and the livor mortis beginning to set in, my professional opinion is that these poor saps are really and for truly dead."

Miles took a couple of steps backward, then sat on a cushioned chair in the waiting area, doing some deep breathing of his own.

"Looking a little green around the gills there, Miles," Lasher said. "If you need to go outside and get some air, do it. But compose yourself first."

He nodded in response and poured a cup of water from the dispenser nearby, sipping it slowly as he breathed in and out.

Lasher shook her head and turned back to the hallway. Walking along the laminate flooring she stepped lightly, peeking into the office, exam rooms, and small surgical theater as she passed by them. There was a slick wetness along the flooring, like a mop or wet towel had been dragged along the length of the hall. Finally, she got to the far end of the hallway to the recovery and kenneling area. She peeked through the window in the door and seeing nothing alarming inside, pushed the door open.

She entered and heard a soft whining from the far end of the room. The cages on steel shelving were mostly empty, but when she came toward the back, she found Barney curled up in the corner of the room.

He was in a recovery cone and had his back to her. But he was also pushing against the floor with his paws, as if he was trying to push himself into a smaller space to hide.

"Hey, Barney," Lasher said softly, calmly. "What a day you've had, huh?"

When he heard her voice, he turned around to look at her, and Lasher swore she saw a caul of black flit across his eyes, like storm clouds scudding across twin moons. He stepped fully into the light, and it was gone.

"What are we going to do with you now?" she said, standing up. When she heard a tiny *meow!* behind her, she turned to see that he wasn't the only foundling. "Oh, and you too, kitty," she said, checking the tag on the cat's cage. There was no medical information on the slip, it simply said "Kenneled" and had the name and number of the owner who'd left it for the weekend. "What a day indeed."

She leaned forward and flipped the latch to open Barney's cage. "Come on, you rotten old dog," she said in as calm and kind a voice as she could muster. "Let's see about getting you out of here."

Barney reluctantly shuffled toward the front of the cage, and Lasher reached out to take his collar. She tugged him forward gently, she saw where his flank had been shaved bare and the bandages taped to his skin. There were spots of yellow and red seeping through from inside, and she realized if she took him with her, she'd be taking care of the dog for at least the rest of the night.

"Maybe Millsap or one of the others knows something about taking care of a sick dog. What do you think of that, Barney?" she ruffled his fur. "Oh, hell, I guess I was going to send Arlen home tomorrow anyway. Let him take care of you."

She led the dog up the dim hallway toward the front of the office. When he saw the two bodies sprawled out on the floor, Barney stepped around them, barely paying any attention to the pair at all. The two EMTs were sitting in the waiting area. Heidi was leaning into her chair, head resting on the back of the seat, her eyes closed. Miles was doing something with his phone, tapping away at the screen. Lasher was about to admonish them both when there was a knocking at the office door from outside.

"Sit, Barney," she said, and he did. "Ummm … good dog."

She opened the door, and Millsap poked his head through. "The camera's here, and West's out front running crowd control. Not a lot of folks though, fortunately."

She motioned him to come inside. He was just entering the room when Heidi opened her eyes, saw Barney sitting in the middle of the room and went over to rub his head. "Good dog," she said. "Come with me," and she shuffled him over to sit on a cushioned chair in the waiting area and out of the way of the cops.

"Thanks, Heidi," Lasher said. "Can you keep an eye on him for a bit while we take these photos?"

Heidi nodded. "Sure thing."

"And Miles, if you're done playing Candy Crush or whatever, maybe go check on the kid out front who found them?"

Miles shot to his feet. "Yeah, you got it." He bolted from the office like he didn't need to be asked twice.

Heidi was scratching Barney behind his ears as she asked Lasher, "When you're done taking photos, I assume these two are going right to the morgue?"

"Unless you think they're going to get up and walk there on their own," Lasher said. She held her hand out, open palm up, to Millsap. "Camera?"

Millsap handed the camera to Lasher. "Here you go. What've we got to deal with?"

Lasher took the camera around behind the counter and started snapping photos. The camera was a high end digital SLR job—another one of Pershing's DHS grant purchases—and the shutter was uncomfortably loud in the silence of the office. "Definitely a 10-54," she said. *Click! Click!* "Very possibly a 187." *Click! Click!*

Millsap got down on his haunches to examine Abby's corpse.

"Hell, you ever seen anything like this? Looks like she was folded up like a pretzel."

"Get out of the way, will you? And be careful where you're walking," Lasher said, looking up from behind the camera's viewfinder. "And no, I haven't."

Millsap stood up and got out of her frame as Lasher zoomed in to get detail shots of the rope-like marks around Abby's neck. "Looks like she was strangled by cords or something. And look at the way her shoulder's bent back like that. Looks dislocated."

Millsap shook his head in disbelief. "Damn shame. You don't think one of the animals they had in here today could've …"

"No," Lasher interrupted. "Unless an angry bear came strolling through or something. But the only patients they had in back were Barney and a tabby cat."

"You think we got the resources for this?" he asked.

Lasher lowered the camera. "I was thinking we might need to call in the state police on this one. But let's see what we can see before we have to make that call."

"Sure," he replied. "So, we've got what, two dead bodies, a couple of possibly missing folks. What the hell's going on in this town?"

"That's the real question, isn't it?" Lasher said, as she kept snapping photos of the bodies. She'd moved on to Hoeger, taking a series of full body photos from different angles before moving in to detail shots. His eyes were bugged out, staring up at the ceiling, and a shiver crawled up her spine as she looked into them, thinking about the conversations she'd had with him that morning. She was closing in on his face when she noticed a crust of dark slime around the edges of his nostrils, and a similar black, scab-like discharge pooled in the corners of his eyes. *Click-click!*

Lasher took a few more photos of the bodies in their death-poses, before handing the camera to Millsap. "Why don't you finish up in here? I'm going to go check on the kid who found them."

"Sure," he said, taking the camera from her. "What about the animals?"

Lasher looked over to where Heidi was sitting with Barney. "We'll figure something out. Maybe see if another vet can take them for a couple of days, or I'm thinking Barney can go with Arlen when we release him."

"Alright," Millsap said.

***

When Officer Lasher finally came outside, she found Miles sitting in the open bay of the ambulance next to the kid who'd found the bodies. Well, not really a kid, she decided. An older teen at the least. He had a blanket wrapped around him and was sipping from a bottle of water. There was no crowd at all by then, and Officer West was talking to the kid quietly.

"He okay?" Lasher asked.

The kid looked up at her, and she could tell he wasn't. "She's dead … they're both dead, aren't they?"

Lasher sighed and nodded. "Yes, I'm afraid they are. Can I ask your name?"

"Martin. Martin Vicks, but everyone calls me Marty."

"Okay, Marty," she said. "I'm sure you've already talked to Officer West, but you're going to need to come down to the station and make a full statement."

"Sure, no problem. Someone should call Abby's folks."

"What's your relationship to Abby?" Lasher asked. "Were you two dating?"

"Huh? No, we're just friends. I was getting off work and swung by here to give her a ride home."

"Okay, we'll still need you to come down and make a full statement."

"Yeah, I get it. I watch *Law & Order.*"

"Alright, why don't you follow Officer West, and he'll take your statement." She turned to West and motioned him over. "West, Marty here's ready to make a statement. Can you take care of it?"

"On it," West said. He leaned in to whisper to Lasher so Marty couldn't hear. "We're not thinking he's a suspect, are we?"

She looked the kid over. Pale and drawn, shaking under the blanket despite the summer heat. "I don't think so," she said. "Get

get his story down and make certain the details line up. I'm going to make sure the bodies get off to the morgue, and I'll get in touch with their families."

"You got it," West said and went off to get Marty moving toward the station house.

Lasher's hands went to her belt, and she turned back to look at the vet's office before going back in. "Christ, what a day."

Soon after, West and the kid drove off to the station house. Lasher approached Miles, the EMT. "I think you're good to start removing the bodies now, if Millsap's done with his photos and secured the space; probably time to take them to the morgue."

The big EMT nodded and said, "I'll check on Heidi." He opened the door, and Barney was sitting inside the office. "Hey, what do you want to do about this dog?"

Lasher approached the doorway and reached her hand out to pat Barney on his head. "Guess you're coming with me, huh buddy?"

Barney licked her hand with a cold, dry tongue, and got up onto his feet.

"Come on, boy," she said, hooking one finger under his collar and leading him outside. It took some coaxing, but soon he was sitting in the back seat of her patrol car. The sun was a distant haze in the horizon now, and the streetlights started to flicker on one by one. The moonless night was going to be dark, and Lasher sighed in the gloom. She figured she could turn Barney over to his owner when she released Arlen from jail. But she also couldn't help feeling like after all she'd been through with Barney in the last twenty-four hours, she had some sort of responsibility for him now.

"Your owner's an idiot," she said, ruffling the dog's furry head, scratching behind his ears. "You know that, don't you boy?"

The dog seemed to smile and *whuffed*.

"Alright, well you stay here and don't cause any trouble, okay?" She cracked the windows in the car slightly to keep air moving through the cab.

A chill breeze blew down the street, fluttering her hair before dying down. She heard a metallic banging from the direction of the vet's office, and when she turned to investigate, saw that Miles and Heidi were loading a body into the back of the ambulance. They'd draped a blanket over it and it was strapped to a bright yellow plastic stretcher. Miles was backing into the ambulance as Heidi held her end up.

"Need a hand?" Lasher said, approaching the ambulance.

Heidi shook her head. "No, we're good."

They disappeared into the ambulance bay. Lasher watched, impressed as the two strapped the body down to a bench along one wall with routine precision.

In barely under fifteen minutes, they'd gotten the second body secured on a rolling stretcher in the center of the ambulance's bay and were getting ready to leave the scene.

Lasher and Millsap were securing the vet's office as the ambulance drivers prepared to leave. "You two all set?" Lasher asked as Miles slammed the rear doors shut with finality.

"Yeah," he said. "We'll zip 'em over to the county coroner's and get them checked in. You'll get the case number by morning."

"I guess we're about wrapped up here for now," Lasher said. She turned to Millsap. "Go ahead and take off. Finish up whatever you've got left to do and clock out. I'll start the report on this when I get back to the station."

"You don't have to ask me twice."

Within minutes, Lasher stood by herself in front of the vet's office. After a few hours of noise, bustle, and controlled chaos, the evening had become strangely quiet. The bodies were on their way to be examined, and they'd gone over the vet's office as best they could. Depending on what the coroner's office said in the morning, they might need to get some state guys out to dig deeper.

Golden Oaks was a small town with small town problems. Killings weren't unheard of, but so rare as to definitely shake things up. If somehow these turned out to be murders, and of someone as prominent and well-liked as Doc Hoeger, who knew what would happen next? She knew she'd be getting a call from Mayor Haines' office first thing in the morning. In fact, she was sort of surprised he hadn't called her cell already. Thanking God for small favors, she slid into the car, sinking into the driver's seat and sighing. It felt good to get off her feet.

She glanced up into the rear-view mirror and saw Barney looking hesitantly at her from the back seat. "Okay, Barney, let's get you home."

Chapter Twenty-One

"So, who are you going with?" Gabe asked as he pulled the car up in front of the *Oro*, the movie theater on the edge of town which was also used for city council meetings once a month. Laurie was sitting next to him in the front of the car, and Kimmie was in the back seat.

The lights from the marquis glowed down across the sidewalk in front of the theater, and the smell of popcorn came wafting in through the car's open windows. *It was a fine, summery smell*, he thought, thinking back to when he was a kid, and the theater was much smaller. Only two screens and shoved into the strip mall. At some point in the late 90s or so, they'd annexed a couple of shops, added two screens, and now it was practically a small multiplex with an ice cream shop on one side and a burger joint on the other.

Kimmie rolled her eyes from under her mop of hair. "Jill and some friends. I told you."

"Right," Gabe said. "I forgot, sorry. Mind's wandering today."

"That's cool you're getting to meet some of the local kids," Laurie said. "Hope they're nice."

Silence.

"Are Jill's brother and sister coming? Or is it only you big …" she almost said 'big kids' but caught herself. "Just the teens?"

Kimmie was scanning the parking lot and the sidewalk in front of the theater but didn't see Jill. "I don't know. Yeah, I guess it's only Jill and her friends."

Gabe unlatched his seatbelt and turned toward her. "So, your mom and I have been talking."

"You're always talking."

Gabe paused, thinking *Someone's got some attitude tonight.* "Okay, sure. I mean, I do enjoy talking to your mother, of course. But we've been talking about maybe keeping the house up here. In fact, we've been talking about maybe the three of us moving up here." No response. "What do you think of that?"

She turned to look at him, but her eyes were flat. He couldn't tell if she was upset, or happy, or what. It was a look she'd developed when she was little, and she didn't want anyone to know what she was thinking. It always reminded Gabe of the scenes in *Star Wars* when the blast doors slammed down and suddenly there was six feet of steel between the heroes and whatever was on the other side.

"I don't know," she said. "It's a lot to process."

Gabe tried not to laugh. Sometimes he forgot she was really growing up until she said something like that, and still thought of her as his little girl. "Yeah, I can understand that, believe me."

Laurie turned around to face both of them. "Look, kiddo, it's nothing to stress out about right now. But think about it, okay? We want to make the decision as a family. And even if we did, it's not something we'd do right away. We're still going back to Alcosta in a few days, and we'd have to sort out the logistics of packing up and moving. It's nothing we'll be able to sort out for a while."

"Okay," she said, flatly.

"Think about it?" Gabe said.

"Yeah, sure." She sat up in her chair, reached for the door lock, and flipped the latch to open the door. "There's Jill," she said and started to bolt from the car.

"Hey!" Gabe called after her.

She leaned back into the car. "What?"

He handed her three folded bills and smiled. "Have fun. Don't make yourself sick on popcorn."

"Okay, Dad."

"What time do you need us to come pick you up?" Laurie asked.

Kimmie stopped. "Oh, Jill said she and her friends could give me a ride back after the movie. Unless that's a problem?"

Gabe paused to think that over. He wasn't thrilled with the idea of her getting a ride from some kids who were practically strangers. But at the same time, he wanted her to make some friends. "I guess that's fine. But listen, if you change your mind for any reason at all, call me and I'll come get you. Your mom and I are going to be here downtown for a while, so it's not a problem. No questions asked, right?"

"Okay, Dad."

"In that case, home by eleven, okay?" Laurie said.

She checked her watch. It was about seven thirty, and the sun was disappearing behind the trees on the horizon.

"Okay, Mom, sounds great. Have fun on your big date night." She shut the door.

Gabe tried to catch her eye and wave to her, but she'd already skipped off down the sidewalk to catch up with Jill and her friend. Who was a boy. *Well, I guess it was bound to happen sooner or later,* Gabe thought, as he pulled away from the curb.

"You okay, mister?" Laurie said, catching his eye as they pulled away.

He shrugged. "I guess I have to come to terms with the idea of her being a teenager and having teenager friends and wanting all that teenager independence."

"Sadly, yes you do, Dad," Laurie said, putting her hand on his knee and giving it a little squeeze. "But don't worry. I can still track her on her phone. She can't get too far." She laughed.

Gabe smiled. "Only in emergencies," he said, with mock seriousness.

"Only in emergencies," Laurie echoed.

***

Jill waved as she and her friend stepped up onto the sidewalk under the Oro's marquis to greet Kimmie. Kimmie gave her a hug and smiled at the boy. "Kim, this is Kevin," Jill said, and Kevin stuck out his hand.

"Hey," he said, as Kimmie took his hand and shook it. "So, you really want to go out and check out the island?"

Kimmie looked over her shoulder, saw her dad's car leaving the parking lot and released the nervous breath she hadn't realized she'd been holding in. "How long will it take to get there?"

The boy shrugged. "Not long, like fifteen to twenty minutes by boat."

Kimmie chewed her lip, thinking. "You think we could get out, look around and be back in a couple of hours?"

He smiled and nodded agreeably. "Oh, sure. There's nothing on the island though, I've been out there a couple of times messing around."

Jill put her hand on Kimmie's arm and squeezed lightly. "You sure you want to do it tonight? Wouldn't you rather go in the daylight sometime? You know, when it's not so creepy?"

Kimmie pulled her arm away. "If nobody's supposed to go out there, we have to go at night so nobody sees us."

"It's no big deal, Jill," Kevin said. "Seriously, we'll be out and back in no time flat. There's really nothing out there to do but hike around in the trees and shit. It's a rock." He turned to Kimmie. "Come on, I'll take you."

Jill didn't look convinced. "Well, I guess as long as we're careful and don't stay long …"

"Sure, come on," Kevin said. He stepped off the curb, waited as a sedan drove by, and jogged across into the lot. Kimmie and Jill followed close behind as he approached his car, a silver two-door Sentra. "Where's your boat?" Kimmie asked, as Kevin opened the door and plopped into the driver's seat.

He leaned across and popped the lock to the passenger door and Jill opened it. She crawled into the back seat, and Kimmie slid into the front.

"There's a private dock up on the north side of the lake," he said. "My family keeps it moored there over the summer."

Kimmie nodded. "Sounds fancy. You guys must be rich."

Kevin started the car, ground the gears into reverse, and pulled out into the parking lot. "Nah, not at all. It's only a shitty little fishing boat. My mom's always bitchin' at my dad about the monthly dock fees. Says with the money they spend keeping it there he could go buy a whole mess of fish from the Raley's and come out ahead anyway. But he says hauling it to the lake's a pain in the ass. And fishing's pretty much the only thing he likes doing. That and drinking beer."

They pulled out of the parking lot and left the cinema and little strip mall behind them. Soon they were cruising along the main street into town, when an ambulance went barreling past them.

The sirens were off, but as it passed them, something about it drew Kimmie's attention. Something tugged at her thoughts as it passed. As if a kindred energy had reached out to her, shadowed tendrils fluttering over her mind, tugging at her like a flailing lover's fingertips before dwindling away. The feeling was gone almost as fast as it had come.

"Someone you know?" Jill asked.

"Hey, you're kinda crowding the driver," Kevin said, smiling, and playfully shoved Kimmie with his shoulder. "Not that I mind, or anything. But you know, safety first and all."

Kimmie blinked a couple of times, and sat back down in her seat. Her head felt fuzzy and cold, like she'd taken too much cold medicine. "Sorry. No … I don't know exactly."

"Just an ambulance," Kevin said. "Didn't even have its lights on, so it's not like anyone was hurt or anything."

"Sure," Kimmie said. "I guess."

"How long till we get to your boat?" Jill asked. Kimmie could tell there was a tinge of anxiety in her voice, and it irritated her. She was trying to figure out a way to ditch Jill when Kevin replied, "A few minutes."

And he wasn't wrong. A few minutes later they'd passed the entrance to the public beach, where Kimmie noticed a hand-lettered "Closed until further notice" sign had been put up over the locked gate.

Less than a mile past that, Kevin turned his car onto a wide gravel road with a sign next to it read "Boat Launch" and an arrow pointing forward. Light poles were placed along the side of the road, their bases lost in the bushes and low-cut trees which obscured the edges of the road. They cast intermittent puddles of yellow light between the stretches of gloom over the roadway as they drove toward the boat launch.

Kimmie could tell they were getting closer because the lights were beginning to filter down through the thin mist off the lake. Soon after that, the road widened into a small parking lot.

At the end of the lot nearest them, a concrete ramp sloped down into the lake. Near that and running across the length of the lot was a tall chain-link fence, reinforced with galvanized steel pipes. Rust-flecked razor wire curled in loops adorned the top of the frame. At the far end of the fence was a gate with a keypad lock holding it closed.

"Here we are," Kevin said and pulled the car into a spot right in front of a large locked gate under one of the overhead lamps. It was the only car in the lot. They got out of the car and approached the gate. Kimmie noticed a dark feather caught in one of the barbed hooks of the razor wire, fluttering in the light breeze. Kevin punched a code into the electronic keypad, and when he hit the final number, an electronic buzz split the silence of the moonless night, causing Kimmie to start.

"You're a little jumpy, huh?" Jill asked. "Having second thoughts?"

Kimmie shrugged. "No, of course not," she said, but her voice shook.

Kevin unlatched the gate and opened it wide. Beyond it was a small platform with stairs leading down to a dock where half a dozen small boats were moored.

"Ladies," he said, holding out one arm and gesturing them toward the dock.

Kimmie stepped through the gate onto the rickety platform. Jill followed behind as Kevin pulled the gate closed and made sure it was locked. She came down the stairs, and a hint of a foulness wafted across her. A green, infected smell of decay and rot. "What's that smell?" Kimmie asked as Kevin began to descend the stairs.

He took a whiff of the night air. "I don't smell anything. Do you, Jill?"

Jill breathed deep through her nose and shook her head. "Nah, smells like the lake to me. Like algae and stuff."

Kimmie wrinkled her nose as she climbed down the stairs. They were attached to the floating dock below and bobbed as she did. "Really? You guys don't smell that?"

Jill took another whiff. "No, sorry. Maybe there's a dead bird or something around?"

"Come on, guys," Kevin said as he hopped onto the deck of a boat at the far end of the dock. "If you want to get out there and back in a couple of hours, we gotta get moving."

Kimmie hustled along the main platform of the dock after him with Jill close behind. She recognized the name stenciled on the side of one boat. "*Shadowfax!*" she exclaimed. "This is Mr. Gaines' boat."

Kevin held out his hand to steady her as she climbed over the starboard gunwale and took a seat. "Do you know Mr. Gaines?" he asked. Jill climbed in after her, and Kevin helped her in as well. "There're life jackets under the hatch at the aft," he said, pointing to a small door built into the rear of the boat. It was a small boat with an inboard motor, and u-shaped built-in bench behind the pilot's seat. Big enough for a family or group of friends to take out for a few hours' fishing on a quiet lake like Oro Lake.

Kimmie flipped the latch holding the hatch closed. "Yeah, sort of," she said. "I was swimming the other day and almost drowned. He was cruising by on his boat and dragged me out of the water."

"Oh, well, that's pretty lucky for you, huh?" He pointed at the rope coiled around the cleat on the boat's edge. "Jill, can you untie that?"

She nodded and set about worming the knot loose.

Kimmie dragged three life jackets from the hatch and let the door fall shut with a slam. "Yeah, it was. We wanted to stop by and drop off some thank you cookies for him earlier, but he wasn't home."

"Huh," Kevin said, as he slid into the pilot's chair. "What'd you do with the cookies?"

Kimmie and Jill both laughed at that.

"Took 'em home," Kimmie replied.

"Okay, we're loose!" Jill proclaimed, unwinding the final coil from the boat's cleat. She slid into the life jacket Kimmie handed her. She snapped the buckles closed and cinched it tight. "Do you know how to put one of these on?" she asked Kimmie.

Kimmie had already fastened the life jacket closed and took a seat in the bench. "Yeah, no problem."

"Alright, me mateys," Kevin said as he fired up the boat's motor from the console. "Have a seat, and we'll be on our way."

"You sure you can drive this thing?" Kimmie asked as she settled in.

Kevin switched the motor to reverse and began backing the boat away from the dock. "Oh, sure," he said. "I've been driving the boat since before I could drive a car. You'll be fine." Once the boat had cleared the dock and backed far enough into the lake, he put the engine in forward and veered slowly out into the dark water. "Come on up front, and I'll show you how to drive it."

Kimmie stood next to him, holding on to the windshield frame for balance. "So, how's it work?"

He pointed to the key. "Ignition's here. Starts the same way as a car. Have you driven a car?"

She nodded. "Mom and Dad have started teaching me. I'll be taking my test before school starts in the fall."

"Okay, so basically the same thing," he said.

He pointed out the throttles, showed her how the steering worked and put her hand on the steering wheel. "Heck, you drive for a while."

"Are you nuts?" she said, laughing.

"It's easy, take the wheel, and we'll go slow. Same as a car, don't make any fast turns. And it's not like there's any traffic to worry about. You've got the whole lake."

Kimmie put both hands on the wheel, staring straight ahead, and gripping it tightly. "Okay. But if I tell you to take over, you take over."

"Deal," Kevin said, and stepped aside.

The moonless night was a riot of stars, reflected mirror-like in the dark lake water as they sped along. Once they had left the shore behind them, Kimmie found it almost disorienting. Stars above, stars below and around, almost like she was suspended in the deeps of space, rocketing through the void to far, distant worlds. While the boat had headlamps pointing forward, they did little to illuminate the darkness more than a few yards ahead of the craft.

"It's really pretty out tonight," Jill said, leaning on the edge of the gunwale, head on her crooked elbow. Her long blond hair was spinning out behind her in the wind as the boat skimmed along the surface of the lake.

Kevin pointed. "The island's ahead."

Kimmie leaned forward, trying to make it out through the gloom.

Somehow, she could tell they were getting closer, even if she couldn't yet see the small spit of land. She felt like a thread from the island reached all the way across the lake and into her gut, tugging her slowly, yet surely, on. She was reminded of reading the story of "Theseus and the Minotaur" in English class. Images of dank subterranean corridors and monsters lurking within them trickled into her mind.

"What's so interesting about that island, anyway?" Jill asked, sliding over closer to Kimmie. "What's the big deal with it?"

Kimmie stared ahead into the night. "Just curious," she said, the wind almost catching her voice and stealing it away into the night. But it was more compulsion than curiosity which fueled her interest. The closer she got to the island, the louder the susurrant whisperings in the labyrinth of her mind became.

Chapter Twenty-Two

Heidi Bogan cruised the ambulance along SR 346, and Golden Oaks vanished in the rearview mirror. Miles sat next to her in a rear-facing passenger's seat, the window rolled down to get fresh air into the vehicle. He was thumbing through a recent *USA Today*, catching up on the news from a few days earlier. Miles never had much time to read the news and often thought it was interesting to go back and revisit events that had already happened a few days after the fact. "I hate pickup duty," he said. "Wish the county Coroners would come collect their own stiffs."

Heidi shrugged. "Small town problems," she said. "We might have waited with the bodies all night before they could send someone. This way, we can take them in and be done with it. Least we're getting overtime."

"Fuckin-a, that's something I guess," Miles said. He glanced up from the paper to look at the bodies stowed in the ambulance bay. The girl, Abby, was strapped into the stretcher in the center of the bay, while Doc Hoeger was lashed to a backboard and strapped down to the bench seat below a wide window. Right in front of him. Miles kept glancing at the sheet-covered body a few inches past his knees, trying not to think about the broken, twisted shape of it. The bodies jostled on their gurneys as Heidi hit a bump in the road. "Gives me the creeps," Miles grunted.

Heidi barked out a short laugh. "Come on, you big baby," she said. "Stop your bitching and maybe I'll take you out for an ice cream after we drop them off at the county office."

He scrunched up his face in disgust and sneered. "Ugh … I'm freakin' starving, but I don't know if I could eat right now."

"Really?" Heidi said. "They're dead guys. You've seen dead guys before."

He shook his head slightly. "Not like that, I haven't." He glanced in the rearview mirror. "What d'you think did it? That's what I'm wondering."

"Beats me," Heidi said. "I'm sure the Coroner will give them a full work up. Probably an animal or something. I mean, it was a vet's office."

"Maybe," he said, thoughtfully. "But I didn't see any claw or bite marks, did you? They looked like they'd been twisted into pretzels."

Heidi was starting to feel a little uncomfortable. Starting to wonder what sort of animal or person could have twisted their joints out of their sockets, could crush bruises into their necks like that. "Now you're creeping me out."

"I'm just saying."

They drove in silence for a few minutes, the warm night air flowing in through the open windows. The ambulance hit a rough patch of gravelly road and shuddered along for a bit, rattling along over the grit. The straps and buckles holding down the bodies in the back jingled slightly as they shook.

Heidi peeked briefly into the rear-view mirror to make sure they were secure.

"I'm so ready for this day to be over," she said. "Drop these stiffs off at the morgue. After that, I'm going to go home, get drunk, and go to bed."

Miles laughed. "What, no hot date tonight?"

"Don't be a smartass," she said.

The highway curved gently around a low hill and in the distance, she saw the bright cone glare of oncoming headlights. Soon she saw they were high, the headlights of an oncoming big rig, probably laden with freight, produce, or packages, crossing the country to parts unknown. "Man. You know, being a truck driver wouldn't be such a bad job. Spend all day on the road like us but at least you get to see different shit every day."

Miles nodded. "Probably get tired of it, though. That's your problem, you're never happy with whatever you're doing."

The truck barreled past, a gust of air slamming into the ambulance in its wake. Heidi gripped the wheel tighter and slightly corrected as the ambulance shuddered and drifted over as the air pounded it. There was a metallic clinking in the back when the buckles shuddered again. She heard a loud thud, and Heidi flicked her eyes to the overhead mirror in time to see the gurney in the center of the bay shift slightly. "You locked down the stretcher, right?"

Miles looked up from the paper again, seeing the stretcher which held Abby shake slightly. "Of course I did. I mean, I'm pretty sure I did."

Heidi shook her head and glanced over at him. "It's a good thing you're pretty, you know that?"

A loud, banging thud and the stretcher shook again. "What the hell? Let me go check." He unlatched his seatbelt, and stood up, holding onto the overhead handrails for balance. He reached out and placed his left hand on the head of the gurney, and with his right checked the straps and buckles. "It's in tight" he said.

Ahead, Heidi saw the sign for the McConnell bridge which crossed the Graham River south of Oro Lake. She slowed as the ambulance curved off SR 346 and took the road toward the bridge which would lead them to the coroner's office in a few more miles. "Well make sure the body's buckled down at least."

"Body's buckled in fine," Miles muttered while he tugged on the straps, cinching them tight.

The shape under the sheet twitched. It shifted and arced, and Miles saw the vague outline of a hand and then maybe the knee pressing against the white linen. "Jesus!" he shrieked, and stumbled back, losing his footing and collapsing into the rear-facing seat.

"What?!" Heidi shouted. "What's the matter?"

There was a ripping noise as the sheet split open and then a spray of cold and wet and red. Miles stared, agog as the body burst open and crimson sluiced over the gurney.

Heidi looked into the rearview mirror and saw long black, spidery tendrils slithering out of the gaping hole in the blood-sodden cloth. They shot toward the ceiling, reached out grasping toward Miles who snapped out of his trance and swatted at them like they were a swarm of stinging insects.

"What the hell?" she shrieked.

The ambulance veered to the right as she turned to see what was going on.

"Oh, Christ it's cold!" Miles screeched. The tendrils had coiled around his arm and were biting into his skin, freezing cold burned where they touched.

The ambulance skidded on the road's shoulder and Heidi's head snapped forward. She fought with the steering wheel, trying to regain control of the vehicle. Cranking the wheel to the left, she overcompensated.

The ambulance veered left, tipping up onto the right-side wheels before slamming into the guardrail at the bridge's edge. Its momentum carried it over the guardrail, sent it careening down the embankment. It caught air, flipping once entirely before slamming down onto the gravel and dirt slope leading into the Graham River.

Miles bounced off the walls as the ambulance spun in space. Heidi heard a sickening crunch as his head slammed against the ceiling, his body twisted a completely different direction, and he was tossed around like a rag doll.

Another turn of the vehicle and Heidi's head slammed against the window next to her. The ambulance rolled over and over and finally fell with a thunderous splash into the river below. The interior lights flickered on and off, and Heidi was in a daze. Her face was numb, and pain lanced through her right thigh. It took her a few seconds to come out of her daze and realize she was lying sideways, mashed against the door. The open passenger-side window was above her and water was trickling into it. If she didn't get up, get moving, soon she'd be submerged.

She unbuckled herself and tried to rise before she realized her leg was broken. Reaching to her thigh she could feel the cracked bone bent beneath the muscle of her leg. When the pain hit her, she screamed out. She thought about all the medical supplies in the back of the truck, the braces, the painkillers, and the irony that she couldn't get to any of them. She stretched her arm toward the radio handset where it hung limply in its cradle on the dashboard. It was an inch out of her reach. She tried leaning up on one elbow, pressing against the window and felt something in her shoulder give way. A lancing, tearing pain and she screamed out again.

The water was a few inches deep now, and she sputtered and spat at it as she tried to bring her face around so at least her mouth and nose were free of the fluid. She saw the reaching, grasping dark tendrils sluicing around the edge of her chair. Creeping down across her right shoulder. The cold clutched, gnawed, numbed as it surrounded her. For a moment, the grinding aches, the searing pains, all the great and small discomforts in her body abated.

In a rush of viscous, freezing darkness, she was engulfed. The chill spread over her body, inched up her neck toward her face and creeping tendrils tickled, slithering toward her eyes. She stared numbly at the open window above her. The stars overhead were bright in the moonless night. The ambulance shifted again, sliding deeper into the river. She heard a crunching, grinding as the windshield spiderwebbed, river water spraying in through the tiny cracks. Her vision clouded, and she began to drift into oblivion. The windshield shattered completely. The cabin was flooded and soon Heidi was completely submerged and choking in a rush of river water.

The dark caul which had engulfed her, freezing and crushing the life out of her, loosened its tenebrous grip. It slid off of her like oil before slithering out through the shattered window and into open water. It sped forth, effortlessly cutting against the oncoming water. Full of stolen life, it drifted against the current away from the ambulance. It darted along beneath the surface of the river, a shadowy predator, full of malice and hunger.

It flowed around and through catfish and river trout, which blackened and decayed in its wake. The darkness slipped up the river, picking up speed until it blurred like black lightning along the riverbed. When it came to the Graham River dam, tendrils of non-dimensional darkness reached out, clutching at the concrete barrier, pulling itself from the water and oozing over the structure like a living stain or bruise. It slithered and crawled, pooling in shadows, reaching out pseudopods to drag itself along before dipping back into the waters of Oro Lake on the other side.

CHAPTER TWENTY-THREE

Shawna Lasher thumbed the transponder button on her squad car's dashboard as she approached the Golden Oaks police station. At this point, she was multiple hours into overtime, her shift was dragging into the night, and she was done with the day.
The gate slid smoothly open, and she pulled into the parking lot and glanced in the rearview mirror. Barney was sprawled out on the seat behind her, staring at her. "How you doing back there, buddy?" she said, craning her neck to watch him as she drove into the lot and found her space. The dog sat up as she exited the vehicle, waiting patiently. She opened the rear door and Barney plopped down in front of her, squatting back on his haunches, looking up at her expectantly. "Is that cone bugging you?" she said as she leaned over to ruffle his head beneath the plastic protective cone. She smiled at the dog, thinking that animals always looked a bit ridiculous in those things. She stood up. "Alright, well, come on."

She turned toward the side door entrance and was almost across the parking lot when she heard a scrabbling above her. Looking up, she saw half a dozen ravens descending on the edge of the roof. Three gripped the lip of the rain gutter, the other three took flight and began circling overhead, almost lost in the blackness of the night, only briefly glimpsed when they flitted under the glow of the sodium lights interspersed around the edge of the lot. The ones on the roof were staring down at her, glaring at her with black eyes as she came closer. Or she thought maybe they were glaring at Barney. Two of the ravens circling overhead landed on the handrails surrounding the small concrete patio outside the station side entrance door. She watched them carefully as she stepped up onto the small platform. When Barney came near, the birds broke into a cacophony of screeches, their wings spread wide, flapping as they shrieked at the dog.

Lasher grabbed her keys from her belt, and opened the door quickly, ushering the dog inside. She waved her arms, big and wide, at the birds. "Shoo!" she yelled. "Go on, get out of here!" She took a step toward the birds, stomping her foot on the concrete slab. The ravens hopped backward, wings still spread as if poised for flight, beaks still wide and screeching.

Lasher entered the station through the side door, pausing briefly to pull it shut tight behind her. The dog trotted ahead of her slowly, its nails click-clacking on the linoleum floor as it padded carefully along, occasionally turning to peek behind, as if worried the birds would follow.

"Don't worry, boy," Lasher said. "They're outside. You're safe in here."

The office was quiet, dark. When she entered the main floor, most of the lights were off. Officer West was on the night shift, sitting at his desk, feet propped up on the nearby paper shredder. The day's news displayed on the computer monitor before him cast a blue glow on his desk. He seemed to be quite enjoying the sandwich he was eating.

"West, how's things?" Lasher said as she approached.

He sat up, put the sandwich on his desk, and wiped his mouth with the back of his hand. "Quiet," he said around a mouthful of salami hoagie. "Millsap came and went, and the phones are quiet. Not that I'm complaining." He noticed Barney at her side. "You brought the dog?"

She nodded and took Barney by the collar, shuffling him around and getting him to sit with a gentle push on his hindquarters. "I was going to release McEwen tomorrow, but I think we can send him home with his dog tonight. Save us the headache." Lasher picked a sealed plastic bag off West's desk. It contained keys, a wallet, belt, and a pair of shoelaces. The accumulated stuff of Arlen McEwen, confiscated when he was arrested a few days before. "I'm sure he'll be happy to have all this crap back. I'll start the paperwork, if you want to go and let Prince Charming know it's time to leave." She began shuffling through her desk for the discharge paperwork and brought up Arlen's file on her computer.

"You got it," West said. "Millsap said it looked like his brother just disappeared?"

"The house looked like he was in the middle of a project, left for some reason, and never came back."

"Huh," West replied. "Well, maybe Arlen'll notice something when he gets home."

"Yeah, maybe," she said.

"I'm going to go tell him the good news and get him out of our hair," West said. He patted the side of his leg to get Barney's attention. "Okay, boy, let's go see your person." Barney *whuffed* and followed him through the office back to the holding cells. He buzzed through and walked toward the cell where Arlen McEwen sat on his cot, eyes glazed over with boredom.

"Alrighty Arlen, we're letting you go. Got enough on our plate right now and can't be babysitting your sorry ass anymore."

Arlen sat up, hopped to his feet, and hustled across the tiny cell. "Hot damn. And I see you even brought me my favorite critter!"

He got down to Barney's level and reached through the cell bars. "Hey, ya dumb dog, how you doin'?" Barney stopped just out of reach. "Heya pooch, let's get you home and get us some grub." He looked at the dog's side. "What's with the stitches, and the cone?"

West handed him the plastic baggie with his stuff in it through the bars, slid a key into the cell's lock and turned. "Didn't Lasher tell you he got hurt? Doc Hoeger fixed him up this morning, but you're going to have to keep an eye on that wound for a while.

Might want to take him in to see … well, a different vet tomorrow. There was an accident at Hoeger's."

"What happened to the doc?" Arlen said, stepping through the door. He got down onto one knee and began lacing up his shoes.

"I'm sure the coroner'll figure it out."

"Oh, damn. That's too bad. He always treated me and Barney right." He stood up and pocketed his key ring and slid on his belt, before tossing the empty plastic baggie into a wastebasket nearby.

West stepped aside, opening the cell door wide to let him through. "Also, keep an eye out for your brother. Still no sign of him, but maybe you'll see something in your house we missed."

"You went in my house?" Arlen said as he leaned down to pet the dog. His hand touched Barney's head, and the dog began to growl. It shuffled back a few inches away from Arlen's outstretched fingers, a snarl on its lips. "What the hell, boy," Arlen said, standing erect and taking a step back. "What's got into you?"

Barney began to cough, a barking hack as if he were choking.

"Hey, Barney, what's going on?" Arlen shot forward, dropping to his knees, as Barney collapsed to the ground. The dog's legs began to paw at the air as his body started to shiver, then spasm.

"Arlen, get back," West said, grabbing him by the shoulder and dragging him backward. Arlen went sprawling, landing on his back as he fell over.

A low growl grew in Barney's throat as West drew his sidearm from the black nylon holster at his belt. The gun glittered coldly in the fluorescent overhead lighting. He aimed it at the dog, but his hand was shaking.

West saw a blackness cloud over the dog's eye. Its mouth opened wide, and he heard a nasally whine come from it. A flood of viscous darkness slithered from Barney's mouth, like a horrible knot of impossibly black snakes or eels. The writhing knot fell to the floor, ropy and slimy and black, a growing pool of darkness into which light fell and was extinguished. It began reaching toward him.

"What the fucking hell?" Arlen shouted, his voice rising to a terrified shriek.

West squeezed the trigger, the gun's retort deafening in the small room. He knew he'd aimed at the center of the darkness, but it had had no effect on the shapeless thing gliding toward him. The bullet had flown into the shadow and simply vanished. Nothing had passed through, nothing had ricocheted off the floor behind it. The bullet had simply ceased to exist.

Twice more he pulled the trigger in rapid succession with the same result. His ears rang from the blasts. West grabbed Arlen by the scruff of his collar. "Go!" he shouted, pointing toward the door to the outer hallway. Arlen didn't have to be told twice. He scrambled to his feet and rushed toward the open door, vaulting over Barney's prone form as he did.

The darkness pivoted and lashed out at Arlen, pseudopodia twitching as it reached toward him. He narrowly escaped their clutching reach and vaulted out the door. West was right behind him. He charged around the slithering pool of darkness and dragged the door shut behind him as he ran from the room.

West turned to look back at the door. Tendrils of darkness slithered under it, boiling in from around the sides and top gap. They whipped the air, searching, crawling, and then congealing and coalescing at the center of the door before dropping to the ground, a huge writhing mass of shadow and nightmare, crawling toward West. He turned and ran, barreling down the corridor after Arlen.

He rounded the corner of the hallway, wet slapping sounds echoing down the hall behind them.

The door clanged shut and Lasher came running down the hall. "What the hell?" she was yelling. "What's going on?"

Arlen ran right past her, not looking back.

West's eyes were wide, wild. With his free hand, he smoothed his hair back out of his face. He turned to the door and back to Lasher. "There's something ... something came out of Barney and ..."

As they burst into the main office area, Lasher saw Arlen banging at the front door. The glass panels shivered and shuddered as he shoved at them with his shoulder.

"Doors won't open!" he shouted, frantic.

West grabbed at the keys on his belt, quickly thumbing them aside until he found the one that opened the exterior doors. "Move," he said, bodychecking Arlen out of the way with his hip and shoulder.

Lasher came running up behind. "West, what the hell's going on, dammit?"

West turned around, his keys left in the door's lock. Over Lasher's shoulder he saw the shadowy mass slithering toward them. It was clinging to the ceiling now, tendrils of darkness reaching out from the shadowy central node and dragging itself along the acoustic tiles with a wet slapping, slithering noise.

"Christ," he hissed, drawing his service revolver from its holster at his hip. "What the hell is it?" He raised the weapon and aimed at the moving stain.

Lasher's eyes went wide as West aimed his revolver in her direction. "West!" she yelled, and dove to the side. Her foot slipped, she lost her balance, and she toppled over toward the front desk. She instinctively reached out to slow her fall, but in the darkness missed the edge of the desk and twisted around, the base of her skull colliding with the desk's hard edge. She fell to the ground unconscious.

Arlen was working the keys in the lock when something black and shapeless slammed into the door on the other side. It flailed and buffeted the glass, and he stepped back, startled, and fell.

He rose, staggering to his feet when he saw a raven outside the door, wings beating against the glass, razor talons scratching and clawing, knife-like beak pecking at the window. With a rush of darkness, it was joined by another pair. Three of the great black birds were assaulting the glass door. Scratching and pecking at the glass. He watched as chips flew out of the thick glass, and cracks began to spiderweb across it.

"What the hell?" Arlen said, eyes darting from the oozing darkness on the ceiling to the frantic carrion birds, and back.

West squeezed the trigger of his gun, the retort deafening in the room. Once, twice, three times one after the other, bullets flew harmlessly into the crawling mass on the ceiling. He took a step back, dumbfounded. "What the hell is it?"

The amorphous dark shape launched itself through the air, colliding with West's torso and knocking him to the ground. Tendrils stretched out and surrounded him, wrapping him in their chill embrace. Arlen scrambled to his feet and rushed over to West. "Oh, God!" West screamed. "It's so cold!"

Arlen tried to grab at the tendrils slipping around West's neck but recoiled at the freezing pain in his fingertips. West choked and gurgled as the black noose constricted, tightening on his throat, the skin around the lashing threads began to turn dark, crystals forming as it froze.

There was a brief still silence. A tenuous calm, like the eye in a nightmare hurricane passing over. A tremendous crash as the door splintered, slivers of glass twinkling down, glittering yellow like sparks of sunlight from the light of the streetlights outside. The ravens burst in.

A rush of air as the three nightbirds vaulted past Arlen, descending on West's prone form. Their wings beating and buffeting as they hopped and scratched and clawed at the caustic darkness which covered him. Arlen turned his face and raised his arms to shield his eyes, and pushed back from West's body.

He got to his feet and was raising a foot to kick at the birds when he stopped. Amid the flurry of wings, the screeching and clawing, he saw the birds tearing at the darkness which engulfed West. The birds used their beaks and talons to tear at the shadowy substance, ripping and rending it. Tearing away long strips of it and swallowing them, gulping them down like writhing snakes.

Arlen ran. He left West and Lasher behind and ran to the glass doors, finally getting them open and leaving the keys behind as he made his escape into the warm night.

Inside, the dark mass pulled back, releasing West and crawling away from the avian assault. It slithered down his torso, dropping to the linoleum floor, no more intimidating than a rather disgusting patch of black mildew. It oozed along, listlessly sending pseudopodia before it to slap at the floor and drag it along. The birds took chase, continuing to rend and tear, bite and swallow, until the shadowy mass was gone.

One of the birds, by far the larger of the three, turned its head toward where Shawna Lasher lay prone. Its dark, brown eyes glittered dully in the scant light as it stared down at her. It opened its beak and shrieked out one long *caw!* before it leapt into the air, flying past her and out the front of the police station. The two remaining birds pecked at the last slivers of darkness, throwing their heads back as they swallowed the snake-like tendrils. And in a rush of wings, they followed their leader through the broken glass door.

As quickly as the birds had come, they were gone and the police station which had just been the scene of such violence and chaos was silent, still.

CHAPTER TWENTY-FOUR

Arlen's foot was pressed so hard on the accelerator that he was almost sitting an inch off the seat of his truck. His eyes were wide with panic, and his blood flushed with adrenaline as he barreled through downtown Golden Oaks.

When he'd run from the station, his only thought was to get out of the area as fast as possible. It wasn't really a thought though, more base instinct fueling his mad dash for survival. He'd raced around the side of the building to where the impound lot was, right next to the lot where the cops kept their cruisers. It wasn't the first time his truck had been locked up for a few days, and he knew the layout well enough. Momentarily stymied by the razor wire curled around the top of the chain-link fence surrounding the lot, it didn't take long before he noticed an area where the fence was bowed in enough he could squeeze through.

So he had, and he'd retrieved the bolt cutters from the back of the vehicle, cut the lock, and smashed through the gate. He wasn't waiting around for whatever that thing was to come after him. As he and Darryl were both known to say, *Our mamma didn't raise any dummies. Except for my brother.*

He blasted through town, constantly checking behind him to see if that slithering darkness was on his tail. That's why he didn't see the stoplights ahead of him turning yellow, then red. And he didn't notice the vintage Chevrolet convertible pull into the intersection. He glanced forward and saw the car and cranked the wheel to the left to avoid it, but it was too late, and his truck bounced off the front of the Chevy, sending that car into a spin to the right, and his own truck in a spin to the left. He overcompensated for the spin, and as he noticed the warning sticker on the sun visor overhead which read "WARNING: Higher Rollover Risk" with a little icon of a truck tipping over, two things went through his mind: the first was that he should've been wearing a seat belt. The second was the bolt cutters he'd left on the passenger seat as the truck flipped over and the cabin collapsed in an explosion of shattered glass and ruined metal.

Pedestrians scattered as the truck rolled and skidded across the street where it slammed into a transformer pole which splintered and fell against the roof of the Ace Hardware as Arlen's truck smashed into the wall. There was a bright light, a flash, and the transformer erupted into sparks. In an instant, the town went dark.

Chapter Twenty-Five

Kimmie and Kevin had switched out driving the boat as they came close to the island, and now Kevin brought it slowly toward shore. He slid the craft toward the edge of the water until the prow bumped up onto the soft sandy beach. After he killed the motor, he pointed toward the gleaming metal fluke anchor folded up nearby. "Kimmie, can you hand me that?"

Kimmie was anxious, jittery. She wanted to get off the boat and onto the island. She picked up the anchor and carried it over to Kevin. It was attached to six feet of steel chain, and a nylon rope which was coiled up in the side of the boat. He unfolded the anchor, took a few practice swings, and tossed it underhand over the side of the boat. The anchor sailed forward and landed spike down into the sand.

"Good enough," he said, and turned to the girls, grinning. "Okay, you want to explore the island, let's do it." He opened a storage compartment with a few simple tools inside, and pulled out a long-handled, matte-black flashlight.

Kevin hopped over the side of the boat, landing ankle-deep in water and clambered over to where the anchor had hit the shore. He picked it up, swung it overhead, and impaled the spike deep into the sand, stomping it down twice for good measure. He tugged the chain, felt it was firm in the beach, and packed more sand around and on top of it to make sure it was secure. Once he was sure it was in tight, he stood up and turned back toward the boat. "We going to do this?"

Kimmie stepped up onto the gunwale and saw a stretch of wet sand below. Lake water seeped and splashed around the edge of the boat, but she was able to jump over it and landed on the beach.

She turned back to the boat where Jill was still on the deck, her brow furrowed. "You coming?"

"I don't know," Jill said. "You really think we should? I mean, it was fun coming over, but maybe we should stay off the island." She looked back the way they'd come, but the far shore was lost in the darkness. She thought she could see a dim yellow glow from the lights on the dock, but it was so far away she couldn't be completely sure.

Kevin had his hands on his hips and glanced from the beach into the trees up the shore. Then back toward the boat.

"Oh, come on," Kimmie said. "Let's check it out real quick, and then we can take off."

Suddenly, Kimmie saw a flash in the distance from the direction of town. A brief silver light burst across the sky, washing Kimmie and Kevin's faces white before vanishing. Jill turned, before they heard a distant booming that passed almost as fast as the flash had.

"What was that?" Jill said.

Kevin shrugged. "Beats me. Looked like it was back in town, whatever it was."

Kimmie was getting antsy. "Come on, guys. We'll make it quick." She looked into the woods, her eyes tracking upward as she looked toward the island's peak. "Up and back, real quick, I promise. I bet you can see around the whole lake from up there." She started across the beach without turning to see if Kevin and Jill were following. A few more quick—almost leaping—strides and she was at the tree line. She tapped on her phone's flashlight so she could see ahead of her.

"Look," Kevin said. "I don't want to pressure you or anything. But it might be kind of cool, right? Besides, she's your friend. And she's kind of weird."

"Maybe I should stay with the boat?" Jill said. "You know, in case the anchor comes loose?"

Kevin turned to look at the anchor buried securely in the sand. "Okay, suit yourself, I guess," he said and turned to follow after Kimmie. "We won't be long, promise." Kevin waved reluctantly, then jogged across the thin spit of sand toward the trees beyond.

"You better not be," Jill muttered. She looked around the small beach, taking in the strange quiet of the night. Normally, the night on the outskirts of town where she lived was filled with at least a murmuring chatter of night sounds. The distant thrum of cars in town, or zipping along SR 346. Pine, aspen, and oak branches rubbing together high in the forest canopy as summer breezes or howling winter gusts caused them to creak and bend. The occasional hooting of an owl, or the bark of the neighbor's dog as something in the night triggered its protective instinct.

But out in the center of the lake, it was disconcertingly quiet. There was no breeze of note, and after the little boat had come to rest near shore, the lake had calmed almost instantly. A slight intermittent bumping thud as the boat bobbed in the water, occasionally banging into the sand and the crunching footfalls receding away from her as Kevin disappeared into the woods. Aside from that, the night was still. Jill crossed her arms in front of her, clutching her elbows and rubbing her upper arms to stave off the night chill.

***

Kimmie trudged through the sparse copses of trees which dotted the island. Her calves were starting to ache as she climbed the incline. Frequently, she had to reach out to push branches out of the way or scramble over a fallen oak log. After she'd been at it for a few minutes, she heard the rustle of footsteps behind her. "Hey, Kimmie, wait up," she heard. She stopped and looked behind, waiting as Kevin caught up to her. He was barely winded by the time he did.

"Hey, you shouldn't run on ahead," he said, as he climbed a few more feet to stand with her. "This place isn't big, but we should stick together so we don't get lost."

"I thought you said you'd been here before?" she said and turned to continue her ascent.

Kevin hustled to keep up with her. "Well, yeah. I mean, I've come out *near* the island. But I actually lied before. This is the first time I've ever really been on it. To be honest, it kind of gives me the creeps."

She looked back the way he'd come. "Where's Jill?" she asked, peering over his shoulder, listening for any sound of footfalls.

Kevin shrugged, his eyebrows arcing comically. "She decided she wanted to stay with the boat. I think the place gives her the creeps, too."

Kimmie stopped and took in the terrain around her. Without a moon overhead, the woods were primordially dark. Tree boughs creaked in the light breeze, branches rustling as they rubbed together. Beyond them, the occasional twinkle of starlight, pinpricks of silver in the dark. "I think it's beautiful."

Kevin looked at his watch. "It's getting kind of late though," he said. "Maybe we should be heading back?"

"Come on, let's go." She reached her hand toward him, and Kevin took it hesitantly. "I promise it'll be worth it."

They hiked in silence up the hill, the only sound their footsteps on the dusty dry dirt path. Kimmie felt a tugging, an urge or compulsion to keep going forward, to keep climbing toward the peak. And deep in her mind, she began to hear a chittering whisper. An insistent buzz, like insects crawling on a sheet of glass, desperate to breach the pane and swarm through. To invade. To infest. Her mind was starting to squirm.

"You seem like you know where you're going," Kevin said.

She turned toward him. His voice was odd, like he was speaking to her from underwater, or from a great distance. Her head felt fuzzy. And she had a slight ache which started in the back of her neck and wrapped around her skull like long, alien fingers. "I guess I do," she said, but her tongue felt thick and clumsy. "Keep going until we reach the top. We'll see what's there. What's there that wants to be seen."

Kevin wrinkled his forehead. "What do you mean? What wants to be seen?"

She laughed. "You'll see!" she said, and slipping her fingers from his, she turned to race up the hill, soon she was swallowed by the darkness.

Kevin doubled his pace, climbing awkwardly in the gloom, swatting tree branches out of the way as he stumbled over roots and rocks. He hissed a curse as a pine bough slapped him across the cheek. He could hear her footfalls ahead of him, light and quick compared to his plodding steps. How was she moving so confidently in the darkness? She was running with full awareness of her surroundings, complete control over her movement. While Kevin was stumbling and staggering along, almost blind in the dark.

After another ten minutes of climbing, the trees began to thin out. His legs were aching as the ground leveled out a bit in front of him, and he saw what looked like an old, overgrown path of sorts. When he got closer to it, he saw it was indeed a crumbling concrete walkway. Knee-high weeds sprang through the cracks in places, and it was strewn with dead pine needles and brown oak leaves. He was panting from his exertion and noticed a smell of dust, of ancient decay which suffused the place.

Looking from side to side, he tried to figure out which way Kimmie had gone.

"Kimmie!" he shouted into the dead of night. "Kimmie, where'd you go?" He walked along the pathway, kicking at clots of rubble and running his hand through the tall strands of grass at the edge of the walkway. "Kimmie?" he called out again.

A hand on his shoulder startled him. Kevin spun around, lost his balance, and fell to the ground. When he looked up, Kimmie stood over him. "Shit! Where were you? Where'd you come from?"

She laughed, a strange, trilling laughter. Then offered him her hand and helped him up. "Guess I got a little bit ahead of you. But you're not going to believe what I found." She tugged him along and started down the pathway. "Come on, it's so cool."

He pulled back a bit, trying to slow her down. "I don't know, Kimmie. Maybe we should head back to the boat. It's getting pretty late."

"We're almost there, come on," she said, tugging his arm. "Come on, trust me, you're going to love this." She turned to smile at him, but her smile was cold, almost spiteful. "And I promise we'll leave soon."

Kevin felt a cold pit open in his stomach. Something about the island was wrong. In the heat of summer, it felt cold. Not a nighttime summer breeze off the lake cool, but like all the warmth and joy of summer was being sucked away. And somewhere distant, the smell of smoke.

"Let's be quick, okay?" he muttered as he followed Kimmie to the island's peak.

Winding through the close boughs of trees, stumbling over roots and rocks, they made their way upward. The old pathway was crumbled to almost nothing here. Asphalt and concrete had been gnawed apart by years of neglect and erosion, and the going was slow as they took the switchbacks toward the top. Finally, the path leveled out, and in the distance they could barely see the trees thinning out. "Looks like it's widening out," Kevin said.

Kimmie skipped ahead, then turned to face him as she jogged backwards. "This is going to be great, right? I bet nobody ever comes up here. We'll be the first to see the top in forever."

He had to hustle to keep up. "Hey-hey-hey! Be careful," he said. "You're gonna trip or something."

She dismissed him with a wave of her hand, then turned and charged forward. "Don't be such a chicken-shit!" she called back over her shoulder, sped around a curve and was lost to his sight.

Kevin slowed down, there was no point in trying to keep up with her now since they were almost to the peak. And he was worried about tripping on the uneven pavement. He kept a steady pace forward until he saw Kimmie standing only a few yards ahead. The trees cleared away from a flat area and there was no more "up" to go. They'd made it to the peak at last.

Kimmie stood at the edge of a wide, flat area.

He looked at the ground before them. A broad concrete slab had been built here at some point in the past, but now it had collapsed in. They were at the edge of the slab, and a large hole yawned open in the center. Spiderweb-like cracks issued from the hole's circumference toward the edges of the slab. Kevin leaned forward to try and look into the hole, but all he saw in it was darkness. "So, what is it?" he asked, turning toward Kimmie.

"A hole," she said.

"I guess," he replied. "Not all that exciting." He turned from the hole, and scanned across the water, along the distant shore of the lake. "You really can see the whole valley from up here. That's kind of cool."

"Come on," she said, stepping toward to him. "I want to see what's in the hole." She stepped onto the concrete and closer to the hole's edge.

"Hey, you shouldn't do that," he said, and took a step forward to grab her arm.

She continued forward. "It's fine. The slab's stable enough." She got right up to the edge, and a few small chunks of concrete crumbled away under her toes, tumbling into the pit with a rattle and clatter. "It's pretty cool, actually," she said, and motioned him over. "Come check it out."

Reluctantly, he inched forward. The slab did indeed feel stable under his feet, relieving some of his anxieties. He came over and stood next to her, staying a foot back from the edge. Looking into the pit he saw darkness and the ghostly shadows of rocks and dirt edging a deep hole. How deep he couldn't see.

"How far down you think it goes?" he asked.

"Let's find out," she said. And Kevin realized she'd stepped behind him as he felt her hands shove him hard. He yelped in surprise as he went stumbling into the dark. He tumbled briefly through the air, then landed hard on his right side. Pain lanced through his arm as he heard and felt something snap. Stars erupted in his vision, pinpricks of white against the blackness of the pit. "Oh, oh! Fuck!" he screamed, as he rolled onto his back. "What the fuck?!" Clutching his broken arm, he rolled over onto his back. Agony. He was having trouble catching his breath and registered a sharp pain in his right side. He reached down to where his ribs hurt with his left hand and felt warm wetness. "What the hell!" he said, craning his neck to look up toward the opening of the hole.

The darkness above him was almost as profound as that which surrounded him. But as his eyes adjusted, he saw a spray of stars far beyond the dome of night. And could vaguely make out Kimmie's silhouette against them.

"So," she asked softly. "How deep is it?"

"You're fucking crazy!" he shouted. "You could've killed me!"

A pause. "I'm surprised the fall didn't," he heard her say.

"How am I supposed to get out of here?" he shouted.

"You're not," she whispered back, her voice echoing off the hard rock walls of the pit.

He heard a rock tumble nearby, the clattering of stone on stone. He reached around with his good hand and pulled his phone out of his back pocket. Sliding his thumb across the softly glowing screen he triggered the flashlight app, and the cave was instantly bathed in a sterile white glow. The rocky wall before him was rough granite, unhewn by human hands. He cast the light around, and saw that the cave-like pit he was in was natural, but with a floor covered with crushed and crumbled concrete. The remnants of the slab above which had collapsed in at some point in the past, and that's what he now lay on.

He was beginning to feel light-headed, but his broken arm had subsided from screaming pain to a throbbing ache. He looked at his phone again, hoping against hope to have some signal, but was unsurprised to see the "No Signal" indicator on the screen.

He heard rocks shift again, and flashed his light in the direction from which the sound came just in time to see a clatter of rubble tumble aside.

There was darkness beyond the gap. And a stench. A wet smell of rot and corruption. Kevin shoved away from the hole with his feet, inching back and trying not to jostle his arm. But as he shoved, pain lanced in his side, and he felt a fresh wave of warm and wet trickling down. A shadow crawled from the gap in the wall. Like roots or tendrils of some awful plant which had spent all its days in the dark places under the earth. Dead black, as if light could not exist in the same place as the slithering shadow. Even in the glow of his phone it retained its void-like emptiness, as if light simply fell into it and disappeared. The shadow seethed over the rubble, dragging forward toward him. His phone's light flickered briefly and went out.

"Kimmie!" he shouted up at the hole in the sky overhead. "Kimmie! Help me!"

A hiss of air behind him, and he turned his head as a crack in the cave wall split open as wide as his body. Shards of granite burst out, rattling off the walls and slicing into his flesh. He screamed again as blood began to pour from a multitude of wounds. Tendrils of darkness burst from the fissures in the rock all around him. Freezing cold coils of shadow gripped his arms, legs, circled his throat and squeezed. Pressure increased and he grew faint. From inside his head, he heard a crack and knew nothing more.

∗∗∗

Kimmie stood at the edge of the crumbling concrete slab, staring down into the darkness below. She'd heard Kevin calling out to her but felt no urge to assist. The slithering darkness was getting stronger, she could feel it. She felt it feeding, draining away the essence of Kevin as it had so many others. And as Kevin's essence was absorbed, Kimmie felt strangely alive. The threads which extended through her body now filling with the energy drained from the boy. She and the darkness in the pit were somehow connected. Like whatever had invaded her was also an extension of the thing in the pit. And as she felt connected to it, she felt connected to other extensions of its core essence. Dead things crawling at the bottom of the lake, clambering out of the slime and muck, infused with the same terrible alien energies which coursed through her mind and body.

The thing in the darkness sensed her as well. Kimmie's mind was now fully connected with whatever passed as the consciousness of the ancient being. She felt pulses of brooding memory, of its journeys through endless voids of space and time. Of its arrival and imprisonment on earth, and of the millennia it spent in the darkness beneath the valley. Yet, she had no clear image of from where it had come. Deep below the crust of the earth? Some distant world far beyond the orbits of the planets in our solar system? Or maybe a dimension of shadow and despair running parallel or slicing perpendicular to our own? The images that barraged her mind were indecipherable. Like trying to glean meaning from the hieroglyphs by blind touch.

She could tell that the shadow and she were bonded. It hadn't drained her essence with its touch in the lake because it hadn't had time. It had gotten a taste of her, but she'd been pulled away too soon. But it saw her as a vessel. Something into which it could pour itself and escape its imprisonment once and for all. For too long it had lurked in the darkness in the warrens beneath the lake. But something in Kimmie's mind was attuned to the same strange alienness of the thing. She knew it was one of the last of its kind, desperate to escape this black pit in which it had been trapped. Needing a human host, it had sent out spores or scouts, minor mirrors of itself to find likely hosts for its full essence. But none of the humans it had encountered before had been able to withstand the melding of flesh and spirit. Until now.

Kimmie could sense that the thing coveted her flesh, her warmth. It could inhabit her, merge with the latent otherness in her and flee the island, the valley, once and for all. Escape into the world of mankind, in which it could feed endlessly.

She stared at the roiling dark coils, ruminating over its existence and purpose. It slunk toward her, squirming along the walls of the pit, inching forward gluttonously. It rose in a wave over the lip of the concrete. Kimmie stepped forward and embraced the darkness.

CHAPTER TWENTY-SIX

Gabe Barnes was tapping his phone furiously as a fire truck raced by, sirens screaming and flashing in the darkness. "She's not responding."

Laurie was holding her phone with one hand as high as she could get it. "I can't get a signal."

"Forget it, let's go find her," Gabe said, putting his hand on Laurie's shoulder and directing her over to where their car was parked.

They raced through downtown and into the parking lot of the *Oro*. They saw the blackout had spread across town and as far as the strip mall containing the theater. Everything was dark, punctuated by the cones of light cast, from their headlights and a few flashing glimmers near the buildings. Slowly entering the lot, they saw ushers with flashlights leading people from the darkened theater. Likewise, the ice cream shop and other places in the strip mall had emptied, and people were making their way with flashlights or the lights of their phones. A throng had gathered in front of the buildings. Numerous people were staring at their phones, tapping, reading, wondering what was going on.

They pulled into a spot near the front. "I'm sure Kimmie's in there," Gabe said, but worry tinged his voice. "I'll text her to let her know to look for us."

Laurie nodded. "Sure. I'll go look." She stepped out of the car, and Gabe followed. They moved through the crowd toward the theater entrance, scanning for Kimmie.

A man's voice, artificially amplified, broke out, "Folks, can I have your attention please?"

Laurie looked around and saw a man standing near the theater. He was wearing the same uniform the ushers and other staff of the theater had on: maroon slacks, and a maroon vest over a white collared shirt. *All very old-timey Hollywood showmanship*, she thought.

"There's been an accident downtown," he continued. "A transformer blew out, and power's out for most of downtown … I was told that the fire department is on the scene, dealing with it."

A worried murmur spread through the crowd. Some people broke away from the throng toward the parking lot. Gabe and Laurie pushed further in. "I'm sorry, but with the power out, we can't open the registers to issue refunds at this time. Come back any time after the power's back on tomorrow, and we can either issue you a refund for your ticket, or a comp to a different show."

People began to grouse about that. One gangly man started barking at the theater manager about his rights and demanding a refund.

"I don't see her anywhere," Gabe said. "Do you?"

Laurie scanned the crowd. "No. Her friends, either. Maybe their movie ended? Or they got bored and left?"

"Shit," Gabe replied, glancing at his phone. "Still no reply to my texts. I'll call her." He thumbed her icon on the phone, and it began to ring. Gabe stuck a finger in his other ear and left the crowd so he could hear better. Laurie opened the "Find My Friends" app on her phone and tapped on the picture of Kimmie. It was an old photo, but she'd never changed it. Kimmie grinning at her in ponytails, hugging Mickey Mouse from when they went to Disneyland when she was seven or eight.

How time flies, Laurie thought, a wan smile crossed her face.

The map that appeared on the screen was wide, showing almost the entirety of Golden Oaks. The phone told Laurie it was 'searching…' and the onscreen map kept zooming back and forth, trying to figure out where Kimmie's phone was.

Kimmie's voicemail picked up. "Hey, kiddo, it's Dad. Where are you? All the power's out through town, and your mom and I are in the theater parking lot looking for you. Call when you can, or come find us, okay?"

Kimmie's status changed briefly from "Searching" to "Found" and to "Searching" again. "What the hell?" Laurie said.

"What is it?" Gabe said, sliding his phone into his back pocket.

Laurie's brow furrowed as she stared at the phone's glowing screen. "For a second the app found her. I guess it's having trouble getting her signal, or sending to mine."

"Great," Gabe said, with a sigh. "Where did it say she was?"

"In the middle of the lake," Laurie replied. "That can't be right. It flashed her icon again near Deer Island, before disappearing again. Look," she said, holding the phone out so he could see the screen.

Gabe looked down at her phone which showed an abstract satellite image of the lake, the town, the surrounding woods. It was still 'searching,' the image scrolling around slightly as the GPS tried to do its work. "Maybe that's a central location," he said. "Maybe the cell towers are sending weird signals. Who knows?"

Laurie lowered her hand and looked at the crowd as it dispersed. With a mix of worry and resignation, people were heading into their cars and driving away from the theater's lot.

"So, where the hell is she?" she asked. "She's supposed to be here at the movie with her friends. The movie's let out, they've *evacuated* the theater. And she's nowhere around."

Gabe shrugged, but he felt growing dread in his gut. "I don't know, babe. They're teenagers, they could have snuck off to do practically anything."

"Oh, hell," Laurie said. "She's been so disagreeable lately, and now this."

A voice crackled out over the loudspeaker again. "Folks, I do have to ask you all to head on out. We won't be reopening until PG&E can repair the transformer downtown, and who knows how long that'll take. Please go find your cars and head home. Or, if you're waiting for a ride, please step to one side over here." He indicated the sidewalk to the side of the theater's marquee where a few people had lined up already.

Laurie grabbed Gabe's arm. "Come on, let's go ask the manager if maybe he saw them."

Gabe had worked at the Coronet theater when he was getting his degree from Cal State Alcosta and was about to let Laurie know that the chances of anyone at the theater having paid attention to the patrons' faces was almost nonexistent. But he could see how worried she was, so went along with her.

She approached the manager as she brought up a recent photo of Kimmie on her phone's screen. "Hi," she said.

The manager turned to her, forcing a smile. His stress was palpable. "Can I help you?"

Laurie noticed that he was still scanning the dispersing crowd as he spoke to her.

"I hope so," she said. "We're looking for our daughter." She held up her phone, showed him the photo. "She was supposed to be here with some friends, but we can't find her."

He nodded. "I see." He took a look at the photograph. "I'm not really sure I can help you, but maybe one of the ushers saw her. What film was she here to see?"

Laurie turned to Gabe, who shrugged. "I have no idea," he said. He stepped back and looked up at the marquee. The four-screen theater was showing a horror film, superhero movie, romantic comedy, and action film. The usual slate; something for everyone. "Could've been any of them, probably."

The manager waved one of the ushers over. A teenage girl wearing the same uniform as the theater's other staff. Her dark hair pulled back in a tight ponytail bobbed side to side as she jogged over. "Roxie, any chance you saw this girl come in earlier? She was with a few friends."

"A boy and a girl," Laurie interjected. "Jill Bridges, and another boy I don't know."

Roxie looked at the phone for a few seconds. "No, sorry, don't recognize her. I know Jill though," she added. "We go to Youth Group together. But I don't remember seeing her come in tonight."

Laurie thanked her and turned back to Gabe. "Maybe they decided to skip the movie."

Gabe nodded agreement. "Let's get in the car and drive around for a bit. We might spot her or at least get somewhere with better cell coverage."

The theater manager turned to leave, then stopped. "Feel free to look around a little more if you need to. But I really do need to clear the parking lot. With the lights out, it's a liability thing. I'm sure you understand."

"Of course," Gabe said. "Thanks for the help, in any case."

Laurie stepped toward the manager, another question on her lips, but Gabe took her hand, holding her back. "Babe, hundreds of people come through a theater like this every night. It's the only theater in fifty miles. She'd be another face in the crowd to anyone working here."

Laurie cast one final glance at the darkened theater. "Sure. Let's drive around and see if we spot her."

They got into the car, Gabe sliding behind the wheel. He saw the look of worry on Laurie's face and put his hand on hers. "Hey, I'm sure she's fine. Teenagers wander off sometimes. They probably got bored of the movie and went for burgers or something."

Laurie stared ahead. "But what if they didn't?" *What if … I don't know. She's been acting so weird lately. Moody, argumentative.*"

Gabe glanced into the rearview mirror and backed out of the parking spot. He felt a chill despite the warm summer air. "She's a teenager, babe. I know it stinks, but that's how they are sometimes."

Laurie stared out the front window. "Maybe they went to Jill's house?" She tapped the screen until Kay Bridges appeared in her contacts. "I'll call Kay and see."

"Good idea," Gabe said.

Her phone rang a couple of times before Kay picked up.

Laurie, hi, what's up?" Kay asked. "Power out for you guys, too?"

"Oh, I don't know, actually," Laurie said. "We're not at home. Kay, listen, are the girls at your place?"

"No, they were going to the movies. Why?"

Laurie let out a long sigh. "We're at the theater. When the power blew, we came to pick them up but can't find them anywhere."

"That's weird," Kay replied. "I wouldn't worry too much though. They probably got bored and went for a drive. I know Kevin, and he's a good kid. I'm sure they can't get into too much trouble."

"Still, could you try and get ahold of Jill? Maybe find out where they are?"

"Sure thing, Laurie," Kay replied. "But don't stress. I'll give her a call and let you know as soon as I hear from her."

"That'd be great, Kay. Appreciate it."

"No problem. Talk soon," Kay said

"Thanks. Bye," Laurie replied, and hung up.

Gabe turned out of the lot onto the road, following the same direction the trucks had gone. Gabe glanced over at Laurie. She was casting her gaze back and forth along the side of the road as the car approached downtown. They drove past a small general store and gas station, but the lights were off there as well. He briefly saw the "Closed" sign in the front window as they sped past. Soon only trees lined the roadsides again.

"We'll find her, Miss. Don't worry."

She slumped back into her seat. "Sure. I'm sure she's fine. Probably hanging out with her friends recording the blown transformer for the clicks or the likes or whatever."

"Right," Gabe said. "It's all about the clicks."

Laurie laughed, and Gabe felt a wave of relief as the tension broke, even if only for a moment. "We'll have to get to know her friends a little better if we move up here, I suppose," Laurie added. "I'd gotten used to all her crazy friends back home, but this'll be a whole new world."

"So, are you thinking this might be the right move for us?" Gabe asked.

"Maybe, Gabe. I don't know. I mean, it could work," Laurie said. "But I don't know if I want to quit my job, pack up, and move us all out into the middle of nowhere. I mean, this is where wildfires happen, you know?"

"I get it," he said. "You're not up for it."

"Look, I get the appeal. It might be kind of nice to live in the country for a while. Have an actual house. Not keep paying money to landlords. It's a lot to think about right now."

"It's not a bad place to live," Gabe said. "Quiet, which I hated when I was Kimmie's age, of course. And it's got its quirks and weirdos like anywhere. But it's not a bad place at all."

She sighed. "Yeah, it's not bad. I promise I'll think about it."

"That's all I'm asking, babe," he said. "Just for you to consider it. Think about how it could be up here. You could find work in town or start your own business. We've got a little savings, enough to keep us going for a while until we land on our feet. Especially if we're not hemorrhaging it to the landlord."

"I get it, Gabe, really. I'll think about it. But for now, can we focus on finding Kimmie?"

Chapter Twenty-Seven

Jill sat on the prow of the boat, her feet dangling over the edge as she splashed her toes in the cool water. Kimmie and Kevin had been gone a while. "Are you guys done making out yet?" she shouted. "Come on, let's go!"

She checked her phone again for the tenth time in as many minutes, but there was still no signal. The darkness, the silence, was starting to get to her. Her imagination conjured stories of people lost in the woods, of the old guy who went missing on the lake a few years ago. What was his name again? He was a local guy; she remembered her dad saying what a shame it was, as he remembered the guy from when he was a kid. Barnes. That was his name, Mike Barnes. "Huh," Jill grunted as she made the connection, wondering if he was related to Kimmie and her family.

She was in thought, ruminating on these details, when she heard footsteps crunching fallen leaves in the distance, coming toward her. When she looked up, she saw Kimmie coming out from a copse of trees. Her hair was mussed, and she was breathing heavily. "You okay?" she called. Kimmie jogged forward and Jill looked past her. "Where's Kevin?"

Kimmie hitched a thumb over her shoulder. "That way," she said, pointing back up the hill. Her voice was low, gravelly. Like she had a sore throat and was forcing herself to be heard. She stomped into the water at the shore's edge. Water splashed ahead of her as she clambered up into the boat.

"Well, is he coming?" Jill asked as she held out a hand to help Kimmie up over the gunwale. "I'm getting cold, it's creepy out here, and I want to go home."

Kimmie glared at her. Smiled, a wide, wolfish grin. "Want to play a prank on him?"

Jill smirked, looked back toward the trees, then back at Kimmie. "Okay, what've you got in mind?"

"Let's take the boat and ditch him," Kimmie said. "Just for a bit. We'll come back in half an hour." Kimmie slid into the driver's seat, reached for the ignition key.

Jill put her hand on Kimmie's. "I don't know if that's a good idea. I mean, do you really think you can drive this thing?"

Kimmie nodded. "Oh, sure. I think I've got it figured out, it's really pretty simple."

"Okay, but we'll come right back, right? Just long enough to scare him?"

"Right," Kimmie said, and turned the ignition. It caught easily, and she shifted the engine into reverse. "Hey, grab that anchor up, will you?"

Jill gave a yank on the fluorescent nylon cable attached to the anchor, and it pulled free from the sandy bank. She pulled on the line, hand over hand, until the anchor had left a runnel in the sand, and disappeared into the water. She lugged it up over the side of the boat and dropped it to the deck. "That thing's heavier than it looks," she said, rubbing her arms. "Guess I can skip arm day tomorrow."

Kimmie gunned the engine, and the boat lurched into reverse, pulling away from the island. She backed up until she was sure she was clear of the beach, put it in forward, and slowly turned it away from the island. She drove into the night slowly, water slapping and lapping at the hull as she did.

"You sure you know what you're doing?" Jill asked, as the boat cruised away from the island. It shuddered and rocked slightly as it chopped through the glassy water.

"It'll be fine," Kimmie said. "A little further."

Jill watched the island recede in the distance. After not too long, it was nothing more than a dark blob, indistinct from the surrounding darkness of the moonless night. "Can we stop now? I think this is far enough."

Kimmie cut the acceleration and the boat slowed to a halt. She left the engine to idle and stood up. "See anything?"

Jill peered into the darkness. "Nope. Can't hear him either. Maybe he hasn't come down to the beach yet."

"Maybe," Kimmie replied. She reached down to the deck, grabbed the nylon cable attached to the anchor and began to coil it.

Jill leaned forward. "Give him a few minutes to worry, but we really should go back and get him." Her phone chirped, the electronic ringing breaking the still silence on the lake. Jill looked at the screen, "Oh, it's my mom," she said. She waggled a finger at Kimmie and said, "Hang on, let me take …"

She cut off mid-sentence as Kimmie dropped the coiled nylon cable around her throat and pulled it tight. Jill dropped her phone, which bounced off the gunwale and then into the water. She grabbed at the rope, tried to spin around and yell, "Hey, not funny!" but all that came out was a choked gargle. Then she saw the anchor fly past her and disappear into the black water.

Hands shoved at her back, and she toppled overboard, splashing into the cold lake. She scrabbled at the coils around her neck but could not get them loose. The anchor dragged her down, and she flailed around with her hands, trying to grab hold of the cable which attached it to her, but her hands found nothing.

Dark spots swam in her vision, and she was becoming lightheaded. Then a surging movement and her face was full of bubbles as she was dragged forward at tremendous speed. She would have drowned if her neck hadn't snapped first.

***

Kimmie gripped the steering wheel with white knuckled fists. The boat sped forward, water erupting behind it in its wake. Dark, nonsensical, nightmarish thoughts squirmed around in her mind as she drove the boat. Anger and hatred crawled like ants through the labyrinth of her brain. She was slowly becoming less Kimmie, and more the Other. The thing in the darkness, the thing from the cave. Its malignancy spreading through her, subsuming her being, her essence.

It wormed through her brain, a strange feeling of wanting an escape, of freedom. To be free of the island, of the lake. To be out in the wider world, free to roam. Free to feed at will. Free to feed.

She saw the shore approaching ahead of her. It wasn't the docks where the boat had been moored up, but it would do. She aimed the boat toward the shore and cut the engine, but the boat plowed up onto the shore just the same. With a thud and a bump, it came to rest a few feet above the water line.

Kimmie hopped over the boat's edge, landing on the sand. She looked behind the boat and saw the yellow nylon anchor cord was taut. *Almost free,* she thought. Or the thing in her thought. They were now almost one and the same, the essence of Kimmie almost completely absorbed by the essence of the Other.

She trudged up the shore and soon was in the woods that surrounded the lake. She caught the scent of smoke on the wind as she rose above the waterline. Distant, but strong. She continued walking forward into the woods, not sure where she was. She thought that she'd come to ground somewhere between the dock where they'd started and the little pier that shot out from the beach at her house.

She was trying to get her bearings when she heard a rumbling and saw a distant light flash by. The road was ahead. The highway that cut through town and ran past her house. That was enough to get her started. She hiked forward, climbing over fallen trees, crunching the detritus of the forest underfoot. Down into the creek, up the other side, and soon she was on the side of the highway. She was standing on the gravel shoulder looking up and down the road when a large trailer truck sped by in a roar of diesel engine and tires grinding on asphalt. She staggered back as a gust of wind hammered into her. The truck barreled toward town, its taillights disappeared around the bend in the road, and it was gone.

To her right, the road would take her back to town. To the left, it wound through the woods toward her house. She wondered if her parents were home. If they'd even noticed she was late, wondered where she was. Or were they still out on their date? Leaving her to fend for herself in a strange town with kids she barely knew? Anger bubbled up in her like a fountain of resentment.

Kimmie—or maybe it was the hate filled entity which was directing her, seeding her thoughts—decided she'd go back to the house. She turned left, to the north, and began the walk through the woods. She'd wait there for her parents, and when they arrived— oh, she'd give them such a big surprise.

CHAPTER TWENTY-EIGHT

Shawna Lasher's head throbbed, and a pulsing ringing in her ears drove her awake as she slowly rose to consciousness. The ringing became clear as the office main phone line, not the aftermath of a head wound. She got up onto one elbow, opened her eyes, and saw the carnage.

Officer West lay broken and twisted on the floor of the office. Shards of glass from the broken windows scattered across the beige linoleum floor glittered like ice from the cold white fluorescent light overhead.

She sprang to her feet as the iPhone in her pocket started ringing. The theme to *Miami Vice*, which instantly let her know it was Officer Millsap calling. She fumbled at the phone with shaky fingers, thumbing the answer button and raising it to her ear. "Millsap, I need you at the station ASAP. West's dead."

A second's pause, then a crackle. "What the hell's going on? Downtown's blacked out, the EMTs are missing, and you say West's dead?"

"Wait, what about downtown?" she said.

"I heard it on the scanner, where've you been?"

"Knocked out," she said. "I'll ..." she trailed off. "I'll try to explain when you get here. I'm not really sure what happened."

"I'm heading into town right now, but the fire department's already there. Sounds like it was a downed transformer, and they're dealing with it. PG&Es on the way. What happened to West? Do you need me to come back to the station?"

Lasher's head throbbed. She looked at West's crushed and mangled body, tried to piece together the events. "No. No, I need you downtown. I'll deal with the mess here. And don't mention anything about West to anyone until I can figure out what the fuck is going on."

"Roger that," Millsap said. "What a fucking night."

"You have no idea," Lasher replied, and hung up. She turned to look again at the destruction in the station's lobby. West's eyes stared lifelessly back at her, dull glints in the darkness, like the shattered glass strewn across the lobby floor. She grabbed the handset on the office phone and dialed the county morgue. The phone rang a few times and then picked up.

"County," the tired woman's voice on the other end said.

"Vera?" Lasher asked.

"Speaking." The line was crackly, distorted. "Who's this?"

"Vera, this is Shawna Lasher over at Golden Oaks P.D."

"Oh, heya Shawna. What can I do for you?"

Lasher took a deep breath and released it slowly. "I've got an officer down here at the PD. I need someone to come pick him up. Discreetly."

"Oh, gee, Shawna, that's too bad. What happened?"

"Can't go into it now. Send Grainger and Bogan back ASAP."

"Hey, speaking of those two, they didn't say anything to you about stopping for food or taking the scenic route, did they?" Vera asked.

"No, not at all. Why?"

"Ain't seen 'em yet," Vera said. "It's only a twenty-minute drive from you to us, and they should've been here an hour ago."

"Yeah, they should have been," Lasher said. "Look, I have to go. Send someone, okay?"

"Sure thing. Their shift was almost over anyway. I'll get someone right out. In the meantime, don't touch the body, etcetera and all that. You know the drill."

"Yeah, I know the drill," Shawna replied. "Thanks, Vera." After she hung up, Lasher took a rough wool blanket out of a storage closet and draped it over West's body. *Screw procedure*, she thought. She wasn't going to let him lie there like discarded furniture until the ghouls at the morgue could come.

Once he was covered, she went back to the door that led to the cells Arlen had spent the weekend in. Through the mesh-reinforced glass window, she saw Barney sprawled out in front of the cell where they'd left him. She couldn't tell if he was breathing or not and had no interest in going in to find out.

She picked up the phone to call the Fire Department and find out what was happening downtown when she suddenly thought about the security cameras in the building. Looking up, she saw the telltale red dots of recording equipment arrayed strategically around the lobby and office. Almost every inch of the building was under constant surveillance.

"Hot damn," she said out loud. The sound of her voice in the stillness of the building seemed odd, almost ghostly. It spurred her into action.

Lasher slid behind the front desk and woke the computer up from its electronic sleep. She logged in, fumbling her password the first time due to nervousness, but soon was into the system. A few mouse clicks and she brought up the cameras' archive files. It didn't take her long to load up the last few hours of recordings and scroll back to where it all started.

She was looking down into the holding cells as Arlen emerged from his cell and squatted to pet his dog. She saw Barney growling, and West pushed Arlen back and suddenly it was chaos. Static filled the screen as the image churned in and out.

She backed the footage up and started it over, but the same thing happened. Something had interfered with the recording; the playback was fine. She watched as Barney began to choke and cough, and fell to the ground. There was a pause while she watched through the pulsing haze of white noise static as Arlen and West stepped back from the dog. West shot at the ground.

It looked like he fired his weapon three times, but with the image distorted by static she wasn't completely sure.

Then through a haze of static, West and Arlen ran from the room, burst through the doors into the office. She watched herself approach, and the ensuing chaos. Saw herself jump out of the way of West's gunshot, and when she cracked her head on the front desk. She thought it was like watching Arlen and West pantomime carnage. West twitched and spasmed and scrabbled at his throat, and was still. The ravens burst into the room and swarmed West's body as Arlen made his escape. And then they were gone.

The events played out on screenas she recalled them and filled in a few missing elements. But it raised more questions than it answered. What had West been shooting at? What caused his frantic retreat from the holding cells? She scrolled back, watched the footage all over from the beginning, trying to make some sense of it. She zoomed in on West choking and saw indentations where it was as if some unseen presence was constricting his throat, saw his skin turn dark as it began to freeze.

She stared at the blanket which covered West's body. How would she explain this to anybody? She thought of the bodies at the vet's office earlier, Abby and Doc Hoeger all twisted and broken. What had Millsap and Vera said about the EMTs missing?

She called back to the Coroner's office from her desk phone. Vera answered on the third ring. "Vera, this is Officer Lasher again," she barked. "Have Bogan and Grainger reported in yet?"

"Sure don't think so," Vera said. "You want me to go check?"

"Yes, right now," Lasher said.

"Hang on." The line went silent as she was put on hold.

Lasher pulled her cellphone from her pocket and began typing out a message to Millsap. *What's going on downtown?* she tapped onto the tiny glowing keyboard. She waited. Being on hold with both was intolerable, and she had a sinking feeling brewing in her gut that the night was only about to get worse from here. A ping from her cell and a message from Millsap said that everything was *Under control. There was a small fire on the roof of the hardware store, but it's out. Power's still out through most of town.*

She typed, *Stay there for crowd control if you think it's necessary.*

Millsap sent back a thumbs-up emoji just as Vera hopped back on the line. "Yeah, no sign of 'em yet."

"Shit," Lasher muttered.

"Shawna, do you think something happened to them?" Vera said. Lasher could hear in her voice that Vera was hovering somewhere between concern and piqued interest.

"Maybe," Lasher replied. "Very possibly. Do you know what route they were taking back?"

There was a pause as Lasher imagined the gears in Vera's head clunking along for that information. "Well, probably 346 south of town, then over the McConnell bridge. That'd get 'em right here the quickest."

"There's no normal route plan or anything?"

"Nah," Vera said. "They'd probably use whatever route their phone map told them to take. And there's never much traffic that way at this time of night. Or a couple of hours earlier, either, I suppose."

"Makes sense. Okay, thanks Vera," Lasher said. "I'm going to go take a quick look, make sure nothing happened to them. If they show up, squawk me on the radio, will you?"

"Sure thing, Shawna," Vera replied. "And let me know if you find them, I'm starting to get a little worried myself."

"Right, will do," Lasher said, and hung up the phone.

She left the office, lowering the metal security shutters across the shattered front doors of the building and locking them tight. Then she was in her squad car, charging out of the parking lot and screaming down 346 with her sirens blaring.

It wasn't long after that she'd pulled over to the side of the road just before the McConnell bridge over the Graham river. She saw the guard rail in her headlights, torn, twisted, and ruined. It reminded her of West, of Doc Hoeger, and Abby.

She got out of the squad car and approached the drop off on foot, shining a flashlight ahead of her. There were tire tracks in the dirt, branches were broken off the trees near the road, sprawled and splintered across the ground. She kept going until she got to the drop off where the ground sloped away down to the churning water below. She could see the rear of the ambulance rising a few feet out of the water. The cab was fully submerged, and the rear doors closed tight, like teeth clamped down to hold in a secret.

Lasher got back into the squad car and called Millsap. "Millsap," she said when he answered. "I think we have a serious problem."

CHAPTER TWENTY-NINE

Gabe was pulling into a parking space in front of the Get Up and Go diner when Laurie's phone rang. It was the distinct gurgling robot ringtone that let them know Kimmie was calling. Laurie snapped up her phone and answered it as Gabe shut off the car.

"Kimmie, where are you?" Laurie asked quickly. "Are you okay?"

"I'm fine, Mom," Kimmie replied. "I'm home. At the cabin, or whatever. I saw you left a few messages. Why's the power off?"

"Your father and I were worried," Laurie said. "Power's off through the whole town. I guess it reached up as far as the house. Are you with Jill and her friend?"

A pause. "No, they said they wanted to go boating on the lake. Kevin's family has a boat at the docks. So, I came home."

"Kimmie, that wasn't a safe thing to do," Laurie said. "You know better than that. You should have called us, and we'd have come and picked you up."

"Yeah, I guess. But I didn't want to interrupt your date night."

"Well, what's done is done," Laurie said. "Stay at the house, we'll be back soon."

"Okay, Mom," Kimmie said, and hung up. Laurie took the phone from her ear and stared at the screen. At the photo of Kimmie, a few years younger, that had come up when she called.

"So, she's home?" Gabe asked, breaking the silence.

"Yes, she's home," Laurie said. "Apparently, Jill and Kevin decided to go boating on the lake, and Kimmie went home instead."

Gabe started the car's engine and pulled out into the empty road. "Well, at least she was smart enough not to get mixed up in that. I don't like the idea of a bunch of kids zipping around on that lake in the dark."

"I'm surprised it's even open this late," Laurie replied.

"My guess is it isn't," Gabe said. "So much the better she didn't go." Laurie picked up her phone and tapped Kay's contact. After a single ring, the other line picked up.

"Hey, Laurie," Kay said. "Any word? I've been calling Jill's number, but it goes to voicemail."

"Kimmie's back at the lake house," Laurie replied. "She said that Jill and Kevin wanted to take his boat out on the lake and go boating."

"So where are they now?" Kay asked.

"I don't know, Kay, sorry," Laurie said. "Kimmie didn't feel comfortable, so she came home alone. We're going there now, and I'll see if I can get any more info out of her. I'll call you in a bit?"

"Yeah, that'd be great," Kay said.

Laurie could tell she was angry. "You okay?"

"Yeah, I'm sure it's fine," Kay said. "The lake's closed to boats at four though. They shouldn't be out there. I'll be having a talk with Kevin's parents about this."

Laurie grimaced. *Better her than me,* she thought. "Okay, well I'll call you soon and let you know if I can squeeze any more details out of Kimmie."

"'Preciate it," Kay said, and hung up.

"Kay's pissed?" Gabe said.

"So pissed," Laurie replied. "Glad Kimmie wasn't involved in any of that nonsense."

"She may be a surly teenager," Gabe replied. "But she's got a good head on her shoulders. Must get that from you."

"Absolutely," Laurie replied with mock smugness.

They drove up the main road, where they noticed a handful of pedestrians walking toward the downtown, where they could barely see the scarlet flashing of firetruck siren lamps. A couple had flashlights, shining their cold white beams along the sidewalk as they made their way among the darkened buildings. Gabe watched the arcs of light slash back and forth through the gloom as he drove. "Guess this is the most exciting thing to happen in Golden Oaks in a while."

Laurie craned her neck to watch the pedestrians as they drove past. "Hot time in the old town tonight, I guess."

Soon the town was behind them, and they were cruising along the highway road toward their house.

"Small and boring aren't always bad," Laurie said. "Gabe, I'm not making a commitment, but I've been thinking about it, and I'm at least open to the idea of moving. Maybe I do need a change of pace. I love my job, but it's a lot. Might be nice to slow down for a while."

"Yeah?" he said. "That's good to hear. There's a lot of logistics to figure out, of course, but I'm glad to hear you're open to the idea."

"At least to talking about it," she said. "Kimmie might not like it at first, but she'll come around."

Gabe pulled across the road, tires juddering and the car vibrating as it went over the small bridge across the creek. "Yeah, she'll get used to it. The school's not bad, and I'm sure she'll make plenty of friends. The new kid's always a curiosity."

"Not always a good thing," Laurie said.

"Not always, but have to hope for the best, I suppose."

"I suppose," Laurie replied. "And you're right; with the savings on rent, what your dad left us, and our own savings, we'd have a cushion for at least a few months while we settle in. It's a lot to think about, but it might work."

"That's all I'm asking for, miss," Gabe said. "Just think about it."

***

Laurie and Gabe entered the house with the flashlights on their phones illuminating the darkness before them. The house was quiet; still. Gabe stepped through the kitchen and was about to call up the stairs for Kimmie when Laurie put her hand on his arm.

"Let me talk to her," she said, softly.

Gabe paused before saying, "Yeah, you know, maybe this is more of a mom and daughter thing."

Laurie nodded. "That's what I'm thinking. I'll go check on her."

"Sure," Gabe replied. "I'll be down here if you need me."

He stepped to the refrigerator and grabbed a beer. Laurie ascended the stairs, saw Gabe disappear into the kitchen, then heard the creak of the back door opening, and the screen door swing shut with a soft bang. She walked through the upstairs hallway, casting the soft light of her LED flashlight ahead of her. The house seemed unfamiliar, ominous in the darkness. When she got to Kimmie's room, she was unsurprised to find the door closed. She knocked softly and waited. "Kimmie, you in there?"

"Yeah, Mom," Kimmie answered from beyond the closed door. "Come in if you want."

Laurie opened the door and stepped in. "Hey, kiddo," she said. "You okay?" She angled the light toward Kimmie who was lying on top of her bedcovers, still wearing the same clothes she'd had on earlier in the evening.

Kimmie shifted to sit up as the light moved toward her. The shadows in the rumpled covers shifted as she moved on the bed. It looked to Laurie almost like the thin dark ribbons of shadow were moving on their own. Like snakes or worms. But when she held the light firm on Kimmie, it was nothing but rumpled covers and bedding. Kimmie raised her hand to shield her eyes.

"Sorry, kiddo," Laurie said, lowering the light. She placed the phone screen-down on the nightstand, so that the light illuminated the room somewhat. "You sure you're okay?" she asked as she sat on the edge of the bed.

"Yeah, Mom, I'm fine. Tired, you know?"

She looked pale, her hair matted with sweat. "What happened with Jill and her friend?" Laurie asked.

Kimmie rolled her eyes, but Laurie opted not to chastise her for that.

"I told you, Mom," Kimmie said, disdainfully. "They decided they wanted to go for a ride on Kevin's boat. I didn't want to, so I came home instead."

Laurie nodded. "Jill's mom's been trying to get ahold of her, but Jill's not answering. Do you have any idea where they might be?"

Kimmie turned and stared out the window. In the distance, the lake; dark in the moonless night. "No," she replied. "If they're still on the lake, they probably can't get a signal."

"I guess," Laurie said. "Kay's worried, so if you know anything more, I'd like to let her know. They didn't say what they'd be doing after?"

Kimmie turned back to look at Laurie. "No," she said again. "They didn't say anything about what they might do later. And I didn't ask. Maybe they went skinny dipping or something dumb like that."

Laurie let out a long sigh. "Okay, well, I guess there's nothing more to do for now. If you think of anything, let me know?"

"Okay, Mom," Kimmie said, and rolled over, facing toward the window again and away from Laurie.

Laurie got up, collected her phone, but as she got to the door, she stopped and turned back to her daughter. "Kimmie?"

"Yeah, Mom?" Kimmie replied.

"I'm not happy about you walking home by yourself, but I'm proud of you for not joining the others on the boat. That was a bad decision they made." Laurie waited for Kimmie to reply, but no answer came. "Maybe take a quick shower before you go to bed?" she suggested. "You might feel better after you clean up a bit." Again, no answer. She slipped out of the room, closing the door behind her.

She went back down the stairs, through the kitchen, and out to the back porch where she found Gabe sitting at the top of the steps to the back lawn. There was a slight breeze in the air, bringing the smell of cool, clean water off the lake. But under that, there was still a tinge of smoke from town.

She'd forgotten how hot the night was. Beads of sweat formed on her forehead almost the instant she'd stepped outside. She sat next to Gabe and reached a hand out toward his beer. Instinctively, with the sort of psychic connection born of many years together, he handed the can over to her. Laurie pressed the cold can against her brow, feeling the relaxing chill wash away the stress which had scrunched her forehead into knots.

"How's she doing?" Gabe asked.

Laurie took a sip of the beer and handed it back to him. "I think she's fine. Maybe a little out of sorts; grumpy and tired."

Gabe drained the last of the beer. "Sometimes I forget how hard it was to be a teenager."

"It was the worst," Laurie said.

Gabe swished the can around, feeling for a last drop or two. It was empty. "What a day. I'm beat."

He crunched the middle of the can, and squeezed it flat between the sole of his shoe and the wooden stair he'd been resting it on.

Laurie reached her arm out and rubbed the palm of her hand over his back. "Come on. Let's go to bed"—she stood up—"Get a good night's sleep, and tomorrow we can start fresh in the morning."

He stood up, took her hand, and opened the screen door. "Sounds great. I'm going to sleep like the dead."

"You and me both," Laurie replied.

***

Kimmie shuffled along the hallway between her room and where her parents slept. Her feet barely rising from the floor as she stepped through the gloom, approaching their door. Her eyes were glazed, distant, as if she were staring through the walls, across space, and into other unseen worlds as she placed her hand on the cold metal doorknob. She paused, listening. Aside from the shallow sound of her own breath and a faint creak somewhere in the house, she heard nothing.

She gripped the knob and turned it slowly, feeling the latch open. With slight pressure, she pushed the door open until it swung free by its own momentum. It opened a few feet and stopped. Kimmie stepped into the room.

A slight breeze rippled the linen curtains over the windows and washed across her. It fluttered her hair against the nape of her neck as she stepped further into the room. In front of her, her parents lay snuggled together, entwined under a thin blanket, fast asleep.

A twitching at the back of her mind, and an itchy, stretching feeling crawled out from the base of her skull and spread across her scalp and back. Distantly, as if in a dream, she felt her hands flex, her fingers spasming open and closed tight in fists. Like she was gripping, squeezing something.

Choking something.

She stepped forward and stretched out her hands, fingers splayed out and brought them toward her dad's throat.

And from outside, far in the distance, a cacophony of squawks and screeching bird noises.

Kimmie took a reflexive step backward, her hands falling by her sides.

She blinked, and suddenly awareness came rushing at her like an oncoming car. Why was she in her parents' room staring at them as they slept? How had she gotten here? The last thing she remembered was talking to her mom before drifting off to sleep. She retreated from the room and closed the door behind her. She had a vague memory of going to the lake with her friends earlier, but that was a blur as well. How had she gotten back to the house?

Standing in the darkened hallway, she felt her heart racing. How had she gotten out of bed, snuck into her parents' room, and had no memory of doing any of it? And why did she come to be reaching toward her dad like she was going to try and strangle him?

Kimmie went back into her room and sat on the edge of her bed. Her head ached, a dull throb which started in the base of her neck and crawled over her scalp to her forehead. Maybe her mom had been right about taking a hot bath or a shower. She slipped out of her clothes, dumping them in a heap next to her bed, and wrapped herself in a soft blue terrycloth bathrobe.

Once she was in the bathroom, she turned on the faucets in the tub, letting it fill slowly with hot water. She sat on the edge of the tub, watching the water rise slowly, churning at the foot of the tub where the faucet poured into it, splashing and steaming. Within a few minutes, the tub was about two thirds full, and the room was thick with steam. She rose, taking off her robe and hanging it on the back of the door. Before getting into the tub, she stood in front of the mirrored medicine cabinet, wiping away the steam built up on the smooth glass. The reflection staring back at her looked small and tired. Dark circles under her eyes, her skin pale, and bruises on her upper arms made her think of a wraith in one of those Japanese horror movies she'd watched at a sleep over a few years ago.

She slipped into the tub, letting the hot water surround her. She felt knots in her shoulders and back slowly release; tension knots she hadn't even realized she had been carrying. Kimmie lay back in the tub, letting the water rise up around her shoulders until she was almost completely submerged. Only her head and bent knees rose above the water.

The water began to gurgle as it flowed into the overflow drain, and she stretched out her legs, placing her feet over the valve to stop the flow. She noticed her ankles and shins, blue and bruised from where they'd become tangled up in the lake only a couple of days before. *What had grabbed me?* she thought. *I wonder what happened to that guy who pulled me out of the lake?* She closed her eyes and lay against the back rim of the tub.

She struggled to recall his name but it came to her: Mr. Gaines, but he'd told her to call him Charlie. She saw his face in her mind's eye, kindly, but sort of sad. Her image of him shifted. His eyes went white, rolled back in his head. His mouth opened in a silent scream, and he disappeared into darkness. But the worst part of the image, the part that startled her upright and threw her eyes wide open, was that it was from her perspective. Not that she *saw* Charlie, but she saw him as if she was killing him. And she knew for certain that he was dead. Dead like Jill and Kevin.

What had happened to them? She had a vague memory of Kevin falling into darkness. Of Jill disappearing underwater. But it was all a glassy, rippling blur.

How was she going to explain the night's events to her parents when she couldn't even explain it to herself?

She was shivering, despite the warmth of the tub. Gooseflesh marched along her arms and back, puckered the skin along her legs. She pulled the drain plug at the other end of the tub and let the water flow away. After toweling off, she snuck back into her room, got into her Taylor Swift sleep shirt, her safety and comfort talisman, and crawled into bed. She pulled the covers up to her chin, rolled over and buried her face in the pillow.

Tears welled up in her eyes and were quickly absorbed by the pillow's white cotton cover. Kimmie was physically and emotionally exhausted. The realization of recent events was pouring through her and she began to feel darkness return in the recesses of her mind. A siren call deep within her, tugging at her thoughts and memories. A ravenous malevolence, gnawing away at her mind and memories and replacing them with something else. Soon, she slipped into darkness.

Chapter Thirty

Officer Shawna Lasher stood under the pale white glow of overhead fluorescent lights, surrounded by gleaming steel walls with innocuous drawers built into them. She wondered how many corpses were held in the refrigerated compartments beyond those doors. She hated the morgue. She'd only been here a handful of times since she started with the Golden Oaks PD, and never with more than one corpse to look at. Now she stood in front of six bodies laid out on metal presentation trolleys. All from the same day. And there was also Peter Guilford, the lifeguard from the lake whose body had yet to be recovered. Not to mention Charlie Gaines and Darryl McEwen, who she was assuming at this point were bona fide missing persons. A slight chill in the cooled room made her shiver as she looked at the bodies.

Four of them had come in together. It had taken some finagling, but a tow truck had finally managed to pull the ambulance from the river, and up the side of the ravine. Miles Granger and Heidi Bogan were both dead in the front seats of the vehicle. Doc Hoeger and Abby were still strapped in tight in the back. They were lined up side by side, and Lasher took in the row of bodies one by one. Each body was twisted and broken in one way or another. Hoeger's head cranked at an unnatural angle on a clearly broken neck. He and Abby both had blackened streaks around their throats, their wrists. The same marks appeared on Miles and Heidi next to them. Eyes wide open in terror on all four.

Next to them was Officer West. His body twisted and torn as Lasher remembered. Arm bent to the side, leg twisted out of shape. The same dark purple burns and bruises across his exposed skin. And finally, Arlen McEwen, the cause of the mess in town. Splinters of glass peppered his face, and his right eye socket was a ruin. A crater of blood and torn flesh, and a distorted eruption of bone where the bolt cutters had torn through the side of his head. The EMTs who had pulled him from his car said he'd died instantly when the cutters had perforated him. The strange angle of his neck and shattered limbs had happened after the truck's cabin had collapsed. *One of these things is not like the other,* she thought, taking in the row of bodies. A door at the other end of the room swung open, and Paul Parsons shuffled through. He'd been the county coroner for a few years now and always looked like he hadn't slept in a week. He was still dragging his lab coat over one arm as he stepped through.

"Hey, Shawna, sorry to keep you waiting," he said, taking a big bite out of a sandwich that smelled strongly of eggs and mayonnaise.

"That's okay," Lasher replied. "I've been taking a quick look at the … what do you call them? Specimens? Bodies?"

He shrugged. "Whatever you want. You're not going to offend them or anything." He popped the last of the sandwich into his mouth, chewed a couple of times, and spoke around the food, "Oh, I should warn you, the Mayor's already on his way down."

"Shit," Lasher grunted. "Just what I—"

"What the hell's going on here today, Lasher?" a gruff voice erupted from the other end of the room as Mayor Tom Anderson burst through the swinging doors. "Six bodies—one a *cop*—and a missing lifeguard in one day? What the hell are we paying you for?"

He came uncomfortably close to her. Close enough that she could smell the sour stink of rotgut whiskey on his breath, noticed splashed drops of the same on his off-white shirt.

Lasher took a deep breath, let it out slowly. "Well, Mr. Mayor, that's what we're trying to figure out."

The mayor put his hands on his hips, a strangely aggressive gesture.

"Well, let's figure it out. Because this town's not big enough for folks to keep dying off at this rate." He turned to the coroner. "Okay Paul, use that big brain of yours and tell us what the hell's going on."

"Right," Paul said. He washed his hands in a nearby steel basin, and put on a pair of pale blue gloves. The tension between the mayor and the cop was palpable and made him nervous. He hated conflict, and fortunately there usually wasn't much of that in his job. *Stiffs don't argue,* he'd often said to his wife.

"I took a look at them as they came in," he said when he was back at the trolleys. "On the surface, what most of them have in common are these dark bruises," he pointed at the dark marks on Doc Hoeger's neck. "They've all got them at various places on their bodies."

"What caused them?" Tom interrupted.

Paul stood up straight. "That, I'm not sure of. They look like constriction marks, like they were tied up tight. Something like that."

"What, with like ropes or something?" Tom asked.

Paul shook his head slightly. "No, not ropes." He grabbed a magnifying glass off the nearby instruments tray. "Take a look closer," he said, handing the lens to Lasher.

She held it up to the bruises around West's throat. "No fibers. And no friction marks."

"The hell does that mean?" Tom grunted.

"It means whatever caused this was really smooth, basically. Like a snake or something."

"So, are we looking for killer snakes? Or someone going around throwing boa constrictors at folks?" Tom asked, incredulously. "That's the dumbest thing I ever heard. Lasher, you were there when West was killed. What the hell happened?"

Lasher stared at the mayor, trying to figure out how to explain what actually happened without him putting her in a straightjacket, slapping her with a 5150, and giving her a one-way ticket to the local psych ward.

She spoke carefully, "It was dark, so I'm not sure exactly. And I was knocked out for most of it. I watched the security tapes, and they weren't much help."

"Well, I suggest you think about it *real* hard," Tom said.

Lasher looked from Tom to Paul, like she was hoping Paul would proclaim some scientific anomaly that could explain it all away. But of course, he didn't. "Arlen's dog was sick. On the video I saw it start coughing up something, that … wait …"

"What?" Tom asked. "What about the damn dog?"

"After we put Doc Hoeger and Abby into the EMTs vehicle, I brought the dog, Barney, back to the station. I was going to release Arlen anyway, and figured I'd give him back his dog while I was there. The dog must've been infested with something, maybe whatever killed West. It must be the same thing that killed Hoeger and Abby."

Paul nodded. "The bruising is similar on all of them. Grainger and Bogan, too. It must've been in the bodies and gotten out when they were en route to the morgue. Killed the EMTs."

"Woah-woah-woah!" Tom exclaimed, waving his hands around like an umpire at a ball game calling someone out. He tapped his open palm onto his upraised fingers and called "Time out!" Lasher remembered that Tom used to coach little league before he became mayor.

"This sounds like some straight-up science fiction monster movie bullshit, and I'm not having it," Tom spat. "I don't care about any monsters, or parasites, or weird snake-throwing carnies or whatever. I'm done here. You two figure this shit out, and make sure it doesn't keep happening."

"Tom," she said, stopping when he glared at her.

"Mr. Mayor, I think we should talk seriously about bringing in the state police."

"Negative. We keep this to ourselves; we fix this ourselves."

"But Mr. Mayor," Paul said.

"End of discussion," the mayor said. He turned before either of them could argue with him any further and stormed out of the office. The wide doors swung shut behind him as he pushed through and disappeared.

Lasher took another deep breath and released it slowly.

"Christ, what an asshole," Paul said.

Lasher burst into laughter. "You said it. I've always hated that son of a bitch."

Paul sighed. "Okay, so we're thinking maybe some kind of parasite? I mean, I've never heard of anything like what you're describing, but who knows?"

Lasher nodded. "It sounds crazy, I know."

"It actually really does," Paul said. "Any idea where it went?"

Lasher leaned back against one of the compartment doors on the wall. "That's just as crazy," she said. "In the surveillance video, West falls to the ground. He's rolling around, choking or something. He's clawing at his throat, and Arlen's helping him. Helping like he's trying to pull something off West, but I can't see what it is. And as West's giving up, these ravens come crashing through the glass doors and swarm him."

"Aren't those doors reinforced?" Paul asked.

"They're not ballistic-rated glass or anything," Lasher replied. "But they should have held up to a bunch of birds."

"That is weird," he said.

"Arlen hoofs it, and the birds, they're swarming around like in that old Hitchcock movie. And the damn birds just disappear. Flew off and that was it. Nothing left behind except for me and West's body." She stared at the cooling corpse of her partner. "Christ, what a mess."

"So, as far as these five go," Paul said, waving his hands toward the corpses. "There does seem to be a commonality in how they died. Strangled and constriction marks all over them. And there's signs of frostbite as well."

"Frostbite?" she said. "That doesn't make any sense. It must've been in the 90s today."

"That's what I'm seeing," he said. "In these bruised areas, the skin is also showing signs of exposure to intense cold."

"What the hell?"

"Indeed," Paul replied. "Of course, with our pal Arlen over here, it's a little more rational what happened. I didn't find any signs on him similar to these others. Seems to have been a simple case of reckless driving."

"Good old Arlen," Lasher added. "He always did march to his own drum."

Paul stepped back from the trolleys and leaned against the edge of a wide desk nearby. "I can run some tests, and investigate further if you'd like. But I gotta tell you, I'm pretty much flummoxed at this point."

"That'd be great," Lasher said. "Give me a call when you have *any* idea what happened."

He stared at the bodies again. "No guarantee, but I'll sure do my best."

"That's all you can do." She grabbed her jacket from where it hung on a hook near the doors. "As soon as you figure out anything, right? Night or day, I don't care."

"You got it ... and hey, if I can make a suggestion, you look beat to hell. Go get some sleep. There's nothing you can do about any of these folks right now."

She nodded. "I'm too keyed up to sleep, but I'll take that under advisement. Doctor's orders, huh?"

"Call it that if you want. Get some rest, will you?"

Lasher tossed a mock salute his way as she left the room.

∗∗∗

Lasher lay on her side of the bed, staring at the ceiling. She occasionally thought it odd that she still thought of it as "her side" despite the fact that she'd slept alone for over two years. She could spread out like a starfish if she wanted to and take up the whole bed. But she still hunkered on one side of the bed like she did when she was still married.

She'd stripped down to her underwear and a sleep tank top, thrown open the windows of her bedroom, and let the cooling night air wash over her. It was warm, even this late at night, but much cooler than it had been earlier in the day.

She was exhausted, but still wired up from the strange events of the day. She'd come home from the morgue intending to spend the next few hours making calls and setting up plans for the following day—until she realized that everyone she needed to talk to was long asleep. Despite wanting to continue the investigation, there really wasn't much more she could do at that point. Not at least until she'd heard back from Paul Parsons.

Tomorrow, she decided, she was going to see about bringing in a team to search the lake for Peter Guilford's body. And what about Charlie Gaines and Darryl McEwen? Echoing Mayor Anderson, she muttered out loud, "What the hell *is* going on in this town?"

Now she really couldn't sleep. She got up, dragged a light bathrobe around her, and headed down the hall into her small home office. It wasn't much more than a computer desk, a bookshelf filled with Tom Clancy, David Baldacci, and P.D. James novels. A few police procedure manuals rounded out the shrine to crime.

She flipped open the laptop on her desk, which sprang to life instantly. It didn't take long before she was logged into the station's network and accessing the files she wanted. She poured a couple of fingers of bourbon from a bottle she kept on her desk into a lowball glass that lived there as well. Taking a sip of the smooth brown liquor, she leaned back in her chair and read the file on-screen.

The police report taken earlier in the day at the lake was brief but detailed. And it listed a few witnesses. Jill Bridges and Kimberly Barnes. She knew the Bridgeses, as she did most people who'd lived in the town for more than a few years. She didn't know the Barneses, but remembered that Gabe Barnes was the guy who Arlen had assaulted a couple of days ago. And Mike Barnes was his dad. His dad who'd also gone missing on the lake. She drained the tumbler of bourbon, felt the warmth spread from her gut.

Shawna Lasher wasn't superstitious, didn't give in to ghost stories and fairy tales. But she also had been around long enough to think there were too many connections here, too many coincidences. All this added up to something weird. She made a quick note to re-interview Jill and Kimberly first thing in the morning.

She poured herself another measure of bourbon. Swirled it in the glass, watched how the light rippled across its surface and thought of Peter disappearing into the depths of the lake. Mike Barnes in the lake. Too many coincidences.

She wanted to know exactly what those kids had seen, but she needed to get someone looking for Peter. Unfortunately, West was the only dive-qualified member of the Golden Oaks PD. There was a team up in Tahoe she could call. It didn't take her long to get them on the phone, even at the late hour. Plans were made, and the dive team lead contact said they'd be in Golden Oaks the next morning.

Shawna drained the glass and stumbled back to bed. She could tell already tomorrow was going to be a long day. May as well sleep while she could. She was out before she knew it.

CHAPTER THIRTY-ONE

Thoughts and images squirmed around in Kimmie's mind. Memories of old friends merged with vistas of alien hellscapes. She had an image of her feet tucked into Chuck Taylor high top sneakers, vaulting forward as she swung on a playground swing. It felt like the swing from her old elementary school, and around her she saw a few yards of the blacktop asphalt playground. But beyond that, a swirling, whirling crimson sky, bat-like reptilian creatures flying across it. Volcanic smoke choking the air, and in the distance, the cry of alien chittering.

Her mind swam with visions of the modern and primeval worlds, melding, merging. Flowing into and through each other like multiple film strips jammed into an insane projection device. Blackness spurted forward in the center of her vision, began to spread out, reaching toward her from some distant point, filling her view until all was shadow and cold.

And a distant ringing. She was vaguely aware of the sound of her mother's ringtone chiming somewhere in the house. Sunlight filtered through the lowered slats of Kimmie's window shades, glowing through her closed eyelids as she slowly rose to consciousness.

Her eyes were gritty and gummy as she rubbed them with the back of her arm. She opened them slowly, adjusting to the over-bright light. Even with her bedroom window facing away from the sunrise, the room felt too bright to her. The sheets irritated her. They felt itchy and rough, and she wondered if her mother had changed them while Kimmie had been out. She peeled back the covers of her bed and lowered her feet to the floor.

The floor similarly felt strange. She felt every knurl, every tiny groove and rough spot in the wooden slats with her feet. Without changing her sleep shirt, she slid on a pair of sweatpants and headed downstairs. Her head throbbed, and she had a sour, acrid taste in her mouth. When she came into the kitchen, her mother was on the back porch talking on her phone. Kimmie poured a glass of water from the cold pitcher in the fridge. She took a mouthful of it, swished it around in her mouth and spat it out into the sink.

She watched passively as dark threads slipped through the water and ran down the drain with the rest of the fluid. She drank the rest of the glass down in two gulps, and poured another. She was finishing the second glass when her mother came in from the porch.

"Morning, Kimmie," she said. Her face had a worried caul over it, her brows furrowed together in a way Kimmie knew all too well. "That was Mrs. Bridges on the phone. Jill's mom."

Kimmie swallowed a mouthful of water. "Sure, I know who Mrs. Bridges is, Mom."

"Of course," Laurie said. "Jill never came home last night, and Mrs. Barnes is really worried. She spoke with that boy's parents, too —Kevin?—He never came home either. And their boat is missing."

"Well, what do you want me to do about it?" Kimmie said. "I told you they were going to go for a ride on the lake, and I left."

"Hey, lighten up on the attitude, miss," Laurie said. "This is serious."

"Okay, Mom," Kimmie said. She felt a tugging at the back of her mind. Like something pushing or prodding her, probing her memories. "What about Kevin's car?" she said. "Did they find that?"

"It was parked in the lot near the boat dock," Laurie replied. Laurie sighed and crossed her arms in front of her. "You sure there's nothing else you can think of? Nothing about what they said they were going to do or where they were going later?"

"Well, maybe they met up with some other people, I don't know. Maybe they ran off to Reno and got married by an Elvis impersonator, or the boat sank or something."

"God, I hope they're okay," Laurie said. "Kay—Mrs. Barnes is really worried. If you think of anything else that might be helpful, please let me know?"

"Okay, Mom," Kimmie said again. Kimmie gazed through the kitchen window, across the small back yard, through the trees, and across the lake. Distantly, a small crest rising above the lake's surface, she saw the island. And suddenly a sense of freedom washed over her. She felt a vague stirring of memory, images of Jill and Kevin, and churning water and darkness. Slipping the rope around Jill's neck. Shoving Jill over the side of the boat and a sense of grim satisfaction as the anchor dragged her under.

Kimmie felt like she should feel some sense of remorse. She knew what she'd done was wrong, but she didn't feel it. It was a curious feeling, not caring. She watched as Laurie poured herself a cup of coffee. Laurie filled the cup, added milk and sugar. Took a sip and looked up, saw Kimmie watching her.

"You okay, kiddo?" Laurie asked. "What are you thinking about?"

Kimmie was thinking about taking the carving knife out of the knife block nearby. About shoving it into Laurie's throat and the blood running out like a scarlet river, splashing and flooding onto the floor. She was thinking about carving her mother's body open, and tearing out her innards, arranging them around her like a hybrid painting of Jackson Pollock and Francisco De Goya. She was thinking about going upstairs and taking an ax to her father's head while he slept in. But what she said was, "Nothing."

And in the back of her mind, a growing buzzing, like a swarm of angry insects rising from a smoke-induced stupor. She shook her head, clearing the cobwebs from her mind. "I think I might go for a walk later. Maybe explore downtown a little more."

Laurie took a box of cereal down from the cupboard. "I can give you a ride, if you want."

Kimmie shook her head, her hair swinging as she did. "No, that's okay. It's a nice walk."

"Make sure to give the road plenty of space," Laurie added. "Cars go pretty fast along that road."

"Sure, Mom," Kimmie said.

Laurie could almost hear Kimmie rolling her eyes. "Well, let me know if you decide to go." She reached into her wallet and pulled out a twenty-dollar bill. "Here, take this, for lunch or an emergency or anything."

Kimmie took the bill and shoved it into the pocket of her sweatpants. "Thanks, Mom," she said, and left the kitchen. She was climbing the stairs to her room when Gabe stepped out of his bedroom.

"Morning, sunshine," he said, yawning. "You sleep well?"

She looked at him standing at the top of the stairs, wearing the ratty old Star Wars bathrobe he refused to throw away because she'd given it to him for Father's Day when she was four. She imagined shoving him down the stairs, of him tumbling as he plummeted down, the snap of his neck and his head twisting around backward as he hit the landing.

"Yeah, I guess," she said, walking around him. "Oh, you should talk to Mom. Jill and her friend are still missing, and Mom's freaking out."

"Oh, hell, that's not good," Gabe said. "You doing okay?"

She turned on him. "I'm *fine!* Why does everyone keep asking me if I'm okay?"

Gabe took a step back as if slapped. "Hey, take a breath there, kiddo."

"And stop calling me kiddo!" she shouted, before storming into her room, slamming the door so hard it shook the frame.

Gabe stared at the door, then continued down the stairs. When he was halfway down the steps, he saw Laurie coming around from the kitchen.

She looked up at him, raised her hands palm up and whispered, "What's going on?"

He got to the bottom of the stairs and shrugged. "Beats the hell out of me. She said her friends are still missing?"

Laurie nodded. "She must be worried."

"I'd imagine," Gabe replied. He took her hand and gave it a quick squeeze. "I'm sure that's it. She's stressed, anxious. Made some new friends, and … well, who knows what happened? Let's hope for the best, I suppose."

"Sure," Laurie said, and took his hand, leading him into the kitchen. "There's hot water for coffee if you want any."

"Absolutely." He went over to the coffee maker, then noticed it was cool, the power light dead black. "Power's still out, huh?" He began to make himself a cup, spooning granules of instant coffee into a mug, then pouring hot water over them.

"Yeah," she replied. "Hope they get it started up again soon. It's going to be a hot one, and I don't want the stuff in the fridge to go bad."

"Keep the fridge closed as much as possible," Gabe said. "I can try and pick up some ice in town maybe. Most supermarkets have a backup generator, right?"

Laurie shook her head. "Maybe a basic one, but that's for running the lights and stuff until they can get customers and employees out."

"Oh, gotcha. I guess that makes sense." He stirred his coffee, the spoon tinkling against the edge of the mug. "Should I head into town and try and get some ice? Before it all melts?"

She shook her head. "I wouldn't bother. If the power went out last night, it'll mostly be melted by now. They're going to have to toss a ton of food."

"That sucks," Gabe said. "I'm starting to wonder if this move is a bad idea."

"Oh, come on. One little power outage. What are the odds?"

"No, not just that," Gabe said. "I wonder if it's the right thing to do. Ripping Kimmie away from everything she's used to, all her friends. It's going to be tough on her." He sipped his coffee. "I don't know. It's such a big change."

"I've been thinking about it too," Laurie said. "But you know, it might be really great. Not only the savings on rent and all, but a place to slow down a little. And I'm sure Jill and her friend will show up. They're teenagers. Think of all the dumb stuff you and I did when we were teenagers."

"Jeez, don't remind me," he said. "I ever tell you about the time some friends and I found a whole dumpster full of paper at the back of our school and lit it on fire?"

"I think you just did." She laughed.

"Yeah, I guess so." He took a sip of the coffee. "You spoke with Kay?"

Laurie nodded. "She's freaking out. She was going to call the cops right after she called me."

"Well, hope for the best, I guess," Gabe said. "Let me know if you hear anything."

"Sure," Laurie replied. "You got plans for the day?"

He shrugged. "Was going to work on sorting out some more of the stuff in the attic maybe. Nothing important, really. You?"

"Nothing major," she said. "Kimmie said she might take a walk into town later. Maybe I'll see if she'll let me go with her and we can talk. Hopefully figure out what's really bugging her."

"Good luck," Gabe said. "I can't seem to get through to her lately."

"Give her time. Hard enough being a teenager, but finding out you might be uprooting and moving your whole life out to the sticks?" She held her hands palm up again, a gesture of resignation. "I'm sure she'll come around, but it's going to be harder on her than either of us."

"Sure," he said. He rinsed out his coffee cup and set it to the side of the sink. Looking out through the window and out over the yard to the lake he felt a twinge of remorse, or maybe nostalgia. He'd played in that yard as a kid, hiked those woods, swam in the lake. All the times, good and bad, that had happened at this house, this town. His eyes landed on the island in the middle of Oro Lake, and a shiver crawled along his spine. That place had always given him a bad vibe.

"You okay, Mister?" Laurie's voice broke the silence, pulled him out of his thoughts.

He turned and smiled at her. A thin, tired smile. "Yeah, thinking about this place, I guess. It'll be fine, really. You're right." He wiped his hands dry on a hand towel. "Once we settle in for good, things'll be fine."

She patted his shoulder and gave him a kiss on the cheek. "Totally."

And at that moment, with the sun streaming through the kitchen window, and the two of them facing into the future together, everything seemed like it really would be fine.

CHAPTER THIRTY-TWO

Shawna Lasher stood at the edge of the pier where the lifeguard had gone under the day before. The scuba team she'd brought in from Tahoe had been diving around the pier for almost an hour with no luck. At this point, they were thinking that if the body was still underwater, it must've floated quite far out, going further and further away from the swimming beach and into deeper water. Out into whatever slime and muck lurked at the bottom of the lake, hidden from her view.

One of the divers broke the lake's surface and waved at her. He popped the shiny chrome rebreather out of his mouth, holding it with the other hand. "Nothing, chief!" he called out. He swam closer to the pier. When he reached the edge, he grabbed onto the wooden slats with one hand and heaved himself up.

Lasher squatted down next to him. "We need to go further out. The body's got to be down there somewhere."

The diver nodded. "Sure, but I mean, it's a big fucking lake. You're sure this is where he went under?"

She nodded. "Yeah, that's what the witnesses said."

He shrugged. "We'll fan out a bit more. See what we can see."

Lasher stood, scanning the lake from side to side. "Appreciate it." She cast her gaze from one edge of the lake across to the other. *It is a pretty big lake*, she thought. Not as big as Tahoe, but still, a body could float off into the middle of it and never be found. And she knew that the longer it took to find the body, the less likely they ever would. It'd been three years and the Golden

Oaks PD still had no idea what exactly had happened to Mike Barnes. All the clues pointed to a boating accident, right here on Oro Lake. But they never found the body. And funny to think that his granddaughter was one of the witnesses to the lifeguard going under yesterday. *Small world,* she thought.

She was watching the undulating ripples of lake water when her radio squawked to life on her hip. "Lasher, you there?" a woman's voice on the other end asked. "Umm, over." Josie, the GOPD office manager sounded flummoxed. Which, Lasher thought, was pretty much her default setting.

"Sure, Josie, what's up? Over," Lasher replied.

"I got a call from Kay Bridges, you know, she's the mom of one of the girls at the lake yesterday?"

Lasher waited for the "Over", but it didn't seem it was coming. "Sure, Josie. What'd she want? Over."

"Well, Jill—her daughter—went out with some friends last night and never came home."

FUCK! Lasher thought, but held it in, maintaining the appearance of the consummate professional. Through gritted teeth she replied, "Text me her number and I'll get in touch ASAP. Over."

"Okay Shawna, roger that. Will do," Josie replied. "Oh, ah, um, 'out' I guess. I'll send that right over."

Lasher slipped her radio back into the hip holster and waited for the text message from Josie. Frustrated as she was, she appreciated Josie coming in early to cover the desk. Lasher had called up a couple of volunteers to help out in the office as well, and Millsap was putting in an extra shift overseeing it all. *Small town cops, small town problems,* she thought. Anything else weird went down today, she was definitely going to be calling in the state police. This was getting too big for her and her rinky-dink department.

Her phone pinged with the text containing Kay Bridges' phone number. She thumbed the digits on her screen and listened to the ringing while she paced on the wooden dock.

"Hello?" a woman's voice asked in distressed urgency. "Who is it?"

"Mrs. Bridges, this is Officer Shawna Lasher from the Golden Oaks PD."

"Oh, thank goodness," Kay said. "Do you have any idea where Jill is?"

Shawna was watching the dive crew work while talking to Kay. "I'm sorry Mrs. Bridges, I'm only now getting up to speed. I know your daughter is missing, but that's about it. Can you tell me exactly what's going on?"

There was a pause. Shawna could sense Kay's frustration over the line. She knew what was coming next.

"I'm surprised they didn't fill you in on the details, frankly," Kay said, coldly. "I already explained to the woman I spoke with earlier."

"I apologize for that, ma'am. But it's been an unusually busy morning. Can you please tell me exactly what you know at this point?"

Another pause. "Certainly," Kay said. "Jill was going out last night with some friends. Kevin Lipton and Kimmie Barnes."

Barnes again, Lasher thought. "Okay, I know them."

"Great," Kay said. "Glad to hear it. They were going to go to the movies, but they didn't. Jill and Kevin took his family's boat out on the lake, but Kimmie decided to go home."

"I see," Lasher said.

One of the divers broke the surface, conferred with someone on their boat, and resubmerged. The guy on the boat stood up and saw Lasher watching him. He shook his head, shrugged, both hands out to his sides as if to say, *nothing yet.*

"What time was all this happening?" Lasher asked.

"After dark," Kay replied. "Jill left for the movies after dinner, and the sun was just going down."

Shawna was about to mention that the lake was closed to boating at that time, but decided she didn't want to start that conversation. "And you know for sure they went out on the lake?"

"I assume so. I spoke with Laurie Barnes earlier—Kimmie's mom —and she told me that's what Kimmie said they were planning. And I spoke with Kevin's parents, and their boat's missing."

"I'll be talking to his parents next," Lasher said.

"Great," Kay said, flatly. "So, what can we do for now?"

Lasher paused to think about it. "Mrs. Bridges, I think it would be best if you or your husband came down to the station and filled out a missing person's report—"

"Oh, god."

"Ma'am, I'm sure the kids are fine, but it'd give us a chance to get a list of their favorite haunts, and maybe some better idea of where to start looking for them. I'm going to call the Liptons and ask them to do the same."

"Alright, thank you. We'll be right down."

"When you get there, you'll speak to Josie at the front desk. I'll let her know you're coming."

"Thank you, so much," Kay said and hung up.

In the next few minutes as she watched the divers go about their duties, Lasher had the same conversation with the Liptons that she'd had with Kay Bridges. They were already on their way down to file a report when she called. She contacted the station to let Josie know to watch out for them all and prioritize their statements over anything else going on.

Too many coincidences, she thought as she waved to the pilot of the dive team boat. He was too far out to hear her but picked up his radio when he saw her waving.

"What's up?" he asked.

"I've got to vacate the premises for a bit," Lasher said. "Need to go ask a few questions. But I should be available by cell, and you have the number, right?"

"Yeah, sure do," he said.

"Reception's not great where I'm going, but send a text if you find anything. I'll be back ASAP."

"You got it," he replied, and gave her a thumbs-up from the boat's deck.

She returned the gesture, replaced her radio on her belt, and strode up the beach toward the parking lot where her cruiser waited for her.

***

Lasher pulled the cruiser to the side of the road across from the Barnes' house on Ringgold Lane. She stepped out of the vehicle and was struck by how isolated it was. Aside from the empty house across the road, and a couple others she knew were further down Ringgold Lane, they were pretty much in the middle of nowhere.

Must be nice, she thought as she approached the Barnes house. She rang the doorbell but didn't hear a chime inside, so she knocked a few times instead.

She heard footsteps approaching the door. It opened, and Gabe Barnes was standing in the foyer.

"Oh, hi," he said, a look of confusion crawling across his face. "What can I do for you, Officer?"

"Mr. Barnes," she said. "I'm sorry to intrude, but I was hoping I could speak with your daughter?"

Gabe's confused look deepened. "Kimmie?" he said. "I guess, but can I ask what this is about?"

"Of course," Officer Lasher replied. "A couple of her friends have gone missing, and I'm led to believe your daughter was the last person to see them. I wanted to ask a few questions that might help us find them."

He nodded, and stepped back into the foyer. "My wife talked with Kay before. Anything we can do to help, of course." He motioned her inside with one hand. "Come on in, I'll get Kimmie."

Lasher stepped inside, and Gabe closed the door behind her. The house was dim, and a breeze flowed through it. Laurie came down the hall. "What's going on?" Laurie asked when she saw the police officer in her house.

"You remember Officer Lasher?" Gabe asked.

"Of course," Laurie said. "What can we do for you, Officer?"

"I need to ask your daughter a few questions, ma'am," Lasher replied.

Laurie opened her mouth to speak just as Gabe said, "About Jill and Kevin, babe. They're still missing."

"And your daughter may have been the last person to see them," Lasher added. "We're hoping she can give us some place to start looking, really."

"Oh, yes, of course," Laurie said. "Come on into the kitchen and have a seat. I'll get her right now."

Laurie led Lasher and Gabe into the kitchen, then climbed the stairs to rustle Kimmie.

"Can I get you something to drink? Water or soda or something?" Gabe asked, as Lasher pulled a stool up to the kitchen counter.

"Water would be fine, thanks."

Gabe pulled a pitcher of water out of the fridge, and an ice cube tray out of the freezer. The ice was melting around the edges and slid out of the tray into the glass easily.

"Power's still out," Gabe said. "But I guess you knew that."

"There's a PG&E crew working on it. Transformer was knocked down last night. Power's out through the whole town."

Gabe whistled, a little trill of surprise. "Man, sucks that something so small can cause such an inconvenience to so many people."

"Hey, how's your head, anyway?" Lasher asked.

He rubbed the back of his skull, felt the slight bump back there.

"Oh, it's okay. Thanks for asking."

"It was the guy who did that who knocked over the transformer, by the way."

"Oh, yeah?" Gabe said. "No kidding?"

She nodded. "Yeah, he'd been released, and ..." she trailed off, thinking about West, about the surveillance footage. "Well, he took off like a bat out of hell, hit another car, and careened into the transformer pole."

"Shit," Gabe said. "He okay?"

Lasher shook her head. "No, he's dead, actually."

Gabe paused. "Oh, well, that's too bad, I guess."

"Yeah," Lasher replied. "Been kind of a crazy night."

Footsteps overhead and descending the stairs alerted them to Kimmie's impending arrival.

"Here she comes," Gabe said. When he saw her and Laurie appear around the stairwell, he waved them over. "Kimmie, do you remember Officer Lasher? She helped us out the other day."

Kimmie nodded once, perfunctorily. "Hey."

"Morning, Kimmie," Lasher said. "I've got a few questions I'd like to ask. Hoping you can help me out here."

Kimmie shrugged and slid onto a stool. "If I can, sure. This is about Jill and Kevin, right?"

"Yes, exactly," Lasher said. "Can you tell me in your own words what happened the last time you saw them?"

Kimmie looked at Laurie, who nodded.

"Go ahead, Kimmie," Laurie said.

"She's here to help," Gabe added.

Kimmie took a deep breath and started talking. "Well, we'd decided to go to the movies last night. Jill said she was going to invite some friends, and it ended up just being the three of us.

"My mom and Dad dropped me off at the movies. Jill and Kevin were already there waiting for me. Once my folks drove off, Kevin said he had the keys to the dock, and we could go out on his family's boat if we wanted to. I didn't think that was a good idea and I told them so. In the end, they decided to go anyway, and I came home."

Lasher was watching Kimmie intently, never taking her eyes off the girl as she spoke. "Did they say if they were going to go anywhere on the lake specifically?"

Kimmie shook her head, dropping her eyes and letting a lock of hair fall across her face. "No."

"Are you sure?" Lasher asked. "I hate to press, but really what I'm getting at here, is if they said anything specific, it might give us a place to start looking. Kevin's car was found in the boat ramp parking lot already, and their boat isn't docked. But that doesn't tell us much."

Laurie placed her hand gently on Kimmie's shoulder. "Honey, if there's anything else …"

Kimmie shrugged off her hand. "No, nothing else. They said they were going to go around on the lake. That's it."

Lasher hooked her thumbs through her belt and leaned back. "Some kids like to go mess around on Deer Island. You know that little island at the center of the lake?"

Kimmie's eyes flashed up at her, and quickly looked away. "I thought people weren't allowed out there."

Lasher was watching her carefully. "They're not. But of course, when's that ever stopped anyone?"

"Why not?" Kimmie asked, keeping her eyes down. "What's so bad about that place, anyway?"

Lasher paused, then said, "It's a mess. Back when the valley was being developed by the WPA, they had an observation tower up there. They could see the whole valley from up on top of it. After the lake was dammed up and flooded, the tower was left to rot. One of these days, we're hopefully going to get the funds together to go clean it all up. There was some talk of turning it into a little camping or picnic area. But it's going to take time and money, and nobody's felt like committing either yet."

"There's some stuff about it in the history museum downtown, if you're interested," Gabe said to Kimmie.

"Not really," she replied.

"You're certain they didn't say anything about where they might be going on the lake?" Lasher asked. "Not even a vague destination or direction?"

"No," Kimmie said, looking up at her.

Lasher thought she saw a shadow pass across Kimmie's eyes. A dark caul flicking across her eyes like the nictating membrane over a lizard's eye. Then it was gone, and she wasn't sure if she'd really seen it, or it was a trick of the light.

Lasher fished into the pocket of her slacks and pulled out a business card. She placed it on the counter and slid it toward the center. "Here's my direct line. If you think of anything else," she cast her gaze on each of them, quickly, "Call me. Any time."

"Of course," Laurie said, picking up the card and pinning it to the refrigerator door with a small "Welcome to Oro Lake!" magnet.

"I appreciate it," Lasher said, heading toward the front door.

Gabe followed along behind her, opened the door. "Sorry she wasn't much more help," he said.

"That's okay. I wasn't expecting to get their GPS coordinates from her or anything. Just a fishing expedition, honestly."

"Well, if we hear anything more, I'll let you know," he said.

"Thanks again," Lasher added, and returned to her car.

Chapter Thirty-Three

Shawna Lasher gripped the steering wheel of the small police boat as it sped along the surface of Oro Lake. She'd spoken to Millsap shortly after leaving the Barnes's house, and he'd let her know the missing persons reports on the Bridges and Lipton kids were in. Nothing that they hadn't already surmised from talking to the parents and her interview with Kimmie and her folks. But it was enough to make Lasher itchy to check out the lake itself. The lake seemed to be the central theme in the disturbances and disappearances over the last few days. She gave some brief directions to the dive team, and then took the police boat out on the lake herself.

It wasn't a fancy boat at all, but it got the job done when they needed it. A town as small as Golden Oaks had limited resources of course, but the lake was big enough that they'd been able to justify it in their budget. Never knew when they might need to take to the water for a rescue. Or a search. Besides, Lasher liked getting out on the water once in a while. She spent so much of her time in town driving around, and sometimes it was nice to get on the water and remember why people came to Golden Oaks in the first place. Oro Lake may have been man-made, but it was still gorgeous. She enjoyed being on the lake at just about any time of the year. From sun-sparkled summer mornings like today, to mist-shrouded winter evenings as the sun crawled below the horizon. She'd taken the boat out a couple of times when it was raining and listened to the rhythmic white-noise hiss of water on water.

There were a couple spots she'd found years ago toward the north edge of the lake where you could still see the trees below the surface, the remnants of what the valley might have looked like before it was flooded. Far enough below the surface that they wouldn't interfere with boating, but still visible to the observant. More so in late summer when the surface of the lake was low. Even though Golden Oaks hadn't yet celebrated its centenary, she often forgot that the town hadn't always been there. That there'd been a whole other world before, a world that had been submerged to make room for the greasy spoon diners and vacation homes that made up the town that she'd sworn to serve and protect.

She was pushing the boat along at a steady clip. Not the speed she'd go if she were responding to an emergency, but not a leisurely afternoon fishing trip pace, either. She'd started by sticking close to the lake's shore, traveling up along the western edge of the lake, past the dam, and around to the north. She waved at the occasional hiker or jogger along the trail that circumnavigated the lake.

And all the time as she was going along the edge of the lake, she kept looking toward Deer Island. She suddenly imagined it as the brooding skull of some strange aquatic giant, peeking above the lake's rippling surface, glaring at her with a singular malignancy. A grim titan from the ancient world, disdainful of the human invaders of its valley, usurpers of its lands. She imagined it reaching slime and root encrusted hands toward her, unseen under the lake's surface until they grabbed the boat and dragged it under.

She shivered at the image, shook her head, and hissed, "Get it together, Shawna," to herself. She increased the throttle, and veered the boat toward the interior of the lake. Toward Deer Island.

The island grew ominously larger as she sped toward it. She'd circled it before, even hiked it occasionally—"police privilege" she'd told a friend once, recounting a picnic hike she'd taken on the island—but now, for some reason, it filled her with dread.

When she'd mentioned the island to Kimmie that morning, Lasher thought she'd seen a flash of defensiveness, of occlusion shadow the girl's face. Lasher's gut told her Kimmie hadn't been telling her the whole story and that something had happened on the island the girl didn't want her to know about.

It wasn't long before Lasher was practically in spitting distance of Deer Island. She cut the throttle and slowed the boat, turned to port and took a slow survey around the island's edge. It looked pretty much the same as the other times she'd been out on the lake. Tangled with oaks and aspens, and a fine fuzz of summer-dry grasses filtered between the trees and scrub.

Her slow orbit of the island took about fifteen minutes until she was back where she'd started. She continued on one more time before angling her boat toward the sliver of shore that was as close to a beach as the island had. Really just a relatively flatter area where she could beach the boat while she got out and took a quick look around.

She got closer to the beach, where she saw a spot where the silty sand had been churned up—almost unnoticeable until she'd gotten closer. She pulled the boat to shore a few feet beyond it and was about to drop anchor when she stopped, staring at the hole in the sand. The anchor's nylon cord was in her hand, and the forked metal anchor dangled a few inches above the lake water.

She hopped over the side of the boat, splashing into water only a couple of inches deep at the edge of the beach. She took a couple of steps up the sand until she was at the spot where it had been turned up. Holding the anchor next to it, her suspicions were confirmed. It sure looked like someone had stuck a small boat's anchor into the beach there. Flat on one side where the anchor had sliced into the earth, and then flat on the two edges but churned up as the anchor had been dragged out.

Next to that, two distinctly different sets of footprints crossing the beach, disappearing into the treeline, and returning back down. The marks were all relatively fresh, edges still sharp and clear. They hadn't had a chance to wear down from wind or water yet.

"Well," she said to the trees as she stood up. "Someone's been here recently." She swung her anchor overhead, driving it into the sandy beach a few yards away from the existing mark. She pulled her phone out of her pocket and snapped a few photos of the indentations, making sure to get clear closeups of the footprints as well as the anchor mark. Giving wide berth to the trail of footprints, Lasher hiked up the beach and into the trees. The footprints weren't easy to follow, but she did manage to catch them frequently enough that soon she'd followed them to the top of Deer Island. The pathway widened out before her until she was standing in front of the broken concrete slab at the island's crest.

She'd been up to this observation deck before, but the slab had been solid the last time she was on the island. The footprints led right up to the edge and around it a little, so she was curious. Stepping up to the crack, she looked down into the depths below. A gaping hole stared back at her. Lasher guessed it was fifteen to twenty feet deep, with fissures and cracks around the edges. She squatted down, put one hand on the edge, and peered into the hole. The sun was about right over her head now, and the hole was fairly well illuminated. Empty all the same. At the bottom of the hole, she saw what looked like mud, or dark water. Maybe seepage from the lake? Or rainwater trapped at the lowest point. Hard to tell from that distance, and she didn't want to go in alone for fear of getting stuck and not being able to get out.

She stood up and surveyed the landscape. If it weren't for the trees intermittently blocking her view, she'd have a perfect vantage point to spy on almost all of the lake's shoreline. Despite a few spots where the flow of the land bent around a curve here and there, she had an almost completely unbroken view.

She stepped away from the platform, and pulled a small pair of binoculars from a pouch on her belt. Raising them to her eyes, she scanned along the shoreline, occasionally lowering them to walk around a tree.

She gazed around the shore. A speck of white in the distance to the southeast, and looking back slowly, she saw a boat run up aground on the shore. There was a yellow anchor cord stretched out taut behind it, angling sharply down, before disappearing under the waterline. The boat itself was leaning at an angle. Like the driver had misjudged the speed it was going, and it stopped of its own accord once it hit land.

"Bingo," Lasher muttered. She started back down the hilly sloped trail to where her own boat waited for her.

***

Lasher drove the boat toward the shore on the southeastern edge of Oro Lake. She reduced speed when she neared the shore, slowing to get a better look at the boat. A small craft, about the right size for a family to cruise around on a lake and do a little fishing. About the same as most of the boats moored at the lake's dock. But this one wasn't at the dock. It was run aground, looking forlorn and abandoned. Shadows cast by trees near the shore rippled along its surface as it rocked slightly in the low, lapping waves.

She used the radio handset on her boat's instrument panel to call in to the station. "Millsap, you there? Over." She waited. "Millsap, respond, over."

"Hey, Shawna," Josie replied from across the radio waves. "Millsap's taking a statement from the Liptons about their boy. Probably almost done though. You want me to go get him? … Oh, um, over."

Lasher rolled her eyes to the sky, pressed the radio mic to her forehead in frustration.

"No, Josie, that's okay. I found the Lipton's boat. Run aground along the shore about two miles from the beach. I'm going to check it out. Let him know and have him get back to me once he's done with the Liptons. Over."

"Okay, Shawna, will do. Over."

"Out," Lasher replied, and replaced the mic in its holding clip on the instrument panel.

Lasher pulled her craft up alongside it and dropped anchor into the water. Once she'd secured her own boat, she hopped overboard to examine the other, landing in a few inches of water. She approached the craft, noting that even though being run up into the sandy beach, it looked to be in fine shape.

When she got closer to the shore, she clearly saw footprints going up the shore and disappearing into the woods. They seemed to be leading left, toward the north. As Lasher got to the edge of the shore where the treeline began, she saw a car and a pickup truck speeding along the main road in the distance. Lasher saw it was easy walking distance to town from where the boat had run aground.

Hadn't Kim Barnes said she'd walked home from town? Lasher went a little further into the woods, scanning side to side as she did. If she kept going straight toward the road, she'd come out about halfway between town and the turnoff to Ringgold Lane, which would take her directly to the Barnes' house. Interesting.

She turned and went back toward the shore, leaves and grass crunching under her boots as she walked across the forest litter. The Lipton's boat was clear in her view. The aft section rose and fell, slowly rocking back and forth with the pulse of the lake's low waves. When she got up next to it, she raised one leg over the gunwale, and slid into the boat. The small deck was clear. Three bright orange life jackets sprawled across the u-shaped bench were the only thing out of place. She checked the instrument panel and noted that the keys were still in the ignition. Whoever had run it aground had either left in a hurry, or without caring about the boat.

It was the anchor line shooting out over the back of the boat into the water which grabbed her attention next. Why did the pilot of the boat crash into the shore, running the craft aground and jammed tight into the sand, and drop anchor? If they were in such a hurry to get away from the boat, why take the extra time to drop the anchor? And the way it was angled away from the craft struck her as strange as well. It stretched back ten feet or so before it disappeared into the green lake water. And it was tight, as if it had been dragging for a while before the boat stopped. Maybe it was caught on something under the water or had been dragging along the lake floor.

She gripped the yellow nylon cord with both hands and gave it a tug. She felt a little give in the line. It was definitely caught on something, even if only dug into the sand down below. She braced one foot against the aft of the boat, got a tighter grip on the cord, and pulled hard. There was a brief resistance, and then she felt the line loosen. She felt it pull free slightly, and she arched back, pulling the cord a few inches out of the water.

She pulled again and felt the anchor coming loose somewhere in the depths. Hand over hand, she dragged the line in, dropping the cord in loops to the deck floor. She pulled the rope toward her and as it coiled at her feet, she saw something large and pale approaching the surface. She recognized it as the outline of a torso, the rope tangled around its neck. A corona of blond hair spread out around the listlessly lolling head as she continued to tug on the rope, it broke the surface, arms splayed out and head shifting to one side.

She ran the rope a couple of times around a chromed steel cleat on the gunwale, tying it down tightly. The body in the water floated at the surface, behind the boat's aft. She leaned over the rear of the craft and adjusted the corpse's head so she could see the features. It was a girl, a teenager as far as she could tell. Looked a lot like Jill Bridges, and Lasher decided it was most likely her. The head lolled over and a small mottled red and black crayfish emerged from the dead girl's mop of hair and skittered across her face. The girl's jaw fell open, revealing another crayfish inside. It crawled over her teeth, down her chin, waved two open claws defiantly at Lasher before dropping into the lake with a faint *plip!*

She jumped over the side of the boat, hitched her hands under the armpits of the dead girl, and dragged her to shore. Lasher lay the body on the dirt beach, well out of the water, and removed the cord from around her neck. It took her a few tries to unloop the cord, as the neck had swollen tight against it. The rope had been twisted with a simple loop, no knot. It looked like it could have been a simple boating accident. Maybe this was why Kimmie Barnes acted so defensive earlier? She'd certainly been acting like she knew more than she was letting on. Could Jill have slipped into the coils? Or maybe they'd been horsing around the way teenagers sometimes do, and it got out of hand?

Lasher put those thoughts aside. This was yet another strange coincidence in a long string of them. She went back to her own boat, grabbed the radio handset, and called in to the station again. "Millsap, I need you ASAP. Over."

Chapter Thirty-Four

By the early afternoon, the heat had become oppressive. Laurie Barnes sat on the back porch drinking a glass of iced tea and reading a tattered paperback copy of Larry McMurtry's *Lonesome Dove* she'd found in a bookshelf in the living room. Must've been one of her father-in-law's books, or maybe it had been left behind by one of their vacation rental tenants. She was wearing shorts and a tank top, and while it was desperately hot, there was a trickle of a breeze. The shade offered by the porch roof and that little breeze offered some respite from the heat. Thin beads of sweat trickled from her scalp and down the back of her neck.

Mercifully, the power had come back on an hour or so before. It still flickered a little, and Laurie assumed that was because the PG&E crew was still fiddling with the transformer. But the house lights worked, and the fridge was cold, and that was good enough for her. Laurie was taking a sip of iced tea when she heard footsteps in the house, and the screen door creaked open. Gabe stepped through. He was wearing black jeans, a burgundy t-shirt, and his favorite sneakers.

"Aren't you hot?" Laurie asked. "I'm scorched."

Gabe shrugged. "I guess," he said, stepping out onto the porch. "Wonder how much it would cost to fix this place up with an AC unit?"

Laurie took a long sip of tea. "Does Kimmie still want to go into town? She was talking about walking in by herself, but I'm not super comfortable with that right now. I thought I might go with her."

Gabe looked back into the house. "Not sure. Haven't seen her in a little bit. I thought she was down here with you, actually."

"Nope," Laurie said. "Nobody out here but us and the trees." She put down her book and stood up, stretching out her back. "I'll check in on her, see if maybe she wants to drive into town and grab lunch. Want to come along?"

"Yeah, that'd be great," he said. "Anywhere it's cool."

"Be right back," Laurie said and went inside. The house was strangely still and quiet, thick with heat. Later in the day they could open up the windows and cool the place down a bit. *Definitely hotter than back home,* she thought as she went upstairs to check on Kimmie. She caught herself in the middle of that thought. Because if things went the way they seemed to be going, she needed to start thinking about Golden Oaks as home. She let out a short sigh as she knocked on Kimmie's bedroom door.

"Hey, Kimmie," she said as she opened the door slowly. "Your dad and I were thinking about going into town to grab some lunch. Want to come along?"

When the door was fully open, Laurie saw that Kimmie was not in her room. The room was hotter than it had been downstairs and had a strange smell to it. A moist, mildewy smell. It reminded her a little like beach at low-tide. The smell of things churned up from deep underwater and left on land to rot in the sun. She went to open a window, and realized the windows to the room were already open. Both the one looking out toward the lake, and the one on the side of the house with a view of the driveway and forest beyond.

"Kimmie?" Laurie called out, a little louder than her normal speaking voice. She checked around the room and saw Kimmie's phone was on her nightstand. She picked it up and clicked the power button, but the phone remained a glossy dark brick. The battery was drained, she realized, so she placed it on a cable to charge up.

She went back downstairs and wandered around the ground floor, calling out to Kimmie and receiving no response. Laurie had a sick feeling growing in her gut. She had a feeling—a mother's sixth sense—that Kimmie was not only not in the house, but in some kind of trouble. She picked up her pace and was soon back on the porch. "She's not in the house," she said to Gabe. "She didn't say anything to you about going out?"

Gabe turned toward her and shook his head. "No, nothing. I assumed she was upstairs reading or taking a nap or something."

"Her phone's on her night stand, too. She never goes anywhere without it."

Gabe stood up and wandered down to the back lawn. He looked up toward the open window of Kimmie's room, turned his gaze toward the woods, and the lake past them. "She probably went for a walk like she said she was going to. She's got to be worried about her friends. She probably forgot about her phone."

"It's not like her," Laurie said.

"Yeah, I know," Gabe replied. "She's been acting strangely for the last few days. Maybe she's still shook up from almost drowning a couple of days ago?"

Laurie was pacing around the yard, looking for any sign of their daughter. "Could be. I should have taken her to a doctor, had her checked out to make sure she was okay."

"I'm sure she's fine, babe," Gabe said. "Let's hang tight here and wait for her to come back. Most likely, in a few minutes, she'll realize she doesn't have her phone on her and come running back. God forbid she's not in constant contact with her friends."

Laurie crossed her arms around her belly and stared out toward the lake. "If she's not back soon, I'm going looking for her."

Gabe nodded. "Sounds good. But I'm sure she's fine. You know how teenagers are. It probably skipped her mind to let us know she was going out. She'd told you yesterday she was thinking of walking into town today. In her mind, I'm sure that meant she'd already told you she was going out."

"I hope so," Laurie said.

***

Kimmie trudged along the shore of Oro Lake, the sun overhead pouring waves of heat over her. The sun's reflection off the lake's surface was painfully bright, causing her to squint her watering eyes against the glare. Her steps were unsteady over the soft and uneven terrain, but they were purposeful. Every step she took seemed to take her closer to some barely known goal. But when she tried to focus on what that could be, her mind became fuzzy and dark. Something was driving her forward, but she didn't know what it was, or even recognize the inimical intent behind what felt more like a strange compulsion.

Her limbs were sluggish as well. Every step was an effort, but she kept going. She had felt better when she'd woken up that morning, but as the day progressed, and the sun rose higher, the fatigue had set in. Up ahead, the path she was walking diverged into a copse of oak trees. When she got into the shade, she felt a wave of relief and a quick pulse of energy. She leaned against one of the old trees for a minute, catching her breath. But it wasn't long before the whispering, chittering, almost vocal essence began squirming through her mind again, black, ropy tendrils slithering around in her brain, confusing her and driving her on.

She felt like her thoughts were infested with angry insects, crawling and skittering through her brain, trying to communicate their alien desires to her. No, not theirs. *Its* desires. Kimmie was slipping away, and the thing she'd met in the pit on Deer Island was replacing her very self. She was somewhat aware of this transition, but not on a conscious level. In her, the being which had been locked away in the darkness for so long had found a perfect vessel. Her mind was already more open to the universe than most. It had been able to touch her in her dreams, communicate with her in visions and images before it had fully made physical contact with her.

And when it spoke to her, it spoke in images, dreams, and in feelings. It reminded her of her insignificance in the world, played on her insecurities. It showed her how small she was, how disconnected.

And when that failed, it simply took over for her. It was the thing that had killed Kevin and Jill, though she bore the guilt and regret. And it was wearing her down. Grinding away at whatever was left of Kimmie Barnes and replacing it with itself.

It wouldn't be much longer before it fully consumed her, replaced her entirely with its own essence. What remained in her mind of Kimmie Barnes had some inkling that the coming moonless evening would give the entity all it needed to subsume her and be free of the valley. Free to roam the Earth, to feed on the lifeforce of anything it met and not be stuck with the scraps it had been forced to survive on for so very long.

Kimmie began walking again. The walking soothed her, quelled the restlessness she felt when the thing in her mind began to squirm with anticipation of its final release. She trudged along the shoreline, walking in the general direction of town.

She came around a bend in the shore when she saw commotion up ahead. Maybe a quarter of a mile down the shore, a police boat had pulled up next to the craft she'd ran aground the night before. A handful of people were standing around the boats, taking photographs and gesturing with their hands. It was far enough away she couldn't quite make out how many, or what they were doing.

But one thing was certain: they'd found Jill's body.

She stepped off of the path, found a tree in the shade, and sat at its base. She could still watch the people working, but doubted they'd notice her from this distant vantage point. She waited, watching them work over the next hours. Watched as they loaded Jill's body onto a stretcher and placed it in the back of the police boat to remove it from the scene. Watched as they wrapped a loop of yellow caution tape around the Lipton's boat.

And as she watched, she felt anger rising in her.

The thing in her mind had a deep hatred for the town that had trapped it. A vengeful rage rose slowly within her, like a pot set to boil. Slow and hot at first, soon rising to a seething ferocity of scalding anger. By the time the police had finally left the scene, the sun was going down in the west, disappearing behind the line of trees. It would still be a few hours until actual sundown. As But the daylight was dying, the shadows growing long, reaching out like bony, clutching fingers.

When the last golden rays of the sun died beyond the horizon, stars began to glitter in the sky. Kimmie stood on the lake shore, her eyes dark and vacant, staring out across the dark rippling water toward Deer Island and beyond.

The lake and shore around her was almost black. No moon overhead, and only the distant stars for light. But she no longer really needed her eyes. To see in the visual spectrum, perhaps. But her mind was attuned to other ways of perception. Almost like she *felt* the presence of the land around her. The slope of the shore, the clusters of trees, the lake's water. And below that, the detritus of the older world. The remains of the valley from before the developers had come along and flooded the place to make it attractive to modern people.

Something within her twitched, spasmed, and slithered. Whatever essence of Kimmie was left was in a stupor. A soporific dream-state, like floating in dark, warm water as the world's events passed right by her. The thing driving her, controlling her mind and body, was cunning and aware. It moved her forward until she stood three yards from shore, in the lake up to her knees. The cold water lapped at her legs, soaking up into her jeans. She ignored the chill. Indeed, the force within her seemed to relish any physical sensations at all.

It extended its mind, its consciousness outside of the meat it wore. Lashing tendrils of thought and intent slithered forth, searching, seeking out the bodies beneath the water. One by one, it made contact, calling to the dead which littered the deep places of the lake. Corpses that had become trapped under the water since the flooding of the valley, if not before, stirred in the muck. Bodies of workers who'd built the dam. Boating accidents. Jilted lovers. And those who'd been dragged under over the years by the thing itself: Charlie Gaines, Mike Barnes, Darryl McEwen, Peter Guilford and so many others.

They crawled from the slime at the bottom of the lake, dragging their water-logged bodies forward. All around the lake, more than two dozen sodden, slime-dripping skulls broke the surface of the water. Cold, hateful eyes in empty sockets glared at the night as the dead marched out of the water. Their limbs shook and jerked as the dark energy animating them directed them, pushing and compelling them onward.

The dead tramped up and along the shore of Oro Lake, crawled up the side of the dam, dragged themselves onto the docks. Some began to trek toward town, others toward the houses and cabins which surrounded the lake.

Kimmie watched as the carrion creatures escaped their watery tomb. The thing in her mind somehow aware of each of the shambling corpses, of its location and direction. She turned away from the lake herself. Shuffling out of the water with great, forced strides, throwing her arms out to her sides for balance.

The night was beginning, and by the time the sun rose, she would be freed of the valley once and for all.

CHAPTER THIRTY-FIVE

Emily was washing down a table at the Get Up and Go. It had been a slow night, but it always was this time of summer. Most of the vacation traffic had slowed down, and she figured lots of folks had stayed home to eat and use up anything in their fridges which was starting to turn due to the power outage of the night before.

The diner had been closed for most of the day, and she'd wondered about even bothering to open it up after the power came back. But since she still couldn't get in touch with Charlie, Emily decided to make an executive decision and open up for the evening crowd. What crowd there was, anyway.

The folks who'd just left had seemed nice enough. A young family on their way up to Reno, stopping for a quick dinner along the way. Nice family, but the kids had left a mess behind. Emily shook her head as she scooped half-eaten french fries off the vinyl booth seat into the washrag she held in the other hand. Kids were always messy, of course. She was used to it, but it still frustrated her.

She gave the table a final wipe with the wet cloth and began to reset it for the next customer. Emily laid down the last of the tableware and returned to the kitchen where Carl McCutcheon, Emily's husband—who she'd roped in as the fill-in cook while Charlie Gaines was missing—was scraping down the grill. "Looks like it's going to be a quiet night," she said. She dumped the detritus of the washcloth into a trash bin and threw the cloth into the laundry hamper in a storage closet to the side of the kitchen.

Carl nodded. "We're due to close up in an hour anyway. Figure if we clean up now, we can leave when we close the place up."

Emily let out a deep, solemn sigh. "If we don't hear from Charlie soon … I'm not sure what we should do. Keep the place open and running it just in case? Or close up until we know what's going on?"

"Beats me. Did Charlie have a lawyer or something? Someone who could maybe give us some idea?"

"I guess he must have," Emily said. "I've gone through some of the papers in his office but haven't found anything helpful yet. I'll look again tomorrow before we open up."

"Hell, take a peek now," Carl said. "It's quiet as a tomb in here. Ain't nobody coming in for burgers and shakes tonight."

"I guess you're right," she said. "But if anyone comes in, give me a holler and I'll be right out."

Emily unlaced her apron and hung it on a hook next to the door to Charlie's "office" as she went in. The "office" was really a corner of the dry goods storage area. A desk in one corner with a phone, ancient computer, and his filing system, which was a cardboard box full of receipts, bills, and other paperwork that perpetually needed to be dealt with. There was also a bank of small lockers behind the door, where employees could lock up personal belongings during their shifts. They were from the high school, and Charlie had gotten them during a remodel back in the 90s.

She'd given a cursory check of his desk earlier that day to see if there was an address book or anything that would point her in the right direction of getting in touch with anyone who might know where Charlie had gone. But all that had turned up was a great big pile of nothing helpful at all. She booted up the computer, waiting patiently while the monitor warmed up, and the Windows logo came across the screen. Another couple of minutes until it finally showed a login screen. She made a haphazard guess at a username and password (trying "Charlie" and his wife's name in various iterations) but nothing worked.

"Well, shit," she muttered. She checked the drawers of the desk, which she'd already checked earlier in the day, and came up with nothing helpful either. She'd hoped to find an address book, or list of vendors, the name of his accountant, or lawyer, or *something* that might give her some clue.

She went to the box under the desk and started flitting through the paperwork. There were bills from food delivery and restaurant supply services, but nothing from "Obviously Charlie's Lawyer, ESQ" at all.

She heard a "ding" from the dining area, signifying someone coming through the front door. She dropped the papers back in the cardboard carton, wiped her hands on her pants, and headed back out.

She heard Carl shout, "Jesus!" and the clatter of metal as if he'd dropped something heavy. A foul breeze flowed through the restaurant from the open door. She stepped out of the office to where it opened up behind the counter and saw the source of the smell.

Two dark shapes came through the doorway, walking toward where the register sat on the counter. And one of them was undeniably Charlie Gaines.

Gaines' clothing was torn and sodden, dripping with foul water. His skin was puffy and wrinkled like he'd spent a week stewing in a bathtub. Reeds and water grasses strung out of his hair and laced through his torn clothing. The other was similarly grim and ghastly, shuffling along on feet which squelched wetly with each step.

Emily shrieked. A long, teakettle scream as her hands went to the sides of her face, and the thing that was once Charlie turned toward her. It had no eyes at all. Only empty vacant sockets, twin pools of blackness.

Carl ran toward the batwing doors which blocked the kitchen from the dining area as Charlie approached her. The second of the lumbering dead rushed toward him. It stalked stiffly forward, limbs jerking and shaking, opening its mouth with a loud cracking sound, and Carl saw slithering black ropy shapes within, like it had a mouth full of squirming black lampreys.

The walking corpse of Charlie Gaines slunk behind the counter and crept toward Emily, a horrible hint of a grin spread across the jaw pulled out of its joints. Lake water oozed from its mouth. Emily grabbed a long knife from where it rested next to a plexiglass display of pies. It had crumbs and raspberry filling streaked along its shiny steel blade, and she brandished it before her. The creature raised thin arms out in front of it, reaching toward Emily, raking the air with cracked-nailed hands. She slashed at it with the knife, taking three fingers off one hand and a spurt of black fluid squirted out of the stumps, spraying across her blouse and the countertop.

In the kitchen, the eyeless creature had backed Carl up against the grill, which was still warm, but turned low. Carl's eyes were wide with panic as he saw a knife block next to the creature. He'd have to dart around it, risk the thing's clutching grasp in order to get something to defend himself. He wondered if Charlie had a gun in this place, and if he did, where the hell it was.

As if it read his mind, the thing reached out its right hand, dragging the largest of the knives out of the block. It turned the gleaming chef's knife over, pointing the wicked tip toward Carl. Then it rushed at him, grabbing his throat with one hand, and sliding the knife into his gut with the other.

"Emily," Carl shrieked. "Go!"

The dead thing dug the knife further into Carl's torso, sliding the blade laterally across his gut and wiggling it sideways until a river of scarlet poured forth. A wide gaping gash opened up across him, like a monstrous smile. Intestines slithered out in great bloody loops.

Carl fell to the side, his arm catching on the handle of an empty fry basket which simmered in a vat of hot oil, and when he fell to the ground, the basket flew into the air. The hot oil gushed across him, sizzling and burning his dying flesh as it did. The foul smell of frying meat filled the room as oil sloshed from the vat and splashed across hit the burners on the grill. In an instant, the kitchen was an inferno.

Emily looked around, wondering if she could get up over the counter as the now-fingerless thing inched toward her. She turned and ran back into Charlie's office, slamming the door closed behind her and leaning against it.

Charlie hammered on the door, a wet, squelching, pounding as it beat its sodden fists against the thin wood. Smoke started trickling through under the door, and she began to hear the crackling of fire beyond the door as the restaurant began to burn.

Greasy black smoke poured into the storage room, making it harder to breathe. Emily began to choke and cough, tears running down her face as she gagged on the thick, foul smoke. Gasping for air, Emily blacked out, slumped against the door, the last thing she was aware of was the sound of fists pounding on the other side.

***

Within minutes, the Get Up and Go was engulfed in flames. They roared through the ceiling, shooting up a shower of sparks which landed in thick piles of elm and oak leaves which had blown onto the roof the previous fall and never been cleared away. The few people on the street who'd been out enjoying the summer evening scattered. A dozen phones called 911, while another dozen were more interested in documenting the disaster.

People began to run as the licking orange flames rose high on the roof of the diner and spread to the hair salon next to it. The blaze spread across the roof, and the dry night breeze carried the flames and sparks to the nearby trees. One of the oak trees in front of the restaurant was aflame, and spreading to the next. Smoke filled the air as fire gnawed through the night, devouring everything in its path.

Chapter Thirty-Six

"Do you smell smoke?" Laurie said, and Gabe nodded. He used to like the smell of wood fire. It reminded him of summertime campouts, s'mores, good times with his friends. But over the last few years, the smell of fires made him anxious. He knew people who'd lost everything in the California wildfires. Gabe remembered when the fires hundreds of miles to the north and south had sent clouds of smoke and ash as far south as Alcosta. The week where the smoke all around the state had spiraled into the San Francisco Bay Area, giving it the worst air quality in the entire world. Choking cauls of airborne filth which blotted out the sun, bathing the town in a dull orange apocalyptic glow.

Gabe went to close the back door as a gust of thick, warm air pushed into the room. The breeze brought a fresh wave of the acrid, burning smell, and he shivered. Laurie was pacing the kitchen, puttering around at getting dinner together halfheartedly. Kimmie still hadn't come home from wherever she'd wandered off to, and Laurie was feeling frantic. Gabe was watching her.

"You want me to go into town and look around for her?" he asked.

"No, that's fine," Laurie said, and emphasized her frustration by beginning to chop a carrot into slivers. "I'm sure she'll be along eventually."

She tossed the carrot pieces into a bowl of lettuce, tomatoes, and other things she'd accumulated for a dinner salad.

"I'm sure she will," Gabe said. But he wasn't so certain either.

Word had already traveled to them that Jill Bridges had been killed in a boating accident, and there was still no sign of Kevin Lipton. Gabe had fielded a frantic call from his parents earlier in the afternoon, answering the same questions about where the kids had gone and did he know anything. He was starting to wonder about the Lipton kid, and if he really was a "good kid" like Kay Bridges had told Laurie the day before.

"Do *you* want to go looking for her?" Gabe asked. "I can stay here in case she comes back."

Laurie stopped chopping. Gabe saw tears welling up in the sides of her eyes, and felt his throat tighten. Laurie nodded, and wiped at her eyes. "Yes," she said.

Without another word, she raced from the kitchen, grabbed her purse, and started fishing around in it for her car keys. Within seconds, she was out the front door, in the car, and racing up Ringgold Lane toward town.

Gabe picked up his phone and grabbed Officer Lasher's card off of the fridge. He dialed it and waited for a ring tone, but after a few seconds, all he got was a recorded voice telling him that "All circuits are currently busy. Please try your call again later. Goodbye." The phone hung up on him.

"Shit," Gabe muttered. He tried the call again and got the same message. "Double-shit."

The house still had the acrid smell of smoke wafting through it, so he spent the next few minutes going around making sure the windows were closed. Checking downstairs as well as upstairs, closing everything up tight. When he got to Kimmie's room, he discovered that the window looking out toward the lake was wide open. He shut it, tight, looking out at the vast swath of woods and wondering if it was safe here. If a fire spread fast, would they have to evacuate? His dad had maintained the defensible space around the house's perimeter, but would that be good enough? The dry moss he'd seen on the roof the other day could pick up sparks easily. He checked his phone, hoping to find some information about where the fires were, but nothing appeared in the local news sites yet. He checked the national fire service page, but nothing was on it, either. Gabe wondered if that meant the fire wasn't big enough to warrant national concern, or if it simply hadn't gotten any attention yet. Or maybe he was being paranoid. Probably someone up the road having a backyard cookout or something.

But through the window of his and Laurie's room when he went to close it, he could see a distant glow. The south-facing window looked out over the driveway, past the trees, and by basic orientation he knew it was pointed in the general direction of downtown Golden Oaks. He couldn't quite tell how far away it was, but there was definitely a ruddy glow beyond the trees in that direction. He hoped wherever Laurie had gone to look for Kimmie, she found her fast.

***

Laurie sped along the highway toward town, scanning back and forth along the sides of the road for Kimmie. But the whole time she drove she saw no sign of her. Suddenly, she heard the shrill screech of sirens coming up on her. A quick look in her rearview mirror showed flashing lights behind her and moving fast. She slowed the car and turned toward the side of the road to let it pass by. A fire truck blazed by, roaring toward town.

After it passed, Laurie pulled back on to the road. She passed by a few lonely shops on the outskirts of town, the strip mall with the movie theater. On a whim, she pulled into the lot and parked near the theater. *The lot was fairly empty; not surprising for a Tuesday night*, she thought. She got out of the car and wandered along the sidewalk, peeking into the windows of the ice cream shop, dipping her head into the lobby of the theater. She quickly checked in each restaurant and shop in the little strip mall before deciding Kimmie probably wasn't there and getting back in the car.

She sent a quick text to Gabe, *Any sign?* After what seemed like an endless few seconds she got back, *Nothing yet. Can you see the fire? I can see sort of a glow from out of the upstairs window. It looks like it's near town, but I'm not sure.*

Laurie texted back: *Looks like something downtown, yeah. Headed that way now.*

She had pulled out of the lot and onto the road when Gabe sent back *Be safe.* She was about to turn onto the road again when another fire truck roared by, sirens flashing and blaring. She gunned the engine and sped along in its wake. She was going a few miles over the posted limit now, but really didn't care. Another few minutes and she was within sight of Golden Oaks, where she could see the glow Gabe had mentioned earlier. A golden corona over the haze of smoke blanketing the town in the distance. The road curved to the left before entering downtown proper, and she saw barricades had been erected about a block beyond.

There were only a handful of cars in front of her now, and they were being redirected as they approached the barrier. The firetruck had been allowed through, but everyone else was being turned away by a couple of men in firefighter uniforms. A police officer was assisting them. Laurie recognized her as Office Lasher.

She pulled the car forward, slowing as she approached the barricade. Beyond it, she could see buildings and trees aflame. Flames licking skyward, sparks drifting into the night sky. The street was a river of water from the firehoses, and the flames reflected from the ground, making for a weird rippling double image. Laurie stopped as she pulled up to the concrete and wooden barriers blocking the road. She rolled down the window, and the cab of her car was instantly filled with dry, smoky air. One of the firefighters was pointing with one hand up a side street and motioning her to "move along" with the other.

"I need to speak with Officer Lasher!" Laurie called out. On hearing her name, Lasher stepped around so she could see into the car and who was driving it. She came toward the open window.

"Mrs. Barnes, I need you to move along. We need to clear the road for emergency vehicles."

Laurie nodded. "I get that, of course. But Kimmie's been missing all day. No chance you've seen her, is there?"

The firefighter directing traffic walked around her car and motioned to the two cars behind her to move around her. One by one, they skirted around Laurie's vehicle and up the street.

"No, ma'am, I'm afraid I haven't," Lasher replied. "When was the last time you saw her?"

Laurie thought back over the day. "Probably in the early afternoon," she said. "After lunch, anyway. She'd said something earlier about maybe taking a walk into town, but she never let us know she was going out."

Lasher's attention was split between Laurie and the firetrucks down the street, which were still blasting water at the roaring flames downtown. "She might be on her way back home?" Lasher said. "Or is there anyone in town she knows and might be visiting?"

Laurie shook her head. "I watched for her as I was driving in but didn't see her. And as far as people in town, the Bridges, I suppose."

"I think the best thing for you to do, really, is head home. I'll put the word out, and if anyone spots her, we'll call you. But right now, we sort of have our hands full with this." She gestured toward the flames just as a gust of wind blew through, and the fire burst upward once again.

"Looks pretty bad," Laurie said.

"The fire department's working on containing it at this point," Lasher said. "The diner's a loss and it's spread to a few other buildings on that block."

"Sorry to hear that. How much of the downtown is shut down?"

"A few blocks in either direction," Lasher said. "Why?"

"Because I'm going to drive around and see if I can find my daughter. Unless that's a problem."

Lasher took a step back from the car. "Not a problem. "Please be aware of the barricades and let the fire department do their jobs. And call me as soon as you find her. I'd like to ask her a few more questions about her friends."

"Sure," Laurie said. "Thanks." She drove the car forward, toward the flames, and turned left at the detour sign, moving further into the town. The vaporous ash and smoke fumes were making her throat raw. Her eyes were watering, but not only from the smoke.

***

Whatever remained of Kimmie's self was buried deep in her mind. Absorbed and merged with the dark presence which had invaded her body and soul, had taken advantage, and finally taken control of her. She was still dimly aware her body had been hijacked by some alien presence, and she put up the occasional psychic struggle against the invader mind, but with every moment it grew stronger and more adept at controlling her body.

Step after step, she plodded along the dark shore of Oro Lake.

She was aware of the bodies which had stirred from the lake bed, the shambling revenants of past victims now lurching with hateful purpose toward the people of the town. She was aware in some way that the town was aflame, that the initial chaos had begun. With luck, the flames would spread and soon the entire valley would be engulfed.

She continued along to the north, stepping along the silty beach until she came to the dock which she knew was part of the Barnes' property. The one she'd swum from a few days earlier when she first caught the attention of the thing. Where she'd almost drowned, and had been rescued by Charlie Gaines, whose lumbering corpse had already caused so much chaos tonight. Turning to the right, she found the path leading to their house.

Despite the presence having spent uncountable years trapped in darkness, Kimmie's physical body was not adjusted to the moonless dark under the trees. The darkness surrounded her, and the thing stepped forward carefully as it entered the forest. Boughs and branches overhead cut down even more on what little light there was. But slowly she made her way forward, staring intently at the dim path before her as she marched along.

Soon she could see a sparkling pinpoint of light ahead of her. It was shifting and shimmering, broken up by the trees and branches between her and it, but she realized it was the back porch light of her house. The distant light was unusually bright against the surrounding darkness but gave her a landmark to walk toward.

She continued through the forest, down into the gulley where the stream gurgled and churned toward the lake. Crossing that, she trod up the other side and onto the lawn. From the edge of the backyard, she saw the house clearly. Lights on in the downstairs, and her father pacing back and forth through the wide windows which looked out onto the yard.

She stalked across the grass, stepped up the stairs and onto the back porch. Kimmie reached out, gripped the metal latch of the screen door in one hand, and pulled it open.

CHAPTER THIRTY-SEVEN

Water bubbled and churned as the head of Darryl McEwen broke the surface. Thin water grasses and clumps of algae streamed from his water-logged hair. His skin was pale and puffy, his eyes pale white orbs like over-poached eggs. He stumbled from the water and up the shore of the lake, hands curled into claws, stretching and flexing and clenching again. They were a killer's hands, compelled to clutch, and rend and strangle. The only thought in his dead mind was a singular hatred of the humans surrounding and infesting the valley. The seething anger which slithered around his cold brain and compelled his body harbored nothing but resentment.

The shell of Darryl trod through the woods, shuffled over the detritus of the forest's shadowed floor. In the distance, he could sense the warmth of the people in Golden Oaks. A hateful vengeance simmered deep within, the vestigial thoughts of the force that had drawn him out of the lakebed, propelled him forward. He stumbled through the woods until he came to the highway leading to town and stepped onto the asphalt.

A bright yellow Jeep came around a curve. The driver tried to avoid him, swerving at the last second, but clipped him anyway, sending him spinning across the road where he landed on his back with a sickening squelch. He rolled and skidded ten feet across the rough asphalt, leaving a smear of rotting flesh and clothing behind him. The driver slammed on the brakes and skidded to a halt. The jeep's doors flung open, and two young women came running out. They were dressed for a night on the town, wearing miniskirts and tank tops.

The passenger was screaming "Oh my God!" over and over while the driver ran to where the prone form lay in the street. She came close and stopped when the stench hit her. A rotting, gassy smell of decay and death.

"*Eurgh!*" she grunted. "God, he stinks. Must be a homeless guy or something."

The other woman came running over, clacking the asphalt in her three-inch pumps. She looked at the body in front of them. "Oh, my God, Debbie. He looks dead. I think you killed him!"

Debbie stepped closer and leaned over him, trying not to gag on the stench. "Hey! Hey mister, are you okay?"

Darryl rolled over. Blind eyes staring at nothing, his slime-crusted hands shot out, grabbing Debbie by the throat.

His fingers began to squeeze.

***

Paul Parsons was eating dinner in the morgue. He was sitting on a rotating stool at his desk in front of his computer, trying to find any information he could about the fire downtown. But all he was able to figure out was that it had started at the diner. The Fire Department was on site and trying to control it. But it was spreading.

He'd brought a container of spaghetti and meatballs, easily portable, and easy to reheat. He had a two-liter bottle of Dr. Pepper he kept in a mini-fridge he'd bought himself and kept in the lab. He'd poured himself a big glass of it and added a healthy dollop from a flask of vodka he kept tucked away in the specimen freezer.

He'd stuffed his third mini-meatball into his mouth when he heard a dull *thud!* from somewhere behind him.

He turned around, spinning in a slow half circle on the stool. Jeff planted his feet on the floor, stopping his turn. He saw nothing behind him except the cold metal wall of morgue coolers. The small doors all latched closed.

He shrugged and began to turn back to his food when he heard the thud again. This time he heard it coming directly from the wall of coolers. Another banging thud, followed by another and another. He saw one of the doors in the center of the wall shudder and shiver in its hinges. It was marked with a "3" for identification. It was the box containing the remains of Officer West.

Another tremendous banging *thump!* and the door blew open and two pale, bloodless hands emerged, gripping the top lip of the opening. The tray on which West's corpse rested slid out as the hands pulled it forward.

Paul shot to his feet, tripping on the legs of the stool and went sprawling. Rolling over onto his back he looked toward the cooler. He saw the corpse of Officer West raising its head to stare at him with gray, clouded eyes. A feral grin spread across its face as it dropped off of the slab and rose to its feet. It grabbed a scalpel from a nearby equipment tray and rushed at him.

***

Water lapped at the dock near the Barnes' house. A steady, quiet rhythmic slapping against the posts and the underside of the dock where it met the land a few feet from the shore. In the distance, in the direction of town, the glow of the raging fire was brighter. A diffuse orange incandescence shining through belching clouds of smoke and ash.

A splashing at the dock's edge, and a wet slap as a pale hand erupted from the water and landed on the wooden planks. It was followed by another. The hands were shriveled, claw-like, finger bones poked through the tips, flesh picked away in spots along the palm and backs. The claw-like bone tips dug into the wood, clenching tight and dragging the rest of the body up. A head, mostly skull, but with scattered patches of bloodless skin still attached came up next. Its eye sockets were like black pits, squirming darkness writhing in their depths. The eyeless face stared toward the woods beyond the shore as the skull was followed by bony shoulders in a tattered, sodden T-shirt. It heaved itself up onto one knee, dragged the other leg up until it crouched at the end of the dock.

Slowly, it stood up. Water gushed out of the torn-open torso to splatter on the dock, flushing bits and pieces of dead meat along with it. It took a step forward, unsteady after so long under water. Step by step, until it was across the dock and onto the shore. Up the shore, with shuffling steps, dragging its feet in the sand.

Mike Barnes was finally heading home.

CHAPTER THIRTY-EIGHT

The screen door to the back porch banged shut, and Gabe jumped, startled. He was in the kitchen, trying the phone again and still getting no connection. When he saw her, he fumbled it back into the receiver and ran over to give her a hug.

She struggled against his embrace, and he stepped back from her.

"Kimmie! Where the hell have you been? Your mother and I have been worried sick. She's out driving around town trying to find you."

"Away," she said coldly. "I had things to do."

"*Things?*" Gabe asked. He pulled his iPhone out of his back pocket and began texting Laurie. "There are kids missing, downtown's on fire, and you went out to do *things?*" Tapping the screen as he spoke, he typed out *Kimmie's home. Come back ASAP.*

"Is Mom on her way?" Kimmie asked, peeking over his shoulder at his phone.

He put the phone on the counter and turned back to her. "Hopefully soon," he said. "I don't know what's going on downtown, or if the fire's spread, or anything."

He glanced again at the phone. Nothing yet. "Do me a favor, go pack a bag in case, okay?"

"Why, you planning on running?" she said.

He glared at her. "Look, you've seen how these fires can spread as much as I have. God forbid, if we have to evacuate, I'd like to be able to do it fast."

His phone rang, Laurie was calling. "Go on, Kimmie," Gabe said as he thumbed the phone to take the call. "Just pack a small bag in case. Probably won't need it, but if we have to move fast, you'll be glad you've got it." He turned his attention to the phone. "Hey, babe, everything's okay. Just come on home."

"Well, that's the thing," Kimmie said, picking the glass pot off of the coffee maker stand. "Everything's not okay. And you're not going to be going anywhere."

"What do you mean?" Gabe asked, just as she spun around and smashed the pot into the side of his head. Glass splintered and exploded as the shards dug into his scalp. Blood ran down the side of his face, dripping into the collar of his shirt. His knees went out and he fell to the ground. "Kimmie…" he mumbled, stunned. "What the hell?" Gabe collapsed onto his back, eyes unfocused staring up at the ceiling. "What are you doing?"

Dimly he could hear Laurie's voice coming from the speaker of his phone. "Gabe! Kimmie! What's going on? What's happening?"

Kimmie raised her foot, and brought it down on Gabe's phone. The screen shattered and went black. Laurie's voice was instantly cut off. Kimmie turned to the counter and drew a large carving knife out of the wooden knife block near the stovetop. She turned back to Gabe. He lay in a growing pool of blood on the floor. A scarlet puddle spreading from the side of his head where his scalp had been slashed open by the broken glass. She stared down at him, flexed the knife in her hand, and squatted down next to him.

A thunderous rushing sound, and something slammed into the screen door. She looked up to see a huge raven beating at the screen with its wings. Its talons and beak tore at the thin mesh, ripping great rents in it. The bird shoved its glossy black head through the mesh and screeched at her. A repeated, deep, rasping, croaking sound.Startled, Kimmie dropped the knife and screamed, falling back against the kitchen's central island and sending one of the stools toppling over.

The raven was pushing through the mesh, squirming and struggling against the web-like tangles. Kimmie grabbed the knife off the floor, gripped it tight in one fist. She stepped over Gabe's fallen form and ran at the door. When she got to the screen, she stabbed out with the knife, piercing through the raven's body, and tugging it back. The raven shrieked, beat its wings furiously against the mesh. When Kimmie pulled the knife completely out of its body, it fell backward, landing on the porch with a heavy *thud!*

She slammed the interior door shut and threw the thumb latch of the deadbolt, locking the door tight. Once it was closed, she peeked out the back window and saw three other ravens had taken roost on the porch railings. They glared at her with their black eyes, as they burst into a flurry of beating wings and croaking noise. They rushed forward, buffeting the window with their wings, and scraping at it with their talons.

Kimmie recoiled from the glass as the birds beat against it. The pane shuddered in its frame as they pounded and thrashed. She tightened her grip on the knife and snarled at them. The thing in Kimmie's mind recognized the ravens as predators. Remembered struggles with them in the past, how for ages they'd kept it trapped in the valley. The strange black birds could see it for what it was, their claws and beaks could pierce its essence and rip and slice it like flesh. They were the only thing it feared, and they'd found it before it had a chance to escape the valley. If it could get away fast, flee the area before more of the wretched birds came, it might stand a chance.

She tried to formulate an escape plan when the front door of the house crashed open, and Laurie came running through. "Kimmie! Gabe!" she was shouting as she ran down the hallway to the kitchen. She stumbled into the room, saw Gabe lying in a pool of blood, and Kimmie crouched nearby with a bloody carving knife. "Oh, my God!" Laurie shouted. "Kimmie, what happened?"

Kimmie whirled around, her dark hair lashing out in a halo like roiling storm clouds. Her eyes were black, feral, her lips drawn tight in a rictus snarl. Laurie imagined the gorgon, Medusa. Cursed gaze, venomous knot of snakes for hair, rage and hatred incarnate.

Laurie rushed toward where Gabe lay prone on the kitchen floor. "What the hell's going on?"

She turned to Kimmie just as she saw a flash of silver, and then a searing pain in her shoulder as Kimmie brought the knife down. If she hadn't moved, the knife would have gone into her neck. But suddenly, she felt a long, searing sting of the blade slicing across her skin. Warm wetness flowed down her back.

Kimmie raised the knife and brought it down again, but Laurie rolled out of the way and the blade stabbed into the floor.

Laurie shoved herself away from her daughter. Pushing with her feet until she was across the kitchen floor. A metallic crash and another burst of pain as her back slammed into a cabinet, dislodging the pots and bowls inside it. Kimmie was working the knife furiously back and forth, trying to unstick it from the wooden slat it had impaled. She wrestled with it until the knife was free, and she turned toward Laurie again.

"My God, Kimmie, stop this right now! What is wrong with you?" Laurie shouted.

Kimmie stalked toward her, back hunched low, knife gripped tightly in her hand. Laurie shoved up with her good arm and got to her feet as Kimmie stabbed out at her. Laurie brought up her arm to deflect the knife, taking a long gash along the palm of her hand. Blood ran warm and wet along her arm.

There was a look of absolute rage on Kimmie's face. She raised the knife high overhead and as she brought it down, Laurie shoved out at her with her slashed hand, pushing Kimmie off-balance. Kimmie took a few staggering steps backward, tripped over Gabe's body and went sprawling.

Laurie turned and ran. Her feet pounded across the floor, took the steps two at a time until she was in her bedroom upstairs. She slammed the door shut, and could hear Kimmie scream in frustrated anger, and her footsteps as she charged after her.

Laurie fumbled for a twist knob lock on her side of the door, but there wasn't one. She grabbed at the chest of drawers nearby and dragged it in front of the door, leaving smears of red on its varnished pine surface as she did. It was light, not having much in it, but it would do. She shoved it tight against the door, and slid to the ground, her back up against it.

A burst of rapid pounding against the door frame as Kimmie began to beat on it with her fists from the hallway. "Come out, *Mommy*," she screeched, the words sour and hateful.

Laurie fumbled in her pocket for her phone. Sticky, bloody fingers taped and prodded the screen as she dialed Officer Lasher's number. It rang five times before it was finally picked up on the other end.

Before Lasher had a chance to speak, Laurie shouted into the phone. "It's Laurie Barnes, oh God you need to come quick. Something's wrong with Kimmie! She hurt Gabe and I think she's trying to kill me!"

"Mrs. Barnes?" Lasher interjected. "Mrs. Barnes, try to calm down. What's going on?"

A loud *thud!* as Kimmie slammed into the door, rattling it in its frame. "Oh, God, come now!" Laurie shrieked. "Please come quick!"

*****

Officer Lasher bolted toward her police cruiser. She slapped Jim Newman—one of the volunteers directing traffic toward the detour downtown—on the shoulder as she ran by.

"Got an emergency," she said. "Can you hold down the fort?"

Jim looked around, waved his hands halfheartedly at the complete lack of traffic. "I think I can manage, chief," he said.

She ran to her car, got into the seat, and started it up, flipping on the sirens and blasting onto the road through town. The fires were dying down behind her, but the town was still bathed in an eerie orange glow, the air still thick with smoke and ash.

Lights and sirens blaring, she charged up the road and out of downtown Golden Oaks. She grabbed the handset radio off the dashboard and called into the station. "This is Officer Shawna lasher. I need backup and EMTs to 307 Ringgold Lane. The Barnes' place. Please acknowledge."

Millsap's voice came on the radio, crackling and distant. "Roger that, Lasher," he said. "I'm on my way. Josie, you send those EMTs, you hear? Over."

Lasher's foot was almost to the floor on the accelerator pedal. Her car raced out of town, came around a curve, and she saw a bright yellow jeep abandoned in the middle of the road on the other side. Its headlights were still on, doors open, and the dome light on as well.

"What the hell?" Lasher said as she sped by, veering to the side of the road slightly to make ample room as she raced around the stopped vehicle. She grabbed the radio handset again. "There's an abandoned vehicle in the road, northbound on 346, about a mile outside of town. Someone needs to clear that shit out of the road before someone gets killed. Over."

She turned across the road and onto the bridge that would put her onto Ringgold Lane. Josie radioed back that she'd add the jeep to the list. Lasher tore down Ringgold Lane, her car bumping and jumping as it hit every bump and dip along the uneven road. The flashing lights on top of the car bathed everything in a sinister red glow. The trees looked bathed in blood as she sped along the dark lane.

Something about Kimmie had seemed off to her when she'd interviewed the girl earlier in the day. Finding the boat, her dead friend. She went missing around the same time the fires had started downtown. Now apparently the teenager was going after her own parents. What had gotten into the girl? Lasher began to wonder if Kimmie Barnes was behind all the chaos and deaths of the last few days. But how did that even make sense? She was a kid, and she certainly wasn't around when the ravens attacked West.

Shawna Lasher didn't know what was going on, but she had a feeling that when she found out what was behind all this, she wasn't going to like it. But whatever it was, Lasher intended to find out, and put a stop to it once and for all.

She hoped she would be in time to stop whatever was happening at the Barnes' house.

***

Gabe Barnes rose to consciousness on the kitchen floor. His head throbbed, and when he turned it to the side it felt stuck to the floor. His hair peeled away from the floor as if stuck in hardening, but not quite stiff, glue. He had trouble seeing out of his left eye before realizing it was stuck shut. He rubbed it with the back of one hand, and it felt gummy, but he was able to get it open. When he took his hand away, he saw it was smeared with clotting blood. His ears were ringing, and he could barely hear yelling and banging, as if at a great distance away.

He slowly sat up, leaning on his hands for support. A wave of dizziness flooded over him, and he almost blacked out again before it passed. Gabe looked around, saw his phone smashed on the ground, saw the shattered coffee pot, shards of glass strewn across the floor, stuck in the congealing puddle of gore and glittering in the reflected overhead lights.

Suddenly it all came back to him. Kimmie assaulting him with the coffee pot, Laurie calling. Where had Kimmie been? Did he ever find out? And a tremendous *thud!* from above, followed by banging and screaming. He got to his feet, grabbed onto the side of the kitchen island to keep from falling again, and unsteadily crossed the kitchen floor. He moved faster until he was running toward the stairs leading to the second floor. He grabbed onto the handrail as he climbed the stairs, wobbling as he did.

"Kimmie!" he yelled out. "What are you doing?"

Another cacophony of banging and pounding, and he heard Laurie yelling from somewhere nearby, "Gabe! Stop her!"

Gabe took a few more steps forward onto the landing when he suddenlysaw his daughter with a bloody butcher knife in one hand, banging and hacking at the door to the room he and Laurie had claimed as their own. He saw the deep, savage gouges in the wood, and the scarlet dripping from her hands.

"Kimmie," he said, holding one hand out in front of him in a placating gesture. "Kimmie, I don't know what's going on, but you need to put down that knife and step away."

Kimmie whirled to face him, and he took a step back in shock. Her eyes were dead black pits, her lips stretched thin and wide in a feral snarl. Thin tendrils of black erupted from between her teeth and danced around the edges of her mouth like squirming, searching worms.

"Kimmie, put down the knife and we can help you," he said again, trying to regain his composure. But he was shaking, his knees felt weak, and a cold dread was creeping through his body.

From behind the door, Laurie said, trying to sound calm, "Kimmie, please listen to your father. Put down the knife."

Kimmie shivered, as if she'd experienced a sudden chill. Her hand which held the knife lowered until the blade was pointing toward the floor. A single drop of blood oozed to the tip of the knife, falling to the ground with a faint *plip!*

"That's it, kiddo," Gabe said, stepping toward her. "Hand me the knife, and we'll figure this all out." He raised his hand again, outstretched to take the blade. He took another step forward. "Please ... put it down, okay?"

She rotated her hand, raising the knife slightly, staring at it like she was seeing it for the first time. The overhead lights reflected off its metallic surface, glittering through the coagulating red smear. Kimmie raised her head, staring at Gabe. She opened her mouth wide, wider than Gabe thought possible. He heard her jaw pop as if it were about to come unhinged, as an otherworldly shriek erupted from the black pit of her throat. A shriek of frustration and hate, and a primeval rage. She raised the knife high above her head and charged at him.

As she brought the knife down in a murderous strike to his neck, his right hand shot up, grabbing her below the wrist. She began to beat him with her off-hand, and he grabbed her other wrist. Kimmie struggled, squirmed, and flailed at him. Gabe felt nicks and slices from the blade in her hand as she twitched and turned, trying to wend her way out of his grasp. The knife flailed and twisted and slashed at his forearm as he kept pushing away at her arm, trying to keep the knife at a distance where it couldn't do any serious harm.

"Laurie!" he called out. "Help!"

Kimmie was strong. Much stronger than Gabe expected. She was still trying to twist her way out of his grasp, but also shoving against him, stamping on his feet, and kicking his shins.

Gabe heard a scraping sound from the bedroom, as of something heavy being dragged across the floor. The door opened, and Laurie came rushing through. "Babe, help!" Gabe yelled.

Laurie ran toward them, and as she was about to grab Kimmie, Kimmie shoved forward, Gabe stumbled backward, and his lower back hit the top edge of the handrail that surrounded the stairwell. He staggered, Kimmie pressed forward again, and suddenly, the two of them were tumbling backward over the railing and into space.

Laurie snatched at Kimmie as they went over. Her fingertips briefly brushing the back of Kimmie's thigh but grabbed nothing but air.

With a sickening thud and a crunch, Gabe and Kimmie landed at the base of the stairs. Laurie grabbed the railing and leaned over, looking down to see Gabe lying on his back, head pointed toward the bottom of the staircase, one arm twisted behind his back. She saw the handle of the knife sticking out from behind his shoulder, then heard a door slam.

There was no sign of their daughter.

Chapter Thirty-Nine

Officer Lasher brought her cruiser to a screaming halt in front of the Barnes' house and flipped off the sirens. The circling lamps over her head beat a steady blood red tattoo across the front of the house. Through the stuttering light, she saw a raven roosting on the front porch railings, and on the roof at least half a dozen more. Disconcertingly, the ravens seemed to be staring at her.

She grabbed the radio handset and clicked the talk switch. "Millsap, I'm at the Barnes' house. Where the hell are you and the EMTs?"

He came back with, "ETA ten minutes."

"Dammit," she hissed. "I'm going in," she said into the radio, and dropped the handset. She threw open the door, got out of the car, and ran across the road to the house, drawing her service revolver as she did. When she got to the front door of the house, she hammered on it with her fist.

"Mr. and Mrs. Barnes?!" she yelled at the door. "This is the Golden Oaks PD, responding to your call." She waited the space of a few heartbeats when she heard a tremendous *thud* from inside the house.

She pounded on the door again. "Mr. and Mrs. Barnes? I'm coming in!"

Lasher grabbed the doorknob and found it turned easily. She pushed the door open slowly with her shoulder, entering the front hallway with her gun held in both hands, pointed low. In the distance, a door slammed.

She stepped through, and behind her she heard the croaking of the ravens out front. She shoved at the door with the heel of her foot, and it swung toward the frame but didn't close fully.

"Gabe!" a woman's voice called from further inside. It sounded like Mrs. Barnes—Laurie, she remembered—and she doubled her pace down the hall. She exited the hallway into the living room. The overhead lights from the kitchen next to the living room were on, and she had a clear view of the space. When she entered the room, she scanned it left to right, and that was when she saw Gabe and Laurie at the foot of the stairs. Lasher replaced her gun in the holster, and rushed over to where Gabe lay at the foot of the stairs, a growing pool of blood spreading from behind him and running down the bottom step onto the floor.

"What happened?" Lasher asked.

Laurie looked up at her, eyes wide with panic. "Oh … Oh, thank God you're here." Laurie looked around the room, over Lasher's shoulder toward the kitchen. She whispered, "Where's Kimmie?"

"I don't know," Lasher replied. She leaned over and saw that there was a long carving knife sticking out of Gabe's shoulder. A steady rill of blood running from the gash. He was nonresponsive when she snapped her fingers in front of his face. She felt his neck.

"He's got a pulse," she said. "It's weak, but it's there."

"What do we do?"

"EMTs are on their way," Lasher said. "Grab towels." Laurie just looked at her.

"Now!" Lasher yelled.

Without another word, Laurie vaulted upstairs. She grabbed four towels off the rack in the bathroom and ran them back down, handing one to Lasher and dumping the rest on the floor next to Gabe.

"I don't want to remove the knife," Lasher said, as she carefully packed the towel around the blade, then pressed it against his shoulder. Almost instantly, crimson blossomed through the white terrycloth as it absorbed Gabe's lifeblood. "But I want to slow the bleeding until the EMTs get here."

She looked at Laurie. "Tell me what happened."

"It was …" Laurie's voice trailed off. "Kimmie." Almost a whisper. Her eyes were wide as she looked past Lasher into the room beyond. Lasher turned her head and what she saw defied her imagination.

Kimmie Barnes was floating three feet off the ground. Her hair fluttered around her head as if caught up in some strange, otherworldly storm. A dark radiance surrounded her. Like a photo negative of a halo glow from a religious painting. A rippling black emptiness at once surrounded and emanated from her.

"Playtime's over," Kimmie said. Her voice was deep, gravelly, and vibrated as if echoing from deep within subterranean caverns under the earth. "Time to die." Arms outstretched, she floated across the floor toward the two women.

Lasher drew her gun and aimed it toward the girl. "Stop!" she yelled. "Stop right where you are!"

Laurie watched all this unfold with numb terror. Black tendrils of energy coursed from the pits of Kimmie's eyes, twitching and twisting around like so many slithering snakes. Kimmie came closer, and a wave of foul-smelling, chill air preceded her.

Distantly, they heard sirens coming closer. Millsap and the EMTs were close now.

"Last warning!" Lasher yelled, pulling back the weapon's hammer with her thumb. Kimmie kept sliding forward, inch by inch. Lasher thought about the absurd weirdness of the situation. For a split second, she imagined herself reading the Miranda Rights to a teenage girl possessed by some sort of weird alien energy.

The front door bashed open with a slam, startling Lasher. Her finger squeezed the trigger, but the shot went wide enough to miss the girl. It tore through the side of her baggy shirt, through a lamp, and out the far window behind her. In a rush, the room was filled with a dozen or more black birds. Ravens cawed and croaked and shrieked as they raced into the room. Flapping wings and clawing talons charged toward Kimmie. Lasher stood up, steadied her stance, and took another shot, and one of the birds exploded into a cloud of black feathers, and a spray of red mist.

The ravens surrounded her, and Kimmie shrieked, an animalistic howl of rage. She swatted at the birds with her hands, but only served to gain herself a few scratches and tears in her flesh when the ravens pecked and clawed back at her.

"Make them stop!" Laurie yelled at Lasher. "They're hurting her!"

Lasher raised her gun to fire again, but stopped. The birds had surrounded Kimmie now, diving in and zipping away. But as they did, she saw they were tearing at the energy which emanated from her. They ripped at it with their beaks and talons, as if they were chewing off shreds of it. She remembered the video she'd watched of West earlier. How he'd been flailing and choking, and then had been swarmed by a similar flock of ravens.

"No," Lasher said, lowering her gun slightly until the barrel was aimed at the floor below Kimmie's feet. "I think they're trying to save her."

Darkness burst around Kimmie, flooded from her pores and skin and roiling out like storm clouds. She fell to the floor, landing on all fours and collapsing to her side.

"Kimmie!" Laurie yelled. "Help her!" she shouted to Lasher. "I can't move!" She glanced down at her hands, slick with blood and holding the red, sodden towel to Gabe's neck. With one bloodstained hand, she grabbed for a fresh towel and carefully switched it for the one pressed to his neck.

Lasher dropped low below the flurry of screeching birds, and duck-walked over to the girl. She reached out and grabbed Kimmie under her armpits, dragging her away from the screeching riot overhead. When she had Kimmie dragged far enough away, she turned back to the dark mass in the center of the room. The ravens were tearing at the floating blackness, ripping threadlike strands from it. They swarmed around it, and the shapeless void drifted toward the back door. It shot out thick tendrils which splattered against the floor, began to squirm under the bottom rail and around the edges. The birds followed, some fluttering down to the floor to continue to rip and shred it at that level. Others still engaged with the mass floating above the ground. It slithered under the door, and Lasher rose to her feet and charged across the room.

She leapt around the birds, stepped around the tendrils, and grabbed the doorknob.

"What are you doing?" Laurie shouted. "You're going to let it get away!"

Lasher threw the door open.

Outside, the black threads stretched across the porch were beginning to slither down the steps toward the lawn. The lengths of darkness killed the grass and vegetation wherever it touched. Burning with freezing cold. The squirming mass in the house fell to the ground and began to pulse toward the outside. It shot out more tendrils to drag its bulk from the house. The ravens followed, tearing and rending, and swallowing the thing piece by piece, strip by strip.

Beyond the house, Lasher heard screaming sirens closing in, tires screeching to a halt out front. She stepped out onto the porch as the pool of roaming darkness trickled down the stairs, reaching out and dragging itself forward while the ravens tore it apart.

More dark birds plummeted out of the sky and trees, diving at the thing. They scattered around the yard, pecking and scratching at the lawn. Lasher knew better. She stepped down the back stairs, watching the birds do their strange work.

When she heard boots running up the front hall of the Barnes' house, she turned and went back inside. She got to the top of the stairs and heard a cacophony of cawing behind her. She turned back once more and saw the ravens were all staring at her, their heads tilted in unison, quizzically.

Millsap called out from inside the house, "Lasher! You here?"

The flock of ravens—an "unkindness" Lasher would remember they were called later and find that label somewhat ironic—took to the sky.

Lasher entered the house and saw Millsap directing the EMTs to where Gabe lay in a spreading pool of his own blood. Laurie was cradling Kimmie who was mumbling something incoherent.

She surveyed the room, and Lasher wondered how she was going to explain this to the mayor. Or how she'd explain it to herself.

Chapter Forty

Gabe rose from darkness to the sound of a steady electronic beep nearby. He opened his gummy, crusted-shut eyes to find himself in a white, sterile room. It smelled of cleaning solutions and fresh linens, and he immediately realized he was in a hospital.

His mouth and throat were dry, and his head was deliciously fuzzy. The last thing he remembered was being charged by Kimmie and going over the railing. After that, everything was red and dim.

Trying not to panic, he looked around until he saw a little red button on a handset which was attached to the wall by a cord. Where the cord went in was a sign that read simply "Call" with an abstract icon of a nurse drawn beside it. He hammered the button with his thumb and waited. Less than a minute later, a large man in pale blue nurse's scrubs entered the room.

"Well, Mr. Barnes," he said. "You're finally awake. How are you feeling?"

"Where are my wife and daughter?" Gabe said and tried to sit up. A dull pain lanced through his shoulder as he leaned on his arm while trying to rise. He fell back on to the bed.

"Hang on there. You don't want to pop a stitch." The nurse pushed a button, and the head of the bed began to slowly rise. "Your daughter's up in neurology. They're doing a CAT scan on her. Your wife is with her."

"CAT scan? Why? What's going on?" Gabe said, his voice louder and more frantic with each word.

"Mr. Barnes, what I can tell you is that your daughter's experiencing some memory loss, and they're running some tests. More than that, I think you'll want to talk to her doctor."

Gabe opened his mouth, but before he could speak, the nurse interrupted with, "Who will be here soon. I'm going to give you the once over, and after that, doc will come in and explain everything."

"So, all I can do is sit here and wait?" Gabe said, leaning back.

"For now." He took Gabe's temperature and blood pressure, asked a few more questions, and was gone.

Gabe sat in the hospital bed and stared out the window at the sun inching its way above the horizon.

***

In a different room of the hospital entirely, Laurie sat next to the bed where Kimmie was sleeping. She was watching her daughter sleep, listening to the intermittent pinging of the monitor nearby.

Hands in her lap, she was nervously rubbing her thumbs over her palms. She'd scrubbed so much of Gabe's blood off her hands when she got to the hospital, but she couldn't help the feeling there was more to clean up. They'd let her know already that Gabe was stable, but since he was out of commission, she had remained with Kimmie. Having to care and advocate for both of them simultaneously had come naturally.

She waited for the doctor to come in and explain everything. To give her the magical key to unlock the cipher of what had happened over the last few days. Because as she ran over her memories of the past few hours, and the days before, almost none of it made sense at all.

"Mrs. Barnes?" a voice asked from inside the room. She turned to see Dr. Botkin, the neurologist who'd supervised Kimmie's intake and CAT scan. He entered the room further when she recognized him.

"Hello, doctor," she said. "Any luck?"

"Hard to say at this time," he said. "But the good news is I can tell you that the scans showed absolutely nothing abnormal at all. From everything I can see so far, she's a perfectly healthy teenager."

A wave of relief washed over Laurie. She relaxed into her chair. "What do we do now?"

The doctor pulled up a chair and sat near her. "I think we should keep her for a couple of days for observation. Run a few more tests."

Laurie nodded. "That's fine. Whatever you need to do."

Dr. Botkin stood up to leave. "Oh, and your husband's awake. He's asked about you and your daughter. I don't think she's going to wake up for a while, if you want to go see him."

Laurie stretched and stood up. "Yes, I would. Please have someone let us know if she wakes up while I'm gone."

"Of course," he said.

They exited the room together; Dr. Botkin went one way, and Laurie the other. It took her a few minutes to trace her way back to the recovery room where Gabe was resting. He was lying in his bed, staring at the ceiling, and for a horrible moment, she thought he was dead. He turned his head to her and forced a thin smile.

"Hey, Miss," he said.

"Hey, Mister," she replied.

She sat next to him and took the hand he held out to her.

"You okay?" he asked. "You look tired."

"You're one to talk," she said and smiled. She glanced at the large swatch of white bandage taped down to his shoulder.

"How's the kid?" Gabe said. He tried to roll over to face Laurie, winced at a tugging pain in his shoulder, and laid back.

"Doc says she's fine," she said. "They ran a bunch of scans and said there's nothing abnormal. Wants to keep her for a couple of days for observation."

"Makes sense, I guess," he said. "I'm sure they'll get to the bottom of it."

"She doesn't remember any of it, you know?"

"What do you mean?" Gabe asked.

"Nothing from the last few days at all. She woke up briefly on the ride to the hospital. She thought she was in an ambulance because she'd almost drowned in the lake. She looked at me and asked me, 'Mommy, did I drown? Did I die?'" Laurie stopped speaking as tears welled up in her eyes and spilled out over her cheeks. "I asked her a couple of questions, but everything from when she went underwater a few days ago until just tonight? She didn't remember anything."

Gabe squeezed her hand, held it tight. "The docs will figure it out, I'm sure, babe." He grabbed a tissue from a box on a bedside table and handed it to her. Laurie wiped at her eyes. Soon, Gabe was weeping with her.

***

Officer Shawna Lasher sat in front of the computer in her office. For the better part of four hours, she'd been staring at the screen trying to decide how to write up the report of the night's events. She was exhausted, and none of it made any sense at all.

How could she write up a report of levitating teenagers possessed by dark spirits? Or a flock of ravens swarming the girl and chasing the thing away? And the girl herself? From what her mom said, the girl had gone berserk, attacked her and her husband. Now the dad and the girl were in the hospital. How would she sort out all that?

She'd watched the security footage of West's death over and over again while trying to make some sense of the report. The way the birds had flocked around him, how they'd torn at the unseen creature she suspected had taken him down.

And there were the bodies found around town. Four bodies burnt to cinders in the Get Up and Go. Darryl McEwen's corpse had been found on the side of the road with a couple of girls from Reno. Weirdest thing about that was that Darryl's body had looked like it had been underwater for a few days when they found it by the side of the road.

She'd tried to get ahold of Paul at the morgue but hadn't had any luck reaching anyone there at all.

Every question led to more questions. Lasher knew it would take weeks to sort it all out, if she ever did. And had no idea at the time, but over the next few years, another dozen corpses would be found in the woods around the lake. Nobody would ever figure out how they got there.

She clicked the cursor into the "Incident Report" box, typed out "Some kind of monster movie bullshit." She sighed and deleted it.

Lasher started formulating a plan. She started coming up with a story about how Arlen went nuts, killed West, and then took off before he crashed into the power pole. It was only a drop in the bucket of all the strangeness, but it was a start. It sure would make her life a lot easier if she could figure out a way to pin everything on the McEwen brothers. She hated the idea of filing falsified reports. But she hated the idea of trying to explain the truth of what had really happened even more.

There were voices outside her door. One loud, angry voice getting closer and closer until her door flew open with a bang, and Mayor Tom Anderson came stomping through. His myopic eyes behind thick glasses glared at Lasher as she rose from behind her desk. Josie followed right behind him.

"I'm sorry, Shawna, I tried to tell him you were busy," Josie said, sheepishly.

"Dammit, woman, this doesn't concern you!" the Mayor bellowed.

Josie stepped back as if she'd been slapped.

"That's okay, Josie," Lasher said. "I'll take it from here."

Josie nodded, and slipped out through the doorway, closing the door behind her.

The mayor trundled up to her desk, fuming. Lasher stood a good foot or more taller than he did. She'd often thought of him like a fat little chihuahua. Pissed off because of his tiny stature, taking it out on the world.

"God-dammit, Lasher!" he shouted. "What the hell's going on in this town? The diner's burned down, we got more dead bodies showing up all the time. I told you to fix this shit, didn't I?"

He was right in front of her desk now, hands on the edge and leaning over it as he yelled.

"Mister Mayor," she said calmly with a voice she'd cultivated over years of dealing with belligerent drunks, meth-heads, and violent crazies. Sometimes she almost missed the big city police work she'd done before she came to Golden Oaks. "I'm going to have to ask you to take a step back."

"You want to keep that badge, you're going to tell me what the hell's going on around here! And what you're planning to do to …"

He stopped speaking abruptly when her fist hit his mouth.

***

Kimmie was released a few days later and was in fact fine. She had no memory at all of any of the events that had happened over the past week. She rested for a day or two after coming home from the hospital, and soon was back to her old self.

Gabe and Laurie had spoken to the police a few times in the interim and told them the whole thing was an accident. Gabe had been making dinner when he'd heard a noise upstairs and had been startled by Kimmie and they'd fallen. Oops. "Whaddya gonna do?" Gabe had said to Officer Millsap with a smile and a shrug. Lasher had nodded, looked him right in the eye, folded up her little notebook, decided it was a domestic dispute, and considered the case closed.

"I saw cops in the woods today," Kimmie said a few days later at dinner. Kimmie had requested burgers and homemade fries, and Laurie had been more than happy to oblige. She'd been sitting on the back porch reading a book when she saw a couple of police in the distance. "I guess they're still looking around for Kevin."

"I wonder if they'll ever find him," Gabe said. He reached for the bowl of french fries and winced as a throb of pain lanced through his healing shoulder. Laurie chided him and told him to rest his arm and dished up the fries.

For the next few days, they often saw police in the woods behind their house. They knew they were still looking out for the Lipton boy, but the longer they searched, the less likely it would be that they'd find him.

What none of them expected was that the police would find the body of Mike Barnes. A mile down the way from the house, slumped under some bushes like he'd dropped dead right there three years ago.

Not long after that, the estate was settled, and Gabe, Laurie, and Kimmie Barnes sold the house on Ringgold Lane permanently. They moved south, near Gilroy where there were no forests or lakes nearby. Nothing to remind them of the strange events of the summer.

It was a quiet place, and they appreciated that.

But once in a while, when the night was dark, and the wind clawed at the walls of their new home, Kimmie Barnes dreamt of squirming darkness, of reaching, clutching dead hands, and woke with the taste of lake water in her mouth.

And on those nights, more often than not, she woke to find her mother watching her sleep.

ACKNOWLEDGEMENTS

Initial and overarching thanks to my wife Beth for everything.

David Ackerman, Bruce Baugh, Cathy Doherty, Anne Rishon, Alastair Sutherland, and George Hearn put up with my incessant texts of the "Which sounds better, *this* or *that*?" variety.

Alex Wu, DVM helped me with details of veterinary medicine.

Todd Stiers helped me with details of how a town would be affected by a blackout if a transformer blew.

I often had Gillian Welch, Alela Diane, First Aid Kit, Mariee Siou, Kate Mann, and the Wailin' Jennys playing while I was writing this book. Lots of Bob Seger and John Mellencamp, too.

Thanks to editor MJ Pankey who took a red pen to my original manuscript like Michael Myers through a fog-shrouded suburb. The book is significantly improved because of her expert eyes.

Kudos to Stephanie Ellis and Lee Murray who's suggestions and support at the eleventh hour helped to polish this story until it shone like blackest obsidian.

And final thanks to Steve and Heather at Brigid's Gate for taking a chance on *The Seething*.

ABOUT THE AUTHOR

Ben Monroe has spent most of his life in Northern California, where he lives in the East Bay Area with his wife and two children. He is the author of *In the Belly of the Beast and Other Tales of Cthulhu Wars, the Seething,* the graphic novel *Planet Apocalypse*, and short stories in several anthologies. You can find more information about him and his work at   or find him on Twitter @_BenMonroe_

363

CONTENT WARNINGS

Gore.
Body trauma.
Drowning.
Violence

MORE FROM BRIGIDS GATE PRESS

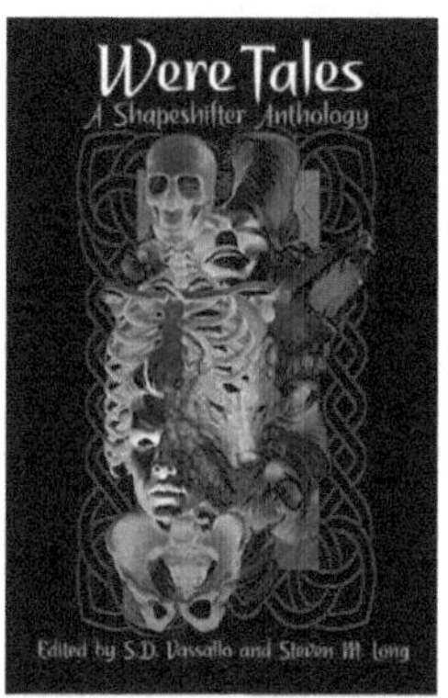

Werewolves. Berserkers. Kitsune. From the most ancient times, tales have been told of people who transform into beasts. Sometimes they're friendly and helpful. Sometimes they're tricksters, playing jokes on their hapless victims. And sometimes, they're terrifying.

Were Tales is a collection of scary, thrilling, dark, mysterious, and even humorous short stories and poems of shapeshifters, from the talented minds of Jonathan Maberry, Stephanie Ellis, Gabino Iglesias, Laurel Hightower, Eric J. Guignard, Michelle Garza and Melissa Lason, Shane Douglas Keene, Clara Madrigano, Kev Harrison, Beverley Lee, S.H. Cooper, Elle Turpitt, Catherine McCarthy, Alyson Faye, Theresa Derwin, Ruschelle Dillon, Baba Jide Low, H.R. Boldwood, Ben Monroe, Cynthia Pelayo, Cindy O'Quinn, Sara Tantlinger, Stephanie M. Wytovich, Linda Addison, Villimey Mist, Tabatha Wood, and Christina Sng.

Malevolent mermaids.
Sinister sirens.
Scary selkies.

And other dangerous women of the deep blue sea.

Dangerous waters takes us deep beneath the ocean waves and shows us once more why we need to be cautious about venturing out into the water.

Featuring stories, drabbles and poems by Sandra Ljubjanović, John Higgins, Patrick Rutigliano, Candace Robinson, Emmanuel Williams, Desirée M. Niccoli, L. Marie Wood, Samantha Lokai, Christina Henneman, Gully Novaro, Christine Lukas, Alice Austin, Dawn Vogel, Victoria Nations, Mark Towse, Kristin Cleaveland, Ben Monroe, Kurt Newton, E.M. Linden, Eva Papasoulioti, Ann Wuehler, Rachel Dib, A.R. Fredericksen, Daniel Pyle, Megan Hart, Ef Deal, Katherine Traylor, Juliegh Howard-Hobson, Simon Kewin, Elana Gomel, Lauren E. Reynolds, Grace R. Reynolds, René Galván, Marshall J. Moore, Ngo Binh Anh Khoa, Roxie Vorhees, April Yates, Kaitlin Tremblay, T.K. Howell, Kayla Whittle, Emily Y. Teng, Briana McGuckin, Tom Farr, Cassandra Taylor, Steven-Elliott Altman, Paul M. Feeney, Lucy Collins, Marianne Halbert, Rosie Arcane, Antonia Rachel Ward, Steven Lord, and Jessica Peter.

Whether in an old weathered mine shaft, somewhere off the beaten path, out in the woods, or right here in the middle of this ghost town, danger awaits. We're going to take you way back, drop you right smack dab in the middle of the Old West at its finest. But we're not just going to give you shootouts and bullet wounds and blood splatter. Yes, those things are prominently featured, but there's so much more to this anthology of western horror.

Maybe it's a well-known creature popping in for a visit, or some new creepy crawly monster sucking out your soul, we're going to turn the Old West inside-out and explore its guts to the fullest. There are new adventures to be had, monsters both familiar and unfamiliar to be thwarted… And we're not always going to be the victors. Life in the Old West is hard, trying at its best, and it can wear you down quick.

So, prepare yourself to be transported back in time. Get yourself up on that rickety stagecoach, draw your guns, and let's get going. There's vast territory to cover here, and your journey begins now.

Featuring the talents of Antonia Rachel Ward, Nick Kolakowski, Villimey Mist & Damascus Mincemeyer, Jonathan Kemmerer-Scovner, Sean Eads & Joshua Viola, Craig E. Sawyer, Lana Elizabeth Gabris, Joel McKay, David Niall Wilson, Ej Sidle,

Brennan LaFaro, Michael Bailey, Amanda J. Spedding, Taylor Rae, P.L. McMillan, Wen Wen Yang, Ben Monroe, and Chad Lutzke.

Following the death of a loved one, Rachelle Collins visits Ferguson Estate, an expansive country mansion which holds many fond memories, and one sinister secret, within its walls. Throughout the course of a single, terrifying night, Rachelle must confront horrors, both psychological and tangible, to prove just how far she is willing to go to keep her family together.

Visit our website at: www.brigidsgatepress.com